RUN RED
WITH
BLOOD

Seasons of War
Come Looking for Me
Second Summer of War
Run Red with Blood

‑❧ *Seasons of War* ❧‑

RUN RED
WITH
BLOOD

a novel

Cheryl Cooper

DUNDURN
A J. PATRICK BOYER BOOK
TORONTO

This is a work of fiction. Any references to historical events, real people, or real places are used fictitiously.
All other characters in this work are fictitious. Any resemblance to real persons, living or dead, is purely
coincidental.

Cover image: Kevin Patterson
Printer: Webcom

Library and Archives Canada Cataloguing in Publication

Cooper, Cheryl, 1958-, author
    Run red with blood / Cheryl Cooper.

(Seasons of war)
"A J. Patrick Boyer book".
Issued in print and electronic formats.
ISBN 978-1-4597-4282-6 (softcover).--ISBN 978-1-4597-4283-3 (PDF).--
ISBN 978-1-4597-4284-0 (EPUB)

    I. Title. II. Series: Cooper, Cheryl, 1958- . Seasons of war.

PS8605.O655R86 2018   C813'.6   C2018-904098-X
                                              C2018-904099-8

1   2   3   4   5   22   21   20   19   18

Conseil des Arts   Canada Council   ONTARIO ARTS COUNCIL
du Canada   for the Arts   CONSEIL DES ARTS DE L'ONTARIO
                                           an Ontario government agency
                                           un organisme du gouvernement de l'Ontario

We acknowledge the support of the **Canada Council for the Arts**, which last year invested $153 million
to bring the arts to Canadians throughout the country, and the **Ontario Arts Council** for our publishing
program. We also acknowledge the financial support of the **Government of Ontario**, through the **Ontario
Book Publishing Tax Credit** and the **Ontario Media Development Corporation**, and the **Government
of Canada**.

Nous remercions le **Conseil des arts du Canada** de son soutien. L'an dernier, le Conseil a investi 153 millions
de dollars pour mettre de l'art dans la vie des Canadiennes et des Canadiens de tout le pays.

Care has been taken to trace the ownership of copyright material used in this book. The author and the publisher welcome any information enabling them to rectify any references or credits in subsequent editions.
— *J. Kirk Howard, President*

The publisher is not responsible for websites or their content unless they are owned by the publisher.

Printed and bound in Canada.

VISIT US AT

 dundurn.com | @dundurnpress | dundurnpress | dundurnpress

Dundurn
3 Church Street, Suite 500
Toronto, Ontario, Canada
M5E 1M2

For my father, Bruce Samuel Evans (1932–2014),
a visionary who, in his time, sailed many ships to far horizons.

PROLOGUE

*T*he night shrouded the carriage in a suffocating darkness as black as the loam of a grave. The rain fell in torrents, pounding against the windows like the fists of a riotous mob. Pools of water had gouged the serpentine road, causing the carriage wheels to swerve and careen, and Emily's head to repeatedly strike the inside wall. She screamed for the driver to stop, but it seemed the carriage had neither driver nor horses — headlong it hurtled along an unknown track, stoked by a ghostly energy of its own.

Across from her sat Lord Somerton in his sombre suit of clothes, his eyes lost in shifting shadows, his mouth nothing more than a grim slash across a pallid jaw. The pitching motion of the vehicle did little to disturb him. Aside from his finger-tapping on the head of his cane, he sat completely still.

"Where are you taking me?" Emily cried.

There was a slight curling of his lips, but silence was his answer.

The carriage escalated its reckless speed. Wet, shivering trees flew past in the darkness — the twisted fingers of their branches scratching at the mournful sky, searching for a way to escape the night. A set of iron gates suddenly appeared and opened like jaws, intent on swallowing them whole.

As they passed through them, Emily grew cold and shaky. She recognized this place. She knew its twisting pathway and the grey, foreboding grounds heaving around it like an angry sea.

Hartwood Hall!

Frantically, she wrestled with the latch on the carriage door. Dear God, no! She had already fled from here once before, stolen away in the night when everyone was preoccupied with dancing and feasting and drinking — no one having seen her except for Fleda, who had wept at her leaving. She had gone looking for Leander and had managed to find him, somewhere near the sea.

The carriage came to an abrupt halt, and the leaden facade of the Hall filled its windows, formidable and startling as an enemy frigate slipping from a swirling bank of fog. Candles burned in the Hall's sash windows, and scurrying figures poured forth from its doors, rushing toward her. Roughened hands dragged her out into the pelting rain; voices shouted: "Hurry! Hurry! You have kept them waiting."

The shadowy molesters prodded her toward the house and into the front entrance where the lights flickered upon a hawk-faced clergyman in his black weeds and white collar. In his pious grasp, he carried the Book of Common Prayer. *Bound in a tight semicircle around him was an assemblage of familiar faces, yet there was no happy welcome in their stares. The Duchess of Belmont exuded indignation; her heavy husband wheezed disinterest; Glenna McCubbin was a clucking hen of disapproval while Uncle Clarence's mood was aloof and dark with bitter disappointment.*

In his extravagant knee breeches and frock coat, Wetherell Lindsay paced with impatience, his high heels clicking upon the marble floor, reflections of candlelight playing upon his bald pate where his wig was normally affixed. Lord Somerton eagerly steered Emily toward him. Wetherell pulled her roughly to his stout side and attempted to lock up her hands in his, but she pushed away, shaking her head in defiance, refusing to participate in their mad conspiracy. Enraged by the rebuff, Wetherell stomped off into a subterranean passage of the house, instructing the wedding guests to follow him, leaving the servants to douse the candles and shutter the doors. Trailing them was Fleda, a haunting, dreadful sadness in her green eyes. As she walked away from Emily, the masonry and mortar of Hartwood Hall fell around her, disintegrating and then vanishing into the earth.

One wedding guest stayed behind. He stood like a scarecrow in the abandoned field where the house had been. The uniform of an American naval captain hung upon his gaunt frame, the wind trifling with the threadbare fabric of his jacket. The brim of his bicorne hat was cracked and moth-eaten. His feet were naked and bleeding; he possessed no mouth, and where his nose should have been there was only a skeletal cavity. He turned to face Emily. His eyes — cold, dark, and merciless — sent icy fingers scuttling down her spine while the distance between them loudly echoed a familiar word.

Pity.

Unable to move, she watched as he raised a black pistol, cocked the hammer back, and levelled it at her pounding heart.

CHAPTER 1

FRIDAY, SEPTEMBER 17, 1813
EARLY MORNING
PORTSMOUTH HARBOUR

Prosper Burgo's teeth rattled as he sat shivering on the planked bench of the ferryman's scow, wishing he had stayed in town rather than risk a crossing of the harbour at this late hour. The world around him was as black as Hades. The rising mists on the still water swirled around him like the wraiths of dead sailors, expelling their chilled breath down his neck. His head was muzzy, his belly putrid, and he could not tell if it was midnight or that hazy, mysterious hour before dawn. Together with losing his money, his coat, and the whereabouts of his ship, he had lost track of time.

The scow did not look reliable. She was sitting awfully low in the water, and in order for Prosper to avoid soaking his shoes in the cold bilge that sloshed about on the boat's ribbed bottom, he had to plant his feet against her peeling sides. Adding further insult to injury, the ferryman, who looked like a mean customer in his bulky oilskin coat against the flickering light of his candle-lantern, was scrutinizing him with his shifty eyes as they rowed upon the steamy water, as if he meant to turn Prosper and his pockets inside out if the fare was not forthcoming when they reached their final destination.

With a mournful sigh, Prosper's thoughts returned to that downy bed in the warm attic of the Ship's Tavern. It had been so comfortable there, so soft, so entertaining ... for a time, anyhow.

"All right then!" said the ferryman gruffly. "Which one of 'em's yours?"

Prosper felt as if he were carrying a hefty boulder upon his scrawny shoulders, the tragic result of imbibing too much of the tavern's Three Threads ale. In vain he peered into the endless sweep of darkness, trying to size up the creaking silhouettes of the ships that stood moored in the harbour.

"How should I know?" he snapped back, his voice shrill and hysterical. "In this light, they *all* look the same."

The ferryman stopped pulling on the oars to scowl at Prosper. "Well I ain't gonna row ya around 'til the sun comes up, so ya better figure out which one's yours."

"Keep rowin' in this general direction. I know I left her 'round here somewhere with that scoundrel, Pemberton Baker, in charge. He wouldn't have *dared* move her if he values his good-for-nothing life."

"Who the hell's Pemberton Baker?"

"He's me second-in-command," Prosper said crossly, praying he would soon recognize his two-masted treasure, the *Prosperous and Remarkable*, in amongst the surrounding jumble of ships that seemed to be mocking him, goading him on in a game of hide-and-seek.

"*Yer* a captain?" There was a startling amount of surprise in the ferryman's voice. "And here I figured ya might be some sort o' corsair."

Indignant to the core, Prosper raised his chin. "I'm a privateer with a letter o' marque, signed by the governor o' Nova Scotia. And me mighty brig, the *Prosperous and Remarkable*, has secured nineteen prizes fer me. NINETEEN o' 'em!"

"Are ya expectin' me to be impressed?"

"Damn right! And if ya succeed in findin' me ship, I'll impress ya further by rewardin' ya with a bottle o' wine, stolen from the French flagship at Trafalgar."

The ferryman gave a loud harrumph. "Ya weren't never at Trafalgar!"

Prosper quickly fired back. "In me mind, I were!"

"I'll gladly take the wine, so long as it be accompanied by payment fer rowin' ya around and freezin' me arse off."

"Fine then!" muttered Prosper. "Now git rowin'."

With that the ferryman fell silent to focus on his strokes — which immensely suited Prosper's pounding head — though, sadly, the blessed peace and quiet was short-lived. As they drifted alongside the hull of a two-masted ship, on their way to study the name on her stern in the hopes that it would prove to be the elusive *Prosperous and Remarkable*, they were very nearly assaulted by an aggressive tongue of orange flame that, through an open gunport, whooshed out at them with sudden ferocity like a cracking whip.

The ferryman let out a long, low growl. "Ya'd better pray *this* particular vessel ain't yours."

Prosper's muddled brains were still trying to process what it was exactly that had nearly struck them both in the head. "Why d'ya say that?"

"'Cause *this* particular vessel appears to be on fire."

Darting a glance over his shoulder, Prosper saw whorls of flame spewing forth from three of the ports on the ship's gun deck — devil's arms, beckoning to those who dared to come closer. Squeals of terror erupted all around them. "FIRE! FIRE! THE SHIP'S AFIRE!" It was only then that Prosper's mind cleared sufficiently for him to fully grasp the situation. With the rising flames illuminating the position of the ferryman's scow on the harbour, he could now see the burning ship's crewmen leaping about on the weather decks, running in circles, crashing into each other in their frenzy to find an escape route. Some of them scrambled onto the bowsprit; some scurried up the ratlines, while a large number fought their way aft toward the stern where the ship's small cutter was suspended over the dark water. In horror, Prosper watched as dozens of them clambered into the tiny boat, causing her to swing wildly upon her davits. They clawed and shoved and began caterwauling, demanding to be lowered at once — as if there were someone standing by with no other purpose than to see them off safely.

As the ferryman's scow rounded the stern and Prosper was able to get a clearer view of the dangerously overloaded boat, he screamed up at them. "Holla! Ya goddamn galoots! There's too many o' yas! That cutter can't handle all o' yas at once! Ya should know better than to —"

But Prosper never finished his tirade. The ominous sound of splintering wood rent the night air. The davits snapped and gave way, flipping the boat over, dumping its shrieking occupants into the harbour much as a surgeon's mate dispenses his bucket of severed limbs over the ship's side.

"Futtocks!" cursed the ferryman, his scow spinning in undisciplined circles before he was able to navigate it away from the burning ship.

"Nay!" Prosper yelled at him. "Bring me in closer!"

"I won't! If those swimmers see us, they'll swamp us."

"Them idiots kin fend fer themselves! Take me to the side o' the ship."

The ferryman was aghast. "Wot?"

"Someone's gotta try and save her."

"I don't dare go back! My scow will catch fire. That ship ... she's — she's gonna blow up! And she'll be takin' us with her."

"Nay! Row me to that ladder yon, so's I kin climb up."

From the bulkiness of his oilskin coat, the ferryman's neck shot up. "Are ya mad? We'll both be killed!"

"I tell ya, man ... there's time!"

"I won't go nearer! Ya can't make me!"

Prosper felt confident in his convictions. "If we're lucky, we might 'ave half an hour afore the guns blow. Might be a chance to douse them flames afore that."

But the ferryman could not be swayed. "I won't ... I won't!" he cried.

Springing to his feet — beyond caring about the destruction of his shoes in the cold bilge — Prosper shoved his fox-like features into the ferryman's glistening face. "Ya either bring me in closer so's I kin climb that ladder," he hissed, "or I'll take me fist and punch another hole in yer bumboat so's ya drown along with that lot o' galoots what are suckin' up foul water through their snouts right about now."

The ferryman shut his mouth and frantically fell upon his oars, suddenly desperate to do Prosper's bidding. Breathing heavily, sounding somewhat like a frightened hog, he paused long enough for Prosper to jump onto the hemp ladder that hung down the side of the unfortunate ship, and then swiftly he pushed off, calling out as he did so: "You're a fool! A right, veritable fool!"

Prosper had already reached the top of the ladder and hooked one of his skinny legs over the ship's rail. Twisting his head around, he glared down at the ferryman and hollered back. "I might be foolhardy, but I ain't never a fool."

Forgetting about payment and the promise of French wine; thinking only of his wife and the breakfast of hot tea and rolls awaiting him, the ferryman ignored the cries for mercy from those faceless heads thrashing about in the water. Extinguishing his lantern flame, he once again took firm hold of his oars and pulled away, extricating himself from the disaster area, hoping to hide his scow somewhere in the blackness, beyond the grisly glow of the fire. As he laboured to put a safe distance between him and the hapless swimmers, he watched the flames growing ever higher on the unknown ship. They had now enveloped the base of the two masts, and were licking at the lowest of the spars. Their reach soon spread to the standing rigging ... the flames advancing up the web of ropes like an army of soldiers.

Despite the chaos and noise, the ferryman could still see and hear Prosper. He watched the fool sprinting about on the main deck; pausing amidships to bellow for water; pausing again fore and aft to scream for the same; dictating orders to and humiliating the crazed, fearful men he addressed as scoundrels and galoots and hedge-creepers. But despite Prosper's efforts, they jumped by the dozens from the upper works, willing to take their chances in the water. In the ferryman's mind, they were the lucky ones, for too many had been caught unawares below deck. Through the open gunports, he could see their arms flailing amidst the voracious flames, their hands begging for help until finally, overcome, they fell away into the fire.

The last the ferryman saw of Prosper Burgo, he was perched like a hawk on the ship's jib-boom, dark and small against the raging fire, still squawking orders — though his words were now lost in the roar — shaking first his right, then his left fist at what ... the ferryman knew not. Seconds later, the first explosion came in a shocking, deafening cloudburst of blackened red, and for a time, the hellish scene was completely — and thankfully — obliterated.

With a violent shudder, the ferryman averted his eyes and continued peacefully on his way.

STILL EARLY MORNING
THE BRIGANTINE INN, PORTSMOUTH, ENGLAND

Emily awoke with such a fierce start she was convinced an omnipotent being had shaken her bed frame and the narrow walls of her room in the inn. Another dream … another harrowing dream, full of tormenting images! She groped for the glass of water she kept at her bedside and drank thirstily, wishing instead for a draught of laudanum, for only its calming properties could erase recollections of horseless carriages, sweating bridegrooms, and the menacing gaze of Thomas Trevelyan. Letting the empty glass fall upon her blankets, she lay back against her pillows, waiting for her eyes — fixed on the dying embers of her coal fire in the grate — to adjust to the dimness as she puzzled over the thunderous reverberation in her nightmare. She could not place the sound, could not identify it. Hartwood Hall had crumbled in eerie silence; Trevelyan's phantom pistol had not discharged, and yet the unsettling noise … it had seemed so near, so real, as if it had occurred externally and not within the inner workings of her mind.

Emily tried to ignore the traces of her nightmare that still stalked the corners of her room, determined to leave her dejected, like a ship caught in the doldrums without its sustaining winds; instead, she tried to remember the day of the week and when it was she had last seen Leander and heard his voice. She had not been successful in recalling either when howls of alarm awoke the slumbering street beneath her windows. Leaping from her warm bed, she tripped toward her heavy curtains, tore them aside and unlocked the shutters. It was still early. Dawn had not touched the western horizon with the wick of her candle, and yet the sky over Portsmouth was bright and billowing with a fiery illumination. Emily felt a gust of the waning night's chill on her cheek, smelled acrid gunpowder in the air, and stared in bewilderment at the crowds scurrying about in circles on the cobbles of Broad Street, carrying torches and lanterns, and chattering to each other in feverish tones of distress.

Dear God! Had a munitions warehouse of Congreve rockets exploded? Were they under siege? Had fleets of French and American ships turned their cannons upon the seaside town and set homes ablaze, hoping to burn the habitants alive in their beds?

"What is it?" Emily shouted to those gathered below. "What has happened?"

From amidst the crowd that swelled in number as she awaited an answer, a breathless, obliging voice struck her ears: "'Tis a fire, Miss! A ship's gone and blown up in the harbour. There'll be dead men everywhere."

Emily withdrew, wavering in shock as she absorbed the intelligence. She gripped the window ledge — for surely the room was spinning around her, the cold floorboards buckling beneath her bare feet — and watched the fire scaling the inky sky, higher and higher, praying she was simply dreaming, entangled in another sequence of the same nightmare.

Yesterday she had learned that her friend, Fly Austen, had been promoted to the rank of post-captain and had taken command of HMS *Invincible*, a 36-gun frigate moored near the dockyard wharves, being quickly fitted out for duty in the American war. Dear little Magpie would be on that ship, his head of curls asleep on his pillow below on the berthing deck, and though she could not be certain of his whereabouts, for they had not met in days, there was a strong possibility that Leander was on the *Invincible*, as well.

That same invisible being that had shaken her awake had now enclosed her heart in its monstrous fists, crushing the life from it.

What if …?

There was no time to light the oil lamp. She felt her way to the corner cupboard and groped through her small pile of clothes for her sailor's slops. As she dressed in the dark, frantic to find her way into the legs of her trousers, her fingers fumbling with the stubborn buttons of her checked shirt, Leander's gentle voice crept into her conscience:

"*Remember, you must stay here. Unless I come for you, do not leave the inn. It is more than likely that your family has sent spies out looking for you.*"

"*I will not go back to Hartwood Hall, Leander — ever.*"

"Then, please, please heed what I say. Give me your word you will not risk it."

"You have my word."

Emily squeezed her eyes shut. She slowed the task of coiling her pale-gold hair beneath a scarf, allowing the pleading voice to tear at the armour of her resolve, imagining the whisperer standing in the musky darkness beside her, his warm breath on her cheek. Pleading ...

But he had not come. And in the days since they had first been reunited, she had seen him but twice and therefore could not be certain of his whereabouts, or whether he would ever come to her again.

Beyond her room, doors opened and closed.

Questions and cries filled the hallways of the inn.

Heavy footsteps hurried downstairs.

Around her, the air thickened with smoke.

She could not stay here. It would be impossible ... not knowing.

This time, Emily would dodge Leander's protective shadow. This time, she would not heed his entreaty, despite having given him her word. Leaving him behind in the blue dimness of her receding night-mare, she quickly searched the bare floor for her shoes, knotted the scarf at the nape of her neck and faced the door. Inhaling courage, she ran out before arms — real or imagined — could stop her.

5:00 A.M.
(MORNING WATCH, TWO BELLS)
ABOARD HMS *INVINCIBLE*
PORTSMOUTH HARBOUR

"Lower the boats!"

"Search for any survivors!"

"For God's sake, where is our bo'sun? Have him raise the men from their beds at once!"

Captain Austen was already dressed and dispensing disquieting orders to his Invincibles who were presently on duty when Magpie, the little sailmaker, arrived on the fore deck, his bandaged arm pressed against his chest, heaving in breathlessness. The shock of the explosion had nearly knocked him out of his hammock and hurled his heart into his mouth, so convinced he was that it had been the *Invincible*'s own store of gunpowder that had blown. Quickly, he adjusted the woolly thrum cap sitting atop his head, so that it didn't weigh down quite as heavily upon the patch that covered his lost eye, and then his gaze leapt over the bulwark of Captain Austen's frigate and across the water where a burning ship lay in the harbour away from the dockyard, engulfed in large, rising volumes of smoke. The flames issuing forth from her gunports looked as hot and hellish as furnaces of coal.

"Kin she be saved, sir?" Magpie asked when the worried figure of Captain Austen appeared beside him at the fore-rail to observe the blaze.

"I'm afraid she's beyond help. She'll burn to the waterline. We can only be thankful that she's standing away from those of us moored near the wharves; otherwise, we may all go up in smoke. But I fear for those two ships lying near her. They'll be scrambling to avoid her fiery reach."

"Do ya know who she is, sir? Where she's from and all?"

"This is a busy port, Magpie, with ships coming and going at all times. I cannot be certain, although I do have my suspi—" Leaving off suddenly, Captain Austen turned his back to roar at his crewmen. "Keep the decks soaked in the event burning debris should land on us. And if we take a hit, secure the hatches to prevent fire from catching below."

"Kin I go out in one o' our boats, sir?" pleaded Magpie.

"It's too dangerous. It won't be long before that ship's shotted guns will heat up and spew their contents in every direction."

"Ya mean a cooking off, sir?"

"Aye, lad."

"But what about the lads yer sendin' out fer the survivors, sir?" asked Magpie, watching his mates lowering the 25-foot cutter on the larboard quarter. "Ain't it dangerous fer them?"

"They'll be careful to stay clear."

"I'd be careful, too, sir."

"Aye, but there — there may have been women and children onboard."

"It won't give me no trepidation, if that's yer worry, sir."

Captain Austen's eyes roved over the woolly worms of Magpie's brown thrum cap. "Remind me again! How old are you?"

"Don't rightly know, sir. I never had no ma to tell when I were born. The Isabelles — they used to measure me up beside Gus Walby, and him bein' twelve, and me a foot shorter, they figured I were maybe ten or so."

"Aye! So young, and yet already you've been acquainted with the worst of our world."

Even in the half-light, Magpie saw something in the older man's eyes that caused him to wonder if he was thinking of Morgan Evans, the carpenter who had once owned the very cap on Magpie's head. A few weeks ago, Mr. Evans had lost his leg and his life to the long guns of their American enemy when they had been so close to England, so close to home. There was such a fierce tug on Magpie's heart whenever he thought of Mr. Evans lying alone in the earth beside Wymering Church, maybe — somehow — aware his old friends would soon be departing Portsmouth to strike out once again across the Atlantic without him.

"What kin I do fer ya then, sir?"

"Tell me first how that injured arm of yours is faring."

Captain Austen's question caused an unwelcome recollection of the condemned Meg Kettle to slither into Magpie's mind. On the day following Morgan Evans's death, Mrs. Kettle — in a fit of knife-wielding rage — had given him a terrible fright and the nasty gash across his forearm. He hoped she was now lying on a damp prison floor with no pillow for her head ... that she was being fed scraps of food fit only for mangy dogs and had a family of fat rats nesting in her skirts.

"It's healin' nicely, sir. It don't hurt much no more."

"Very well then, you can assist Biscuit in the galley. We are so short of able-bodied men, Magpie, and already our cantankerous cook is overwhelmed with the task of feeding us. And yet, he means to feed the survivors, as well — if, in fact, there are any."

With that, Captain Austen departed so abruptly, he did not see Magpie's respectful salute nor hear him chirp, "Aye, sir."

Delaying his hike to the galley where Biscuit would be swearing and fussing over his Brodie stove — for already the cook had asserted it did not handle half as well as the one he had coveted, then lost, when HMS *Isabelle* was burned off the Carolina coast — Magpie lingered near the fore-rail. He was morbidly mesmerized by the distant blaze. Its silvery-orange and black bellows devoured the ship's rigging like a lion ripping apart its kill and revelling in its bloody innards. That poor ship! *Those poor men*, he silently bemoaned as he stood witness to large numbers of them, many on fire, jumping into the harbour to flee the inferno. So few of them could swim! Would the boats be able to reach them before they were sucked into the salty sludge of the cold harbour?

Roosting overhead in the ropes of the fore shrouds was Jim Beef, the man who had Magpie convinced he was a spectre until he had saved his throat from Mrs. Kettle's knife. Magpie looked on as Mr. Beef rose up, his lanky arms and legs clawing at the tarred ropes, his long, stringy hair and beak-like nose a ghoulish silhouette against the brilliant fire. Into the shattered morning he bawled his now-familiar pronouncements as if he were standing in a high pulpit before a cowering congregation.

"Death and woe! Death and woe and despair to the lowly wretch caught in the fires of hell."

Magpie tried calling out to him, encouraged him to come down from the shrouds, but Mr. Beef did not hear, so disoriented he was in his own wasteland of madness.

A barrage of cannon-fire suddenly cracked through the air, sending shock waves around Portsmouth. Magpie hit the deck.

Just as Captain Austen foretold, the guns of the unfortunate ship went off in a succession of thunderous blasts. The foundations of the town shuddered. Magpie was certain he could hear distant windows imploding. Glowing-hot debris shot skyward before unpredictably showering down upon the water like a fireworks display gone horribly wrong. The *Invincible* rocked frantically on her anchoring cables, reminding Magpie of a dog struggling to break free from its leash. He drew himself up into a tight ball, like a threatened woodlouse, terrified that flaming spars and sails would come crashing down upon his head, or worse still, an errant round of grapeshot would cut him in two. How long did he lie there in that curled position, listening to his heart pound in his throat? Only when the explosions had ceased, their quaking din still echoing in his ears, did he risk peering up and having a look around, so thankful to see that the *Invincible*'s timbers were still intact.

Etched against a sky of glaring gold, he could see Jim Beef climbing toward the mizzen platform, his resonant mutterings now incoherent and impotent. Near the *Invincible*'s wheel, Captain Austen was hailing that disagreeable midshipman, the one with the pink cheeks of a schoolgirl, who, Magpie surmised, had earlier been sent out in one of the ship's cutters to discover what he could about the accident.

"Mr. Brambles!" shouted Captain Austen as the midshipman loped toward him. "What news? What news?"

In breathless snatches, the midshipman gave his answer. "Sir! She's a brig from Canada with — with one of the *queerest* names I've ever heard."

Hearing this, Magpie stiffened like a lump of ice.

"I did not have to go far, sir," Mr. Brambles went on. "I met a fisherman in the harbour who was familiar with her, having provisioned her yesterday afternoon with fresh bass and mackerel. He told me she had a crew of less than sixty, and that there were no visitors on board. The Portsmouth Polls ... er ... I mean to say the women had all been ordered ashore the previous night. Apparently, her commander was planning to weigh anchor at some point today and head out to Spithead to await favourable winds for sailing. Oh, and what's more — on the subject of the commander — my source told me that —"

Captain Austen convulsed with impatience. "And that queerest of names would be what ... if you please?"

Mr. Brambles's forehead shot up. His lower lip dropped, and his cheeks darkened as if he were affronted by the sharp tone to which he was being subjected. But seeing the deepening frown on his captain's face, he quickly sobered up. "Sir, she was called ... the ... the *Plentiful and Fantastic.*"

Magpie saw the corners of Captain Austen's mouth turn downwards. "Are you quite sure, Mr. Brambles?"

"On second thought, sir, it was the *Profound and Impressive.*"

"Mr. Brambles," said Captain Austen after a powerful exhalation, "I hope you are correct in this, because *if* you are wrong —" he allowed the words to hang heavily between them.

Magpie pushed himself up from the deck and scurried toward them, desperate to know. "Beg yer pardon, Captain Austen, I know it ain't me place," he said, rushing his panting words, "but I wondered if Mr. Brambles thought it might've bin the *Prosperous and Remarkable* what blew."

With a glare of indignation, Mr. Brambles jostled Magpie aside with his hip before delivering up his final answer. "Forgive me, Captain!" He stuttered with embarrassment. "With all the excitement! Aye! To be sure ... that ... *that* was the name of her."

CHAPTER 2

6:15 A.M.

Fly Austen hurried to the Camber Dock on Portsmouth Point where the boats were bringing in the wounded and the dead in droves, and placing them into horse-drawn carts. Searching their ghastly cargoes, he was relieved that Mr. Brambles's report had proven accurate. There were no women or children among the dead or those still clinging to life, wailing and groaning in their agonizing pain. Fly had hoped to find Prosper Burgo, the audacious commander of the *Prosperous and Remarkable* — preferably alive — but meeting with no success, he proceeded to the green space surrounding the parish church of St. Thomas of Canterbury, its lawn both a makeshift hospital and charnel house for the victims. A number of the town residents had already descended upon the green, bringing with them lanterns and blankets and food. Those with any knowledge of medicine — physicians, surgeons, apothecaries, mates, and loblolly boys — had set to work attending to scorched flesh and broken limbs, the latter having been effected by those forced to jump from the flaming shrouds and spars in order to escape the doomed brig.

Amidst the chaos that lay in the shadow of the church, Fly found his friend, Dr. Leander Braden, on his knees in a scattering of autumn leaves, a single lantern burning beside him. He was attending Pemberton Baker — Prosper Burgo's jack-of-all-tradesman — whose upper body was badly burned, and who, despite his unimaginable pain, did nothing more than heave an occasional sigh. Dropping down beside Leander in the leaves, Fly began arranging the rolls of linen bandages into convenient piles, keeping his eyes averted from Pemberton's oozing welts and blackened lips, particularly gruesome in the flickering glow of lantern light.

"Dear Mr. Baker, I am most distressed by the news of your ship and to see you have been grievously injured. I can assure you, you are in the very best of hands."

Pemberton moved his large head in a listless nod and closed his eyes, which — as good fortune would have it — had been spared from the fire's barbaric corruption.

Fly lowered his voice considerably as he addressed Leander. "I figured you would still be snoring in your bed at your Aunt Eliza's at this hour ... or did you steal away from a certain Brigantine Inn when the accident occurred?"

Leander kept his focus on the careful wrapping of Pemberton's left arm. "I think you know me better than that, Mr. Austen."

"Aye, sadly I do."

"If you must know, I was summoned to the home of my Aunt Eliza's friend in the middle of the night. The woman is suffering from a nervous complaint and just happens to live nearby on Lombard Street."

"Providential, indeed, though I prefer to think you were lying contentedly in the arms of your Emily."

Leander's quiet hoot of laughter was a sarcastic one. "Between you, my demanding aunt, the Sick and Hurt Board, and the Transport Office, I have been successfully kept from her. In the two weeks since our reunion in Wymering, I have scarcely seen her. I may as well be sailing still on the Atlantic."

"My dear old fellow ... sniveling does not suit you."

"Is that what I am doing?" Leander turned his frown upon Fly. "Perhaps, Mr. Austen, rather than admonishing me, you could make yourself useful by organizing a transportation of the wounded into the church. They will all catch a chill lying in these dews. Find the clergyman and ask him to open its doors. And — and please have word sent to the Haslar hospital in Gosport of our desperate situation here."

"If there is the slightest chance that some of Prosper's guns have not yet exploded, Haslar's ferrymen will not likely attempt to cross the water."

"Maybe not, but they must prepare beds, for their numbers shall soon rise." Leander sighed as he surveyed the scenes of suffering around him. "We need more medical supplies! As it is, the contents of my chest are already depleted. There must be an apothecary nearby, one that has not yet been plundered. If you must, raid the cockpit cabinets of every ship at or near the wharves — your own included — and know that I require bandages, more lanterns, olive or linseed oil, vinegar, tar-water, and ointments particularly kind to burns."

Fly rose to his feet, eager to be away. "Consider it done, old fellow."

"Oh, and while you're at it, some red wine might serve a purpose."

"For you? Or for your patients?"

Leander did not smile. "I believe red wine contains extraordinary curative powers."

"I will send out a search party for your necessary supplies, Doctor, and try to find our friend, Prosper Burgo, in this mess. Let us hope I do not come upon his strewn and blackened bits."

Pemberton Baker lifted his head to speak, his voice a croaky whisper. "Nay, ya won't, sir. Prosper weren't on the ship when she blew. Ya see, ya see, it were like this —"

"There now, Mr. Baker," said Leander gently. "That knowledge is a great comfort to us, but please lie back and rest. You can tell us what happened later when you have quite recovered."

Obliged, Pemberton closed his eyes again and grit his teeth as Leander lifted the melted ruins of his other arm and began applying a healing ointment with the greatest of care.

Fly scrutinized the shadowy crowds of volunteers and gawkers creeping through the mists around the church. "In that case, my guess is Prosper is around here somewhere, either in shock and wandering in circles or cursing like a costermonger and slamming anyone who crosses him." He jumped out of the way as two more victims, being hefted on canvas stretchers, were hastily set on the cold ground beside Pemberton Baker. One of them, screaming obscenities, tried to take a swing at the head stretcher bearer, who was in a rush to leave. The other one, naked, his flesh disastrously roasted from the waist down, was either dead or had lost consciousness. Feeling his stomach starting to heave, Fly glanced away.

"Please do not forget my supplies, Mr. Austen," said Leander, rustling the fallen leaves as he shifted on his haunches to examine the lifeless man.

"I shan't disappoint you." Fly attempted a smile. "And then later, when you are done here, perhaps I might treat you to a decent meal. I daresay you shall have earned one that includes at least five or six courses."

"And what is your reason for so generous a proposition?"

"We have further business to discuss."

Leander twisted his neck around to stare at him, lines of suspicion disfiguring his brow. "Of what nature, I pray you?"

"I shall be leaving England again soon, the minute the *Invincible* has been adequately manned and provisioned, but I am still in need of a ship's doctor — one who knows what he's about. In my experience I have found they are, indeed, a most rare breed."

6:30 A.M.
PORTSMOUTH POINT

In the aftermath of the explosion, the town was in an uproar. It seemed every inhabitant of Portsea Island had descended upon Portsmouth Point, clogging the smoke-filled streets in their unwholesome search for details of death and anguish, chattering and speculating at once about the accident. Some claimed it had been two ships that had blown, others claimed it was an enemy schooner "what drifted stealthily into the harbour under cover o' darkness," while others still claimed hundreds had been killed — "women with babes in their arms" among them. With each shrill proclamation, dread burrowed deeper into Emily's heart.

For some time, she had stayed in the shadow of the Brigantine Inn, too fearful at first to venture far. Now, desperate and determined to find her own answers, she struggled down Broad Street, her breathing shallow, her knees barely able to hold her upright; elbows nudging and jostling her as they had in her dream of Hartwood Hall. Between buildings and bodies cloaked in silvery pools of mist, Emily caught snatches of the rosy glimmer on the horizon. Oblivious to the destruction that had breached the hour before dawn, the sky was brightening in its heralding of the day. The lamp light of tea houses and taverns spilled into the streets, inviting the street dwellers to take refreshments within their warmed walls. Emily wished she could exile her cares and seek refuge in one of them to wrap her hands, already stiff with cold, around a mug of something hot. But she pushed on, allowing the momentum of the crowds to propel her forward.

Some were heading for the very tip of Portsmouth Point, eager for an unobstructed view of the conflagration in the harbour; others were moving toward the church of St. Thomas of Canterbury; all of them scampering with purpose like a pack of hounds, impassioned by the scent of fox blood. Emily followed those going in the direction of the church. It was there they were taking the injured, she had heard someone shout. Massaging warmth into her arms, she kept her line of vision lowered to the cobbles. Far too many passersby had ogled her, their glances widening in surprise when they realized her sailor's garments were disguising a female figure. It only raised Emily's alarm. What if someone had spotted her stealing away from the inn? What if someone was lurking in one of the many alleyways still layered in night gloom, hoping to spy the granddaughter of King George amidst the heaving crowd of humanity, and eager to report their fortuitous sighting to her family back in London?

Breathless and shaky, she arrived on the grounds of the old church and paused beside a walnut tree, waiting for the crowds to scurry past her, to wherever it was their curiosity was leading them — her senses heightened by the stirring branches that seemed to sigh in quiet communion with the catastrophe in the harbour. Looking up at the church tower, she saw the large clock and the bells in their lofty cupola. Sailing high above them was the weather vane — a three-masted ship, its imaginary course determined by the wind, its golden veneer reflecting the first fingers of sunlight.

Fearing the worst, Emily's gaze reluctantly fell upon the foretold destruction that lay veiled in blankets upon the ground around her. Small groups of men criss-crossed the lawn, dragging their feet through dried leaves as they collected the deceased and arranged them in tidy rows — an unsettling reminder of the line of dead on the decks of the *Isabelle*. Later on, they would be disposed of … not in the sea, but in unmarked graves or open pits in Kingston churchyard on the outskirts of the town. Emily could see that those still clinging to life were being carried into the church through the tower door, around which so many of the curiosity seekers had gathered. Wringing her hands, she wandered around in the green darkness of the tree, debating the wisdom of following them through that door into the vaulted interior of the church. She could not risk being seen, yet surely the answers she sought would be found within those stone walls.

The biting cold of the morning was mind-numbing, making it impossible for her to think clearly. Catching sight of a discarded blanket in the dewy grass, she scooped it up and retreated beneath the walnut, crouching down upon its knobby root mass. Wrapping the blanket tightly around her, she waited for the blood to return to her frozen limbs and for a shot of courage to carry her onward. But while she waited, staring miserably at the wisps of mist prowling the grounds like ghosts of the newly departed, she was startled by the appearance of two fashionably attired gentlemen who stopped to gossip a few feet away from where she sat.

"Apparently, it was not one of ours. It was a damn brig … a privateer from Canada."

"Thank goodness. I daresay the crew was all inebriated. One of them was most likely breaking into the stores of spirituous liquor and realized too late he was alongside barrels of gunpowder."

"Seamen are a dim-witted lot. 'Tis no wonder our navy suffered so many resounding defeats in the first year of this American war."

29

"Wait! I thought you said the unfortunate ship was from Canada."

"I did! You *do* know that those in Canada are helping us fight the Yankees?"

"Yes! Yes! Of course! How silly of me to forget!"

"Adding insult to injury, they say her guns killed a few of our lads on a neighbouring ship. A fine mess! And I further overheard someone saying their commander had survived the ordeal."

"Where was *he* at the time?"

"Not on his brig, that's to be sure. Rumour has it he was holed up in the second floor of a tavern with the publican's buxom wife, who had provided him with a warm bed and plenty of ale."

"What a beastly imbecile!"

"A veritable jackanapes!"

"Did you catch the name of this luckless brig?"

"It was something silly and pretentious. I — I can only recall that it began with a *P*."

Their loud guffaws scratched Emily like a hair shirt. So, too, did their overall attitude. It was unsuitably jocular, best befitting a Sunday stroll in Hyde Park, where one promenaded in the hopes of being seen. As they went off on their way, Emily was left sinking in despair. A brig from Canada! A privateer! For pity's sake! She didn't have to hear its name declared on the scornful lips of a stranger. She knew. It was the *Prosperous and Remarkable* — the impregnable *Prosperous and Remarkable*.

Two weeks ago, when they had all met again in Wymering, Leander, Fly, and Magpie had shared their stories of the heroics of Prosper Burgo and his Remarkables during their last voyage. Had they not — through extraordinary circumstances — found themselves on Prosper's brig, they would now be prisoners of war, withering away in damp, diseased American jails alongside Captain Prickett and his ill-fated Amethysts. Emily owed everything to Prosper Burgo. *He* was the one who had brought *her* men safely home. Had the explosion occurred a week ago when they were all still on board Prosper's ship — but no! She could not go there ... she could not contemplate the unthinkable.

High above the walnut tree, chimes began playing a hymn, jolting her with fresh fears. She had been in Portsmouth long enough now to know that the clock chimes of St. Thomas struck up a hymn every four hours. But, really, was it eight o'clock already? If so, she had lingered here for too long a time. Back at the Brigantine, the innkeeper would soon be carrying her breakfast tray of tea and toast to her room, and if Emily was found to be missing, she would surely organize an immediate search party from among the gang of inebriates who frequented her establishment.

Heartsick in the knowledge that her quest had not been successful and knowing that a nauseating anxiety would torment her until she knew for certain that both Leander and Magpie were still alive, she reluctantly began retracing her steps to the inn. The crowds on the streets had thinned. Save for the smoke that crested the town and stung her nostrils, all seemed normal once again. Laughing boys rolled hoops over the cobbles with barking dogs close on their heels. Peddlers plied their trade from their portable stands, sonorously extolling the virtues of their wares. Clusters of men and women stood around chattering or were cheerfully getting on with their daily shopping. As Emily sped along the sidewalks, she felt exposed and unprotected, for the rising sun had swept away the twilight of dawn, and she could no longer move freely about, a shadow among shadows.

A block away from the Brigantine's front door, she ducked into the nearest alleyway. Her heart racing, her stomach souring, she prayed her eyes were playing a cruel trick. If not, had she seen *him* before he had seen *her*? Hugging the wall of mortar on the edge of the alleyway, she peeked into the street to observe him. There ... there, standing in the archway between two bustling shops, was a man she had hoped never to see again. He was not dressed as one might expect. The style and shabby manner of his shirt and pantaloons, as well as the cap pulled low upon his forehead, would indicate to anyone taking note that he was most likely a dock worker, enjoying the excitement and variety of the morning, happy for a reprieve from his dismal chores. But it was *him*. Emily was sure of it. Furthermore, he was carefully scrutinizing the faces of those who passed him by; evidence that he was ... on *watch*.

Hoping to find a circuitous route back to the inn, Emily wheeled about and fled toward the smouldering harbour, wondering why — of all people — they had chosen to send *him*.

8:00 A.M.
ABOARD HMS *EXPEDITION*
PORTSMOUTH WHARF

Having been ordered to stand down and go below to fetch his breakfast, Thomas Trevelyan stopped at the rail of HMS *Expedition* to sniff the irritating air that fell heavily upon the harbour. His feet — gratefully housed once again in shoes — kicked nervously against the bulwark as he looked out over the debris-laden water to the place where the exploded remains of the Canadian brig lay like a dead whale. Later today she would most likely vanish from view and sink into the harbour to join the forgotten wrecks of the *Royal George*, the *Boyne* and the ancient *Mary Rose*. Trevelyan silently celebrated her demise. It had been the pesky *Prosperous and Remarkable* and her crew of ruffians that had brought about his downfall on the coast of South Carolina back in June. He could not regret the loss of life and hoped the detonated limbs of her commander — that mouthy shrimp, Prosper Burgo — had now washed into the waters of the Solent, providing its sea creatures with a feast of overbroiled meat.

Trevelyan's eyes travelled to the upper works of the neighbouring frigate, HMS *Invincible*, sitting companionably next to the *Expedition* just out from the wharf. Not once having left his own ship since joining its crew two weeks ago — thinking it wise he show a preference for chores such as swabbing the deck rather than risk venturing beyond the safety of her timbers — he had collected his information on the *Invincible*'s particulars from the *Expedition*'s clerk, one of the few on board with whom he bothered to speak. Trevelyan had been dismayed to learn the captain of the *Invincible* had been struck down by apoplexy four days ago, and her new commander was Francis Austen. And it was more than likely that Mr. Austen's physician was still Leander Braden, that grave academic for whom *Princess* Emily had harboured an ignominious infatuation. Trevelyan had crossed battle paths in the Atlantic with Austen and Braden. And it was just his luck! Of all the thousands of men employed in the Royal Navy, these two were the most acquainted with him. These two were the most capable of recognizing him — notwithstanding his present emaciated appearance — and uprooting his falsehood of being the New Bedford, Massachusetts–born Asa Bumpus who had willingly elected to join the enemy navy rather than rotting in an English prison.

How much longer could he go on unnoticed on the decks of the *Expedition*? Trevelyan wondered. How much longer could he safely use the assumed name of Asa Bumpus? Surely now the news of his escape — and the displacement of Mr. Bumpus — was common knowledge, if not among the general public, then among the highest officers of the Royal Navy. Surely there were spies out everywhere, searching for Thomas Trevelyan, the traitor responsible for the sinking of HMS *Isabelle* and HMS *Amelia*; for the death of countless British sailors, and the kidnapping of a granddaughter of King George. Surely the Admiralty — angered and humiliated by his clever evasion of naval authorities during a transportation of captives from the prison hulk *Illustrious* — was determined to find him. And when they did, they would seek swift justice.

Noticing the *Expedition*'s clerk scurrying along the starboard gangway with a stack of registry books in his arms, Trevelyan hoped the man might prove useful.

"With respect, Mr. Croker, might I delay you a moment?" he asked, pushing away from the ship's rail.

The clerk stopped short, his eyes narrowing as he looked Trevelyan up and down. "Ha! Mr. Bumpus, is it? Well then, what do you want? I am a very busy man. If it's a complaint regarding your messmates or your grog rations, ya best take it up with the bo'sun."

"Just an inquiry, sir: I thought it had been Captain Uptergrove's intention to put to sea immediately when I first came aboard. That was two weeks ago now, sir."

"Ha! Eager to quit English soil, are ya, Mr. Bumpus? Or is it a fear ya have that our ship might blow up, same as that hapless brig from Canada?"

"'Tis neither, sir," said Trevelyan, lying through his teeth. "I am simply at my happiest whilst on the waves."

"Then you are a rare one, Mr. Bumpus. Ha! Must be the Yankee blood flowing in your veins. Most of *our* lads are happiest in the taverns and grog shops, regardless of the country they're in at the time."

Trevelyan faked an appreciative smile. "And has the captain made a decision, sir, as to when we'll get under way?"

Mr. Croker frowned and pursed his thin lips before offering up his theory on the subject. "Well, as you should know, Mr. Bumpus, our initial unease concerned fogs and unfavourable weather, but now it has become Captain Uptergrove's pleasure to meet with Captain Austen of the *Invincible*. It seems this Captain Austen has been away visiting his young family and much preoccupied with Admiralty affairs, but as he and Uptergrove share a common friend in the late Captain James Moreland of the lost *Isabelle*, our captain is most anxious to dine with Mr. Austen at his earliest convenience."

Trevelyan felt an unpleasant tug in his belly. "Then you believe it may be a day or two before we weigh anchor?"

"At the very least! In the meantime, be ever vigilant for all manner of incendiaries abandoned or strewn carelessly about. We do not want to suffer the same fate as the *Prosperous and Remarkable*." Mr. Croker cleared his throat. "Now, if you'll excuse me, Mr. Bumpus, I am a very important man."

As the clerk went on his significant way, Trevelyan returned to the rail and gave the bulwark another kick. He shot a scorching glance at the neighbouring *Invincible* and muttered obscenities under his breath. Until the *Expedition* took her departure from Portsmouth, it would be essential that he lay very low.

CHAPTER 3

8:00 A.M.
MILE END TERRACE, PORTSMOUTH

"If that explosion resulted in multiple injuries, Arthur and Leander may be a long while yet," stated Miss Eliza Braden while digging about for her sewing scissors in her leather etui. "In the meantime, its flames will soon be heating up all of Portsea Island."

Gus Walby, who sat shivering on a blanket box in the bow-window of Miss Braden's sparsely furnished culinary sitting-room, was made more miserable by her cold pronouncement. How he wished she would just agree to warm the coals and the cast-iron hob grate in her bricked fireplace so they could boil the copper kettle and have their tea. But Miss Braden, who was presently sitting on her customary chair behind him, sewing a length of delicate lace onto a gown that belonged to a wealthy woman of Portsmouth, had previously informed him that the tea would remain locked away in her cupboard until the moment when her brother and nephew returned home. Gus wondered if the real reason for delaying their breakfast was the fact that she did not completely trust him, and believed he might try to run off with her precious canister of tea, a gift from her brother, Dr. Arthur Braden, upon his arrival on her doorstep more than two weeks ago with his crippled, young charge in tow.

Craning his neck, Gus searched the views beyond the window, hoping to see the old doctor and his son, Leander, hastening toward the small rectangle of garden wedged between the street and Miss Braden's front door. Minutes after the first explosion, the old doctor had departed from the cottage and struck out in the pearly mists, determined to learn what had happened, and hoping to accelerate his journey to the harbour by hitching a ride on a curricle or a cart heading in the general direction. Young Dr. Braden had been called away in the night to the bedside of a friend who — according to Miss Braden — lived on Lombard Street, in the vicinity of Portsmouth presently engulfed in smoke. Gus's stomach boiled with fear. What if something terrible had happened to them? What if Emily or Captain Austen or his shipmate, Magpie, had been gravely injured? Gus had begged to go along with old Dr. Braden, but Miss Braden had insisted his crutch would be a hindrance, and told him to ease his mind with diligent occupation.

"The dishes must be set out, Mr. Walby," she had said sternly. "The table must be scrubbed, the sugar grated, and the bread and cheese arranged for the men's return."

Gus blew his warm breath into his hands to thaw them as he continued his watch at the window. Out on the street, the neighbours — in their smocks and shawls — were huddled in groups, speculating upon the explosions while their carefree children played games in dizzying circles around them. The sun was peeking over rooftops and chimneys, spilling rays of fiery-orange upon Miss Braden's little garden, warming her dew-soaked vines and climbing roses. But these scenes of domesticity and beauty were soiled with plumes of smoke as if their invisible creator — in a fit of rage — had besmirched his canvas with black paint.

Still there was no sign of father and son.

"One cannot dispute the fact, Mr. Walby. It will be a ship that has blown in the harbour. I have seen it before — more times than I care to remember. The worst explosion was the *Boyne* back in ninety-five, but then there was the unfortunate accident that befell the *Royal George*. She sank in eighty-two, taking a thousand lives with her."

Gus's fear escalated. He turned around to gaze shyly at Miss Braden. He did not like being left alone with her. She possessed none of the warmth and vitality that her older brother and nephew had in abundance. In her late fifties, she was a thin, cheerless woman whom Gus had never seen wear anything but brown dresses and mob caps that tied under her chin, and who frequently peered at him through a double-lensed, single-handled prospect glass. Occasionally, a lone iron-grey curl slipped from beneath the frilly edge of her cap, but her mouth was permanently pursed in opinion.

"That is why *you* must reconsider your career choice, Mr. Walby."

"Why, Miss Braden?"

"You are a clever boy, but your intelligence will go to rot in the Royal Navy," she said, peering at him over her sewing. "You should become a physician like my brother and nephew."

"I don't believe I have the constitution for it," said Gus weakly, hearing his stomach rumbling in sympathy.

"If you stay in His Majesty's service, your life will surely be cut short. There are far too many hazards at sea. If your ship doesn't catch fire, a storm or disease will finish you off ... or a Frenchman or American will kill you with his long guns. Think how close we came to losing Leander on his most recent Atlantic crossing. Shot and starved! That wrathful ocean's waves have already deprived me of one brother —" Her voice trailed off into the chilly pockets of the sitting room.

Gus watched her bend her head over her work and stitch furiously as if exorcising a memory. "You should become a physician," she added, with a decisive nod of her cap.

"My uncle is a sea captain, Miss Braden, with no prospects of prize money. I am afraid he would not have the funds to send me to school."

"There are benefactors to be found."

An uncomfortable tightness settled inside Gus's chest. Words began tumbling unchecked from his mouth. "I want to return to sea with Captain Austen and your nephew and my friend, Magpie, and with Emily ... if she's allowed to go."

Miss Braden set aside the gown and picked up her prospect glass to stare at him with her fearfully magnified, light-grey eyes. "I shall expend every ounce of persuasion to make certain my nephew *never* sails again." She went silent for a time to allow her words to sink in. "Your friend, Princess Emeline, is unknown to me; however, if she has any comprehension of decency, she will abandon this imprudent scheme to hide out here in Portsmouth and return home at once to her family. Otherwise, people might mistake her for a Cyprian."

"Beg your pardon, Miss Braden ... what's a Cyprian?"

"A woman of," she caught herself, as if taking care in the selection of her words, "easy virtue."

Having never heard the word *virtue* before, Gus did not fully understand, though Miss Braden's tone hinted at something objectionable. "But her family means to marry her off to a fat marquess named Wetherell Lindsay."

"That is her family's prerogative. Her future must be charted for her."

"But he wears a wig! And wigs are terribly outdated and unfashionable."

"What the Marquess wears on his head is of no concern so long as he provides *her* with a good home and a good name, befitting her royal birth."

"Oh, but, Miss Braden, I have met the Marquess's mother and two of his brothers."

She blinked at him. "What is your point, Mr. Walby?"

"They are *all* so very mean-spirited."

"I am certain the Princess shall win them over ... in time."

Gus could help neither his whine, nor its rising amplification. "But — but Emily loves your nephew. And he loves her."

Miss Braden's laugh was mirthless. "Princess Emeline has as much chance of marrying Leander as she has of marrying Lord Nelson."

"Lord Nelson is dead, ma'am."

"Precisely!" Her eyes went flinty. "Mr. Walby, a union between my nephew and a granddaughter of King George is inconceivable. The very idea of it is ... why, it's absurd. Remove it from your head this instant."

Bewildered by her opinions and sensing the gavel of justice had just come down hard upon his own, Gus resumed his worried watch out the window, praying he would not have to bear Miss Braden's severe company alone for much longer.

2:00 P.M.
THE SHIP'S TAVERN, PORTSMOUTH POINT

Magpie shrank in the doorway of the Ship's Tavern behind Biscuit, who was busy doing a sweep of the perimeter with his odd eyes. They had been searching for hours and the last thing Magpie expected to hear from the lips of the Scottish cook was a raucous hoot of victory, the sudden shock of which very nearly caused him to leap out of his new leather shoes.

"Told ya we'd find him sooner or later," Biscuit laughed, giving Magpie a knuckle-rub on the top of his head.

Clutching his thrum cap, Magpie followed Biscuit's eyes to the lonely corner of the tavern where Prosper Burgo appeared to be hiding behind an enormous earthenware pitcher of drink. He ran to him at once. "Prosper! We bin lookin' fer ya all over the place."

Biscuit approached the table at a more leisurely pace. "And we're mighty relieved to find ya much as we left ya two weeks ago, 'cause Cap'n Austen feared we'd stumble across yer heap o' charred bones."

Without meeting their gaze, Prosper gestured with an open palm for them to join him. "If that'd bin me end ... I might 'ave bin better off."

Magpie sat down on the bench opposite the privateersman, who reeked of smoke and brine, and looked much as shirts do when put through a wringer, and watched as he poured himself another mug of brown ale. After the initial joy of their discovery had abated — Prosper's black mood not conducive to celebrations of a prolonged nature — Biscuit fell into a quiet conversation with him. Magpie let his eye wander around the tavern. It had been three months since he had spent time inside a drinking establishment. The last time — in Charleston, South Carolina — had ended badly when an unexpected encounter with Thomas Trevelyan and that unscrupulous turncoat Octavius Lindsay had led to them terrifying him within an inch of his life, to the point where he had chucked the contents of his stomach all over Mr. Lindsay's Hessian boots.

Biscuit had told him that the Ship's Tavern was popular with local seamen, but he was ever so thankful it possessed nothing of the sweltering pandemonium and terrors of Charleston. It was peaceful here; the crowds that earlier jammed the public houses had moved on with their regular routines. Even so, Magpie did not like the look of the four old rustics with their dried-apple faces, spread out upon stools around the cold, brick hearth in their torn stockings and wooden clogs, chewing on bread with their mouths open and their rheumy eyes fixed upon Magpie's table. Nor did he like the publican's wife, who swished around the high-ceilinged room, refilling the glasses and tankards of her few customers, her hairy chin lifted so high in the air, Magpie fully expected — at any moment — to see her trip up and perform a somersault. She was a painful reminder of the hateful laundress, Meg Kettle. Why, the woman's sour mug and hip width were so similar to Mrs. Kettle's, Magpie wondered — with an involuntary shiver — if the two women shared a kinship. For a time he found entertainment in the funny black bird that alternately tweeted and cussed in its bamboo cage on the wall above his head, but a sudden outburst from Prosper swivelled him toward his companions.

"I should never 'ave left me ship. I ain't sure I kin ever forgive meself. Have ya seen her? All that remains o' me spunky *Prosperous and Remarkable* is a blackened shell and one blackened mast, pokin' out o' the water like the pathetic arm of a drownin' man." Prosper lowered his face into his earthenware mug.

"Ach! We're mighty sorry fer the loss o' yer lads," said Biscuit, his lazy eye rolling in his whiskery face.

Magpie was fascinated by the throbbing purple veins on Prosper's bald crown as he delivered his sibilant reply. "Me lads? Why they're nothin' but a damn lot o' galoots and jackanapes. Sure as it were a barrel o' rum what caught fire! If I'd been aboard in the first place, the *Remarkable* never would've blown."

"But, Prosper, what about Pemberton Baker?" ventured Magpie. "Ya must be so relieved knowin' he's gonna pull through."

"Why, he's the biggest puddin' head o' them all. I left *him* in charge whilst on shore." Prosper growled. "Ah, but what good is he to me now, anyways? I ain't got no ship, and even if I did — swaddled in all them bandages — Pemberton would be as useful as one o' them mummies from Arabia."

Magpie stroked the woolly thrum cap in his hands. He couldn't understand Prosper's insensitivity. If the moon were his to give, Magpie would gladly relinquish it to have his friend, Morgan Evans, come back to life. How he ached to hear Morgan sing one of his sweet Welsh songs about the sorrow of parting.

Prosper was still shaking his head, his narrowed eyes looking at nothing. "When I think o' the treasures I'd amassed in me hold … all gone to waste."

Treasures! What treasures? All Magpie could recollect of the *Prosperous and Remarkable's* darkest parts were the barrels of stinky cheese and the rats and the rumour that — rather than bury them respectfully at sea — Prosper had stored his dead Remarkables down there and covered them over with shovelfuls of shingle.

Biscuit's curiosity was piqued. "Well, don't keep us waitin'! Tell us! What did yer hold … *hold*? Gold? Diamonds? Ambergris?"

Prosper exhaled a long, drawn-out sigh and spoke mournfully as if he were listing the qualities of a woman he had loved and lost. "I had it all: Madeira, port, rum, gin, all varieties of beer. Why I could 'ave retired from privateerin' and set up me own tavern. But nay! 'Tis gone, and the few farthin's I had on me … I gave to that pus-faced wench over there." He flung a scornful glance at the publican's wife, leaving Magpie's imagination in a muddle. Hadn't Prosper, in the not too distant past, harboured a burning devotion to that woman's *twin* — Mrs. Kettle?

Biscuit's large hands suddenly clamped down upon Magpie's ears so he could whisper to Prosper. "Ach! Were ya lyin' with that wench when her husband weren't around?"

"I were!" hissed Prosper. "But never agin. She played rough with me parts!"

Magpie weaseled out of Biscuit's iron clutches. He didn't want to miss a word, especially now that Prosper had fixed his eyes upon *him*. "Little sailmaker … I'll tell ya right now … keep yer distance from them *vile doxies*. They'll rob yer coins right outta the pockets o' yer trousers whilst they're smilin' sweetly with their bosoms pushed up so hard in yer face ya can't breathe. Next thing ya know, they'll be the cause o' ya losin' yer crew, yer ship, and yer livelihood."

Magpie did not know too many women, aside from Mrs. Kettle and Emily, but he didn't believe that Emily was one of these vile doxies.

Biscuit threw his head back and hollered at the publican's wife to bring them "a skillet o' cheese and bread," ignoring her flagrant tongue-sucking response. Then, looking serious all of a sudden, he nodded at Prosper. "Now, let's get some vittles in ya so's we kin talk a shade o' business."

Prosper gaped at the Scottish cook as if he had sprouted a tuft of whiskers on the bridge of his nose. "What business kin I talk with me ship already disintegratin' in the harbour and no letter o' marque to continue me privateerin' with?"

"Well, ya see, Mr. Austen — who, be it known, is now Cap'n Austen — were just given orders to take command o' the *Invincible* on account o' the previous cap'n comin' down with the apoplexy and —"

"The *Invincible*? Ahhh! Don't tell me she's another lumberin' seventy-four like the *Amethyst* what belonged to that blunderbuss Cap'n Prickett?"

"Nay, Prosper," cried Magpie, "she's a frigate!"

Prosper rearranged his skinny rump on the bench. "A frigate, ya say? One o' yer Royal Navy's *fast fighters*?"

"Aye! And she's got thirty-six guns!" added Magpie.

"A scanty thirty-six?"

"And — and she's got a Nelson chequer on her hull."

"What the devil's that?" hissed Prosper.

Magpie beamed with knowledge. "She looks like a checked shirt! Her gun deck's painted yellow and all her gunports black."

Biscuit lent some clarification to his description. "That way, from afar, her gunports always look open — ya know — to frighten off potential foes."

Prosper looked circumspect. "And where's this frigate o' yers headed to?"

"Back to the American coast to do more fightin'."

"And do ya think she'll 'ave any effect against one o' them heavy American frigates, one o' them forty-fours?"

"Guess we'll find out soon enough. Our navy's sendin' all the ships it kin spare in the battle against Old Boney. But we gotta find enough men to man 'em."

"Think I'd rather be privateerin'. More chances to git rich; less chance o' gettin' killed."

With a snarl, the publican's wife set the plate of ordered food between them and then flounced off, the great swish of her skirts blowing up a draft of wind strong enough to ruffle Magpie's hair. For a long while both Biscuit and Prosper watched her go.

"Ach, man! What were ya thinkin'?" Biscuit was appalled. "That wench could keep a ship's sails billowin' in the doldrums with them hips o' hers."

"She looked a good sight better when the candles were doused." Prosper stuffed a lump of bread into his mouth and chewed on it in a way that suggested he was doing some heavy pondering. "This frigate ... the *Invincible* ... might Cap'n Austen be lookin' fer a seasoned helmsman?"

Biscuit's face broke into a whiskery grin. "Aye! He were hopin' ya might consider —"

"'Cause I won't join his crew unless I'm helmsman o' the ship. Not interested in bein' the cox'n o' the cap'n's launch or one o' them cutters. Too piddlin' fer me what's brought down nineteen prizes in this American war. By Jove! Might 'ave been twenty if Trevelyan's *Serendipity* didn't decide to keep company with the ocean floor."

"I think ya've got yerself a new post, Mr. Burgo," said Biscuit, extending his hand to ratify the transaction.

But Prosper did not heed it, for he had more to say. "I won't be takin' no orders from no one 'cept Cap'n Austen, so's if I agree to it, he'll have to make me the sailin' master, as well ... with all the privileges. I won't be sleepin' nor takin' no meals with the common lads. And I'll be wantin' a ticket into the gunroom and great cabin."

Even Magpie knew that Captain Austen was short on officers and masters, but it was not Biscuit's place to promise Prosper Burgo a seat at his supper table.

"When we finish up here, ya kin tell all that to the cap'n himself," Biscuit said with some trepidation. "Ya just may find he's agreeable on all accounts."

Magpie turned on the bench to look up hopefully at Biscuit. "Kin I tell 'im the rest?"

"Ya go right ahead, lad!" said Biscuit, treating himself — now that the official part of the meeting was over and the outcome successful — to a thick wedge of dark yellow cheese. "But make it fast! We've gotta run our errands fer Cap'n Austen in town and git back to the ship."

Magpie gazed at Prosper, his eye round with excitement. "Tomorrow ... at nightfall ... Cap'n Austen's sendin' a few o' us out on shore. We're formin' a *press gang*."

A queer expression took hold of Prosper's face. "'Ave ya ever bin out with a press gang afore?"

"Nay, sir."

"Do ya even know what they be about, little sailmaker?"

"Nay, sir, haven't a notion. But Cap'n Austen says I kin go ... so long's I stay close to the ship's cutter."

Prosper reached for his mug of ale and howled like a dog. "Ha! I took ya on that reconnaissance mission in Charleston and ya nearly soiled yer drawers."

Magpie hated being reminded of that. "I've growed up a lot since then," he said quietly.

Prosper howled a second time. "It'd be wise to 'ave me come along. And I will, but I 'ave two stipulations."

Biscuit swallowed his mouthful of cheese so he could blurt out the word: "Stipulations?"

"Aye! First off, ya settle me account with the publican fer me beer and vittles; second off, ya put *me* in charge o' leadin' the gang." Prosper locked his arms across his thin chest and gave them a puffed-up smile. "I'll show ya all how it's done!"

CHAPTER 4

4:00 P.M.

THE BRIGANTINE INN

E mily hovered near the window of her little room, struck by the loveliness of the late afternoon. The shock of the early morning seemed all but forgotten by the sun, casting its rosy glow upon the people strolling below on Broad Street. Though the essence of gunpowder still laced the air, the smoke in the harbour had dissipated, and from her vantage point Emily could see nothing of the ruined *Prosperous and Remarkable*, for which she was thankful. She studied the faces of the strollers and those who loitered on the cobbles, wishing she might find Leander among them … that he would see her standing by her lonely window and raise his arm in a jubilant wave to assure her all was well. But the faces on Broad Street were neither familiar nor suspicious. Feeling a cloying despair in her breast, she dashed the shutters across the glass panes that looked out upon the world, plunging her room into darkness. Another long, empty evening awaited her. There would be no joy in taking her dinner — her stomach was a veritable butter churn — and her only available distraction, Jane Austen's volumes of *Pride and Prejudice*, could not possibly hold her attention, her mind being aflutter with something akin to madness.

Emily lit the oil lamp on her small bedside table, shovelled more coals onto the horizontal bars of her grate, threw her shawl around her shoulders and sadly gazed around for something more to do. The last thing she had expected was to hear a sharp rap upon her door.

"Mrs. George?" said the distinctively depressed voice of the innkeeper. "Ya have a visitor, ma'am."

Emily scrambled across her bed to open the door. "Who has come?"

The innkeeper answered with a concise shrug. "All's I know is ... I don't like the look o' him."

"Why then did you let him in?"

"He insisted that he knew ya well, and that he had been *sent* to speak with ya."

"Sent? Sent by whom?"

"Sure as I don't know!"

Emily's pulse raced. "Did he not give you his name?"

"He were evasive on that account," the innkeeper said with a toss of her frizzy head. "I'm not sure I believed him."

Emily glanced at the window, wondering — should it be necessary — if she could successfully climb down to the street level without breaking a leg or reinjuring her ankle, the one she had snapped after leaping from the shattered windows of Trevelyan's ship back in early June.

The innkeeper huffed a great sigh. "Come see fer yerself, ma'am. He's waiting for ya in the private sitting room we call the *Blue Peter*. If ya say the word, I'll send him packing on the next merchantman bound fer the East Indies." Hiking her skirts up, she began trudging down the hall toward the stairs.

"Wait!"

"What's it now, Mrs. George?"

"Tell me! How — how is he dressed?"

The innkeeper turned back, mouth downturned and nostrils flared as if she smelled a rat. "Like a street urchin or one o' them filthy little powder monkeys ya always see on them warships. Only this one ... well, he's only got one eye."

4:15 P.M.

When Emily crossed the threshold of the sitting room, Magpie wanted so badly to jump into her arms. But Captain Austen had earlier warned him that he must always bear in mind that she was a princess, "a grand-daughter of our King George," and it was improper to exhibit affec-tionate behaviour unless she were the one to initiate it. Often at night, before sleep overpowered him, he liked to relive the rare moments when she had rewarded him with a warm embrace — like the time when she first learned he had survived the sinking of the *Isabelle*. But given the events of the day, he figured she might not be in the right frame of mind to give hugs to a little lad who was desperate for them. That was all right; he was overjoyed just to have her to himself. In the weeks since they had all reunited, there had only been one opportunity to visit with her. The problem was ... there had been too many others present, all clamouring for her attention, all talking to her at once. Magpie thought Emily's face was too pale, as if she had not seen the sun for days, and her shoulders too rigid, as if she were waiting for someone to pounce upon her. But as soon as her glance fell on him, she lit up like a candelabrum.

"Magpie!" she cried, shutting the door behind her and urging him toward the sofa where they both sat down. "It *really* is you!"

With all he had to tell her, Magpie was a bundle of excitement, and as such he failed to notice the tears in her brown eyes. Words flew out of his mouth like an overturned bucket of ice.

"Oh, Em! I'm so glad I knew ya was goin' by the name o' Mrs. George. I remember when some o' the Isabelles called ya *Mr.* George and thought ya was a man."

She let out a little laugh. "With all this subterfuge, I'm beginning to forget who I am!"

"I kin remind ya if ya forget." Jamming his hands between his knees, he peered up at her, his smile wavering. "Yer innkeeper didn't like the look o' me and told me I needed me hands scrubbed, and said I should be addressin' meself as *Mister* Somebody, not namin' meself after a naughty bird what no one likes."

"Then she simply cannot recognize a gentleman when she sees one."

"I were so worried she were gonna send me away, 'cause I brung important messages with me."

Emily lunged toward him, her eyes pleading. "Tell me ... please tell me he is safe."

"Ya mean, Dr. Braden? Oh, he's safe and sound, Em."

He heard her sharp intake of breath. Her head rolled backward and her lips began moving as if in prayer.

"He's bin at the St. Thomas church since early this morning, helpin' all the men what got burned. Captain Austen and I brung him some supplies. He ain't had a moment to breathe."

"Of course!" She beamed. "Where else would he be?"

"Oh, but, Em, I gotta tell ya ... the *Prosperous and Remarkable* —"

"I know. I have heard. Everyone out on the streets —" she hesitated and started again. "Everyone here at the inn has been speaking of it."

"Did ya know Prosper's alive? I just saw him. He's in a tavern and his back teeth are well afloat, but he's alive. And Pemberton Baker is, too, though hurt real bad." Magpie woefully shook his head. "So many o' the Remarkables didn't make it, Em. They might've bin ruffians, but they was all good men."

"The very best," she said gently. "Now, tell me ... have you eaten anything today?"

"There weren't no time to. Cap'n Austen needed us to fetch some provisions fer him, and earlier I were busy helpin' Biscuit boil up and transport pots o' burgoo fer the survivors."

"Oh no! Not Biscuit's horrible burgoo? Those poor Remarkables!"

"Nay, Em! Biscuit got fresh stuff from the Weevil Yard and he —"

"The Weevil Yard?" she grimaced.

"It's what they call the Vittlin' Yard 'round these parts."

"Oh, I see."

"And — and Biscuit added butter and molasses to the mess. Tastes a whole sight better."

Emily jumped up from the sofa, instructing him to "Sit tight and wait here!" He scarcely had time to study the colourful collection of flasks and bottles displayed upon the sideboard when she returned, holding high a tray of steaming tea, cold chicken, bread, and butter. Her cheeks, he noticed, had now fully regained their pink colour.

"The innkeeper made all that fer me?"

"No! I did! You see, I'm on good terms with her and she occasionally lets me into her kitchen … as long as I press a shilling into her palm."

"Does she know yer a princess?"

Emily set the tray down on the sideboard and placed a finger to her lips. "She thinks I am a hopelessly frightened woman whose husband is away at sea fighting the Americans." She poured and handed him a cup of tea. "Now I have it on good authority that the tea leaves are fresh."

"Are ya sure the innkeeper doesn't add floor sweepins' to them?"

"I don't believe so."

Magpie lifted his cup to his nose and took a sniff. "It don't smell like horses."

Emily laughed quietly as she sat down with her own cup. "I believe you'll find it much improved over the tea Prosper Burgo offered you on your journey back home."

"Prosper boils the same leaves fer weeks on end."

"Despite the expense, the innkeeper is surprisingly particular about her tea. Apparently, she purchased this set of china at Wedgwood's showroom and buys her leaves at Richard Twining's warehouse in London."

From the way Emily spoke of them, Magpie figured they must be places of importance, frequented only by the cream of society.

While they enjoyed their food and drink, they speculated on the fate of the *Prosperous and Remarkable*, discussed his recent eye examination, conducted thoroughly and kindly by Dr. Arthur Braden — "*who said I were healin' good*" — and ended off with Magpie giving her a complete description of Captain Austen's new frigate, HMS *Invincible*. When these subjects had been exhausted, Emily returned her cup and saucer to the tray and looked at him — kind of nervously — as if she was working up to ask him something.

"Did you have your visit to Captain Austen's house?"

Magpie felt a rush of happy remembrance. "Oh, Em, I bin just bustin' to tell ya 'bout it."

"Was Mrs. Austen kind to you? Did you meet all of the children?"

"Mrs. Austen spoiled me with pound cake fer breakfast and lemon cheesecakes fer me supper and gave me chocolate coffee 'cause she was upset when she found out Mrs. Kettle had given me a fright with her big knife. And Mary-Jane — she's Mr. Austen's eldest — played Ninepins and Jackstraws with me, and thought I were a pirate on account o' me eye patch. I made the three little babes laugh until they had to go to bed, and then Miss Jane sat down on the sofa with me and read from a book called —" Magpie had to catch some air before continuing "— *The Life and Strange Surprizing Adventures of Robinson Crusoe*. She said she thought I might like it on account o' me knowin' about the sea and life on ships and such."

"Miss Jane?" Emily's face had turned very red, as if her hot tea had heated her through.

"Cap'n Austen's youngest sister. She were visitin', too … just like me. And, oh Em, Mr. Austen told me *she's* the one what wrote that book we was readin' on the *Isabelle* about them two sisters, Miss Dashwood and Miss Marianne, what had problems with money and men."

"Yes. I know." Emily's voice fell to a whisper. "What is she like?"

Magpie took a moment to gather his thoughts. "She has brown curls all over her forehead and shiny eyes and she smells like them little white flowers what come out in spring."

"Lilies of the Valley?"

"Aye! Think so! And she made me laugh just like I done with Cap'n Austen's babies. Oh, and she wanted to know all about ya. But I didn't tell her ya was here in Portsmouth 'cause Cap'n Austen said we was to tell no one o' yer whereabouts."

"Was — was Dr. Braden there, too?"

"Nay, not when I were there."

Emily reached for her teacup and brought it to her lips without taking a sip. It was some time before she spoke again. "Please tell me you won't be sailing for a long while. I cannot bear the thought of being separated from you just now."

Magpie's stomach dropped. "But won't ya be comin' with us?"

Her chest heaved a plaintive sigh. "I am afraid not."

"But what will ya do?"

"I do not know exactly."

"Ya can't stay here in Portsmouth fer always, Em."

When she glanced up from the floor, there was a wild look in her eyes. "No? Can't I?"

"Nay! They'll find ya here, hidin' out in this place, and take ya back to Hartwood Hall. And that wicked duchess will make ya marry her son — the one ya said wore powdered wigs and shoes with them high heels."

"They cannot force me back there, even if they threaten to take me to the roof and dangle me by the ankles over the stones of the street."

"Aw, ya just gotta come with us, Em. Cap'n Austen needs more men and yer as good as ten. Biscuit's always sayin' that yer every inch a true sailor, 'every hair a rope yarn.' Tomorrow night, we're formin' a press gang to try and find us some more sailors and Prosper Burgo's gonna lead us through the alleyways."

Emily angled her head and frowned. "Did Captain Austen give you permission to go out with them?"

"Aye! So long's I stay with the cutter at the Camber Dock."

"Oh no, it is far too dangerous."

"I'm gonna be the lookout, and I kin help row all the men what they round up back to the *Invincible*." Magpie did some thinking as he savoured his last bite of bread and butter. "They could use some help agin in the hospital, Em."

"Why? Is Captain Austen short on surgeons and loblolly boys, as well?"

"Right now he's only got Mr. Duffy and Dr. Braden."

She gazed at him as if she were going to apologize. "Oh, Magpie, I don't think Dr. Braden will be making the next cruise with you."

"Why not?"

"Because he was weakened from his ordeal on the *Amethyst*, and wants to stay with his father. Remember, he only just learned, upon arriving home two weeks ago, that his mother had passed away."

Magpie scratched his head in confusion. "But I don't understand, Em, 'cause I overheard Cap'n Austen sayin' that —"

"*What* did you hear him saying?" There was a flash of fear in her eyes.

"He said there weren't no doubt in his mind … that it were all settled … that Dr. Braden would be comin' with us."

Emily stared around the room in disbelief and then slowly struggled to her feet just as an elderly woman would. She made toward the window that looked upon the ships in the darkening harbour and stood there for the longest time, her arms folded around her body, a blank expression upon her face. Magpie sat very still, watching her, afraid of making the slightest noise.

"How soon are you all planning to leave Portsmouth?" she finally asked, her voice despairing.

"On Monday," he gulped. "At the — at the very latest."

6:00 P.M.
ABOARD HMS *INVINCIBLE*
PORTSMOUTH HARBOUR

Leander rued the moment he had agreed to dine with Fly. He didn't want to hear what his friend had to say. For the time being, he'd had quite enough of the Sick and Hurt Board and war and the meaningless loss of life. Of all things, he desired to stay in England … near Emily. But he didn't have to ask himself why he was here on the *Invincible* — Fly's new command — and not visiting her at the Brigantine Inn. He knew only too well the reason, and loathed himself for it.

What Leander did not understand was why he so keenly scrutinized the cabin's spartan perimeter as he hung his overcoat on an iron hook beside the door and settled upon an old Hoop-back Windsor chair with a badly cracked seat.

"It seems to me the furnishings are inferior to those pieces on the *Isabelle*," he remarked, running his palms over the rough wood grain of the dining table, all set and arranged for supper. "And what's all this? Pewter and creamware dishes? Where is the silver plate, Captain Austen?"

He watched Fly drop down heavily into a chair that looked far superior to the one he would be forced to sit gingerly upon all evening, unless, of course, he did not mind walking around later on with a tremendous snag in the bottom of his best breeches.

"These are hard times, Dr. Braden," Fly replied stoically. "I do not possess a fat purse; neither, it seems, did the captain before me. These are *his* dining implements, not mine."

Leander did another quick sweep of the cabin. "It certainly is not as roomy as Captain Prickett's quarters on the *Amethyst*."

"Nay! But I shan't have Prickett and his swag-belly dining with me. The important thing is … there is room for you, old fellow. You fit rather nicely at my table." It was Fly's turn to do the scrutinizing, his eyes moving disparagingly over Leander as if he were a weevily biscuit. "I was, however, hoping to see you fattened up by now."

"Extravagance is not to be borne at my Aunt Eliza's table," Leander lamented. "She occasionally forgets I was nearly starved at sea. And as much as I have tried, I have only managed to insult her frugality by suggesting I could assist with both the purchase and preparation of food."

Fly's frown was a threatening one. "I will not have you spending your days baking bread and becoming a drudge."

"Even though I might benefit from a few abundant meals?" Leander fired back.

"Perhaps *this* will help!" Fly began pouring them both a bumper of Madeira. "And I am most assured that the royal feast Biscuit has prepared for you will add some beef to your scanty bones."

"Dear God! Biscuit hasn't boiled up a pot of his lobscouse, has he? Or that white pudding sausage? Or, heaven forbid, his soused pig?"

"How ever did you guess, old fellow? Knowing they were your favourites, I asked him to cook up all three."

"I suppose beggars should be no choosers," said Leander, brightening somewhat as he eyed the goblet of amber-hued drink Fly slid toward him. "But I *do* appreciate the wine, even if you were negligent in supplying it for my *medicinal* purposes earlier today."

Fly chuckled at the reference to their morning conversation on the grounds of the church. "Ah! But you gave me quite a lengthy list of items to fetch, Dr. Braden. Still, it is astonishing that I forgot the wine! Well then, hopefully I shall not disappoint you in my promise to provide you with a decent meal, although I must apologize for asking you to come *here* to dine rather than seating you in the best chophouse Portsmouth has to offer."

"It crossed my mind that your game, Captain Austen, was to impress me with the weatherly beams of this ship, hoping that, in a reckless fit of feeling, I would accept your offer to add my name to her muster-book."

"Aye! Guilty as charged! But further to that, the simple truth is, having inherited a crew that includes more madmen than skilled seamen — my presence is sorely required on these decks. But I shan't disappoint you on all accounts." Fly threw his head back and roared, "BISCUIT!"

On cue, the captain's cook waltzed into the cabin, juggling a tray of steaming, savoury dishes — loin of veal, fried onions, diced turnip, and warmed rolls — and placed them on the table as near as possible to Leander so that his nose could appreciate their delicious aromas. And while the feast beckoned and Leander salivated, he suddenly found Biscuit leaning over his chair and whispering in his ear.

"I even made ya a pound cake fer dessert, sir ... an Austen family favourite," he said with pride, giving his thatch of chest hair a good scratching. "It's got a dozen eggs in it. The recipe called for some vanilly extract, but I couldna' locate any so's I added a splash or two o' rum. Didna' think ya'd mind."

Leander extended his warmest regards. "I am forever grateful, Biscuit."

When they were alone again, Fly quickly raised his goblet in a toast to King George's health and then winked at his guest. "And if there is any chance the Prince Regent is in town, sniffing around the streets for his wayward niece — the fair Emily — his nose is sure to lead him here to our fine repast."

"I could do without *his* convivial company."

"Do not fear it! He shall be barred from boarding. I may be short on sailors, but I cannot abide a *bon vivant* who would devote his days to the pursuit of pleasure. Now, please, help yourself."

As they enjoyed their feast they spoke of the sorry business of the *Prosperous and Remarkable*; Mr. Burgo's willingness to join the *Invincible*'s crew, albeit, with countless conditions; the bratty nature of

Fly's gaggle of young midshipmen — Mr. Cadby Brambles, the son of a minor aristocrat, was particularly obnoxious; and news that had recently come to their ears regarding British losses against the Americans on both land and sea. Only once they had cut their slices of the rum-laced cake and filled their cups with tea did Fly sidle their conversation toward more urgent matters.

"I'm afraid, old fellow, I will not be able to feed you every night in such style; otherwise, at the conclusion of our cruise, I shall be sent to the debtor's prison at Marshalsea."

Leander shook his head helplessly. "And I am afraid I do not know how to answer you. If you were leaving in a month or two ... but knowing you have been given orders to depart as soon as possible —" His stare shifted past Fly toward the cabin windows that overlooked the lights twinkling on the deep blue stillness of the harbour. "You can hardly have had any time with your family. Your poor children! How many do you have now?"

Fly grinned as he held up four fingers. "And Mary is again with child. She is due in January."

"Are you quite certain it is yours?"

"If memory serves me correctly ... yes, I do believe I was home at the time of conception!"

Leander gave him a watery smile. "How, then, do you bear it?"

"I do not bear it at all. To be parted from our families is a curse, but one that is owned by men of the sea. The reality is ... this damn war is not going away. And sitting here in Portsmouth is not helping our efforts any, especially since our efforts heretofore have been apathetic at best. I have long wanted to command a frigate. Now that I have my chance, I can hardly tell the Admiralty I would rather stay home to await the birth of my fifth child."

For a time Leander was quiet, though conscious of Fly's fingers drumming the table. "I am trying to reconcile the death of my mother, and my father ... he is growing old. How could I leave him?"

"Bring him with us."

Leander's eyes jumped back to his friend. "He is nearing seventy!"

"I am quite certain our Bailey Beck was older than that, and Captain Moreland ... not much younger."

"But Pa has taken on the guardianship of young Gus Walby. He would never leave the boy behind."

"Then bring them both!" Fly exclaimed, giving the table a fervent rap with his fist. "Think of the assistance they could provide … your father in the hospital and Mr. Walby … perhaps in the clerk's office or as one of my attendants. There is no end to the ways they could be useful to us both, Lee."

Unable to share in his friend's enthusiasm, Leander said nothing. He could only stare at his empty cup, wishing Fly had not strained the tea so that, maybe, he could find answers in the patterns of its damp and dark leaves.

Fly yanked at his buttons, peeled off his jacket and flung it upon cushions under the galleried windows. When he fixed his sights on Leander again, his mood had unfavourably altered. "Do not pretend your main worry does not lie with Emily."

Leander's face grew hot. His heart leapt at the mention of her name, unleashing all sorts of sensations inside him. "She has endured so much of late, and I — I have had so little time with her."

"Why the devil did her family send her to live with the family of Octavius Lindsay? Of all people!" Fly railed. "And then try to foist her upon his eldest brother the very second they had secured for her an annulment from Trevelyan?"

"It is all beyond me."

Some of Fly's pleasant humour reappeared. "Is this eldest brother *really* as bad as all that?"

"If the Marquess of Monroe were worthy … if he were a decent sort … if Emily had felt an ounce of attraction toward him, I do not think she would have escaped Hartwood Hall in the middle of the night in a barouche with an intoxicated woman."

"Is Monroe anything like the obnoxious Octavius?"

"According to Emily, aside from the family arrogance, Monroe is nothing like his brother. *He* has a fondness for fashion and jewellery."

"Is he a fop?"

"Perhaps more of a fribble."

Fly laughed out loud. "Our poor Emily! No wonder she finds her penniless doctor so attractive."

Leander exhaled in mock exasperation. "Just once could you offer me a measure of compassion?"

Pushing aside the pewter plates and goblets scattered before him, Fly folded his arms upon the table and assumed a serious expression. "Look, Lee ... Emily is safe in Portsmouth, tucked away in her little inn. You said she has enough money to keep her comfortable for a long while. If the arrangement makes you uneasy, have her stay with your Aunt Eliza until you return. Your aunt may feed her nothing beyond tea and broth, but surely there is no fear of her taking up a speaking trumpet and announcing to her neighbours that King George's grand-daughter is holed up in her cottage."

Leander's gaze clouded over as he contemplated his half-eaten dessert.

"You *could* marry her, you know."

"She is nineteen, Fly. Without her family's consent I would have to wait until she is twenty-one."

"I shall have you back before her twenty-first birthday."

"That is truly comforting. I wonder if I would live that long. The last time I cruised with you on the Atlantic, I *twice* came within inches of death."

"If memory serves me correctly, Dr. Braden, the second time was not entirely my fault." Fly's sharp glance softened, so, too, the delivery of his words. "I promise you ... this will be the last time. I shall not ask you again."

Leander flinched. "I need time to think ... to settle my affairs."

"I shall give you two days."

"How very generous!"

"And during your two days, I have a favour to ask of you."

"Oh God! What now?"

"Prepare yourself!"

Squeezing one eye shut, Leander braced for the blow.

"The Admiralty has requested that you and I pay a visit to one of the prison hulks here in the harbour."

Leander was aghast. "Whatever for?" he cried. "To play cards with the prisoners?"

"I suppose that could be arranged."

"How can you jest, Fly? With all that must be done before you set sail ... when, henceforth, every hour counts ... you are being asked to set aside time for a social visit?"

"This particular prison hulk is the one upon which Thomas Trevelyan was being temporarily incarcerated."

The room suddenly felt cold, as if someone had thrown open the windows and ushered in the brisk September breezes. "You are saying this in the past tense," stated Leander, his scalp tingling.

"Very observant, Dr. Braden!" was Fly's retort. "And since there is no one in the Royal Navy more intimately acquainted with Trevelyan, *we* have been asked to go in search of answers." He fixed his gaze upon Leander for too long a time.

Glancing away, Leander reached for more Madeira, feeling his hand starting to shake. "Answers?" he whispered. "Why? Where is he? Where is Trevelyan now?"

"To tell you the truth, Lee ... we do not know."

CHAPTER 5

From the stern of the jolly boat, Biscuit watched one of the *Invincible*'s cutters gliding past him as it pulled away from the frigate and began its journey to the Weevil Yard in Gosport for provisions. He hailed the man in charge — that nestle-cock of a midshipman named Cadby Brambles.

"Don't forget the soft bread fer the officers, Mr. Brambles," he bellowed across the steely waters of the harbour. "And make sure ya don't get scalped fer the price o' sugar neither."

Amidst laughter from his cutter mates, Mr. Brambles indignantly raised himself up on the boat bench and averted his head in a show of pomposity and disdain for the cook's warning.

Biscuit grumbled aloud. *He* should be the one overseeing the provisioning. Entrusting that most important duty to Mr. Brambles, who had not yet sprouted whiskers on his upper lip, would most certainly prove to be a mistake. Chances are the dolt wouldn't resurface until nightfall, not knowing his way 'round the Yard, and wouldn't have the slightest idea how to properly haggle with the suppliers. It was well accepted — and often remarked upon by the lads — that "*there weren't no one who could haggle and dicker quite like our Biscuit*," something of which he was most proud. But on this morning, Captain Austen had asked a favour of him, and he couldn't very well let the captain down simply to display his prowess in the victualing yard for the benefit of the new greenhorns.

As the jolly boat neared the wharves, Biscuit scoured the designated area for the person he had been asked to meet. He didn't know her name, and neither did Captain Austen, the note she'd sent to the ship having been signed only as *A Lady*. Praying she would prove to be a real beauty — lustrous red hair, striking green eyes, maybe a sprinkle of freckles across the bridge of her perfect nose — Biscuit was crestfallen when there was only one *lady* standing there, who seemed to be anticipating his arrival. As misfortune would have it, she didn't in any way resemble the comely young lass he had envisioned.

As the coxswain and his mates tied up the jolly boat, securing the ropes around the fat bollard on the wharf, Biscuit politely bobbed his head in her general direction. Coming forward expectantly, she called out a cheery welcome.

"Yoo-hoo! Are you Captain Austen, sir?"

"'Fraid I ain't, ma'am," said Biscuit, clambering out of the boat and hitching himself up and onto the wharf. "Our Cap'n Austen's a sight more smart lookin' and he don't got a skewed eye like me," he said, suddenly worried she might find his deformity off-putting. "But as he's away on business this mornin', he asked me to come in his stead." Standing upright on terra firma, he towered over her and gave her a big, mossy-toothed grin. "They call me Biscuit, ma'am."

"Good heavens! Why?" she asked kindly, seemingly unfazed by his inelegant appearance.

"'Cause I'm known fer the delectable biscuits what I occasionally bake fer the lads," he said, swelling up with pride. "It's the pinch o' sugar and shot o' rum I adds what makes 'em special."

The woman surprised him with a loud chortle. "How delightful! Shall we sit down, Mr. Biscuit? My bunions are an aching nuisance today."

She sidled away, signalling to him to follow, and selected a place on a stone retaining wall where they could view the harbour and the scenes of life unfurling in the little channels between the tethered ships. As Biscuit sat down, making certain there was a respectable amount of space between them, he openly inspected her, his steady eye taking in every detail of her dress and person. She was a stout, middle-aged woman with a pleasant face and clear complexion. There were indications of good humour in the crinkles around her eyes, and from beneath the hem of her gown, he glimpsed well-turned out ankles. But some of her more interesting parts were covered up in a Kashmir shawl and an outrageous, feather-infested turban, making her resemble — in Biscuit's mind, anyway, not being up to date with ladies' fashions — some sort of heavy-set sultan of the Ottoman Empire.

"How kin I help ya, ma'am? Did ya want me to carry a message back to Cap'n Austen fer ya?"

The woman laughed again. "Oh, no! Not exactly!" She hesitated and suddenly transferred her gaze from him to the *Invincible*, swaying gently upon her moorings. Her lips were parted, but nothing came tumbling out.

"Well then, are ya lookin' fer someone?" he asked, starting to feel the stirrings of restlessness. "A son? Yer husband, maybe? And ya thought he might be with our crew o' lads?"

"Heavens, no! I have neither son nor husband."

"Ach! Ya've left me at a loss then, ma'am."

"That makes two of us, Mr. Biscuit, for these matters are quite foreign to me." She emitted a few dainty *a-hems* and gave her head a determined toss. "I have been informed that the *Invincible* shall soon be sailing. Is this true?"

"Aye! Ya've heard correctly, ma'am."

"That is very good, because I should like to come with you … you know, be one of your passengers." She loosened the strings of her embroidered reticule and with a lacy-gloved hand pulled out a few banknotes. "May I give you the money now?"

Biscuit was taken aback. "With due respect, ma'am, the *Invincible*'s a fightin' ship. Might not be the best place fer a woman o' yer … sensibilities."

"Oh! But I have heard that Captain Austen has carried female passengers before."

"Not as a common rule, ma'am."

The harbour breezes violently shivered the long feathers of her satin headgear. "It is common knowledge, Mr. Biscuit," she continued, her voice growing shrill, "that Captain Austen protected Her Royal Highness, the Princess Emeline Louisa, throughout his last voyage."

"Aye, but we came across the Princess quite by accident. She were driftin' in the sea and bleedin' badly. We couldna very well 'ave left her there to drown, now, could we 'ave?"

"No! Of course not! But the fact remains that she was protected and returned to England with all her limbs intact, and — I should like to believe — unmolested by the sailors." Her plump face suddenly flared with colour. "Therefore, I shall travel with no one but Captain Austen."

Biscuit eyed the necklace of diamonds the woman wore around her throat. "Might I ask yer business in wantin' to cross the Atlantic, ma'am?"

"By all means!" she swiftly replied, giving the skirt of her gown a brisk smoothing down. "I have a daughter in New York. A year ago she gave birth to my first grandchild and though I desired to travel then, I was advised to postpone my journey and wait for this *squabble* with America to end."

"Sound advice, ma'am."

"But you see I am getting on in years," she sighed and then paused, gazing wistfully at Biscuit's face, perhaps hoping he would dispute the fact. "And — and since my daughter took forever to produce this grandchild in the first place, I cannot wait for the *squabble* to be resolved. It might be ages before that occurs."

Unsure what to tell the woman — realizing it was not his place to discourage her from her program of action — Biscuit stiffly rose to his feet. "Beg yer pardon, ma'am, I needs to git back to the ship to cook up dinner fer the lads. But rest assured … I'll relay yer wishes to Cap'n Austen, and he'll send word to ya at yer place o' lodgin'."

She stood up quickly and looked somewhat forlorn that their interview was nearing its end. "Oh! Very well then! Tell him I'm staying at The George in High Street."

"Right! And might I know who I'm havin' the pleasure of speakin' with?"

"Heavens! Did I not introduce myself?" she cried, surprising Biscuit by placing her hand on his upper arm and leaving it there for much longer than was truly decent. "You, sir, are speaking to Mrs. Arabella Jiggins."

"Pleased to make yer acquaintance, Mrs. Jiggins." He felt his own cheeks heating up as he performed another awkward bow. Anxious to depart, he rushed the delivery of his final question. "And ma'am? Should I tell the cap'n that yer plannin' to sail alone?"

Her smile was positively provocative. "Tell him — there is a strong possibility — I will be accompanied by my nephew. Knowing that I shall be properly chaperoned whilst on board his ship may give Captain Austen some *much* needed peace of mind."

10:00 A.M.
Aboard His Britannic Majesty's Prison Ship *Illustrious* Portsmouth Harbour

Fly and Leander waited for the lieutenant-in-charge of the prison hulk to return, having been momentarily called away to settle an argument below deck. They stood uncomfortably on the officers' side of a bulk-head of solid planks that separated them from the prisoners' exercising area, horrified by the large-headed nails that studded the bulkhead on the prisoners' side like a menacing wall of iron. Fly shook his head as he peered around him, his eyes moving critically over the jumble of crude sheds, lines of tattered laundry, and decomposing timbers of the abomination that was once the Royal Navy's proud *Illustrious*.

"If it were not for her barren masts and the surrounding harbour," he said bitterly, "I would be hard pressed to believe we were even standing on a ship."

Leander had never been on a prison hulk before, but he had long heard stories of the abject suffering within their spheres — "more foul and fetid than the holds of slavers." His eyes followed his friend's, absorbing every hideous detail. "She is like a woman who was once a beautiful actress of renown," he said pensively. "And has now been ravaged by time and poverty. Look! Just look at those poor souls."

Wordlessly, they observed the large tangle of prisoners getting their air and exercise upon the hulk's narrow spaces bordering the open waist — scornfully referred to as "the Enclosure" by the miserable residents. They dragged their weakened bodies about, trying to avoid the forecastle deck where the chimneys belched their nasty coal smoke. Some were attired in the sickly yellow-orange clothing distributed by the Transport Office; most were clad only in their knee-length drawers or wore nothing at all. None of them spoke. Was the effort to keep one foot in front of the other all they could manage or was it the presence of musket-wielding guards at every turn that quashed their inclination to seek fellowship?

A wave of depression hit Leander. "They are still young, yet they are bent and arthritic as if they had reached fourscore years."

"As hard as it is for you to stomach, Lee, please remember we are here to gather information on Trevelyan, and not to reform the prison system. *That* you can do later … in your next life. Now, hush! Here comes that bumbling lieutenant-in-charge again."

"Gentlemen, please accept my apologies," said the lieutenant, breathing heavily from his foray into the decks below. "I had a Frenchman and an American going at it … their scrawny hands on one another's throats over the disputed ownership of a scabrous blanket."

"Do they not each receive a blanket of their own?" Leander asked, bewildered.

A great deal of eye-rolling accompanied the lieutenant's reply. "Aye, they do, but the idiots gamble away any and all valuable possessions, including their clothes, as you can tell by the amount of exposed flesh what's presently walking about."

"How did you settle their dispute?" pressed Leander, starting to fume.

"I confiscated the blanket and told them they'd lost their meat rations for a week."

Hastily, Fly resumed his questioning to thwart whatever was about to fly out of Leander's mouth. "So, you believe it would have been impossible for Trevelyan to have escaped before the transportation of prisoners that took place on Wednesday, August twenty-fifth."

"There's no possible way," the lieutenant insisted sharply. "At six the previous evening we took up our iron bars — as we always do — to make certain there were no fresh holes cut away in the hull or tampering done to the grilles on the gunports. An hour later we counted the sheep out on the deck. They were all accounted for."

Fly wrinkled his brow. "But that occurred the day before. You said the transportation was accomplished in the middle of the afternoon on the twenty-fifth."

"Aye."

"Was fresh water delivered on the twenty-fifth?"

"Nay! The water boats come on Fridays."

"So then Trevelyan could not have escaped by hiding himself in one of the empty water casks returning to shore," said Fly, more to himself than anyone else. "What about the contractors who provide you with meat, fish, and bread? Do they not come to you on a daily basis?"

"Aye! But we would have seen Trevelyan if he'd tried to filch a ride to shore in one of *their* boats. What do you take us for, sir?"

Fly was suddenly livid. "Frankly, I haven't been able to figure that one out, especially under such extraordinary circumstances, when you have managed to lose track of England's most notorious prisoner." He continued after an interval, hoping his words had struck humiliation in the lieutenant, pleased to see the man avert his blinking eyes and not know where to place them. "When the men who were to be moved had mustered on deck, do you recall seeing Trevelyan among them?"

The lieutenant tugged on his neckcloth with a greasy finger. "I might have."

"But you cannot be certain."

"Other prisoners later testified that Trevelyan had cut his hair all off ... smeared tar on his face ... that he'd disguised himself in various ways."

"Were any other prisoners found missing?"

The lieutenant's eyes lit up. "Aye! A twitchy bastard named Bumpus, or something like that. I can't rightly remember. Anyway, *he* was slated for transportation to Dartmoor, but showed up at Newgate, dressed in breeches believed to belong to an American naval captain."

Fly's lifted his chin. "Why have I not heard of it? This is most significant. Has the man been questioned?"

"He was brought forward for interrogating, but took an apoplectic seizure on the spot and has been mute ever since."

Leander made a sucking sound of annoyance. "How wonderfully convenient!"

"You said he was slated for Dartmoor. Are they short a prisoner there?"

"Aye, they are."

"Then our *friend*, Thomas Trevelyan, did not simply switch places with someone else. It seems there were a number of layers involved in his plan of escape." Lost in thought, Fly massaged his jaw with his hands. "Besides Newgate, Woolwich, and Dartmoor, where else were prisoners being sent on that day?"

"To Portchester Castle, and to hulks moored in Plymouth and on the Medway River."

Fly groaned in dismay. "And when the prisoners were forming their various lines on deck on the twenty-fifth, did you let them leave for the boats before you had done your counting?"

"Nay! Aye! Maybe I did!" The lieutenant's voice rose up in a whine. "It was a hot day, and prisoners kept collapsing under the sun. We had to remove several bodies. A few had died on the spot, and I was forced to count again and again." He glanced away, vehemently shaking his head. "I don't know! I just don't know."

It was Fly's turn to fume. "We are done here," he said in a voice edged in anger and disdain. "You may now return to what you know best ... solving arguments over blankets." He watched the lieutenant creep away to the shelter of the officers' shed on the hulk's battered stern like a child who had narrowly escaped a thrashing from a wrathful parent. "That man should be discharged and dispatched to Newgate for the rest of his incompetent life."

"Perhaps! But what now?" asked Leander, throwing his arms in the air. "Are we to search every prison hulk in England?"

Fly looked out upon the long line of wretched hulks held captive in the mud of the harbour like chained animals awaiting their slaughter, but soon shifted his sights toward the white mists far out at sea. "Nay! It would prove a waste of time, for I believe it unlikely that we shall find him there."

CHAPTER 6

Gus Walby looked up from his dish of potato stew and across the table at old Dr. Braden and his son, Leander, and gave silent thanks for their safe — though long-awaited — return. It had been a chilly nine and twenty hours staying alone with Eliza Braden in her cottage. Conversation had been doled out parsimoniously between lengthy periods of awkward silence. The only exception had been the moment when the distressing news of the *Prosperous and Remarkable* had reached those who resided on Mile End Terrace. With renewed zeal and a great deal of finger-wagging, Miss Braden had then revisited her treatise on why Gus must "re-evaluate" his choice of a career in the Royal Navy. In a prolongation of his agony, Gus had had to wait an extra hour to hear all the news, for, upon their arrival at the cottage, father and son had requested a private meeting with Miss Braden in her garden, the details of which he was not yet privy.

As they ate their meal, the atmosphere in the little culinary sitting-room was as sombre as Miss Braden's face. It was all out of respect for the loss of life on Prosper Burgo's ship. Or so Gus thought. Still, he couldn't help but be fascinated by the doctors' solemn recounting of the events of the last day. He listened, hanging on to their every word — even the horrible and heart-rending ones — wishing he, too, had been there, lending a hand, or been the one to have had the good fortune to find Prosper alive in the Ship's Tavern.

When their stew and buttered bread had been consumed, young Dr. Braden produced a paper-wrapped parcel he had been concealing from them on the unused chair at his side, and set it upon the table amidst the scraps of his aunt's dinner.

"Yesterday held one bright spot," he said in a hearty voice that ameliorated the tense atmosphere in the kitchen. He grinned mysteriously at Gus as he untied the string holding the parcel together. "I was invited to sup with Captain Austen on his new command, the *Invincible*, and Biscuit baked us a pound cake. As the two of us could not possibly finish it, Captain Austen wondered if I would like to take it home for 'the young Mr. Walby with my compliments.'" Picking up the bread knife, he began cutting generous slices.

Gus eyed the buttery-yellow confection with its golden-brown top. "Oh, sir! Does Captain Austen really remember me?"

"Indeed, he does!" said young Dr. Braden, offering up the first slice to Miss Braden, who showed her disinterest with a vigorous shaking of her head. Winking, he carefully placed it upon Gus's empty plate. "Not only did he inquire after your health, he asked me to extend to you an invitation."

Gus perked up. In no time at all, he was imagining Captain Austen inviting him — as he had Magpie — to his home in Southampton before the *Invincible* sailed, or to attend a meeting of the Admiralty at Whitehall. "An invitation, sir?" he whispered, trying to rein in his galloping excitement.

Young Dr. Braden glanced knowingly at his father, but seemed to go to grand lengths to avoid his aunt's hardened stare through her prospect glass. Undeterred, he returned his attention to Gus. "Would you like to sail again, Mr. Walby?"

Gus's heart was thudding in his chest. "Sir! Would I!"

"Even if it meant taking on duties other than those of a midshipman?"

"I would be grateful to work side by side with Biscuit around his Brodie stove, sir, or live on the orlop deck and spend my days making oakum if it meant going back to sea with all of you," he sputtered happily, his eyes beginning to blur.

Miss Braden's contemptuous snort made Gus all the more appreciative of her nephew's kind smile.

"I believe Captain Austen has something more consequential in mind for you, Mr. Walby."

Quite certain his chest was about to explode, Gus swivelled on his chair to look at old Dr. Braden, his countenance and demeanour so similar to those of his son. "Might I go, sir? My cough is so much better now and I do feel a bit stronger."

For an endless time, old Dr. Braden studied the ceiling and rubbed his chin as if Gus had asked him to name the root causes of disease. And when he did finally give his answer, it was a long, drawn-out affair, spoken with measured solemnity. "Well now, let me see. I believe ... it is in your best interests, Mr. Walby ... nay, perhaps it is in *my* own best interests. Ah! Let me start again. The truth is ... I wonder ... if you do not come ... I shall be quite at a loss, for I shall need *you* at my side to explain the workings and configurations of the ship."

It took a moment to interpret the old doctor's words, but when a mirthful glint appeared in his faded blue eyes, Gus thought he would burst into tears. "Oh, sir! Do you mean ...? Are you going, too?"

"Against my better judgment, Mr. Walby; however, someone must make certain Leander here does not play the hero and set out once again in one of the ship's boats when the seas are inhospitable."

There was an explosion of scratching and scraping sounds as Miss Braden rose from her chair and began clearing the table. The abruptness of it all halted Gus's gurgling laughter in his throat and wiped the air clean of happy celebration. Like a white swan traversing its peaceful pond, she floated across the room, her head held high, but when she reached the sideboard next to the washing sink she set the stack of dirty dishes down with a disquieting crash.

A pall fell over the room, as thick and hideous as the smoke that had choked Portsmouth the previous day. Gus scrunched his toes up in his shoes, waiting for her tongue-lashing to hit them all like a destructive spray of grapeshot. The Drs. Braden did not dare look toward the place where she stood. Saying nothing, they picked up their forks and quietly ate their slices of cake, thus spared from having to witness the disturbing scene that unfolded in front of Gus.

Gripping the edge of the sink, Miss Braden doubled over as if she were about to vomit. One trembling hand reached up to massage the area around her heart, and her pointy face — ordinarily devoid of all emotion beneath that formidable mob cap — contorted with some form of physical agony. Then she slowly straightened up and it was over. The pained expression was gone. And the only thing her brother and nephew noticed was the back of her as she drifted silently from the room like the ghost of the woman who had once lived there.

8:30 P.M.
THE BRIGANTINE INN

Emily was just leaving the Brigantine's kitchen, having prepared for herself a light supper with the intention of taking it up to her room, when the innkeeper's voice — buoyant and teeming with uncharacteristic intonation — startled her from behind, rattling the dishes upon her tray.

"Aren't ya the popular one, Mrs. George!"

Emily stopped to stare at her. "Why do you say that?"

"Ya have another visitor, waiting for ya in the *Blue Peter*." She jerked her frizzy head at the closed sitting room door.

"At this late hour? Has little Magpie come to see me again?"

"Nay! This one's full grown with both eyes in his head still."

Emily's heart began jumping in her ribcage.

"It's a rare occasion when a man — the likes of this one — passes through my humble door, Mrs. George. If ya ask me … he's rather attractive … in a rakish sort o' way ,.. like one of them bucks in the novels I likes to read before blowing out the candle at night."

Emily's laugh was a nervous one. "In that case, perhaps I should go upstairs and change."

"Into what?" The innkeeper lifted her arms to channel Emily toward the *Blue Peter*. "I've only ever seen ya wear one gown and one shawl, Mrs. George. And it seems to me yer in 'em now."

"It just so happens I do possess a second gown!" said Emily haughtily, detesting the feeling she had to defend herself. "And I should very much like to go upstairs and —"

"Nay, Mrs. George! I'd say the man's been waiting long enough."

The woman's heavy arm enclosed her shoulder like a clamping tool; her hips blocked her avenue of retreat, and before she could remonstrate, Emily had been successfully navigated through to the sitting room.

"Here we go then, Mrs. George!" It was a squeal of victory. The woman could just as easily have shouted "Huzzah!" and been spectating a Royal Navy frigate leading an American prize into the harbour. In two deft movements, she had relieved Emily of her supper tray, bestowing a blushing smile upon the visitor as she did so, and swept out of the room, closing the door crisply behind her, locking them into — what Emily sensed was — a musty jail cell in the hold of an ancient ship.

She watched him rise from the Chippendale chair in which he had been waiting. He was dressed far differently than he had been when she had first recognized him yesterday morning on the streets of Portsmouth. His cap and labourer's pantaloons had been replaced with his more usual attire: fine wool breeches, a cutaway coat, and a starched neckcloth, and his dark hair was freshly cropped in that forward, dishevelled style he favoured. He stood before her, his hands locked behind him, his feet spaced upon the room's woven rug, a stance with which Emily was familiar, and which seemed to signal his readiness to do battle. Those close-set eyes of his watched her intently, as if expecting her to flee or have a go at him with her fists. Emily remained composed — on the outside at least — and, feeling no compunction whatsoever to act civilly, waited for him to speak.

"You must have known we would find you ... sooner or later ... *Mrs. George*," he said, giving the plain skirt of her blue-and-white striped gown a disdainful going-over.

71

Emily moved farther into the room to seek the sofa she had earlier occupied with Magpie, certain, if she did not sit, her legs would collapse in betrayal. "Yes, I suppose I did. What I did not expect was to see *you*, Lord Somerton."

He remained standing. "Your uncle, the Duke of Clarence — being sick with worry — asked that I find you."

"Why then did he not come himself?"

"I am guessing his many *duties* as Admiral of the Fleet took precedence over searching the countryside for his headstrong niece."

Emily snuffled. "Is that what *you* have been doing these past two weeks?"

He seemed reluctant to answer. "It was difficult at first, not knowing where you had run off to. But when your uncle received word that your *friends* had returned to Portsmouth, I had no doubt you would be found here."

"Clever deduction! And who, pray, is minding Hartwood Hall in your absence?"

He shifted his stance on the rug. "My father and Wetherell ... between them both."

"Oh! Then you have left your estate in most competent hands while you play the intrepid investigator. Although I am surprised your father could muster the energy, and your brother ... the motivation for such a grand responsibility."

There was swift retaliation for her sarcasm. "I am taking you back to Hartwood Hall tonight."

Emily eyed him while she delayed her reply, ignoring the gasp of surprise that erupted from behind the closed sitting room door, concrete evidence of an eavesdropper. "What is the point? I shall only further frustrate your family and mine."

"Once we arrive back in the City, the Regent and his mother plan to pay you a little visit."

"The Prince Regent? And my grandmother, Queen Charlotte? My goodness! Such regal artillery!"

"Together they will do whatever is required to bring you to your senses."

"I am quite in control of my senses, Lord Somerton."

Glancing around him, he scoffed. "Really? Holed up in a third-rate hotel? Fetching your meals from a filthy kitchen, wearing vulgar clothes and passing yourself off as *Mrs. George?*"

Emily said nothing, but made certain her eyes did not vacillate away from his.

"I have a post-chaise waiting. I shall give you twenty minutes to gather your belongings, although I daresay you will require no more than five. It astounded us all to find you had taken so little with you when you left Hartwood ... in Mrs. Jiggins's barouche! The poor woman was a wreck when she learned she had inadvertently conveyed you to London on that night."

"You mean ... when she learned she had helped me to *escape* on that night."

"*Escape?* Heavens! Such a strong word!" He turned his back on her to finger the collection of bottles and flasks on the sideboard, carelessly clinking two of them together. "Were we really all that unpleasant, Emeline?"

"No. Your father was always generous in spirit and your sister, Fleda ... I quite adored her. In the absence of a governess, had you allowed me to instruct her, I might have stayed on ... rather contentedly ... despite your bad behaviour and your mother's little scheme to make me Wetherell's wife."

With a sniff of impatience, Somerton consulted his pocket watch. "We can quibble in the carriage. Now, be a good girl and go fetch your things."

But Emily did not move from the sofa, could not move with her mind swirling in agitation, weighing and discarding her options. What if she went to her room and refused to leave it? She could try to smuggle out a note to Leander in the night. But where was *he?* At the home of his Aunt Eliza? She did not know the woman's address! Was he already on Fly Austen's ship? Perhaps. But then Magpie had mentioned something about him staying with an ailing friend on Lombard Street, so close by, though where exactly she had no idea.

She gave Somerton a blank stare, so at odds with her stomach, roiling as if she had ingested a rotten potato. "I have never taken orders from the second son of a duke, and I shall not begin to do so now."

He returned to his chair and rested his haunches on its front few inches. "Ah! You are going to be difficult then! Must I send word to your uncles and summon them here at once?"

"To do what? Lash me publicly on Broad Street until I acquiesce?"

One dark eyebrow arched in amusement. "If need be."

Again, the eavesdropper behind the door could not help herself. But this time the woman's cackle of enjoyment only served to embolden Emily.

"Go home, Lord Somerton, and tell them you could not find me. Tell your brother, Wetherell, the time has come for him to set his cap at another rich woman. I do not believe the Prince Regent's daughter, Charlotte, has been spoken for yet. And then there are my four spinster aunts: Augusta, Elizabeth, Sophia, and Mary," Emily said drolly, enclosing her hands around her knees. "Princess Mary is still youngish, and so anxious to permanently escape the austere halls of Windsor Castle for the excitement of London, that Wetherell may find, when it comes to selecting a husband, she is not excessively particular. Of course the notion of sacrificing any one of my relations to your brother is a revolting one, and I would say his chances of rejection are indeed high, but should he fail in his pursuit, he could always try something completely novel and work at paying back his own debts."

Somerton's mouth assumed souring lines of annoyance. "I shall not leave here until I have you packed and in my waiting carriage."

Emily ignored him; her thoughts now tripping down another tangent of possibilities. What if she agreed to go quietly with him back to Hartwood Hall? Could she escape again? There was no doubt his mother, the conniving Duchess of Belmont, would hire an armed contingent of servants to surround the house at all hours until the wedding was a *fait accompli*, and their unhappy union had been ... consummated. But even if she were to succeed in giving Lord Somerton the slip en route — perhaps when they stopped to rest the horses at a posting-house — how long would it take her to make her way back to Portsmouth? Captain Austen's ship would be sailing in two days. Two days!

"Surely you must know it is impossible, Emeline."

"Nothing is impossible."

"You cannot fight *all* of us."

"Are you so sure of that?"

"Not unless your *army* is greater than the King's Own Royal Regiment."

Emily searched Lord Somerton's smug face, her impulses screaming at her to "*Flee! Now! Get away ... far from him!*" making it necessary to prevail upon her dwindling reserves of discipline to hush them. Oh, how she itched to fire a volley of recrimination at him ... at his family ... at *her* family; to shout and decry and castigate. But it was then that an idea came to her. Something Magpie had said earlier rose to the surface of her frenzied thoughts like a smooth bubble in water, calming her, restoring some hope.

She sat quietly, staring at Lord Somerton's leather boots; hoping to make it appear she was in the agonizing throes of defeat. In order to piece together some sort of plan, she needed to stall for time before picking up the unravelling threads of their discourse. While she waited, a gust of silence churned between them. Emily welcomed it, mostly for the effect it had on Somerton. He could not stay still. One foot tapped upon the woven rug. His hands fiddled with the cuffs of his coat and then gripped his knees. From the corner of her eye, Emily could see him shooting scowls at the door as if he expected someone, aside from their female eavesdropper, to come bursting in and butcher his well-laid plans.

"Admit it, Emeline," he finally said in exasperation, "you have neither the resources nor the fortitude to go into battle against so many."

She looked over at him in mournful resignation. "You are right. I do not."

His eyes skittered back to the bottle collection to mask his stupefaction. But surely the hardest part for him was tweaking the hostility, which up to this point had been so prevalent in his voice. "I — I *had* hoped you would see, without the guiding influence of parents, how very much you still need to be taken care of by your family. They are devoted to your welfare ... as are others who have only your best interests at heart."

Emily waited for his wandering eyes to meet hers. "Marrying Wetherell is *not* in my best interests."

"At least come home."

"Hartwood Hall is *not* my home."

"All right then!" He stood up, a little too eagerly. "Allow me to take you back to your family. That is where you ought to be. And when you are safely under their protection, I am certain they will allow you to plead your case ... to state your wishes and desires ... and come to some form of a mutual agreement."

The urge to laugh aloud was steadily building in Emily. Such ignorant assumptions! Gathering up the skirt of her gown, she levered herself from the sofa in such a way as to appear beaten and exhausted by the weightiness of their interview.

"Wait here and amuse yourself as best you can, Lord Somerton," she said serenely. "I shall not be long."

At the entranceway of the sitting room, with her hand already on the door latch, she paused to glance backwards. It was enough to incite a spasm of suspicion to crawl across his face. His lips parted, his neck reddened, and once more that square chin of his was thrust forward like a weapon of intimidation.

"Perhaps, *Mrs. George*, you should be forewarned that your innkeeper has kindly agreed to keep watch on all of the doors and exits."

CHAPTER 7

"Now I needs ya all to shut yer faces and wait fer the word," muttered Prosper Burgo to those who had followed him from the wharves into the obscurity of a damp alleyway somewhere beyond the populous Portsmouth Point. Magpie was among them. Captain Austen had demanded he stay with the cutters and not journey through the dangerous streets with the men. It was Prosper who had insisted he join them, "*so longs ya bring yer dirks with ya … in case someone jumps ya.*" In Magpie's stead, a young midshipman was left behind with the boat at the Camber Dock.

Across the way from a snug but lively tavern, Magpie was crouched on his heels behind a rain barrel. Beside him was Cadby Brambles, breathing heavily and stinking up the air around them with a noxious odour reminiscent of Prosper's stores of rancid cheese. Magpie's own heart was working hard in his chest, and his throat was so dry that it was hard to swallow. He watched the stooped forms of Prosper and Biscuit, furtively approaching the tavern's window so they could scope out the potential pickings amongst the seamen who sat unwittingly, revelling in their grog and ales in circles of convivial women. The cheery music of a fiddler and flutist filled this dark but otherwise quiet corner of Portsmouth, and soon it was joined by the patrons' drink-laced notes of song:

> We be three poor mariners
> Newly come from the seas;
> We spend our lives in jeopardy
> While others live at ease.

When the tune ended and the subsequent peals of laughter had rolled away, Magpie heard a shivery recital of words rise up from the blackness beyond the warm glow of the tavern's lighting, prompting the hairs on his neck to stand at attention.

"Death and woe! Death and despair! Hell fires! The Divil ... he shall cometh in the Middle Watch."

Cadby Brambles seized Magpie's shoulder. "What the —? Who's that?"

"Not to worry, sir. It's only Jim Beef. He were once a patient o' Bedlam."

"Bloody hell! You mean we've got a lunatic with us?"

Being well acquainted with Mr. Beef's skills in the realms of brute strength and aggression — the man having demonstrated such while saving Magpie from Mrs. Kettle's slashing knife — Prosper had asked him to come along, too, to stand guard in the event their gang was caught in the act of pressing seamen and attacked by a horde of irate citizens, armed with brickbats. Magpie wondered whether the mad Mr. Beef would prove useful, or whether he would get drawn into his own ghoulish world and wander off into the shifting night mists.

A door opened and a beam of strong light illumined the alleyway, throwing the areas around it into darkness. A litany of swearing followed. Muffled mutterings came next. A yelp. Then a scuffle. Magpie tightened his clammy hold on his dirks. He could not see where it was Prosper and Biscuit had got to, but he soon heard Prosper questioning two drunken gentlemen in snarling whispers.

"Landman or sailor?"

"I ain't gonna tell ya I'm a sailor 'cause I know what yer all about."

"What ship is ya with?"

"I ain't gonna tell ya the ship I'm with 'cause I know yer game."

Prosper guffawed and the subsequent scrabbling upon the cobbles seemed to indicate he was shoving the man about. Then the same questions were fired at the second man. "And what about this here galoot? Landman or sailor?"

"Neither!" cried the galoot.

"And yer ship?"

"I'm nothin' but a ferryman with a broken scow!"

"Then ya knows how to work the oars!"

"Aye! Aye, 'tis true but, please, have mercy for I have a little wife at home."

This time Prosper's guffaw was raucous. "Then I suspect she'll be content to be free o' ya fer a year or two."

An afflicted howl pierced the night air.

"Prosper," hissed Biscuit, "both o' them got traces o' tar on their hands."

Prosper's reply was a triumphant one. "Right then! Guess yer both comin' with us, ya Jack-puddins."

Another scuffle ensued. Someone was pushed hard to the cobbles. The hapless sailors cried out for assistance, but their voices were sheared off, most likely by wads of cloth being shoved down their gullets. The next thing Magpie knew, Prosper had dropped down behind the rain barrel to communicate his gruff instructions.

"Stay here, lads. We'll be back shortly."

"Where are you going, Mr. Burgo?" There was pure terror in Mr. Brambles's voice.

"Gotta take our new recruits to our rondy fer more questionin'. And I needs to check up on the others ... see how many they've managed to round up."

"What should we do if another seaman leaves the tavern while you're gone?"

"Steer him into that there narrow alleyway," said Prosper, pointing into the dark web of the widespread night.

"What if he protests?"

"Knock 'im about the head, but mind ya don't kill 'im."

"What if he fights back? What if he has a cutlass on him?" Mr. Brambles sounded like a whinnying horse.

"He'll be full o' the drink. Unarm him!"

"And what should we do if a number of seamen leave the tavern all at once?"

Prosper's patience came crashing down. "What are ya ... an imbecile? A blockhead? Do us all a favour the next time there's men's work to be done ... stay behind on the ship and play with yer dolls and toys!" Prosper up and left, leaving Magpie alone with a vexatious Mr. Brambles.

"I don't like that man!" he mewled. "For a privateersman who just lost his ship, he's awfully haughty. Does he know *who* he is addressing? Does he understand the naval hierarchy? I may only be seventeen, but he has no right to speak to —"

"Sir! Look!" Magpie was relieved he had reason to divert Mr. Brambles's attention. The tavern door bounced open again. A group of revellers stumbled out and into the street, collapsing into one another, still warbling strains of "We Be Three Poor Mariners." Despite the theme of their song, their silhouettes sliding before the glow of tavern lights made it difficult to determine their numbers and if they were, in fact, sailors by profession.

"What should we do?" whispered Mr. Brambles, who had huddled so close to Magpie, the sailmaker could not escape an assault from his malodorous fear.

"Stay hidden 'til Prosper and Biscuit return. We can't tackle 'em alone."

"Are you quite sure? Won't Mr. Burgo be out of temper if we miss this opportunity?"

Above their heads the air quivered with a strident voice that snatched the breath from Magpie's lungs.

"And what do we 'ave here? If it's worms yer lookin' fer, lads, ya won't find 'em 'round these parts."

Shivering like a curled autumn leaf, Magpie peered up. The man was faceless against the backdrop of bright light from the tavern. Magpie could see nothing beyond a round hat, bowed legs in loose-fitting pantaloons, and cucumber fingers reaching out toward … *him*! Before he could gather his wits, the hand had seized his arm and pulled him roughly to his feet, whereupon a coarse-skinned visage with a heavy jawline jumped frighteningly into view.

"Was ya plannin' to murder someone then?" the man snorted, eyeing Magpie's dirks.

"Oh, no, sir!" Magpie's voice was weak and reedy.

"Maybe the person what plucked out yer eye?"

A great chorus of drunken laughter rose up around Magpie, providing an opportunity for Mr. Brambles — who had been making a series of whimpers and gulping sounds behind the rain barrel — to spring up and take off running, his heels stumbling and skidding about on the cobbles before he could gain enough traction to flee.

"Huxley! That one was wearin' a uniform o' sorts."

"Then ya better go git 'im!"

Inky-black figures tore off into the darkness to give chase to Mr. Brambles, shrieking obscenities that would wake the Portsmouth dead as they disappeared into the dreadful holes of the alleyways. It was Magpie's bad luck that two stayed put, intent on detaining him. The one called Huxley locked his fat fingers around the length of frayed rope that held up Magpie's ragged trousers, while the other — another faceless shape — unburdened him of his dirks and took great pleasure in brandishing them before his terrified face.

With a chilling crow of laughter, Huxley adjusted his grip on Magpie. His heavy face lunged forward in a cloud of stale, sudsy breath, and for the first time Magpie could see his eyes, frightening and flinty with suspicion.

"Now then," Huxley seethed, seizing one of the dirks from his companion's grubby clutches and pressing its pointed tip into the soft skin beneath Magpie's chin, "while me lads are skinnin' yer friend alive, ya kin tell us what yer all about." Magpie stayed very still, aware of the drops of his own blood rolling down the front of his shirt. "And ya better give us the real story … else ya won't be seein' another sun risin' in the west."

9:00 P.M.
MILE END TERRACE

Hearing the slow step on the creaking floorboards of the hallway just beyond the culinary sitting-room, Leander shook off his reverie and pulled his distant stare from the sputtering candle in the centre of his aunt's table. He watched his father walk past him and make his way to the chair opposite him, wondering why he had not previously noticed the slight stoop in his back and the craggy lines of fatigue on his face.

"Where is Mr. Walby, Pa?" he asked, massaging the kink in his neck.

His father lowered himself into the chair and stared at his half-eaten slice of pound cake, still sitting where he had left it earlier. He took up his mug of tea, which had long since grown cold. "In bed, though I doubt he will get much sleep tonight."

"And Aunt Eliza?"

"She is in her room, sitting rigidly in her rocker, staring out into the night."

"Did she say anything?"

"No," his father said grimly. "I did the talking. She would not even look at me."

Leander slowly inhaled. "We can hardly expect her to understand, Pa. I do not understand it myself. I only know that Mr. Austen has a talent for persuasion."

"Surely, if Mr. Austen's talents had not worked on you, those belonging to the Lords Commissioners of the Admiralty would have."

Leander spread his fingers over his mouth. "How can I, in good conscience, stay here when so many of our countrymen are spilling their blood in our fight against France and the United States? When so many of our ships are sailing without skilled surgeons. If I can save a few more lives —" He broke off to glance at his father. "Are you having second thoughts about going?"

"Well, I am not physically fit and my eyesight is not what it should be," he replied, after giving the question considerable contemplation. "But I am still of sound mind — I think — and I do truly believe I could be more of a help to you than merely a hazard or a hindrance."

"Bless you, Pa. I shall benefit from having a loved one near, in more ways than one."

His father gave him a fond smile and speared a bite of cake with his fork. "So, when do *we* sail?"

"Monday at the latest. Fly is anxious to get under way. I have been told we shall be cruising once again in the company of the little mail packet, the *Lady Jane*, and with Captain Uptergrove of the *Expedition*. Apparently, Uptergrove is anxious to depart, as well, which means I shall have to resign myself. Until there is peace between England and our foes, there is little use in dreaming of another life."

They stayed silent, entranced by the frolicking of the candlestick's tiny flame, until the clock on the wooden mantelpiece above Eliza's red-bricked fireplace announced the half-hour with a single, penetrating bong. Leander let loose a mirthless laugh. "The good news is, upon our return, Mr. Austen has promised to put forward my name for consideration as Physician to the Fleet."

His father pushed away his cake plate and began fiddling with the handle of his mug. "Which fleet?"

"Whichever one is in need of a presiding physician!"

"And does Mr. Austen's good name hold significant sway?"

"The final decision would rest with the Navy Board, naturally."

"Naturally!" A small smile began pulling on the sagging ends of his father's mouth. "And does the post pay well?"

"Not well enough, I'm afraid, to provide for —" Leander looked helplessly across the table.

"When will you go to her, my son?"

"First thing in the morning."

"You cannot leave her without some form of an understanding."

Leander bit down on his lip and slowly shook his head. "The problem is ... I do not know what to tell her. I do not know what I should say."

"You must prepare yourself, son."

"For what?"

A gleam illumined his father's old eyes. "For an uprising as fierce as Queen Boadicea's against the Roman Empire."

9:10 P.M.
THE BRIGANTINE INN

Dashing away tears, Emily cleared the last of her belongings from the corner cupboard and stuffed them into the pillowcase that housed her meagre belongings, bracing herself for the knock on the door that was sure to come if she did not act swiftly. If only Leander had come rather than sending Magpie as his representative. She could have warned him that Lord Somerton was in Portsmouth, that she had spied him hanging about on Broad Street the morning of the explosion. She would have risked raising his ire for having left the sanctuary of the Brigantine, but at least he would have known what to do. He might have taken her to his aunt's home, or found her lodgings in a different section of town, somewhere far from the enticing views of three-masted ships and the blue rim of the sea. As it was, she could think of no other recourse.

Stripping off her gown, tearing a button off in her haste, Emily hurried to pull on her checked shirt and trousers over her underclothing. Once again, she was coaxing her hair under a scarf and trading her silk slippers for leather shoes with silver buckles! She wanted to scream. Her head ached. Her throat felt thick, and a desire raged in her to hurl her belongings into the air, and kick the coals in the grate. The only thing stopping her was the certainty that listening ears were attached to her door.

Banishing her destructive thoughts with a fierce shake of her head, Emily calmed herself so she could think clearly. She looked around her. Had she collected everything? Could she leave now? The bed was pulled together and tidy; her account with the innkeeper was up to date; Jane Austen's cherished volumes had been retrieved from the bedside table; and the remainder of the money she had won playing at whist with the unlucky Wetherell — a generous £38 4s. 6d. — was tucked safely away in a pocket at the waist of her trousers. That was it, then. Tying off the pillowcase — praying those in the streets would recognize it as a sailor's ditty bag — she made for the window and urged it to be quiet as she eased open one of its mullioned sides.

The September air blew fresh in her face. "Oh, blessed, blessed darkness," she whispered, assessing the structural features of the inn's slate roof. It was as wet and slippery as a water sluice; its pitch exceedingly steep. If she had the misfortune of sliding off, she would surely attract a crowd and frighten the horses hitched to the four-wheeled carriage on the pavement below, the one waiting to carry her off into the night.

It was a chance she was willing to take.

CHAPTER 8

I f he could spew the contents of his belly all over the pantaloons belonging to that man called Huxley, just like he'd done to Thomas Trevelyan and Octavius Lindsay in that Charleston tavern, Magpie figured he had a chance. Shocked by the assault of vomit, wouldn't Huxley instantly unhand him? And then he could flee, for there was no doubt in Magpie's mind that he could outrun the man. The trouble was he couldn't persuade his stomach to come up, most likely because Huxley and his toad-eater, the one who had pilfered his dirks, had managed to drag him back into the tavern and presented him to a gaggle of unsavoury women. Almost at once, the women pulled him down upon their bench, peeled off his thrum cap and began stroking his head.

"Where'd ya find this one?"

"Ain't he lovely? Such soft curls!"

"Irresistible, more like!"

"How did ya lose yer eye, wee pet?"

Magpie felt arms groping him, inching him dangerously close to enormous sets of bosoms spilling out of low-cut gowns. He couldn't breathe with the pervading smells of unwashed bodies, smoking tobacco, stale breath and cheap perfume. Hadn't Prosper warned him yesterday at the Ship's Tavern … about "all them doxies wantin' to get at yer money"?

"I don't got no money on me," he cried out, trying to fend off their frightening mounds of flesh.

"We ain't int'rested in yer money, pet. Just give us a cuddle." Magpie's head was seized, his hair was roughly tousled and then — oh, horror! — a smelly, wet tongue began licking his cheek as if he were a loaf of sugar.

Huxley began elbowing the doxies. "Leave 'im be. We're takin' 'im with us."

"Nay! Let us play with 'im a bit longer," squawked one of the women. "He's sweeter than a kitten, and I 'ave a notion to take 'im to me bed."

The blood in Magpie's small face drained to his feet; his eye enlarged like a pewter plate as the woman drew back her filthy skirt to reveal a dimpled and bounteous thigh. "What d'ya think o' this, pet? Would ya like to touch it? Here! Give me yer hand and I'll show ya how it's done."

Snatching back his thrum cap, Magpie sprang up and backed away from the doxie and her lewd notions, swiping at his face with his shirtsleeves to rid himself of her sticky drool.

"Where is ya takin' me?" Magpie demanded of Huxley though his voice was nothing but a vanquished squeak.

"We're takin' ya to sea."

Having learned something from Prosper Burgo, Magpie did his best to put up in protest. "Nay! I ain't a seaman!"

"Yer a wee liar," growled Huxley.

"I'm a farm labourer," cried Magpie, "whose poor old ma will be ill at her stomach if ya takes me away. I'm all she's got."

Huxley shoved his deeply pitted face into Magpie's shrinking one. "A labourer, my arse! Why that thrum cap o' yers belongs to a ship's carpenter! Can't fool me! Ya have the look of a seaman with yer eye patch and yer tar-blackened fingers and all. Yer familiar with the ropes, by Jove!"

The tavern's fiddler and flutist, who were stationed far from Magpie in a corner of the room blanketed with grey clouds of pipe smoke, and who therefore had no inkling of the crisis that had befallen him, once again took up their instruments. It was not long before the walls were thrumming with more boisterous song:

> Farewell and adieu to you, Spanish Ladies,
> Farewell and adieu to you, ladies of Spain,
> For we've received orders to sail for old England,
> But we hope in a short time to see you again.

The air grew stiflingly hot. The wheel of candles, hanging from the ceiling of the room, swung back and forth like an erratic pendulum. The music and singing and dancing pounded upon Magpie's ears like the drums of war. His head felt as woozy as if he had downed a tankard of ale on an empty stomach, and he feared his uncontrollable tremors were the beginnings of an apoplectic fit. Rouged faces licked their lips and blew him kisses. Strange faces, marred with ulcers and scars and pustules, moved in and out and side to side to leer or laugh at him.

Huxley seized a fistful of his shirt and kicked him to the tavern door as if he were a tomcat being transported by the scruff of his neck and about to face disposal. Where were they taking him? Who would know? Mr. Brambles had run off, and Prosper and Biscuit had gone to do business at the *Invincible*'s rendezvous. Terrifying images thrashed about in his brain. What if he were put on a vermin-plagued Spanish galleon destined to set a course for one of those mysterious Asian seas, or even worse, for that place called Madagascar where the Duke of Clarence's young son, Henry, had drowned in the black depths of the Indian Ocean. Magpie felt his stomach flip and heave. But it was too late now for vomiting to have any effect. Already he was outside on the street, and the only thing looming before him were the fearsome shadows of the unknown.

9:30 P.M.
(First Watch, Three Bells)
Aboard HMS *Expedition*
Portsmouth Wharf

Overhead, on the aftermost beam of the forecastle, the quartermaster of the glass clanged the ship's bell three times. Its lonely peals echoed through the stillness of the evening. In his dusky corner on the gun deck where he sat, propped up against a gun carriage, Thomas Trevelyan looked up from his book. It was getting late and the flame in his candle-lantern was guttering. Soon he would have to make a move and seek his hammock on the airless berthing deck that reeked like a basket of soiled undergarments. The night hours would pass swiftly, but it was imperative he be well rested, for tomorrow he would be reporting to his new post in the clerk's office on the quarterdeck.

Mr. Croker would expect him to draw up watch and station bills for the first lieutenant, and assist in copying letters and missives for Captain Uptergrove — the ones Mr. Croker felt were insignificant and therefore beneath him, being as he was a very important man who had been blessed with his very own sleeping cabin. Having proven to be one of the more literate among the *Expedition*'s landmen, Trevelyan would be saved from the tasks of hauling sails and cleaning the heads and swabbing decks, which only *he* knew were demeaning for a man of his superior education and rank. How lucky he was to have secured such a post. But he was not alone in his philosophy for survival. His seven messmates on the *Expedition* were all American, former prisoners such as he, keen for a second chance at life. They had been only too happy to quit their prisons at Plymouth with their heads held high, impervious to their compatriots who had taunted and cursed and spit upon them for their treachery and cowardice.

A few feet away from the spot where Trevelyan relaxed alone were four of his American messmates. They were sitting on casks arranged around a single, shining lantern, sharing stories of their previous lives and grumbling about their present lot over their tins of beer. Two of them, like him, were reluctant to retire to bed; the other two would be relieving the gangway and cathead lookouts at four bells. Rather than joining in, Trevelyan pretended to be absorbed in a dog-eared copy of a Henry Fielding novel which Mr. Croker had loaned him from his prized bookshelf in the clerk's office. In reality, he was eavesdropping on his mates' grumbles, delivered in undertones as the closed door of the great cabin was dangerously nearby, and it was evident from the voices and occasional laughter within that the captain was in residency.

"Word has it we may end up in either New York or Boston."

"I thought we was headed fer Halifax."

"Aye, but I overheard Cap'n Uptergrove tellin' the master that we would be negotiatin' the release o' prisoners in one o' them places."

"I'll jump ship the minute we're tied up in a friendly harbour."

"Ya don't think maybe the captain will release us then? Ya know … exchange us fer some o' their prisoners?"

"Fat chance o' that happenin'. He'll be hopin', by the time we reach America, we'll all be pals with each other and forget we were once drinkin' on opposite sides of the table. That the only thing what matters is … we're sailors. And sailors stick by each other."

"Ha! Still think I'll take me chances and jump ship."

"Is it true we're sailin' with Cap'n Francis Austen and the Invincibles?"

Trevelyan stiffened, hardly daring to draw breath. *What was this then? He had not heard of it!*

"Aye! 'Tis true! Safer in numbers while crossin' the sea, so we don't invite sea wolves to plunder our happy ship."

"Who's this Austen then?"

"He's the one what caught that English traitor, Trevelyan, the one responsible fer the burnin' of two Royal Navy ships, and kidnappin' a granddaughter o' King George … all while he were commandin' an American ship."

"Ha! Sounds like he's some kind o' *hero*."

Soft murmurs of laughter enlivened their discourse.

"So, whatever happened to this Trevelyan?"

"Most like he's tethered to an iron ring in a windowless cell at Newgate or his severed head's sittin' on a spike on display fer all to see on the Southwark gatehouse o' London Bridge." The speaker paused to hail Trevelyan in his place of isolation, away from their circle of casks.

"Ho, there, Mr. Bumpus! What's yer opinion? Where d'ya think our hero is now?"

Trevelyan, his belly stirred up like a roiling sea, laid down his book on the planks next to his long legs and calmly faced his messmates. "I imagine they disposed of him the minute he reached English soil. I suspect he is long gone by now, though, frankly, the man's fate is of no interest to me."

It seemed that none of the others were truly interested either. They grunted and shrugged in mutual agreement, and changed up the subject, someone suggesting they play a round of faro before they dispersed for their beds and night duties. Trevelyan was just as happy to have the attention removed from him, for surely, despite the feeble lantern light, they could see that beads of sweat had formed on his upper lip. And his face! He had felt its transformation. Why, it must be as glaringly white as the quarter moon drifting over the harbour. His heart drummed in his skull. What was he going to do? Sailing with Captain Austen? How could that be? It had been three weeks since his escape from the prison hulk. In all that time, surely Mr. Austen had learned something of the methodology adopted by Thomas Trevelyan in executing his disappearance? The question was: had Austen yet heard the name of Asa Bumpus? Damn! Perhaps he should have changed up his alias long ago. But it was too late to worry about that now.

His messmates had only just cut the cards for their game when the door of the captain's cabin flew open. Into the pool of light cast by the silver candelabrum on the dining table stepped Uptergrove and his guest. Seeing who it was that walked alongside the captain gave Trevelyan another shocking jolt. Yanking his legs to his chest, he drew back into the shadows of the gun carriage.

"Good evening, men." Captain Uptergrove's nod was curt, his face unsmiling, as his short, slight frame marched past their small gathering on the gun deck, leading his guest toward the companion way that would take them up to the quarterdeck.

Instinctively, fists flew to foreheads in respectful salutes, though the reply of his messmates lacked any measure of enthusiasm. "Evenin', sir."

Trevelyan peered around the gun carriage to watch the retreating figures of the two men. He could see their heads bowed together in quiet conversation. What was Uptergrove telling him? That those "shiftless bumpkins back there" were some of the newly acquired American prisoners of war? That one of them, known as Mr. Bumpus, upon the discovery of his uncommon talent for words and letters, had been assigned assistant to Mr. Croker? At the precise moment when Trevelyan was craning his neck to get a clearer view, Uptergrove's guest glanced back over his shoulder to survey the small circle of men. For a horrifying instant, their eyes met. Crippled with fear, Trevelyan held his breath and waited, still watching as the guest proceeded on his way and mounted the ladder behind Uptergrove, expecting at any time to see him pause mid-step, his head jerk up in disbelief and recognition, and swing around for a second look.

"Woulda bin nice if our cap'n had introduced us to his friend," whispered a voice full of spite and sarcasm.

"Who was that with him?"

"That's our sailin' partner … Cap'n Austen himself."

On the quarterdeck, Trevelyan could hear Uptergrove shouting at his men to lower the launch to take his guest the short distance back to the *Invincible*, and when his vociferous orders had died away, Captain Austen thanking his host for the "splendid supper." Murmuring his own words of thanks to no one in particular, Trevelyan clutched at the ropes of the gun carriage, concealing his face against the cold metal of the gun as he calmed his ragged breaths.

There had been no second look.

CHAPTER 9

11:00 P.M.
MILE END TERRACE

Leander was so weary he could scarcely summon the energy to rise from the kitchen table in his aunt's little cottage. It was late, and he had to be up at dawn, for there was much to do. He would have to pack for his upcoming departure from Portsmouth, and assist his father in writing letters to make certain the house in Steventon would be taken care of by the housekeeper and trusted neighbours while they were away from England. Later, he would have to take stock of the medical supplies in the *Invincible*'s dispensary, purchase any items that had been overlooked, and then perform his first task as ship's doctor: the examination of the newly impressed sailors to make certain none of them were carrying the typhus. In amidst it all, he had to go to Emily. How he dreaded it! Sleep, he knew, would not come easily. The hours of the night would drag on while he imagined the conversation — nay, argument — they would have in the sitting room of the Brigantine Inn, she in tears, he trying his best to convince her to stay with his aunt until he returned. He had risked his life to see her again, and now once more duty and war would wrest them apart.

With a long sigh, he finally made a move, whispering "shhh" to the legs of his chair that insisted on making a racket as they scraped along the stone floor, worried he would awaken both Gus Walby and Eliza, who had small bedchambers on the other side of the hallway. Once upright, he stretched the muscles in his shoulders and back — all knotted in defiant protest of his medical rigours over the past two days — and reached for the candle to light his way up the steep stairs to the garret room he shared with his father. He was about to mount the steps when he heard a disturbance in Gus's room. Halting to listen, he heard a bump, and then a thump and then a bang. Knocking quietly upon the door, Leander was not surprised to see it swing open at once, revealing a flush-faced, somewhat guilty-looking boy, leaning on his crutch.

"Are you aware of the time, Mr. Walby?"

"I am, sir."

Leander peeked past Gus into the bedchamber. The bed was still made, and Gus's sea chest lay open upon its patchwork quilt, stockings and shirts hanging untidily over its sides like drunken sailors in a scow. He brought his eyes back to the young lad standing restlessly before him. "You should be in bed."

"I know, sir, but I am so jumpy I cannot sleep. Did I drink ten mugs of coffee at suppertime?" Gus smiled. "I thought it best to pack my chest now, so come morning I can help you and your father pack yours."

Leander shot a disparaging glance at Gus's sea chest. "If you are going to help with mine, I will first *insist* upon giving you a lesson in the art of packing clothes ... properly."

"When I am done here, sir, you'll be impressed with my skills. I promise."

"I hope so. In the meantime, perhaps you could do your business with less bumping about. We don't want to wake Miss Braden."

Gus's smile vanished. "No, sir!"

"Good night then."

"Good night, sir."

Leander was waiting to hear the door latching shut when Gus stuck his blond head out into the hallway. "Sir? I thought I would rise early to light the fire and lay out everything for our breakfast so as not to trouble Miss Braden."

"Excellent!" Leander nodded approval before continuing on his way toward the stairs. But for a second time the small cottage rocked with a disturbance. He was on the cusp of cursing the exuberant Mr. Walby when he realized the noise had come from farther down the hall ... from his aunt's room. Tiptoeing to her door, he could hear her heavy footsteps criss-crossing the floorboards. Evidently, she, too, was awake, though it was beyond him what she was getting up to at this hour. Trying on clothes? Throwing old books into a rubbish bin? Rearranging the furniture? Leander shook his head in wonder. Most likely she was diffusing her anger with activity, letting those still awake know of her extreme displeasure at their decision to return to sea.

Unarmed for a late-night argument, he decided against further investigation, and conserved his waning energy for the ascent to the garret, and the more *trying* encounters that would come on the morrow.

11:00 P.M.
ON THE CAMBER DOCK

Prosper Burgo hovered on the edge of the old Camber Dock and lifted his lantern high above the *Invincible*'s bobbing cutter, half-obscured in the rising mists scudding across the harbour. With a grunt, he narrowed his eyes to scrutinize the occupants huddled together on the boat's benches to ward off the night's creeping cold. Some were snoring, their heads fallen backwards, their mouths open to the stars; others were eerily quiet, and had most likely taken a hit to the head to subdue them so they could be easily transported to this place without mishap. As he counted their numbers, Prosper chose to ignore the steely eyes of one, who — being sober — was cognizant of his situation, and therefore stewing in his outrage. Thankfully, his bound hands and the wad of cloth stuffed in his mouth precluded him from shouting for assistance.

In addition to the two midshipmen, Cadby Brambles and the younger one assigned to watch over the cutter while the men had gone off to do their evening's work, Prosper concluded the successful impressment of eight seamen. First-rate! Then it had been a profitable night, for already they had carried nine back to the *Invincible*. Feeling a generous spirit rise up in him — in spite of his conviction that these new recruits had been single-handedly mustered by Jim Beef and his terrifying decrees of death and woe — Prosper bestowed felicitous approbation upon Mr. Brambles.

"Well I vum! For a nestle-cock, ya've done us proud."

A surprised Mr. Brambles sprang to his feet, causing the cutter to rock wildly. "Oh! Thank you … sir! It was nothing … quite easy, really!"

"All right, ya fish flake, sit yer double juggs down," growled Prosper, "so's ya don't dump our catch into the drink." At the sound of approaching footsteps, he spun around, fully expecting to see Magpie, Biscuit, and Jim Beef returning to the boat. But it was only the latter two who emerged from the gauzy shadows. He looked to Biscuit for answers. "Where's Magpie?"

"Ain't he here with ya?" Biscuit's eyes fell upon Mr. Brambles, who had obediently retaken his place on the cutter's thwart. "Where's Magpie got to? Last we seen o' him, he were with *you!*"

"I — I haven't a notion."

Prosper stockpiled a mouthful of sputum and spewed it on the ground. "Tell us somethin' we don't already know!"

"I — we — we were separated down an alleyway," stuttered Mr. Brambles.

"*Where* exactly?"

"Near that tavern where you left us to return to the rendezvous."

Prosper eyed Jim Beef. There was no point in questioning *him*; he had a queer expression on his face, as if he were listening to conspiratorial voices in his demented head.

"I think Magpie was quite frightened, sir," Mr. Brambles added solemnly. "I think I saw him run off when a large group of sailors came out of the tavern all at once."

"Ya *think*, do ya?" Though the night served to cloak it from the others, Prosper's face had turned purple with rage. "And did ya *think* to go after him?"

"Why no, sir! I — I stayed behind to round up the recruits. Somebody had to!"

Biscuit howled his disgust. "Ya never shoulda left the lad's side."

Mr. Brambles's voice rose in shrill defiance. "I shall not have the ship's cook tell *me* what I should have done!"

"Then I'll tell ya, Cadby Brambles," said Prosper, hissing his own brand of venom. "Yer a damned jackanapes, a galoot, a chowder-headed, blustery bag o' wind o' the first order!" When he was done, he calmly singled out the younger midshipman who was looking on from the cutter's stern, swallowing hard in fear, though he himself had done nothing wrong. "Take Mr. Beef with ya and row these men to the *Invincible*. Then come straight back here and wait fer us."

"Aye, sir! Right away, sir!"

Mr. Brambles gazed around indignantly, his hands fumbling about on his hips to create an impression that he still held some sway. "And what about me, Mr. Burgo?"

"Yer comin' with us."

"Where — where are we going at this late hour?" he sputtered.

"Where d'ya think? To quaff a jug o' corn juice in the nearest wobble shop!" Prosper snorted in annoyance. "And should ya disobey, I'll be advisin' Cap'n Austen ya remain a midshipmite fer life." Giving Biscuit the signal to follow, he set off toward the winking lights of the town, forcing the distressed Cadby Brambles to scramble out of the cutter on his own and break into a run in order to catch up to them.

Annoyed by the negligence of Mr. Brambles, and fixated on the task ahead of him, Prosper was hardly aware of the lone figure who silently scurried past him on the dock, hunched over under the weight of a ditty bag. It was only later that it occurred to him — he should have paid more heed.

CHAPTER 10

Fly Austen paced the larboard gangway of his ship with his worrying thoughts. As it was Sunday, the church service had been held early that morning, but for the remainder of the day there could be no rest for the wicked mariner. The Admiralty was adamant that he get under way, back to America, and yet he wondered how his company could do so with precious little time to prepare. The main concern was men ... and the lack thereof. In addition to his quota of marines, he required a crew of at least two hundred and fifteen to adequately outfit the *Invincible*, and notwithstanding Prosper Burgo's press gang bringing to their numbers a further eighteen, there was still a serious shortage. He shook his head woefully. They would just have to muddle through.

His eyes skimmed the forecastle and quarterdeck where the Invincibles were working with a feverishness normally reserved for the readying of battle stations. A small herd of pigs was being harnessed and lowered, one by one, onto the lower deck by block and tackle, their frightened squeals an amusing contrast to the men's hoots of laughter. Landmen were scurrying up and down the companion ways with baskets of freshly greased round shot which would, at some point, fill the shot garlands of the carronades and bow chasers. Hammocks were being stowed in the netting atop the bulwarks and covered over with hammock-cloth for protection. Clothing was being washed in large buckets of rainwater with hard blocks of coarse soap, made from brine. Eggs were being collected by the cook's mates from the chicken coops stacked up beside the ship's bell, and nearby the marines, organized in a disciplined line in their working dress, were practising with small arms under the supervision of their lieutenant. Well, some of them were at least. There were others contentedly polishing the brass finish on their muskets to create an impressive shine. Fly looked skywards to see his topmen on their footropes, hauling up the reefpoints of newly affixed sails, while beneath the oaken planks upon which he stood, he could hear the pulsing thrum of barrels being rolled along the decks. Again he sighed.

Catching sight of the ship's purser, Mr. Philpotts — a jowly, bespectacled fellow — lugging his portable desk and ledgers in the direction of the starboard rail, sitting broadside to the wharf, Fly assumed the boats had returned. It was Mr. Philpotts's responsibility to carefully record all supplies — food, drink, clothing, bedding, lighting, and sundry — brought onto the *Invincible*, and he would be at his task for hours. Fly crossed the quarterdeck to assist him in arranging his recording station near the mainmast, and then proceeded to the rail to see the barge and two cutters landing alongside the ship with more cargoes of provisions. He searched their crews of men, compressed between sacks of biscuit, wooden crates of vegetables and limes, and casks of ale, hoping to spot Biscuit and Prosper Burgo among them. Aggrieved that their late night search had proven fruitless beyond discovering that the little sailmaker had been "snatched from the tavern by a ruffian called Huxley," they had promised not to return until they had found him. But they were not sitting there in the boats below. Racked with stabbing panic, Fly gazed at the thicket of ships bobbing in the harbour, moored to the north and south of the *Invincible*, and finally toward the far-reaching fingers of the sea. Where — where could the little lad be?

Quitting the rail, he wandered back to Mr. Philpotts, thinking he could alleviate his despair by engaging the man in small talk. But the purser pounced on the opportunity to bend his captain's ear, firstly on the subject of his immediate requirement for a competent assistant — preferably one who could add and subtract — and, secondly, on the inflationary prices of salted beef, which, in *his* estimation, would likely ruin him in the long run. Relief, therefore, arrived only when Leander appeared at his side, seemingly from out of nowhere.

"Old fellow! Wherever did *you* come from? Did a bird drop you on the deck?"

"I arrived just now in the barge. Did you not see me when you were standing at the rail?"

"Evidently not! But then I was not expecting you." Fly moved with Leander away from the purser's desk. He did not like the shadows beneath his friend's eyes, nor his uncharacteristically dishevelled appearance. His cravat was improperly knotted; there was a tear in his coat, and one of his shoes was missing its silver buckle. Perhaps it would be wise, thought Fly, to delay in divulging his fears concerning Magpie. "Now that you are here, you must know ... you look like a dingy street-seller of second-hand curiosities."

"As good as that?"

"Have you been in a fight?"

"Only with my conscience."

"Does this mean you have been to see Emily?"

Leander looked sheepish. "No. I thought I should first examine the impressed men ... get some things done here, and then —"

"I cannot pretend it will be easy," Fly firmly interjected. "My Mary was incensed when I told her I was setting off once more; the children in tears."

"Aunt Eliza is staging a silent protest against our leaving," Leander sighed. "If she had lashed us with her tongue and smashed the kitchen crockery, we might have borne it somewhat better."

"I suggest you do only what is necessary here, and then swiftly make your way to Emily."

"There is time. I had a messenger take a note to her at the Brigantine Inn, telling her I hoped to come by midafternoon."

"And what was her reply?"

"I — I did not think to ask for one."

"Then you have no idea if she even cares to see you, or if she has returned to London, fed up with waiting for you to come to her." Fly admonished him with a firm shake of his head. "Sometimes I despair for you, old fellow."

Looking beaten, Leander's eyes glazed over. "Yes! So you have told me a hundred times."

Taking pity on him, Fly attempted to raise his friend's spirits, though goodness knows his own were sadly flagging. "Our cruise across the Atlantic shall not come without its pleasurable diversions!"

"How so?"

"We shall have a woman travelling with us."

"Oh, well, that news has just made my day," said Leander with sarcasm. "And what is *this* woman's reason for cruising on the *Invincible*? Is she aware of the dangers?"

Fly grinned. "According to Biscuit, she refuses to travel on any ship but ours since news reached her that Princess Emeline managed to travel unscathed amongst our company."

Leander lifted an eyebrow. "Those were *not* the dangers I had in mind." He heaved an impatient sigh. "I had better get below to see to your new recruits, and while I'm there I pray I shall find the dispensary adequately stocked."

"I believe you will find the previous captain did a most decent job on that score. You should not have to part with the meagre contents of your purse to cover off what is lacking. Now then," said Fly, flicking his fingers at Leander, "off you go."

Fly was about to head off himself when he saw Cadby Brambles approaching with two strangers whom he presupposed to be his passengers: a stout woman bundled up in a Kashmir shawl with an elaborate turban upon her head, and, following a few steps behind, a scowling, dark-haired man in a finely cut suit of clothes. Young Mr. Brambles looked anxious as if he had been given the task of wringing the goose's neck for their supper.

"Excuse me, sir. Please pardon my intrusion. I wonder if I might present to you Mrs. Arabella Jiggins?"

Fly bowed to the woman whose face was as jolly as a sun-ripened tomato, and whose body seemed to be undulating with excitement beneath her shawl. "Francis Austen, your servant, ma'am."

Mrs. Jiggins flounced forward eagerly. "I am honoured, Captain Austen, truly honoured to meet you, *and* to be sailing with you. Oh! To think of the adventurous weeks that stretch before me!"

"Welcome aboard the *Invincible*."

"I hope your ship *does* prove to be invincible, Captain Austen. The very thought of sinking in the Atlantic and losing all of my earthly possessions is not a gratifying one," she teased, hooking the arm of the dark-haired man and pulling him into their circle. "Now then, allow *me* to present to you my esteemed nephew, Mr. —"

"Shipton Ludlow," the man put in quickly, his scowl having undergone a magical transformation. Aside from the elevation of his chin, he looked rather pleasant when he smiled.

"How do you do, Mr. Ludlow?" said Fly, mustering his enthusiasm. "When we are under way, I do hope you will both join me in my cabin for a welcoming feast. It shall give us a chance to get better acquainted. For now, make yourselves comfortable. Mr. Brambles here will show you to your quarters, and answer any questions you may have."

Mrs. Jiggins placed her silk-gloved hand lightly upon his arm. "Thank you, Captain Austen. You are *most* accommodating," she effused.

Fly bowed and watched as they set off with Mr. Brambles. Following in their wake, struggling to keep up, was a huffing gaggle of servant boys, laden with trunks and assorted boxes, and what appeared to be a collection of art easels. It was only then that he noticed Leander, stepping out from behind the mainmast.

"Ah! You have not yet gone below, Doctor. Have you taken to spying?"

"I wanted to get a good look at our female passenger."

"Well?" said Fly, his eyes widening in question. "Might Mrs. Arabella Jiggins give Emily a run for her money? I judge her age to be more in keeping with yours."

"Good gracious, the woman is as noisy as the bo'sun's shouts that daily awaken the dead. If you have any thoughts of matchmaking, I shall disembark immediately." Despite Leander's words, there was a twist of amusement on his lips. "However, from what I could see, she has already taken a liking to *you*."

"I am a married man. You, sir, are not." Fly glanced over at Mr. Philpotts to see how the man was getting on with his record-taking of the supplies that were being brought aboard in chaotic droves all around him. "And what of Mr. Shipton Ludlow? Have you formed an opinion of him?"

"Hot-tempered and demanding," opined Leander. "I watched him surveying his surroundings, his nose twitching with disdain. He did not seem pleased to see goats running about on deck."

Fly gave a half-hearted shrug. "Perhaps Mrs. Jiggins and Mr. Ludlow will lend some vibrant colour to our dreary lives ... as a young woman named Emily once did on the *Isabelle*." His eyes strayed as they caught sight of Mr. Brambles loping across the quarterdeck in their direction, his cheeks redder than usual. "What on earth?" he muttered. "Don't tell me Mrs. Jiggins has already made unwanted advances toward our young, foolish midshipman." He glared at Mr. Brambles. "Yes? What is it now? Have our guests found fault with their quarters?"

"No, not yet, sir!" Mr. Brambles looked uneasily toward Leander. "Actually, Dr. Braden, it is you I have come to fetch. I am afraid your assistance is urgently required."

"Where?"

"In the hospital, sir. There seems to be some sort of curfuffle afoot."

10:30 A.M.
MILE END TERRACE

Gus rested on his crutch in Aunt Eliza's little front garden, an expanding feeling in his chest, making his tight midshipman's jacket all the more uncomfortable. His eyes combed the street for the wagon and driver that would convey old Dr. Braden and him to Portsmouth Point.

Already he had hauled his sea chest outside, it being immaculately packed — certain to meet young Dr. Braden's high standards — and awaiting its next journey on the garden stones beneath the tangled gooseberry vines. Old Dr. Braden was inside finishing up his letters at the table, and Aunt Eliza, who had not made an appearance at breakfast, was keeping to her room. Gus was just as glad. He did not want her gloominess destroying the first happiness he'd known in a long while.

There was the wagon! Gus could see it in the distance, trundling along the cobbles behind a single horse. Hobbling to the panelled front door, he called into the sitting room. "Dr. Braden. It's here! It's here, sir!"

"Such impeccable timing," remarked the old doctor, pulling on his old brown Carrick coat, and tucking into a hidden pocket his sealed letters, which he would post once in town. He hurried into the passageway where his own chest had been temporarily stowed. "Now, Mr. Walby, help me with this unwieldy monster if you can, and we shall be off."

Gus gazed up in surprise. "But, sir, shouldn't we say our good-byes to Miss Braden?"

The old doctor patted down his grey, thinning hair before taking his broad-brimmed hat from its wall hook and ramming it on his head. "I think not," he said solemnly, reaching up to take down his traveller's cape, which he draped over his arm. He stooped to lift one end of his chest while Gus scrambled to pick up the other without collapsing his crutch. Saying no more on the subject, they slowly carried it to the curb just as the driver halted his horse before Aunt Eliza's red-bricked cottage.

With old Dr. Braden's assistance, Gus followed his own sea chest into the back of the uncovered wagon, and contentedly sat down beside it, leaving the front box free for the men. While he waited for them to climb up, he stole a glance at the house, wondering if Miss Braden would be found standing in one of the two ground-floor windows, grimly observing their departure. Sure enough, she was there. But she was not in the window. She was in the garden. Gus sat forward and blinked, not certain at first it was really her. She had shed her distinguishing mob cap and mud-brown weeds for a smart redingote and matching bonnet — of a shade that reminded him of freshly grated cinnamon. White kid gloves covered her hands. Her leather etui was tucked under one arm and the canister of tea that old Dr. Braden had brought her as a gift under the other. At her feet lay two bulging carpet bags. Just as her brother was settling in on the box seat, she called out sharply to the driver who had already taken up the reins.

"Wait!"

Old Dr. Braden turned his head and stared at her. At first the lined features of his face were overspread with unease, but outright astonishment soon set in. At a loss for words, he sat as if paralyzed and watched as she locked the front door and concealed the key under a loose stone in the shadows of her withering roses.

"Eliza!" he finally gasped. "What are you thinking? Surely you cannot mean to —"

She fixed her brother with a challenging stare. "Are you going to help me, Arthur? Or must I load my luggage into the wagon by myself?"

10:30 A.M.
ABOARD HMS *EXPEDITION*

Magpie bolted upright on his bed of straw, his heart pounding as he lashed out at the darkness with his fists. A rat had just scuttled over his body, he was sure of it. He had felt its ropey tail trailing over his bare ankles, and could smell the stench of mustiness and fecal droppings it carried with it. Only when he heard the rodent's tiny clawed feet skittering away along the rotting timbers did he cease to fight the dark spaces that had settled upon him like the black veil of a moonless night. He didn't care what that rat found to gnaw upon — a cask of ale, the wood of the ship's hull, a severed limb — so long as it wasn't him.

Magpie peered into the darkness, listening for approaching footsteps over the sounds of the creaking ship, and hoping someone might come with food and water. He feared he had been forgotten. He reached up to feel the painful tenderness of his swollen left cheek, igniting memories of his ghastly night. Soon after leaving the tavern, the man called Huxley had delivered the blow to shut him up so he could drag a scratchy old biscuit sack over his head. Magpie had then been roughly toted through the night-shaded alleyways under the man's arm, keeping alive a prayer that the tavern doxies, those who had taken pity upon him, were in close pursuit and would attempt a rescue by knocking out Huxley with a salvo of brickbats. But when no one had come to his aid, he had been deposited here in — what he figured were — the fore regions of a foul-smelling orlop deck. As the dark hours wore on, no one had crept to his corner to check on him, even though there were people moving about. At one point in the night he had seen men and lanterns, only yards away from him. He had heard the men joking as they collected dry oats from open barrels in the steward's room. Later still, someone had been searching for nails in the drawers of the carpenter's store. It gave Magpie a measure of comfort knowing he wasn't on a prison hulk or a slaver or a ghost ship.

And his dreams ... they had been fitful, full of unfamiliar figures moving slowly and silently around the squalid decks of a ship, unfurling the sails for faraway lands. He had dreamed about Morgan Evans, thrashing about on a surgeon's table with his leg cut away. His lips were blue, his eyes had been gouged out, and he had reached out to Magpie, begging him to help, to take away his pain. But Magpie, frightened by the look of him, had backed away and tumbled off a platform, expecting to be smashed upon the ballast of gravel and stones in the ship's bottom. He was still falling when the marauding rat had awakened him.

Magpie lay back down, curling up once more on his straw bed, trying to shrug off the horrors of the past hours and ignore the dampness that had seeped into his clothing. He thought of the lemon cheesecakes and chocolate coffee that Captain Austen's wife had so kindly prepared for him during his visit, hoping their sweet memory would appease his rebellious stomach. If only he could go to sleep again, and have pleasant dreams, so for a time he could forget his discomfort, and the unbearable reality that he would likely never again see Emily and Dr. Braden, and his best friend, Gus Walby. But, unexpectedly, the darkness began to lift around him, and he watched as the lumps and shapes on the platform — all varieties of nightmarish objects to Magpie's tormented mind — slowly revealed themselves to be nothing more than burlap bags of coal, stacks of firewood, and an assemblage of portable stoves. Winding through the lot, like the tail of a giant alligator, was a length of the anchor cable. As the light grew stronger, the carpenter's heavy set of oak drawers and the cheese rack became apparent, as did the realization that someone was sneaking up on him. Magpie lay still, too terrified to look; especially when the creeper's strident voice severely scrambled his brains.

"Here. Put these on."

A heap of sailor's slops was dumped on the floor beside him. Magpie stared at the fusty-smelling breeches, shirt, and jacket. "But I — I already got clothes, sir," he said, ashamed of his voice, a mere whisper. He couldn't help it. He was certain that the man standing over him was Huxley, and if irritated, he might take a fist to Magpie's other cheek.

"We're takin' no chances that what ya got on ain't full o' lice. And just so's ya know … the cost o' them slops will come outta yer pay."

"Me pay, sir?"

"Aye, pay! Wot? Did ya think we was gonna treat ya like a lord and master on our ship?"

"What'll ya have me doin', sir?"

"First off, the surgeon needs to check ya over, make certain yer not runnin' a fever or have the *itch*." His rumbustious bark of laughter seemed at odds with the cold cheerlessness of the orlop. "And if ya pass muster, ya'll be put to work cleanin' up the officers' roundhouse."

Magpie raised himself up on one elbow and slowly looked around to see the floating silhouette of Huxley's round-hatted head above the orange circle of lantern light. "Sir? Would ya be kind enough to take me to see yer cap'n?"

Huxley jerked backwards with a howl. "Wot's this? The cap'n?"

"I needs to have a word with him, straightaway, if ya please."

"Nay! The cap'n ain't got no time fer a gypsy beggar."

Huxley might as well have punched Magpie in the stomach. But the captain needed to know he didn't belong on this ship. The Invincibles would be waiting for him, maybe even worrying about his whereabouts, and quite unprepared to sail until they had found him. Sinking very low, Magpie dropped his expectations a notch. "Would ya mind tellin' me the name o' this ship, sir?"

Huxley thrust his face in closer, enabling Magpie to positively identify the heavy jaw and deeply pitted skin of the man who had pressed him into service. "By all means!" he replied, grinning ghoulishly. "She's called His Majesty's Ship *Bloody Flux.*"

Magpie shuddered. "Where're we goin' to, sir?"

"First off, to the Barbary Coast, and then on to Pandemonium by way o' the River Styx."

In an outburst of guffaws, Huxley stomped off toward the ladder, shouting further instructions over his shoulder. "I'll be comin' back soon to fetch ya fer the surgeon's examination. Get dressed in them slops, sit tight and keep yer ale-hole shut."

As the lantern light receded, Magpie's world went black; the objects around him once again became the fearful inventions of his overactive imagination. Magpie had never before heard of those places Huxley had named off, the ugly sound of which struck such terror in him. Rocking back and forth on his bed of damp straw, he tried to be strong and hold back his tears.

CHAPTER 11

Requiring no escort, Leander excused Mr. Brambles and made his own way to his new hospital in the forepeak of the gun deck. Long before he had arrived at his destination, he could hear the uprising of quarrelsome voices, the most offensive belonging to his assistant, Mr. Duffy, who Fly had warned him had no more education than that of a loblolly boy, and who tragically had a penchant for liquor and laudanum. It was enough to propel him forward.

"I'm not goin' to ask ya again!" yelled Mr. Duffy in a rage. "Strip down! I gotta look ya over like I do all o' the men to see if ya got any protrudin' hernias."

Upon entering his hospital, Leander found the new recruits — an omnifarious lot — standing about in front of the cots slung over an 18-pounder gun. They were dressed in nothing beyond their pitiful underclothing, their arms crossed upon their bare chests to stave off the harbour chill wafting through the open gunport. Mr. Duffy stood huffing before them as if he were a drill sergeant, brandishing a wooden peg leg. Behind him was a slender-made loblolly boy at work, probing the ear canals of one poor recruit with a tool designed for teeth. On the other side of the angled bowsprit, which served to divide the hospital in half, was a delicate-looking, fully dressed sailor, who had turned his back on them all in a defiant stance.

In the hopes of gaining the attention of his assistant, Leander banged the hospital door shut behind him. "Please lower your voice and your *weapon*, and explain your predicament."

Mr. Duffy, who owned a face immutably etched with exasperation, prefaced his narrative with a long, drawn-out exhalation as if he had just finished filling the shot locker. "It's a simple order, Doctor! I'm readyin' these idiots fer yer examination. And *this* one —" jabbing his thumb at the troublesome recruit "— won't do as he's told. I asked him if he'd prefer to have *me* yank his clothes off, to which he put up an unruly protest and insisted upon bein' taken straightaway to Cap'n Austen. Now I made it clear that every man's gotta be washed up and checked over for ruptures and lameness, but *this* one insists there's no need, 'cause, accordin' to him, he ain't got no scurvy, nor the typhus, or lice, or any conditions such as *lues venerea*." Mr. Duffy dragged one of his giant hands through the tight, sun-bleached curls on the top of his head, and shot a disdainful glare at the troublesome recruit. "Ain't that right, Mr. *George*?"

Leander followed the path of Mr. Duffy's glare to scrutinize the recruit who had now turned around to face them all. He was clutching a stuffed pillowcase against his chest in a way that suggested someone had threatened to pilfer it. His huge eyes, glittering with hope, locked on Leander as if *his* entry into the hospital had signalled the coming of a saviour. The lad's flushed cheeks, soiled with splotches of tar, and a head scarf, which completely covered his hair, could not possibly disguise him from those who knew him well. For a moment a faint disorientation filtered through Leander, comparable to the awakening from a dream and not recognizing one's surroundings. His heart lurched uncomfortably. But aware that the undressed onlookers had fixed their curiosity upon him, all eager to witness his reaction, he made certain his expression did not betray him.

Mr. Duffy came sidling up to him to mutter his opinion. "If ya ask me, Doctor, this Mr. George is a sight more *fee*-male than male … if ya catch my meanin'." He winked, his tongue hanging out the side of his mouth.

"Continue with your preparations, Mr. Duffy," said Leander gravely, retreating from the man's grog-laced breath. "But first, give me the keys, and I shall lead Mr. George through to the dispensary —" he turned to frown at the unruly recruit "— where *he* shall feel the *weight* of my reproof."

11:15 A.M.

Ill at ease, Emily watched Leander close the canvas door to the cramped quarter that housed the dispensary, hang the lantern he had brought with him upon a ceiling hook, and walk past her to push up the heavy gunport to allow in the natural light. Then he stood back, eyes on the closed door, and waited until the noise in the hospital had crescendoed to its normal level before he spoke.

"*What* were you thinking?" There was an undertone of anger in his voice.

Emily threw back her shoulders. She had expected a warm reception, happy surprise, perhaps an anxious inquiry after her health, but not this. "I had no choice."

"Why? What has happened?"

"Lord Somerton paid me a visit last evening at the inn. He said he had a carriage waiting to take me back to my *family*, and had, most likely, made it worth the innkeeper's while to keep a close watch on all exits so that I had no other recourse but to go quietly with him."

Leander swept his fingers across his mouth. "Someone must have betrayed you."

Emily did not dare tell him of her rambles around Portsmouth Point on the morning of the explosion. "Yes. Perhaps."

"How ever did you manage to get here?"

"I returned to my room under the guise of packing my things, got dressed in these garments, climbed out the window and headed for the wharves. I knew, from Magpie's visit, that a press gang was being sent out from the *Invincible* and that one of her boats would be waiting at the Camber Dock."

His hand fell away from his face to stare at her in astonishment. "So you — you clambered into the *Invincible*'s cutter alongside the impressed men?"

"I did."

"No one questioned you?"

"Not a one. There was a frightened midshipman in charge, but he said nothing at all. I am guessing he thought I already belonged to the crew."

"How did you even know you were getting into the right boat?"

"I — I just knew," she answered, her fingers reaching up to massage her throbbing temples.

Leander's tone hardened again like the cold steel of the long gun at Emily's side. "And so you came aboard and spent the night in the company of all those malmsey-nosed maggots standing *naked* out there in the hospital?"

"Goodness, Doctor!" she said, attempting to smile. "You sound like Prosper Burgo! And anyway, last night they were all fully dressed." Her amusement expired as his glance left her to skitter over his shelves of powders and potions, leaving a gulf of uneasy silence between them.

"I shall take you to the home of my Aunt Eliza," he said at last. "You will be safe there, I assure you."

"I do not wish to be *foisted* upon your aunt."

He turned back to her, his features strained and ashen in the grey morning light. "You cannot come on this journey, Emily."

She looked up at him, tormented by the recollection of their joyous reunion two weeks before. What had happened since then? Was his heart no longer beating as rapidly as hers? "I did not risk my neck only to be told I cannot come. I refuse to hide out here in Portsmouth while you are gone for months, maybe years, sailing an ocean teeming with enemies. Do not ask me to endure that again."

"Captain Austen would forbid it."

"Then do not tell him I am aboard until we are well out at sea."

"Emily," he said, his voice wilting, "you must remember that back in June the Isabelles rescued you from dangerous waters in the aftermath of a battle."

"Yes! So what of it? Do you sometimes wish you had left me in the Atlantic, Doctor?"

For a second his eyes blazed. "Don't be ridiculous! Of course not! But back then ... on that ship ... we enjoyed an existence created under extraordinary circumstances, free from the societal rules that dictate our behaviour and our choices."

"I am not particularly fond of my *present* existence."

"No," he quietly concurred.

"What are you trying to say, Doctor?"

"Can you not see? If you were to come with us this time ... Captain Austen and I would be accused of kidnapping. I care nothing for myself, but I cannot, in good conscience, risk Fly's good name."

"Were I not a granddaughter of King George, would you feel differently?"

"It *would* lighten the enormity of the situation ... considerably." He looked past her and through the gunport to gaze upon the churning harbour. "Perhaps it is time we return to reality, and attempt to live within its confines."

Any enthusiasm for further debate drained away through Emily's toes. There was a knot of constriction in her ribs, as if she were bound in an overly snug corset. She was trembling all over, and felt certain she would faint away if she did not soon sit down. "Was I wrong to believe you were going to come to me and inform me of your plans?"

"No, you weren't. I had hoped to visit you this afternoon."

"Really? Or were you simply going to sail away and say nothing at all, and have your Aunt Eliza swing by the inn for tea to break the news of your leaving?"

"I would not have done that to you."

"Maybe not." There was a weary sadness in Emily's voice. "But either way your message would have caused me great injury."

Leander seemed as restless as a horse left too long in its stall and anxious to bolt free. He answered her with an obliging formality that was reminiscent of the many butlers she had known throughout her life.

"If you will excuse me, I must leave you here for a time. I shall lock you in so no one disturbs you, and tell Mr. Duffy that your case must be discussed with Captain Austen." He hesitated by the door, his hand on the latch. "May I bring you something to eat or drink when I return?"

When had she last eaten? She could not tell. But having no appetite for sustenance of any kind, and unwilling to ask for anything, she shook her head. With a polite nod, he slipped away as if he were quitting her world to permanently return to his own. The noise in the neighbouring hospital filled the terrible silence he had left behind. Mr. Duffy's shouts rose up, vulgar words and invocations of sacred names shivering the air upon his discovery that one of the recruits had venereal disease.

"Ya bloody devil, ya have the clap! So! Ya've been playin' at rumpscuttle! I'll have to give ya an antaphrodisiac. And if I successfully cure ya, know this, ya leper! Ya'll owe me a pretty sum o' yer pay."

Emily covered her ears to shut out Mr. Duffy's tirade and, more significantly, the sound of the key in the lock. She sank down upon a three-legged stool nestled up against the long gun and rested her burning cheek upon its cold barrel. She needed to think. She had to plot her next step, whatever that would be. But the pounding in her head curtailed clear thinking, aside from the one certainty which filled her with a sense of shame.

It had been a mistake to come to the *Invincible*.

She knew that now.

NEAR NOON

By the time Leander reached the weather decks, it was drizzling out. The sky hung low over Portsmouth like a wasteland of grey ice, a portent of heavier rain to come, but he did not mind getting wet; in fact, he welcomed its freshness. It served as a slap in the face for his bumbling behaviour in the dispensary. He felt so foolish, but he could not master his jumble of emotions. The thought of Emily travelling on the *Invincible* and subjected once again to the horrors she had witnessed on the *Isabelle* was unbearable. And to think she had passed the night in the hospital, her head on the mouldy floor, surrounded on all sides by snoring, filthy men! It made him physically sick. Dear God! How easily they could have discovered she was *not* who she claimed to be.

He paused beside the ship's wheel to scan the decks for Fly. Though he had expected to find him among the sailors hanging about with the stores of food they had brought on board, waiting for Mr. Philpotts to record all in his ledgers, Leander could not see his distinguishing figure anywhere. Neither could he find any of the men with whom he was well acquainted. Where was Biscuit? Come to think of it, Leander had not noticed his head of untamed hair amongst those in the galley when he went down to the hospital. Where then was Prosper Burgo? Had he not agreed to sail with them? It was practically customary to hear Mr. Burgo's cursing long before his bald pate came into view. And what about Magpie? He always seemed to be about, scampering here and there like a contented puppy, but there was no sign of his woolly thrum cap weaving through the crowds.

Leander's searching stopped abruptly on the starboard rail, near the spot where four sailors were raising barrels up the side of the ship by means of a parbuckle. To his surprise, Mr. Shipton Ludlow was standing there, presumably having required fresh air after seeing his noisy aunt settled into her quarters, drawn to this place by his curiosity to watch the sailors at work. Catching sight of Leander, Mr. Ludlow turned away from the parbuckling and began scrutinizing him with his dark eyes, as if sizing up his only competitor in a running race. Acknowledging him with a pleasant nod, Leander stepped away from the ship's wheel to continue in his search for Fly, but Mr. Ludlow was now coming forward.

"I take it you are the ship's doctor," he said not unkindly.

"Yes! I am."

"I gathered as much. You stand out from the others."

"How so?" asked Leander, locking his hands behind him.

"Your attire is markedly different, and you have the aspect of a learned man. I do not believe there are many on board who could boast of having much in the way of a formal education besides your Captain Austen."

Leander was about to launch into a protest to defend the sailors whose knowledge of navigation and the sea was far superior to his own, but was not given an opportunity to squeeze in a response.

"How do you do, Dr. Braden? My name is Shipton Ludlow. I have been on the *Invincible* no more than an hour, and already your good name has preceded you."

Earlier, while concealed behind the mainmast, Leander had noted Mr. Ludlow's patrician face, and the fine cut and fabrics of his suit. He now wondered ... was he a wealthy merchant or a member of the landed gentry? If the former, it would explain his forwardness, but if the latter, why would he even stoop to speak to the ship's doctor? Ah, but then they were not on land where the provoking business of etiquette was far more rigid than it was on the sea. Thoughts of Emily resurfaced, hitting Leander with a new wave of anxiety. It was imperative he not be long away from her.

"Welcome aboard, Mr. Ludlow," he said, hoping to make swift excuses and dart off, but it seemed the man was in favour of further delaying him.

"Thank you. Are you aware I am travelling with my aunt?"

"Yes! And I wish for you both clear skies and calm seas."

"Having looked around the decks, would I be correct in supposing that we are your only passengers, Dr. Braden?"

"I believe so."

"Ah! And here I had hoped there might be a lady or two aboard. You know," he added quickly, "to enliven our mealtimes as we cross the Atlantic."

Leander was now desperate to leave. "I am sorry to disappoint you, Mr. Ludlow, but with all respect, this is a frigate, a man-of-war — not the most suitable place for our fair sex."

"Of course! How silly of me!"

"Well then, I had better be off. Good morning, Mr. Ludlow."

Leander had only just turned himself around when his attention was riveted to the rail, just beyond the place where the sailors were labouring with their barrels. Having been hoisted up from the water on an arrangement of pulleys, one of the ship's cutters was now swinging level with the deck. Sitting up straight on its stern bench, as proud as a puffed-up peacock, was young Gus Walby, who greeted Leander with a dignified nod of his blond head. Beside him sat Leander's father, looking every inch an adventurous world traveller in his broad-brimmed hat and greatcoat. It was the third individual on that stern bench who gave him consternation. Though unsmiling, the face was a familiar one, and yet Leander could not register to whom it belonged, too confused was he by the bonnet and its jaunty adornment of ribbon bowknots.

Despite the fact that he had rather surprisingly — and abruptly — taken a few steps backwards and was now standing partially shielded by a stack of vegetable crates, Mr. Ludlow had followed Leander's gaze. "More passengers, perhaps, Dr. Braden?"

"Yes! No! I cannot be sure," Leander replied, still in the grip of disbelief.

"Are you acquainted with the *woman* in the boat?"

"I am," he said, feeling defeated as if he had been named the loser in that running race. "She is — she is my aunt."

"How lovely for you! Then we shall both have our aunts on board."

Scarcely had Leander recovered from the shock of Eliza's arrival when Mr. Duffy appeared at his side in a state of agitation. "Beg pardon, sir. Could I entreat upon ya to return to the hospital?"

"I told you, Mr. Duffy, I have business to discuss with Captain Austen. Only when I am done shall I return."

"Well then, ya better know this, sir. I heard a disconcertin' kind o' sound in the dispensary."

Alarm seized Leander by the throat. Had Emily tried to escape through the open gunport?

"So's I thought it best to investigate, sir."

"What? But I have the keys!"

"I've got me own set," said Mr. Duffy with a grin, dangling them before Leander's eyes. "Like I was sayin' … unlockin' the door, I found our Mr. George on the floor. It seems he fainted dead away. Ya better come, sir. He ain't at all well, and I suspect he has somethin' catchin'."

Leander gazed distractedly at his family. They were waiting to disembark from the cutter, and, from their expressions, aware of his having received troubling news.

"Yes, yes, all right, Mr. Duffy."

"And sir, there's somethin' else ya should know."

"What *is* it?" snapped Leander, wishing that Biscuit would appear on deck with an enormous decanter of wine.

"Ya'd better prepare yerself fer what I'm about to tell ya, sir." Mr. Duffy paused for effect, his narrowing eyes darting around the quarterdeck as if he were gearing up to divulge his esteemed theories on the origins of life. "Ya see, our Mr. George ain't a mister at all. He's — he's a *woman*, sir! Of the highest quality! And I foresee trouble, big trouble as the lads'll be wantin' to git their hands on her and —"

"Thank you, Mr. Duffy! That is all the information I require for now," hissed Leander through his teeth, giving his assistant a push in the direction of the ladder down to the upper deck. Worried that Shipton Ludlow was within earshot, Leander glanced behind him. Sure enough! There he was, still positioned near the vegetable crates, nodding his tilted head in Leander's direction, his face all aglow with rosy satisfaction.

CHAPTER 12

Fly trudged along the mess deck, dreaming of the hour when he could seek refuge and sanity in his cabin and take his supper alone, far from the cares and exigencies of the day. As always, there was much to do before he could rest his feet and calm the black closet of his mind. One of his servants needed his personal instruction on the maintenance of both his civilian clothes and his undress uniforms. Mr. Philpotts's ledgers had to be studied, and any shortfalls of supplies duly noted. A message had reached him that Leander had been looking for him, requesting a meeting in the hospital. And finally, if he could squeeze in the time, Fly hoped to speak with the quarterdeck watch to learn if there had been further news of Biscuit and Prosper Burgo. Since the rating of these chores, in order of their importance, fell to him and him alone, he chose to begin with an agreeable one: welcoming aboard his most recent party of passengers, Dr. Arthur Braden and his sister, Eliza, and congratulating Gus Walby on his return to sea.

Their lonely dining table — wide, wooden planks suspended by ropes affixed to the deckhead — was tucked away in the fore narrowing of the mess, which was mainly empty except for the few whose job it was to clear, clean, and store the tables. The sailors had finished their meal at two bells, and those who had no immediate duties had headed off to various sections of the ship in search of entertainment. Shipton Ludlow and his aunt, Mrs. Jiggins, who had not yet had the pleasure of meeting their fellow passengers, had asked to dine later, a request Fly had found particularly irksome. Tonight he would let it go. But in future they would be given clear-cut reminders that they were on a frigate, and, consequently, not eligible for flexible dining hours.

As soon as Mr. Walby had masterfully handled the introduction of Miss Braden, Fly invited them all to resume their seats. With displeasure, he eyed and sniffed the ragout heaped upon their square wooden plates: lumps of potato, onion, and anonymous meat, swimming in a greyish, congealing gravy. "I do apologize. My cook is away at present, but I promise you better fare upon his return," he said, doubting his own words.

"It is sufficiently adequate, thank you, Captain Austen," said Miss Braden, dabbing at her mouth with a tidy square of linen. "You shall receive no complaints from me. And as you can see, I have brought along my own store of tea." She reached over to tap a red and gold chinoiserie canister which, for safekeeping, she had set at the end of the table, beneath the cutlery rack. Fly concluded she had heard stories of the alarming quality of tea offered up on Royal Navy ships, or more specifically, Prosper Burgo's peculiar recipe for the stuff.

In the glim of their solitary candle, Gus's eyes were shining. "Where is Biscuit, sir? I do hope he shall be joining us. And where is Magpie? I thought he might have been waiting to greet us when we all first came aboard."

"In good time, Mr. Walby," said Fly, taking care with the phrasing of his answer. "We are all hard at work, trying to achieve our objective to sail tomorrow."

"Captain Austen, while we are at sea, might I have your permission to help out in the hospital?" asked Arthur Braden, his shapely hands clasped around an earthenware mug of ale. "I may be a man of many years, but I do recall a thing or two of medicine."

When Fly had first met the old doctor two weeks ago in Wymering, he had taken an instant liking to him. He had the same sagacious face and warm smile of his son, and looked just as Fly imagined Leander would in about thirty-five years. "By all means! It is my understanding that you personally undertook the responsibility of restoring the health of our Mr. Walby."

Old Dr. Braden angled his head to look fondly at Gus. "I had my concerns about that cough of his, but what truly inspired me was how hastily he pulled himself together upon receiving confirmation he would be cruising on the *Invincible*."

Fly's glance grew serious as it fell upon the boy. "We must find some other clothes for you, young man. You have quite outgrown your midshipman's uniform; besides, it will not do if you are to become my clerk."

Gus's mouth dropped open.

"Our purser, Mr. Philpotts, also requires assistance. I think between the two of us, we shall succeed in keeping your nose to the grindstone." The mute disbelief on Mr. Walby's face delighted Fly. "You didn't really think I would have you trapping rats in the hold now, did you?"

"Sir! Thank you so very much!"

Miss Braden's disarming, light-grey eyes peered up at Fly. "As I do not wish to be a burden to anyone, it is my fervent hope that you might consider some manner of occupation for me."

Fly studied the severe face framed in its abundant mob cap. She was wearing a white shawl tucked into the belt of a deep-grey woolen dress, which reminded him of a seventeenth-century Covenanter. Most likely she was younger in age than she appeared, though he did not judge her to be a woman predisposed to flirtatious behaviour. Perhaps she could teach Biscuit a thing or two in the galley and keep him in line at the same time. "Tell me, Miss Braden, how are your cooking skills?"

She pursed her lips while she considered his question. "I assure you, Captain Austen, my sewing skills are far superior."

"Well, *that* is exceedingly good. 'Tis true that every man on board is expected to understand the mechanics of a needle and thread. Sadly, experience has taught me otherwise. You shall be a tremendous help to us. All *three* of you shall!" Fly forced a happy smile. "Now I will take my leave and let you finish your meal. I do hope the cook's mates have prepared some sort of sweet treat for you."

With a slight bow, Fly stepped away from their table, but not before catching the look — the silent communication — in Mr. Walby's young eyes, as if the lad sensed that all was not well.

5:45 P.M.

Hearing someone rattling the latch on the hospital's main door, Leander put aside his medical journal and blotting paper, and popped his goose-quill pen back into its inkwell. When he glanced up, Fly had entered his office and was standing before him, looking drawn, discontented, and humourless.

Suddenly nervous, Leander rose from his chair and tried his hand at levity, hoping to extract a smile from Fly. "There you are, Captain! Where have you been all this time? I was beginning to wonder if you had abandoned ship, for no one seemed capable of finding you this afternoon."

Dodging the question, Fly lifted his jutting chin to study Leander. "You've cleaned up. You now have less of the look of a street-seller about you."

"For that I am grateful."

"And I see you have finally acquired some new spectacles. Well done, Doctor! Do they have hinged sidepieces?"

"They do." Leander removed his glasses from his nose so he could show them off. "I found them in a toy shop of all places, amongst the penknives and pocketbooks."

"How much did they cost you?"

"Four shillings."

"How fortunate you are that the Navy Board at Somerset House saw fit to give you your back pay. If I recall correctly, you had nothing at all when we pulled you out of the Atlantic and onto the decks of Prosper Burgo's privateer."

"Nothing but my life," said Leander with a shudder of remembrance. He took a deep breath to introduce the troubling subject of his state of affairs, but Fly had wandered off to poke about the hospital's perimeter.

"I do wish you would move all *this* below, Doctor," he said when he was done inspecting the cleanliness of the hammocks, the contents of the oak cupboards, and the sturdiness of the bowsprit. "I can think of a dozen other purposes for this space."

Leander's shoulders sagged. "Surely none as important as being near the gunports and thus able to provide clean, fresh air for both the sick and the healthy. You have long been privy to my theory of the benefits of arranging a ship's hospital on the upper deck. Evidently, my predecessor agreed with me. I did not set up this space. He did. Now if it pleases you, when enemy frigates appear on the horizon, I shall work below the waterline, for I cannot perform amputations while sidestepping cannonballs and grapeshot."

Fly nodded absently, as if his mind were now strolling along the beloved Wood Walk behind his childhood home at Steventon. "I see you have no patients. What have you done with the recruits?"

"As per your orders, they are being safely guarded below until we are at sea. Remember? You did not want any of them trying to swim to shore in the night."

"Ah! Good! Because I had worried I would come down here to find an unbridled contagion had felled a dozen of them."

"Thankfully, there is nothing quite as bad as that. I did come across three cases of rheumatism, so I have asked that they be given flannel, and further asked that the portable stoves be put in place to keep the decks as dry as possible. In addition, there was one case of venereal disease, the treatment of which has already been administered and shall be ongoing until the man recovers, hopefully."

Fly raised a suspicious brow. "So then, Doctor, why the summons?"

Gesturing for Fly to follow, Leander anxiously led him through to the dispensary where he had left a lantern burning. They walked to the side of a cot that had been slung over the gun, and together observed its slumbering occupant. Her cheeks were flushed, her breathing slightly shallow, and her long hair lay untidily upon her pillow like knotted lengths of corn silk.

"I see," sniffed Fly. "Does the entire crew know? Am I the last to learn of this?"

"That is more than likely sure."

"Did you drug her so you could smuggle her aboard?"

Leander huffed quietly with annoyance. "Does that truly sound like something I would do?" He looked down again at Emily, unwilling to admit or show just how relieved he felt that she was here, safe under his protection. "She managed to travel from the wharf in one of our cutters."

Fly was incredulous. "What? When? Today? With the incoming supplies?"

"No. Last night."

"With the recruits?"

"Yes." Leander raised his eyes to him. "You don't appear to be surprised."

Fly met his questioning gaze. "Were *you*, Doctor?" He took a few steps backwards to lean against the dispensary wall — beside Emily's pillowcase of belongings which had been deposited upon the three-legged stool — and tightly locked his arms across his chest. "Well? Out with it! What is her story?"

Beginning with the disturbing appearance of Lord Somerton at the Brigantine Inn, Leander swiftly recounted the events that had led to Emily's arrival on the *Invincible* and her ultimate admittance to the dispensary bed. When he had finished the retelling, he eagerly sought out Fly's reaction, but his friend had now moved beyond the sphere of lantern light and into the darkness.

"You said that Mr. Duffy found her here on the floor."

"I believe she fainted from a lack of food. She could not tell me when she had last eaten."

"So with some gruel and tea she should be restored to good health?"

Leander hesitated. "She is suffering from exhaustion and anxiety," he said softly. "She has a headache and a mild fever. And, in the past two hours, she has developed a dreadful cough."

"What is your diagnosis then, Doctor? Pneumonia? Bronchitis?" Fly's voice quivered with impatience.

"Perhaps. It is too soon to tell."

"Both of which are contagious."

"Yes. Then again, it may turn out she has nothing more than a bad cold. At this stage, I simply do not know."

Fly returned to Emily's cot, his eyes frozen in a glassy stare. "What is your plan, Doctor?"

"My *plan* was to leave her with my Aunt Eliza, but as you now know *she* had other ideas. Were Emily not sick, I would suggest taking her to shore ... finding her safer accommodation, away from the wharves. Regrettably, I have no other kinsmen here in Portsmouth, no one to whom I could entrust her."

"Then you are telling me that I must either delay our departure or find myself another doctor."

"Would you — would you consider waiting until Friday to leave? As it is, I cannot abandon her."

Fly smirked. His tone was scornful. "You should know by now, Doctor, that it is bad luck for seamen to set sail on a Friday."

Leander watched his friend move toward the dispensary exit, waiting tight-lipped and on tenterhooks for the unleashing of a reprimand; a tirade on royal princesses travelling on frigates in the time of war; a stark reminder that stealing a lamb could mean execution with the dead body afterward being offered up for dissection. Fly walked like a weary traveller, one who had completed his journey, not one about to embark on it. He paused to rest his hand upon the door frame, allowing his fingers to lightly drum the thin wood, and half turned toward Leander, but their eyes did not meet, and no further words passed between them. Withdrawing, Fly left his friend stung by the strident echo of his heels on the hospital floor, and the crisp closing of the outer door.

9:00 P.M.
(FIRST WATCH, TWO BELLS)

Biscuit and Prosper Burgo were ushered into the great cabin, along with a howling gust of wind, and stood quietly, twisting their rain-drenched cloaks in their hands. For a brief, expectant moment, Fly, who had just sat down to his supper, gazed upon them. But there was no need to inquire; he could tell all from their downcast expressions. Slowly, he put down his fork and stared at his warmed-up meal — the same ragout Mr. Walby and the Bradens had been feasting upon in the mess; disgusting, in spite of its presentation on a delicate creamware plate. With his forearm, he pushed it down the length of his table — beyond his sense of smell — and seized his goblet of wine, gulping down the contents before his glance returned to the men.

"There must be something more we can do?"

Biscuit could not make eye contact. "I dunno what, sir. We've searched every tavern, every ship near the docks; even made queries at Haslar in Gosport."

"Must've questioned a hundred or so people," added Prosper, dashing away the dampness from the top of his head, his voice uncharacteristically grave. "No one's heard the name o' the little sailmaker."

"Or claims to 'ave seen him," added Biscuit.

"No one?" said Fly scornfully. "No one's seen a small boy with a head of dark curls wearing a green eye patch, Biscuit?"

"Nay, sir. Problem is — if this man who goes by the name o' Huxley did indeed steal our Magpie — in a seaside town such as this, aside from them doxies at that tavern, anyone in possession o' information ain't likely to own up to it. Any more than we'd admit to the takin' o' them sailors last night."

Fly watched the rainwater pooling around Biscuit's sodden shoes and Prosper's crumbling boots, creeping along the timbers to meet that which sluiced through crevices in the deckhead around the cabin's skylight. His imagination ran wild, stopping only in morbid places of danger and darkness. Was Magpie padlocked and starving in a Portsmouth garret? Was he chained in the hold of a man-of-war with a guard of marines glaring down upon him through a hatchway, their loaded muskets fixed upon him? Was he lying beaten and bleeding in a decrepit basement, unfamiliar with his surroundings, unable to find his way back to the wharves?

Prosper prepared to put his cloak back on. "Would ya like us to go out lookin' agin? 'Cause we can search 'til we sail, if ya want."

Unable to trust himself to speak, Fly turned in his chair to look upon the galleried windows. Rain poured down the windowpanes, and periodically the groaning wind snatched it up, ramming it against the glass like a fist coming down in frustration upon a hard surface. He felt the ship rolling on her moorings; heard her timbers railing in protest of their severe pounding. His gut clenched in sympathy for little Magpie; his mind dimmed with the lonely images of Morgan Evans's graveside, still green, but unloved and unvisited. A few days ago, he had thought it was all coming together nicely. Now, like a worn pair of stockings, the threads of his efforts were unravelling. Fighting off a quiver of emotion, he turned back to the waiting men.

"No," he said coldly. "We have our orders. We must push on."

CHAPTER 13

"All hands ahoy!"

The rousing cry of the boatswain's mate jarred Gus Walby awake. For a few moments he had lain in his cot, wedged in the cramped closet to which he had been assigned on the berthing deck, trying to recall where he was, his mind clearing only when the subsequent cry of "Up all hammocks ahoy" had resounded throughout the ship. Then, as quickly as he could, he quit his bed and eagerly felt around in the dark for his clothes, dragging on his trousers and jacket, slipping his cold feet into his leather shoes, and collecting his crutch, for he was on a mission — to find Magpie. Last night at supper, he had accepted Captain Austen's explanation that everyone was busy in preparation to sail, but he could not believe he had been on board so long without seeing hide or hair of the little sailmaker. Even if Magpie had had to finish up a hundred tasks and done his searching at midnight when all except for the Middle Watch were snoring in their beds, it was in keeping with the lad's character to have been the one to seek out Gus.

The berthing deck was dimly lit with nothing more than a few oil lamps placed at intervals, scarcely enough light for the men to see their way about as they stumbled from their cabins. Gus flattened himself against a framework of canvas to study the shadowy faces of those who passed him by, hoping to recognize someone he knew. Meeting with failure, he finally flagged down a fat-faced midshipman who was struggling into his single-breasted, blue coat as he hurried along the deck, and asked if he could trouble him for directions to the sailroom. Lifting an arrogant brow, the midshipman examined Gus from stem to stern, wrinkling his nose as he beheld Gus's ill-fitting uniform and walking stick, his mouth puckering like a prune as he deliberated upon the wisdom of obliging him.

"One deck down. Forward platform," was his surly reply before he dashed off, shooting a parting scowl at Gus.

Aside from its piles and rolls of canvas, the sailroom was empty. The only sign of a sailor's existence was the ditty bag hanging from a hook in the deckhead, but with no distinguishing tag or label Gus could not be certain to whom it belonged. Shaking his head in speculation, he decided to hunt down Biscuit. If anyone knew of Magpie's whereabouts, it would be him. And surely, by now, the Scottish cook would be in the galley, terrorizing those who dared to interfere with his breakfast routine.

Gus scurried up the ladders to the gun deck, hampered by the straggling mess cooks, those who were late in drawing their oatmeal rations from the steward's room and were now heading in the same direction as he, the ponderous wooden buckets they carried, known as mess-kids, threatening to launch him and his crutch cleanly off the slippery rungs. When at last he had reached the galley and set eyes upon Biscuit — whose shock of rust-coloured hair was conspicuous in any crowd — Gus felt a constriction in his chest. He had not seen Biscuit for weeks, not since their parting in Bermuda in early July when he had returned to England with Emily and the Duke of Clarence, leaving his friends behind on HMS *Amethyst* to continue their warring on the North American coast. As expected, Biscuit was flitting around his Brodie stove — the black, hissing, spitting, steam-breathing monster given pride of place on many Royal Navy ships — inspecting his baking loaves of bread, stirring the coppers of boiling burgoo, and flipping Captain Austen's eggs over in a cast-iron pan. Unexpectedly, he was singing "Scots Wha Hae" while he worked, a rather mournful tune for him as he was more inclined to begin his workday by rending the galley air with cheerful profanity.

> Scots, wha hae wi Wallace bled,
> Scots, wham Bruce has aften led,
> Welcome tae yer gory bed,
> Or tae victorie.

Abruptly, Biscuit left off his singing to organize the mess cooks into a line — those now swarming his stove — all of them anxious to have their mess-kids refilled with cooked rations and delivered to their howling messmates who had not eaten since yesterday afternoon.

"One at a time! One at a time, if ya please! Skillagalee and Scotch coffee this mornin' fer yer dinin' pleasure!" Though his words sounded exuberant, his voice did not.

Jumping out of the way, Gus waited for a chance to speak to Biscuit beside the steeping tub where the meat for the midday meal was being soaked. Almost immediately, his attention was yanked away from the Brodie stove and riveted to the seaman standing over the flat surface of an oak cabinet in the galley alcove, mixing together flour, sugar, and raisins in a wooden bowl. In spite of the man's enthralling appearance, which seemed at odds with the meekness of his task, Gus figured he was a cook's mate. As the alcove was incommodious, he was stooped awkwardly over his bowl, his shirtsleeves shoved to his elbows, exposing an array of queer tattoos. His legs were as skinny as the spindles of a Windsor chair; his nose was beak-like, bumpy and prodigious; his lips were heavy and swollen and his hair fell near to his waist in a stringy, unwashed braid. There was something unsettling about him, his aspect eliciting comparisons with the disagreeable individuals who laboured in the bottom of the ship in the noxious waters of the bilge. Here, in the lively atmosphere of the galley, he seemed out of place. For a time, with his interest piqued, Gus watched him work, slowly, almost indolently, measuring and adding to his mixture, and then, without warning, the man began to mutter, words that only Gus could hear in the noisy confusion.

"Death and woe and despair."

Thinking he could not possibly have heard him correctly, Gus made a polite inquiry. "I beg your pardon, sir. What did you say?"

The man rolled his head backwards in a ghastly angle as if he were dangling from a hangman's noose, his eyes — round and discerning — darting everywhere before landing upon Gus. "Woe and despair. Suffering and wretchedness," he said in low, arresting growls. "And they shall mourn those who perish in the *autumn gales*, beneath the violent sea."

The hairs on the nape of Gus's neck began crawling; it felt like someone had unleashed a colony of spiders upon him. Blinking rapidly, he backed away, knocking into Biscuit who had just finished filling the mess-kids with burgoo, and was now wiping his hands on his greasy neckerchief.

"Stand easy, Mr. Walby! There ain't much room to manoeuvre in these parts."

"I am so sorry!" cried Gus, convinced the strange man would creep up behind him and spew more pronouncements into his ears.

Biscuit displayed both his rotting teeth and some good humour in a wide grin. "Well, here ye are! And ain't ye a sight fer sore eyes! Now tell me, 'ave ya come to fetch me, so's I kin break bread with ya? Or 'ave ya come to drag me off so's ya kin introduce me to the bonny and lusty Miss Eliza Braden?"

So great was Gus's distress at hearing the words autumn gales uttered from such hideous lips, he did not have the wherewithal to set right Biscuit's misinformation regarding Miss Braden. "I have looked everywhere," he said, his voice breaking with a sob, "but I cannot find Magpie. Do you know where he is?"

Like the steam circulating around the cooling stovepipe, Biscuit's smile evaporated. Gently, he pried Gus's fingers off his arm. "Calm yerself now, Mr. Walby. Yer overwrought and forgettin' yerself. Come away from here, and I'll tell ya what I know." With a wave indicating Gus was to follow, he trudged off toward the lift by the companion way where the gun deck was less burdened with heat and bodies.

Disregarding the melancholy note in Biscuit's voice — so relieved to be rescued — Gus scrambled after him. And only when a safe distance from the galley alcove had been achieved, did he risk a backward glance. But the strange, muttering man and his mixing bowl were now nowhere to be seen.

10:00 A.M.
(FORENOON WATCH, FOUR BELLS)

The gunport was open, ushering in sunshine and a cool, whispering breeze. Emily's cot had been arranged over the long gun in such a way that she could delight in both the sights and sounds of the outside world. In the morning light, Portsmouth Harbour was a sapphire. Like wisps of diverging clouds, seagulls circled in the blue sky before swooping down to play in and around the wilderness of masts bobbing on the water. Voices at work called and heckled, laughed and badgered. Smaller vessels — punts, lighters, and bumboats — plied the ruffled channels between the anchored ships, some of them bearing loads of provisions, others carrying their trumpery baubles and wares, their owners haggling with the sailors on their decks in the hopes of finding those willing to part with their golden guineas. The scenes of life and adventure were entertaining, and yet Emily had never felt so low.

"Would you like some breakfast now?"

The voice was gentle, almost tentative, as if aware of its intrusion on her thoughts. Emily turned her head to find Leander hovering near the foot of her cot. He was wearing an open-necked shirt, its white, linen sleeves rolled to his elbows, and in the crook of his arm he carried a wooden bowl of steaming oatmeal. She had not heard him enter the room. How long, then, had he been standing there, she wondered? Hauling herself up into a sitting position with some difficulty — her limbs as weak as those of a newborn lamb — she pulled her pale-blue, silk-embroidered shawl up around her shoulders and pushed aside a messy tangle of hair from her face.

"Thank you," she said reservedly, reaching out to accept her meal, relieved to see that it had been sweetened with a splash of goat's milk and sprinkle of brown sugar. Her head felt as weighty as a 36-pounder, her chest like a section of the mainmast, but her stomach appeared to be very much alive, grumbling its annoyance at having been denied food for so long.

Leander fetched a spoon for her from a small drawer in the dispensary cupboard, Emily relishing the warm brush of his fingers as he placed it in her hand. "I remember seeing silver-plated spoons in Captain Moreland's cabin on the *Isabelle*, but I don't recall seeing them in your hospital, Doctor."

"I came upon it in the same shop where I found myself a new pair of glasses." Leander gave the spoon a speculative glance before adding, "It holds the scuffs of a century, but I thought it fine ... and rather regal."

No doubt, thought Emily, saying nothing of her suspicions that, at some point in its history, it must have been stolen, for it shared a remarkable resemblance to the collection of dessert spoons that were once laid out at the Prince Regent's banquets at Carlton House. She ate in silence, her sore throat making the oatmeal's journey to her stomach an uneasy one, her right leg bouncing nervously as she waited for Leander to broach the subject of dispatching her from the ship. Having delivered her breakfast, and perhaps not of a mind for small talk, he had turned away to see to the confusion of bottles that someone — most likely his assistant, Mr. Duffy — had hastily dumped upon the lowest of the dispensary shelves, organizing them into neat groups according to their contents. Able to decipher some of the wording on the bottles' paper labels from her bed, Emily could see that his stock included Madeira wine, French brandy, lemon-flavoured cordial, Daffy's Elixir, and Wessel's Jesuit Drops, the latter two surely containing little beyond alcohol. She gazed at Leander as he worked; astonished at the overabundance of his spirituous tonics, contemplating yet incapable of making a flippant remark on her observations, having no vivacity to form the words while beset with worries of leaving. She tried sitting taller in her cot. Well then, if Leander was plotting to take her ashore, he would doubtless have to act fast, for hadn't Captain Austen planned to sail today? Hadn't a high tide already filled the harbour, enabling them to safely head out to Spithead? Training her ears upon the voices of the Invincibles on the overhead decks, she listened for calls to make sail or to raise the anchor, for any change in the tempo of activity which would indicate they were getting set to depart from Portsmouth. To her dismay, all seemed far too peaceful and ordinary.

With a sinking heart, Emily set her spoon and bowl down upon her blankets, and stared listlessly out the gunport. Where was she going to go? Of all those vessels out there, which one was preparing to sail away from these unloved English shores, and — more importantly — planning to steer a course toward North America? If she could locate that ship, how many of her precious pound notes would she have to press into the palms of its captain so that he may welcome her aboard? She looked back at Leander only to find him looking at her, one fist concealing his mouth, his blue eyes glazed over as if deep in thought.

"And how are you feeling this morning?" he asked.

"Quite well, thank you," she lied, pulling her shawl tightly around her.

His eyes came to life, flickering with skepticism.

"Why do you look so surprised, Doctor? Did you think I was on my last legs ... that I would succumb before the midshipmen picked up their sextants to do the noon observation of the sun?"

"While a ship lies motionless in harbour, there is little requirement for a sextant as her position on the sea has already been determined."

"Thank you for that, Mr. Wiseacre," she said, with an indignant toss of her head. "Did you by chance hear my death rattle?"

"No." He frowned. "Although you *were* making some disturbing sounds as you slept."

Emily coloured. "What — what sort of sounds?"

"Croaks, snorts, and snuffles," he replied, linking his arms upon his chest, "which have consequently led me to conclude you are suffering from a deplorable respiratory ailment."

Emily's face grew hotter. She rummaged through the rooms of her tired brain, hoping to stumble upon a witty rejoinder to preserve her respectability, but was foiled by a sudden, painful fit of coughing, forcing her to scramble for a length of her shawl to help muzzle the attack. And so, when the canvas door rattled with an alarming staccato of knocks, stealing away at once the doctor's attention, she could not help feeling a twinge of exasperation. Given permission to enter, Mr. Duffy came striding past Leander and into the dispensary, his eyes rolling around the room on swells of curiosity, rubbing his hands together as if anticipating his ration of grog.

"Beg pardon, sir. I've brung a note fer ya from Cap'n Austen." He handed it off — or rather, stuffed it into Leander's waiting palm — and rose up on his heels in a kind of pirouette, to bestow an expression of profound pity upon Emily, anchored mouth, knitted brow, and all. "And, naturally, I were wond'rin' how the miss were farin'?"

"Thank you, Mr. Duffy, but there's no need for you to worry yourself sick where the *miss* is concerned."

"Well, it's like this, sir —" his pity giving way to rising excitement "— I thought maybe she needed to be bled, purged, and blistered."

"Oh, I see." Mildly amused, Leander threw a glance at Emily. "Certainly not until she is done eating."

"All right, sir! When it's time, just holler. I'll be standin' by, ready to *pin* her down to the bed so she don't flail about."

Horrified by the thought of such a healing procedure — if that's, in fact, what it was — and resenting the men's chatter — you would think she was sitting on deck, not a few feet away from them, helplessly imprisoned in her cot — Emily opened her mouth to protest, but instead, stopped to gape at Mr. Duffy. He was winking at her in a most lecherous way, every feature of his face getting in on the act. Thankfully, Leander's response was swift. Giving the winker a twirl about, he navigated him through the dispensary door and pushed him into the shade of the hospital. It was not long before she heard the outer door click. Then she waited, listening for Leander's returning steps, seizing the opportunity when they did not come. Climbing from her bed, she landed on wobbly legs and crept to the stool to collect her pillowcase of belongings. Already dressed in her trousers, she had only to find her shoes and a scarf with which to fix her hair, so that, when and if he did return, she would be standing ready to face her fate.

Within minutes, the dispensary door opened wide and in he walked. His eyes were lowered, absorbing the contents of his letter from Captain Austen, an enigmatic and somewhat boyish smile playing upon his face. As soon as he became conscious of her, wavering bravely beside her cot, he stopped in his tracks. "What are you doing?"

"I'm waiting."

"For what, pray?"

"To be rowed ashore." Emily held on to the side of her bed for support and remained resolute, despising the uncomfortable thumping of her heart. "You have made it abundantly clear that I am to be put from the *Invincible*."

His auburn brows arched in bewilderment, as if the words "*Have I?*" would soon tumble from his open mouth. Instead, whatever amusement he had gleaned from Captain Austen's letter dried up, its replacement the familiar physician's countenance — staid and stern — normally reserved for wayward patients who had not heeded his earlier advice. With an exclamation of impatience, he stepped toward her.

"As I have no desire to have to peel you from the floor a second time in four and twenty hours, I suggest you get back into bed." He held out a steadying arm, but did not touch Emily nor look at her as she did as she was told, falling into the canvas pit of her cot and lying back upon her pillow, shutting her eyes in exhaustion as the last of her dignity drained away like unwelcome waves of water through the scuppers of the decks.

"And then later, when you've had more sleep, we shall discuss this business of you going ashore."

She heard him leave and lock the door behind him. What she did not see was the return of his smile as he strolled from the room.

10:00 A.M.
ABOARD HMS *EXPEDITION*

Magpie lifted his ears and listened to the alteration in the hum and hustle of the ship. He knew the shouts, the orders, the reason for the running feet, and the frisson of excitement in the air. Even in his dark prison down in the ship's entrails, submerged in the cold harbour, he could tell that they were getting ready to leave Portsmouth.

The Bloody Fluxes were heading for their stations — to the capstan aft of the mainmast and fore to the hawse holes and cathead to begin the arduous task of raising the anchor. Magpie was certain he could hear the sails being unfurled and slapped awake by the September wind. His overwrought imagination pictured the sailing master and the helmsman together at the wheel as two fearsome figures: one a skeletal giant in a black, hooded cloak, the other a one-legged dwarf, consulting their harbour charts and discussing the various obstacles they would have to steer clear of as they made their way to Spithead, one of which would surely be the freshly charred bones of Prosper Burgo's once brave warrior, the *Prosperous and Remarkable*. And somewhere on deck that odious Mr. Huxley would be jabbing his cucumber fingers into the flesh of the landlubbers, threatening to whip them to within an inch of their lives with his cat-o'-nine-tails if they didn't work faster.

Had things been different — had Magpie been standing on the forecastle of the *Invincible*, listening to Captain Austen calling out to his rallying men; hearing their voices rising in unison, singing verses of "Heart of Oak" as they heaved upon the capstan pawls; smiling as the new sails came fluttering down upon their spars — every sound would have filled him with elation. But he wasn't aboard the *Invincible*; he was in a ship called the *Bloody Flux*, bound for the Barbary Coast on the bottom of the earth — or so he thought; home to merciless, salt-sea pirates and dark-skinned slave traders — or so he'd heard tell. As it was, each and every one of the ship's shuddering movements champed on his innards as if the rats that haunted the hold's hiding places were making a meal of him. Pulling the thrum cap from his head, Magpie gently rubbed its woolly worms against his swollen cheek, trying to soothe away his tormented imaginings of the miseries about to poison the coming days.

The shocking sound of multiple footsteps on the ladders sent him scrabbling into the shadows behind a stack of firewood, abandoning his thrum cap to the squalid floor. Through an aperture in the dried kindling, he watched a large party of surprisingly ordinary-looking sailors invade his prison, their lanterns throwing light on the area around his mean bed of straw as they positioned themselves to stow and handle the incoming anchor cable. Plugging his nose against the stink of rotting fish that snuffed the air, he listened to their banter as they passed the strong, thick cable between them, lifting it from the harbour like an oily sea serpent from its sunken cave. Their vitality and murmurs of contentment puzzled him. For pity's sake, didn't they know they would soon be sailing in savage waters, fighting sweaty battles with pirates and slave traders, and God knows what else? Had their captain hoodwinked them into believing they were heading for their homeport — wherever that was? If that weren't the case, these Bloody Fluxes were a stout-hearted lot and a faint-hearted sailmaker such as he had no place among them.

Before every fibre of his being plunged into a pit of despair, Magpie was resuscitated by seeds of hope, leading him to wonder. If he were to join the ranks of these men when the cable had been successfully stowed, could he flee with them up the ladders to the upper deck? With all the abounding activity afoot, surely no one would notice him. And maybe, once he had reached the forecastle, he could clamber down a tow rope, or — if need be — fling himself over the bulwarks and pad-dle his way to the mooring buoy of another ship where — being as he wasn't much of a swimmer — he would appeal to passing boats to stop and pick him up. It was worth attempting, he figured, even if he were stripped of his shirt and dragged before Mr. Huxley, who would gladly oblige him with a hundred lashes of his whip.

Overhead, the ship's bell sounded, each resonant clang giving Magpie an awful belly-punch of anxiety. His clammy hands pressed against the firewood, his eye glued to the peek-hole, he agonized over when and how to slip in amongst the men. It was a cruel lifetime before he heard the heavy anchor thumping into place on the cathead and the subsequent outburst of triumphant cries signalling the completion of the task. The sailors dispersed. In twos, they ran up the groaning ladder, full of raucous chatter, all puffed up and convinced their efforts had earned them an hour of recreation and an extra ration of grog. And, at long last, when Magpie judged his chance had arrived, he ruined it with his sudden, exuberant movements, his elbow knocking a chunk of wood from the pile. As it hit the floor with a sickening thud, he cringed and cursed. Oh, why hadn't he tried to fall in with the men when dozens of them were still on the platform? Why had he waited so long? The castigating voice of Prosper Burgo pounded the inside of his skull like a migraine. "*Yer a galoot, ya little sailmaker, of the lowest ... fumble-fisted ... order.*"

Peering again through his peek-hole, Magpie's skin began to crawl. The last two sailors to gain the ladder had come to a grinding halt and swung around. One of them carried a lantern and was holding it aloft to search the darkness that had quickly closed in behind him. His mate took a cursory glance around the platform. "Ain't nothin' down here but goddamn vermin, and my guess is they're already chewin' through our stores o' food. C'mon!" he said, stumping up the rungs.

But the sailor with the lantern stayed rooted, and for a second time, he let his light sweep the area, in a wide arc to reveal the lonely nooks and crannies. There was a moment when the travelling beam of light passed over the sailor, exposing the lineaments of his face. Magpie felt as if a deliberately aimed arrowhead had struck him. Ducking swiftly, he grappled with the burbling howl about to erupt from his lungs. Blinking into the darkness, reeling with disbelief, he tried to make sense of it all.

"C'mon!" the ascending sailor barked again. "What's yer concern? Don't see no one about determined to slit yer throat! Ya've no enemies here beyond the bloated rats what'll one day, no doubt, turn up cooked in yer breakfast pies, their wee stiffened paws pokin' through the pastry." He laughed, but when his coaxing proved ineffectual, he continued on alone with bold steps to express his disgust.

In the breathless silence left behind, footsteps slunk across the timbers — coming ever closer to the place where Magpie was cowed with terror. Periodically, the lantern rose up, brightening the ship's bleak landscape like a full moon when it sails clear of cloud cover. Magpie squeezed up against his defensive wall of wood. The sailor now stood on the opposite side, so near to him he could smell his unwashed body. Magpie pleaded with the gods. "*Please! Please!* Make him go away!" Intoning over and over again, as if reciting a magic spell, one in which the intoner is forced to act fast in order to achieve a favourable outcome … or else!

Magpie heard the soft creaking of knees, as if the sailor had crouched down to retrieve something from the floor. Expecting at any time to be seized and cuffed about the head, Magpie was startled when a grunt of satisfaction crackled the air above the woodpile. What did it mean? Would the man go away now? Magpie hoped so, though nothing could entice him to take an investigative look through the peek-hole. Blessedly, the waiting was soon over. The lantern light fell away and receded, and footsteps were heard pacing up the ladder, slowly at first, and then with increasing alacrity. Sinking to the floor, Magpie drew in breath, his little chest finally permitted to heave with relief. Gathering his knees up in his arms, he stared into the tomb-like blackness and shuddered in remembrance.

The face he had seen — hideously illumined by the lantern light — was ravaged with old scars; the eyes, shrewd and vigilant. In a crowded tavern in Charleston, back in early June, those same eyes had sliced through Magpie with the vengeful stare of a king intent on sending a disloyal subject to his death. Their owner was a fiend, a familiar one, having trod heavily through so many of Magpie's nightmares. His abundance of straw-coloured hair might be shorn, and his clothes grotty and inferior — long gone were the gleaming epaulettes and blue uniform of an American naval captain — and yet, though he only possessed the sight of one eye, Magpie knew for certain. There could be no mistaking. It was Thomas Trevelyan … in the flesh.

CHAPTER 14

L eander adjusted his neckcloth, tugged upon the hem of his amber-coloured waistcoat and stared blankly at the door to Captain Austen's great cabin. He had little desire to dine with Fly's passengers, especially as he had already decided Mrs. Arabella Jiggins was a noisy, coquettish affair who likely had a bunch of bodily complaints and would require an inordinate amount of his attention on this voyage. On the other hand, although odd and somewhat unpleasant when they had met on deck yesterday, Mr. Shipton Ludlow had piqued his curiosity. Why was a man such as him travelling on the *Invincible* in wartime? Was he an armament dealer? Did he supply military stores? Was he a shipping magnate? Was he a spy? Or was he simply keeping his aunt under surveillance as she crossed the Atlantic to visit her daughter in the United States? Leander wondered, and meant to find out … somehow. Admittedly, had he been given a say in the evening's planned events, he would have far preferred to have stayed near Emily. It would not be long before the effects of the laudanum would wear off, and she would awaken to find they had already put to sea. He wanted to be there to see her face upon the moment of discovery.

Fly must have heard him thinking aloud outside his cabin and figured he would flee, for the door was suddenly flung open and he was pulled inside by his exuberant friend. Before Leander could even utter a single word, Fly had dispensed with the introductions and seated him in the privileged position next to Mrs. Jiggins. He had hardly settled in upon his chair — no surprise it was the Hoop-back Windsor with the cracked bottom — when he noticed Biscuit and Jim Beef standing quietly near the door, awaiting their orders for food and drink. Leander had been privy to Fly's scheme to have Biscuit keep Mr. Beef in tow, but to bring the unhinged man into the great cabin to serve exalted guests was a stretch — a potentially hazardous one. He wondered how long it would be before Mr. Beef began muttering his woeful proclamations, which would surely terrify Mrs. Jiggins and have Mr. Ludlow demanding they return to port at once. Then again, perhaps that was the idea.

"Dear Doctor, I was so worried you were not going to join our little party tonight, and I did so want to meet you." Mrs. Jiggins's voice was warmly effusive as if she were greeting a long-lost relation, the plump ostrich plume atop her gold-braided turban nodding in rhythm with her head as she spoke. Leander was amused by her dress. In jewels and a white, low-necked Empire gown, adorned with short puffy sleeves and turban-matching braiding, she appeared prepared for an elegant soirée — not a third-rate meal prepared in the galley of a frigate. "And as you can see," she added, her mouth and teeth stained red with wine, "we already have our drink in hand. Mr. Biscuit! Do come forward and fill Dr. Braden's cup to the brim."

As Biscuit raised the decanter of Madeira wine over Leander's pewter goblet, he quietly said, "Beg pardon, ma'am, it's just plain Biscuit. No need fer the *Mister.*"

"How very curious!" said Mrs. Jiggins with a giggle before raising her own goblet to her eager lips.

"Now that the good doctor is with us, you can bring in our feast, Biscuit," said Fly, taking his place at the head of the table.

Leander glanced over at Mr. Ludlow and was surprised to find the man's heavy-lidded eyes assessing him. What surprised him even more was the question he posed.

"And are you a *good* doctor, Dr. Braden?"

Grasping helplessly for a reply, Leander was relieved when Fly intercepted. "He most certainly is! We are fortunate to have Dr. Braden on our ship. During your stay with us, should you have a toothache or a stomach pain, or have the misfortune to fall from the shrouds, he shall take *good* care of you."

"That is excellent news indeed!" Mrs. Jiggins declared, giving Leander a grateful smile before leaning against him and taking him into her confidence. "For you know, Doctor, I have excruciating bunions, and at times I suffer dreadfully from nervous headaches."

Fly smiled reassuringly at her. "We will be sure to keep you safely below deck when the weather turns against us."

Mr. Ludlow rolled his shoulders in his cutaway coat. His challenging gaze moved away from Fly and once again fell upon Leander. "Where did you take your training, Dr. Braden?"

"In Edinburgh," said Leander, reaching for his wine.

"Did you earn a medical degree? Or are you a surgeon apothecary?"

"I earned a degree."

Mr. Ludlow's dark eyebrows shot up to meet his hairline. "Is your father a gentleman? Was he able to afford to send you there for all those years?"

"I was lucky enough to have a benefactor."

"How is it a physician finds his way into the navy? Was your benefactor unwilling to set you up in a consulting practice?"

Leander felt his blood starting to simmer. "The generosity of my kind benefactor ended with the acquisition of the degree."

"There was no patron waiting in the wings to assist you?"

"Sadly, there was not."

"So, then, you chose the navy?"

"Yes. At some point I did, Mr. Ludlow."

"Correct me if I am wrong, Dr. Braden, but wouldn't the Royal Navy have been the least attractive option for a man of your education?"

"Oh, dear nephew, do hush now!" scolded Mrs. Jiggins, twisting in her chair so she could watch the parading Biscuit and Jim Beef returning with platters of hot food. "See now! Our supper has come. Let us discuss more tantalizing subjects such as war and politics."

Unnerved by Mr. Ludlow's questions, Leander was happy to have the attention diverted. What issue had brought on such impertinence? What could the man possibly have against a naval doctor? He looked over at his antagonist only to find him looking back and very pleased with himself. Determined to waste no further time speculating on the nephew, Leander switched his thoughts to his supper of lamb, roast potatoes, peas, and buttered spinach, having taken no sustenance that day beyond a cold meat sandwich and coffee.

When everyone's plate had been heaped with food, their goblets replenished, and Biscuit and Mr. Beef dismissed, Mrs. Jiggins reached over to pat Fly's forearm, the diamond bracelet on her pudgy wrist sparkling in the candlelight. "Captain Austen, tell me, this war we are embroiled in ... what exactly is our argument with the Americans?"

Leander could see the hesitation on Fly's face. Earlier, when Fly insisted that Leander join their little party — reminding him he was owed a great favour — he had expressed his hopes that the evening would pass quickly. He had planned ahead to make some polite small talk with his guests; stick to harmless subjects such as health, hearth, and family; enjoy a few glasses of wine and a decent meal; and excuse himself, all within the space of an hour. An endless evening that required the partaking of too much wine and resulted in a fierce headache the next morning was not to be borne. What Leander did not know was that, prior to his arrival, Fly had already made his polite inquiries and learned very little, Mrs. Jiggins having continually steered the conversation around in her quest for information on the ship's men with whom she would be sailing.

Setting aside his knife and fork, Fly sighed. "I cannot give you an easy answer, Mrs. Jiggins, for there are many reasons why we are at war with the United States, one of them being the fact that many Americans have a thirst for more farmland, and hope to secure it by invading the territories of Upper and Lower Canada. There also exists an issue surrounding our strong influence over American Indians which has resulted in much anger. But, I suppose, if you were to ask an American, they would tell you outright that they had declared war upon us in June of last year in the name of free trade and sailors' rights." He looked at Mrs. Jiggins with a hopeful expression that his brief answer had satisfied her and they could now get down to the business of eating. Unfortunately, the wheels in her turban-clad head were rolling forward.

"Sailors' rights?" she said, her affable features rigid with interest. "Do tell us more, Captain Austen."

"The Americans have long been unhappy with our practice of halting their ships to search their crews for deserters."

Mr. Ludlow interjected with an exclamation of impatience. "The problem has been and continues to be the fact that our Royal Navy has been accused of stealing men who are not deserters ... that they have simply helped themselves to hardy, healthy-looking Americans to make up for their own shortage of able-bodied men."

Fly said nothing, for it was the truth.

"Dear Aunt," Mr. Ludlow continued, "are you aware that our navy does the same with our own Englishmen, their press gangs stealing whomever it pleases just to make up their quotas? I hear men are often taken as they leave public houses late at night — too drunk to put up a fight — and others from their homes, in front of their families, sometimes on the very day they return after having been at sea for months." He ended his dissertation shooting a smug glance at Leander as if believing he had made an impression with his comprehensive knowledge of things political and naval.

Mrs. Jiggins looked horrified. "Oh, well, that does not seem fair, Captain Austen. No wonder the Americans are not pleased with us."

Leander was astounded by Mr. Ludlow's tone. It seemed the man had no appreciation for propriety. Could he not have waited a day or two before hitting Captain Austen with his trenchant opinions?

"I am curious, Mr. Ludlow," said Fly, swirling the wine in his goblet, "how is it you are apprised of these matters? Are there any seamen in your family? Or do you speak from personal experience?"

"Certainly not!" he answered with hot indignation.

Fly's dark eyes dulled. "Whether one agrees with it or not, impressment is a requirement of the service."

"Perhaps, but it seems to me it is nothing more than a legalized form of slavery." Mr. Ludlow swung toward Leander. "Is that what happened to you, Doctor? Were you a victim of impressment?"

It was Fly who answered, in a voice laced with fervour. "Aye, Mr. Ludlow! He was! One moonless night, as he was leaving the Brigantine Inn on Broad Street, stumbling about as he was full of drink, I seized upon him, knocked him on the head with a brickbat and smuggled him aboard the *Invincible* in a sack of sailcloth."

The room went quiet. Leander cleared his throat while Mr. Ludlow and his aunt exchanged subtle glances. The noise of Fly's chair pushing back from the table seemed as jarring as musket-fire. "If you will excuse me, there is a matter I must see to straightaway," he said, struggling to temper his voice. "Do not rush through your meal and do not leave before Biscuit brings you some coffee and a sweet. Dr. Braden will stay to keep you company." He shot an unspoken apology at Leander and strode from the cabin.

Knowing his friend well, Leander suspected he was about to blow and needed time to cool off. He was sympathetic, but not eager to be left alone to entertain. If only Biscuit and Mr. Beef were still in the room. Had they been, in the absence of Captain Austen, perhaps Mr. Beef might spout off his decrees of doom and drive away the cabin's occupants to the far corners of the ship. But as there was little hope of them returning any time soon — their meal only just begun — Leander had to make the best of the situation. Thinking he might succeed in fending off further impertinence — as well as have a chance to taste his supper — he made a few harmless inquiries of his own.

"Tell me, how was your first night with us? I trust you were comfortable."

While Mr. Ludlow, who seemed to have tucked away his belligerence for the time being, replied that his quarters were adequate and that he had slept well enough, Mrs. Jiggins had a tale of woe to share, her bejewelled hands fluttering about the folds of her neck during its recounting.

"I am not used to such confinement, Dr. Braden, and I have never before slept in a room without a window. I felt quite pent-up throughout the night. With that and the excessive heat, I was awakened again and again. And here I had expected the nights to be cool, especially at this time of year. But I suppose, with all those sailors — hundreds of them — sleeping cheek by jowl in their hammocks right outside my cabin door ..." her voice trailed off, down some sentimental laneway, before resuming with renewed vehemence. "And those bells and whistles! Why do you not silence them during the nights, Dr. Braden? How do you ever manage a wink of sleep? Dear Lord! And the awful odours and vapours! I daren't guess what causes such effluvium! Had I not brought my smelling salts with me, I am positive I would have fainted dead away."

Leander smiled. "I assure you, after a while you will grow accustomed to the whistles and the tolling of the bells and not hear them at all. Regrettably, I cannot say the same for the ship's odours nor for your confined quarters. On the latter score, however, perhaps it will help when I tell you that you are among the fortunate for few of the men on the *Invincible* can boast of a cabin of their own."

"I understand your aunt is aboard, Dr. Braden. Does she have her own cabin?"

"She does, Mrs. Jiggins."

"I do look forward to meeting her for I have such hopes that we shall become steadfast friends."

Leander flinched, knowing his aunt would have little interest in making *her* acquaintance. He could picture Eliza, reaching for her double-lensed prospect glass in order to examine Mrs. Jiggins's rouged cheeks and the low neckline of her gown.

"Does she paint, Doctor?"

"I don't believe so."

"Then I shall teach her! We shall set up our canvases and pots of paint on the quarterdeck, near the ship's wheel. It may inspire some of the seamen to gather around us and ask if they, too, can learn."

Leander bit his lip to keep from scoffing at the absurdity of her enthusiastic scheme, but when he caught sight of Mr. Ludlow's furrowing brow as he shuffled his peas around on his plate, he feared a cross-examination was in the works.

"What about the woman in your hospital, Doctor? The one you first thought was a Mr. George?"

"What about her?" Leander said, steeling his voice.

"Will she be forced to reside on the lower deck with Miss Braden and my aunt, or is there a cabin set aside especially for her here on the upper deck?"

Leander would like to have been able to deny the existence of such a woman, but lamentably Mr. Ludlow knew otherwise. His main challenge now would be to keep Emily away from this odious man until they reached the American coast. That being another four weeks or so, perhaps Mr. Ludlow would have the mischance of coming by an accident or drowning in the ocean.

"At present, no arrangements have been made for her," Leander said evenly with no hint of his pernicious musings.

"Goodness, Doctor! Don't leave me gasping in suspense. Who is she? What is her story?"

There was something in the way Mrs. Jiggins posed her question — a peculiarity in that, for the first time, she did not stick her fluttery eyes into his when she asked it — that left Leander wondering if she already knew the answer. He turned toward Mr. Ludlow to study him — their eyes locking for a moment — and wondered the same thing.

The precipitous knock on the door could not have come at a better time. Without servants about to answer it, Leander was only too happy to assume the honours. The messenger was a loblolly boy with a mouth full of crooked teeth, come to inform him that one of the cook's mates had received a dreadful scalding in the galley, and required his administration as his assistant, Mr. Duffy, had no idea how to proceed with treatment. There were times when Leander resented these intrusions upon his personal hours. They always seemed to give rise to unfinished conversations, interruptions of sleep, and half-eaten — or in this case — untasted meals. This, however, was *not* one of them.

Realizing he was leaving, Mrs. Jiggins raised a strident protest. "Dr. Braden! First Captain Austen and now you? Surely someone else can see to the scalded sailor. Tell him you are having supper and amusing guests and will see to him later on."

"I do apologize, Mrs. Jiggins, but you may as well know right now that interruptions of all kinds are a frequent occurrence around here. You must not be offended by them." Leander bowed in her direction, intentionally avoiding Mr. Ludlow's displeased stare — he who was still awaiting a reply to his probing question — and hurried out the door.

7:30 P.M.
(SECOND DOG WATCH, THREE BELLS)
MIDDY'S BERTH

"Sit down and shut up, you muttonheads, or I shall not give you a share of the captain's pudding."

Gus Walby squeezed back against the canvas wall of the middy's berth as Cadby Brambles came bounding in, bellowing orders and clutching a tray with a wobbling pudding on it that was shaped like a peaked mountain. It was commonplace for Captain Austen to share the remains of his pudding with the midshipmen, but this pudding did not appear to have been touched at all. Gus wondered if it had something to do with its greyish-brown colour — Captain Austen having found it unappetizing and deciding against serving it to his supper guests, whom Gus had not yet seen, but who were rumoured to be a haughty pair.

The berth was a hive of lively activity thanks to the six boisterous midshipmen who were tripping over each other in their noisy games and pranks. Mr. Brambles, being taller than all the others and, by the looks of it, having a good five years on them all, appeared to be the self-proclaimed master of the midshipmen and commander of their berth. Thinking it might ease Gus's pain in losing Magpie, Captain Austen had suggested he might spend some time with the midshipmen, especially since, not so very long ago, he himself had been one. But already, Gus had decided he didn't like these other lads. They were an undisciplined, obnoxious lot who could not sit still long enough to soak up orders and instructions — delinquents who would inevitably wind up on Captain Austen's blacklist. He had sat quietly and observed them pulling on each other's noses and punching each other in the back, heard them cursing and hurling obscenities, and — feeling nothing beyond exasperation — had judged it was time for him to leave when Mr. Brambles had arrived, blocking the entranceway with his fleshy girth. Spying Gus, he glowered down at him.

"What are *you* doing here? You don't belong among us," he said, setting the tray upon their narrow table and shoving aside two scrawny midshipmen to plunk down his heavy bottom upon the rickety bench opposite Gus. "Captain Austen said the pudding was for us; therefore, you shall not get a share of it."

"I did not come here to eat your pudding," Gus said weakly, fiddling with the balloon sleeves of his new shirt that the purser, Mr. Philpotts, had given him on the proviso that the cost would come out of his wages.

"Then why did you come here at all? Don't you have some top-secret memorandums to compose?"

The other lads fidgeted on their benches, still throwing the occasional punch despite Mr. Brambles's warnings. Not one of them seemed the least bit bothered by — or curious about — the foreigner sitting in their circle.

"I thought I might come to meet you all as some of you are near in age to me."

Mr. Brambles gave Gus a gruff going-over. "Well, it's obvious that I am *much* older than you. I remember seeing you earlier today. You were wearing a middy's uniform then, and yet you're no midshipman. You're a clerk to the captain."

"At one time I was a midshipman."

"Why aren't you one now? Did the captain find you unworthy of becoming a full officer?"

Gus bristled, but was not about to defend himself to this overgrown buffoon. Nodding toward his crutch, he calmly said, "I had an accident back in June."

"Well, don't get above your station just because you have around-the-watch access to Captain Austen, writing his letters and all."

"Oh, I wouldn't think of —"

But Mr. Brambles did not await his answer. Already, he had turned away to divide up the pudding, shouting at each midshipman to "shut your face and mind your manners" before handing them their dish of dessert.

Thinking no one would even notice his departure if he slipped away, Gus could not believe it when Mr. Brambles, having given himself the largest portion of the pudding, began speaking to him as if they had been chums at school.

"Have you heard? Dr. Braden has a woman locked away in the dispensary."

Gus had indeed heard, having learned the news directly from old Dr. Braden that morning, but only after they had breakfasted with Miss Braden in the forepeak, the old doctor believing the intelligence a bit beyond his sister's sensibilities. However, Gus had no intention of telling Mr. Brambles this.

"Who is she?" he asked, playing along, at ease now that Mr. Brambles's mood had grown more congenial.

"No one knows. Seems she disguised herself as a man and jumped right into our boat carrying the new recruits on Saturday night. It is astounding that I did not see her."

"Why is that?"

"I have sharp eyes. I rarely miss seeing anything of importance, Mister — Mister — what is your name?"

"Walby," Gus put in quickly. "Were you part of the press gang?"

"I was!" Mr. Brambles sat up straighter on his section of the bench. "It was me who brought in several of the recruits."

"Bravo! Well done!" said Gus, unable to embrace the ebullience of his words.

Mr. Brambles leaned across the table as if to impart a deep, dark secret, and for the first time, Gus noticed his groggy breath. "This morning, while taking a message to Dr. Braden in his hospital, I caught a glimpse of her. She saw me, too, and gave me a little smile. I think she found me very handsome." He grinned in remembrance.

"I do hope she is not too ugly."

"Oh, she is not at all ugly, Mr. Walby!" Mr. Brambles let out a shrill whistle of approval. "I can tell you she's a sight better than that heifer, Mrs. Jiggins, and that shrivelled prune, Miss Eliza Braden, with whom, I believe, you are acquainted."

"How old do you think she is?"

"Eighteen, nineteen? Hard to say for certain. At present she is ill and contagious, but when she has recovered, I mean to make her acquaintance. She will be pleased to know that my father is a baronet who holds extensive properties. His baronetcy was granted in 1611 by King James, you know." He shovelled a generous spoonful of pudding into his mouth and sucked it down. "Compared to all of the young men on this ship — lieutenants included — I shall shine very brightly. You, of course, do not stand a chance with her. She would never be interested in a stripling who has to carry a crutch."

Mr. Brambles could not have caused Gus more pain if he had trampled on his poor leg. "Bully for you, Mr. Brambles!" he hissed, though to himself only, adding aloud in an effort to shake it off: "You said you had formed part of the press gang … did you go into Portsmouth with a boy named Magpie?"

"Magpie? Who the hell is Magpie?"

"He is a sailmaker of maybe ten years. He wears an eye patch and he —"

"Oh, that little clod!" Mr. Brambles growled, licking his lips. "He was with me all right, and he ran off at the first sight of drunken sailors coming out of the tavern. He left me to round them up on my own."

Gus felt such a pang of silent grief he could hardly utter his words. "What — what do you suppose became of him?"

Mr. Brambles glanced around the middy's table to make certain no one else was listening in, and then he snickered. "He got caught! Ha, ha! The little clod was supposed to be rounding up men for Captain Austen; instead, he got pressed by a couple of naval miscreants!"

10:00 P.M.
(FIRST WATCH, FOUR BELLS)

Leander finished up with his medical notes and rubbed his shoulders as he rose from his desk to unhook the oil-lantern from the deckhead. He was bone-weary and dreaming of his bed, but a final observation of his patients was necessary before retiring for the night. In addition to the scalded sailor who had providentially hastened his departure from Mrs. Jiggins and Mr. Ludlow — and left him bereft of his lamb and roast potatoes — he'd had to admit three more into his hospital: one who had tumbled down the companion way and struck his forehead on a post, a direct result, though denied, of swigging an abundance of ale; another afflicted with gut pains; and a third one who had come to him complaining of seasickness. Of them all, the latter caused Leander the most consternation, for on this night the sea was running calm. How the poor man would suffer when she was blowing hard. With his hands full, Leander had been forced to ask Mr. Duffy to see to Emily and administer her tonics. Mr. Duffy had proven keen to the task, quitting post-haste and without entreaty a favourable card game with his mates. But fearing he could not trust his assistant and therefore tormented by thoughts of overdoses and erroneous medications, Leander was determined to look in on her.

Assured that his four new patients were all sleeping soundly in their swaying cots like babies in their cradles, he crept toward the dispensary and opened the door as quietly as he could. Raising the lantern to his eyes, he found Emily's cot empty and her standing to one side of the open gunport. Her face was fixed upon the sea, silvered under the moon, and the lights of England shimmering in the distant darkness. Her shawl had slipped from one shoulder, and the evening winds were playfully lifting and scattering tendrils of her hair. Despite his best efforts at stealth, she turned around, looking wild and beyond reach like something from a dream world. Her dark eyes were huge and unseeing in her pale face, as if she had been listening to the fitful sighs of the English Channel or communicating with elfin voices only she could hear, and was now trying to assimilate the footsteps that had dragged her reluctantly away from them. Without saying a word, she slowly returned to her cot, seemingly determined to show him that she could manage well without assistance, and when she was settled in and sitting up, the shawl wrapped around her once more, she looked over at him. In the dim half-shadows, Leander could see the warmth that had rushed to her cheeks, the gleam of a smile and the light of discovery in her eyes. Feeling a fierce pull in his chest, he wanted to laugh, to utter the words gathering eagerly on his tongue, but there was no need for conversation. In silent communion they held one another's gaze until she reluctantly lowered hers and snuggled down beneath her blanket, ending the night's bewitching spell.

CHAPTER 15

TUESDAY, SEPTEMBER 21
11:45 A.M.
ABOARD HMS *EXPEDITION*

"Git up, ya gypsy beggar! Time fer ya to leave yer hole down here and git workin'. Now it ain't normally my responsibility to show new recruits the ropes, but I bin asked to, so git a move on 'cause I got better things to do."

Magpie had watched Mr. Huxley descending the ladder, knowing even before the wavering candle-lantern had confirmed it that the hunched silhouette in round hat and wide pantaloons did indeed belong to him. He scrambled to his feet, but was reluctant now to leave behind his straw bed and the protective wall of the woodpile. The idea of messing with and working alongside the Bloody Fluxes made him shudder. Besides, no longer did he mind the rats, having found some solace in their late-night foraging so long as they left him alone, their presence having prevented his imagination from straying toward notions of corrupted bodies buried in the shingle below his platform, just like it was — or so the rumour ran — on Prosper's privateer. Though he longed to take in clean air and catch a glimpse of the sea, Magpie now knew that more terrifying things prowled outside the limits of the *Bloody Flux*'s black hold. For somewhere up there, Thomas Trevelyan was walking the decks.

"C'mon, then, collect yer blanket and stuff."

"I don't got no stuff, sir."

Mr. Huxley's cucumber fingers latched themselves to his thick middle, and he let out a surly harrumph as if Magpie had been bold in his reply and told him off. "So where's that woolly hat ya was wearin' when ya first came on board?"

Magpie could only shrug; he didn't know. Yesterday, when the Bloody Fluxes had come down to stow away the anchor cable, and the sight of Trevelyan had nearly given him heart failure, he had misplaced it. All he could surmise was that at some point he had dropped it and one of the sailors had kicked it off the platform and into the yawning hollow of the hold. He was heartsick about its loss. Wearing the woolly thrum had kept the memory of Morgan Evans alive and near to him; it was all he had that once belonged to his poor, dead friend. Believing its final resting place to be the foul, sluggish waters of the bilge was depressing, but it was far too dark and scary down there to go looking for it.

Clutching his blanket, Magpie nervously followed Mr. Huxley up the ladder and along the ship's decks. He felt like one of those Welsh coal miners Morgan Evans used to tell him about, having just spent long hours toiling in the black earth and now returning to the unfamiliar world of daylight and humans. Worried that his green eye patch and head of curls might be glaringly recognizable, he kept his head down, not daring to look up lest he found himself meeting the eyes of someone he did not care to see. If only the ship's surgeon had discovered his hair crawling with lice and had to shave it cleanly off, thereby affording him some manner of disguise. But what a stroke of luck it was to find most of the men gathered around their mess tables, awaiting their midday meal. Hungry and full of lively chatter, none of them seemed particularly interested in the timorous mouse running past them behind the plodding figure of Mr. Huxley.

As soon as Magpie had been outfitted with two hammocks, a pillow, and an old mattress that had an evil, pervading stink — there being a strong likelihood it was stuffed with chopped rags saturated with contamination and infection — and shown his fourteen inches of sleeping space on the lower deck, Mr. Huxley handed him a bucket of soapy water, a scrub brush, and some tattered washcloths. He then marched him forthwith to the captain's cabin beneath the poop deck. Crossing its threshold, Magpie breathlessly eyed its contents. It was a richly decorated space with fine oak furnishings and red velvet chairs, and there were interesting paintings in fancy frames set upon easels. Leather-bound books lined a shelf, and a beautiful, burnished desk of reddish-brown wood was neatly laid out with quills in blue ceramic inkpots. Light streaming through the galleried windows reflected tiny squares of sunshine upon the gleaming oval of the captain's table and frolicked upon the ornate branches of his silver candelabrum. There was no sign of clutter, no nautical charts, papers, clothing, or the remains of meals strewn about the floor or furniture, no decapitated heads of enemies nailed to the walls or implements of torture dropped upon the velvet cushions of the window seat. This was not what Magpie had expected to find in the great cabin of the *Bloody Flux*.

"The cap'n's gone down for his dinner with his officers in the wardroom, but he's never long at eatin' so ya don't have much time," said Mr. Huxley as he strutted across the floor, a length of rope known as a boatswain's starter firmly locked in his right hand. Thinking he was in for a flogging, Magpie was ever so thankful when Huxley stopped before a curtain hanging on the ship's side and threw it open, exposing a small gallery that housed the captain's lavatory. Approaching, Magpie could see the formidable round hole that topped the crude wooden seat and opened onto the sea.

"Ya gotta scrub down all o' the surfaces and finish up with the floor timbers. And pay particular attention to the area around that there hole. Can't be no turds anywhere. The cap'n won't stand fer it. He'll flog ya if he sees any brown gobbets or streaks, and I'll be sure to tell him who it was what's responsible." He gave his starter a menacing shake. "And when yer done here, ya can scrub down the officers' lavatory on the upper deck. The stench in that one'll knot the hairs on the tip o' yer nose. But I suppose yer a lucky one!"

"Why's that, sir?" asked Magpie, thinking he was anything but lucky.

"'Cause ya don't have to handle the jacks' necessary buckets and dump 'em over the side. Not today, that is!"

With a sigh of resignation, Magpie set to work the minute Mr. Huxley and his throaty howls of laughter were gone, scrubbing and polishing with his brush and rags. The confinement of the gallery made him anxious, but it was neither the tight space nor the off-putting smell. Having once been a London climbing boy, he was used to being holed up in tighter, smellier places than this. Nay, it was the fear that the captain would return at any moment and explode in anger when he found someone crouched over his privy with a scrub brush. Oh, but then maybe — maybe if he proved his worth here, if he made certain the captain found no turds in or around the *hole*, he could ask to be transferred to the sailroom. Better still, maybe the captain would take pity on him and agree to listen to his story, that Magpie really was a seaman, that Francis Austen was his true captain, and that he had been wrongfully pressed into service on the *Bloody Flux*.

After ten minutes or so, Magpie stood up to stretch and rub his knees, and peek out the lavatory's little mullioned window. Not yet used to the brightness of day, his eye watered as he squinted through the squares of glass. It seemed the *Bloody Flux* was already a fair piece from the English shore, which was now nothing more than a ghostly horizon of faded blue against the bleached expanse of sea. And lo and behold! There was a ship sailing near to them! Rising up on his toes for a better look, he was surprised to see not one, but two ships, one much larger than the other. Were they all travelling together in the same direction — toward the Barbary Coast and River Styx — or was it just a coincidence? Magpie had been told that Captain Austen had planned to sail alongside the little mail packet, the *Lady Jane*, as well as HMS *Expedition* because it was safer in numbers. Maybe all of England's ships were now sailing together so that American and French men-of-war would think twice before attacking them. But then, he thought, what good had it done Captain Prickett and the Amethysts to have had the very best, the *Prosperous and Remarkable*, sailing alongside when the American fleet had pounced upon them?

Magpie tried to bolster his spirits with the vistas of distant shores, and by cheering on the two ships, hoping one of them would soon sail past the *Bloody Flux* so the name on her stern would be visible. He never expected to hear voices beyond the closed curtain quite so soon. Had the captain returned from his dinner? If so, he was not alone. Praying neither of the men were in need of easing themselves upon the lavatory hole, Magpie could do nothing but eavesdrop upon their conversation.

"Well done, Mr. Bumpus. I must admit I am most impressed, and I appreciate you having completed everything so quickly, especially when your help was needed yesterday to raise the anchor cable and prepare for sailing." In spite of his friendly words, the voice — which Magpie assumed belonged to the captain — was cheerless and aloof.

"Thank you, sir. I am only too happy to be of service."

"I am aware that you are an American, but what I do not know — and am most curious to discover — is how high on the naval ladder you were able to climb."

"I — well, it just so happens that I *was* a clerk, sir," said Mr. Bumpus after a slight hesitation.

"Ah! That explains your excellent literary skills, and obvious familiarity with naval reporting. Our Mr. Croker will have to watch himself. He has a gifted competitor for his post."

"Not at all, sir."

Confident the two men were conversing on the far side of the cabin, Magpie pushed aside a stitch of curtain to have a look. In the brilliance of the stern windows, they were standing in front of the desk over which was now spread some sort of document. The one in the uniform — surely, the captain — was short and slight, and there was a thinning patch of wiry, grey hair on the back of his head that reminded Magpie of a bird's nest. In comparison, the man with whom he spoke was a beanpole of a giant with no hair at all, perhaps on account of lice being discovered when he first came aboard.

"Now I have countless other assignments that I would like to discuss with you." The captain twisted his neck to peer up at the thin giant. "Is this a good time?"

"If you like, sir," Mr. Bumpus replied, his profile now clearly visible to the interloper in the lavatory.

"Have you taken your dinner yet?"

"No, sir, not yet."

The captain moved toward his door, the giant obediently following like a horse being led by his dwarfish master. "While you have your meal, I shall take care of some business with Mr. Croker. Be sure to meet me back here in half an hour. And make certain you are prompt, Mr. Bumpus."

Together they departed from the cabin, leaving the door ajar and Magpie in a state of agitation. Dropping the curtain back into place, he grabbed handfuls of his hair, baffled by what he had seen and heard. Mr. Bumpus? Whoever was Mr. Bumpus? What ruse was this? Could it be that the captain of the *Bloody Flux* was completely unaware he was carrying a condemned English traitor upon his ship?

2:00 P.M.
(AFTERNOON WATCH, FOUR BELLS)
ABOARD HMS *INVINCIBLE*

"There you are, Miss Braden! I am certain I have worn myself out searching for you."

Gus shaded his eyes against the commanding pear shape of Arabella Jiggins, who was wavering before him on the forecastle. Ordinarily, he took no interest in women's fashion, but it was hard to feign disinterest in hers. She was swathed in a pink floral shawl and floating yards of white muslin with an expansive bertha collar edged with rather ominous-looking points of lace. Sitting high on her head of short, salty-brown hair was a pink hat that resembled a bowl of fruit with its outpouring of artificial grapes, cherries, strawberries, and plums. Over it all she carried a frilly, white parasol, most likely to guard her complexion against the strong sunshine and contain the sparkles of her diamond bracelets. Wandering about the decks, amongst livestock and the plain, muted colours of the seamen, she could not escape notice. And sure enough — as Gus's swift inspection confirmed — every Invincible toiling within a square mile had their eyes trained upon her, openly appreciating her feminine finery. It would not surprise him in the least if, across the water, she had riveted the Lady Janes and Expeditions, as well, those lucky enough to possess spyglasses and able to eyeball her through their magnified lenses.

Sewing primly on an overturned crate beside Gus was Miss Braden, draped in a brown homespun dress, her mob cap tied in a neat bow under her chin. Assessing the two women, Gus could not resist comparisons. Miss Braden was the parson delivering a dry sermon in a dismal country church while Mrs. Jiggins was the colourfully clad Mrs. Jordan, performing *Hippolyta* on the stage of the Drury Theatre on a Saturday night. His bleak impression of Miss Braden notwithstanding, Gus could only feel gratitude for her on this day. Not once since they had departed from the cottage on Mile End Terrace had she revisited her antagonistic notions of the Royal Navy or railed about him throwing away his life in returning to the service. Gus wondered if her remarkable behaviour had something to do with her taking pity on him now that she knew he had lost his good friend, Magpie. Maybe. But then old Dr. Braden had only informed her of the sad news that morning. What was even more intriguing was the fact that she was already hard at work on her first sewing assignment — a cerulean-blue serge coat for "Captain Austen's young clerk." Having finished sewing on the sleeves, she had recently summoned him from his office for a fitting. Gus smiled to himself, knowing that she had chosen to do her sewing here in the shadow of the bowsprit owing to her belief that the forecastle deck would be an unlikely location for a woman such as Mrs. Jiggins — a woman of whom, up to this point, she had only heard stories — to take exercise and fresh air when it was heaving with seamen. She had claimed that Mrs. Jiggins would be more disposed toward the quarterdeck where she could keep company with the officers and offer up navigational advice to the sailing master.

"Apparently not," Miss Braden muttered to Gus from one corner of her mouth.

"I am Mrs. Arabella Jiggins. How d'ye do?"

Miss Braden made no attempt at cordiality. Her voice was flat and dry as if she were addressing a tax collector. "Are you already in need of some mending? Is that why you have tired yourself out searching for me?"

"Heavens, no!" gushed Mrs. Jiggins, beaming when Gus jumped up to offer her his crate, but assuring him with a flutter of her gloved hand that she was content to stand. "I am in search of friendship. On a ship of men, one does crave the conversation of another woman. So imagine my happiness when I learned that you were on board."

"I regret to inform you, Mrs. Jiggins, that I am not on a holiday," said Miss Braden, taking up her needle. "I will not have time for leisurely chats when I shall be kept quite busy with my mending and sewing."

"Come now, my dear Miss Braden! We have weeks of sailing ahead of us, and you must plan for some enjoyment. I was ever so disappointed when you and your brother — whom, regrettably, my nephew, Mr. Ludlow, and I have not yet met — were not invited to sup in Captain Austen's cabin last evening. Such a shame! We were fed so bountifully and treated to a delectable apple-cinnamon cake for dessert!"

"Has your nephew managed to seek out friendship for himself?"

"Not as of yet, but I am assured he will. He hopes to find much in common with your own nephew, Dr. Leander Braden."

It was perhaps best that Miss Braden's sniff was inaudible to Mrs. Jiggins. "Until that friendship is steadfastly formed, how does Mr. Ludlow plan to spend his days?"

"Oh, he shall keep himself advantageously occupied writing his letters of business and reading books that benefit his superior mind, and maybe — at my suggestion — even try his hand at a little sketching now that he is aware of Captain Austen's competency in this field. But let us not concern ourselves with my nephew, Miss Braden," she said, clapping her hands together in a girlish display of excitement. "Let us make plans of our own. Now then, if on the morrow the afternoon is as pleasant as today, I shall set up my paint-box and canvases, and you shall join me."

Miss Braden looked horrified. "Doing what? Painting? Mrs. Jiggins, I have never, ever held a paintbrush in my hands."

"Then I shall be overjoyed to show you how it is done."

"And what — what do you propose we paint?"

"Miss Braden! Look around you! There is a wealth of enchanting subjects here at our disposal!" She cast admiring glances around the ship, and laughed in delight when she spied the topmen observing her from their yards. "But if you prefer, we could begin with castle ruins and dark forests. Now, today you may return to your sewing as I have agreed to drink green tea shortly with Mr. Ludlow, but let us arrange to meet here tomorrow at the same time. I shall have all the necessary paraphernalia set up and will arrange with Mr. Biscuit to serve us some light refreshments. Cheesecakes and syllabubs would not go amiss. Oh! What fun we shall have! Until then!" She bounded off, humming away happily, smiling at the men who fell across her rambling path.

Miss Braden's light-grey eyes rolled under the mighty brim of her mob cap. "Cheesecakes and syllabubs! Lord above! Next she will be demanding pies and oysters be delivered from Thomas Rules's bar in Maiden Lane! Well, I will not be painting canvases with her tomorrow."

"With all respect, Miss Braden, then why didn't you tell her so?"

"Mr. Walby! You do not say *no* to a woman such as her."

"Why ever not?"

"She is not acquainted with the word." Miss Braden reached down beside her, picked up her canister of tea — which seemed to travel with her everywhere — and hugged it protectively against her flat bosom. "If that woman thinks I shall be agreeable to sharing *my* tea with her, she has another think coming."

Gus nodded his approval and settled back upon his crate to watch Miss Braden make her skillful stitches on his new coat, but it was soon Emily who garnered his thoughts, and ultimately, his sympathies. For all her extravagant clothes and jewels, Mrs. Jiggins seemed a needy sort of person who required an audience for her tireless tongue — Biscuit claimed the woman could talk the shillings out of King George's silk breeches — and if Miss Braden were to spurn her society, the moment Mrs. Jiggins discovered there was a princess on board … there would be no leaving *her* alone.

4:00 P.M.
(AFTERNOON WATCH, EIGHT BELLS)

Fly Austen snapped his spyglass shut and stepped away from the quarterdeck rail, satisfied that all seemed as it should be on the decks of his sailing companions, the *Expedition* and the *Lady Jane*. They were a picture of perfection, an artist's dream, travelling within close range to one another on sun-dappled waters under a cloudless sky and a full complement of billowing sails. Navigationally speaking, his only complaint was the wind, which did not meet his approval for strength, but given the time of year it would inevitably blow harder in the days to come when they were in the open waters of the North Atlantic Ocean and no longer under the protection of England and France.

Before heading to his cabin, Fly paused to admire Prosper Burgo. He was standing at the helm, looking uncharacteristically pensive; his roughened hands caressing the spokes of the ship's mahogany wheel, eyes squinting into the distances. Sunshine had bronzed his fox-like features. The sea breezes ruffled his scant curls, and rippled his loosely fitted shirt like the pennant on the masthead. If Prosper had been wearing a hat, something with a leather visor or a pre-eminent ball of wool, Fly would swear the mariner of his boyhood daydreams had sprung to life in his image.

"Are you settling in well, Mr. Burgo?"

Prosper lifted a fist to his forehead in salute — a rarity for him, not being one to heed Royal Navy ceremony — but his eyes never left the sea. "So long's I'm standin' right here I feel at home and in command o' this ship — meanin' no disrespect to you, of course, Cap'n. And every once in a while, one o' me old ruffians happens by. Gives me a chance to berate him and tell him he's a galoot, just like old times. Helps me forget what I lost back there in Portsmouth."

Fly pondered his helmsman's words. Wouldn't he love to have something to help him forget what he had lost. Morgan Evans and Magpie were constantly sitting in the front seat of his mind. When his spirits were running high, Morgan was alive, his face wreathed in mischievous smiles or beautifully serene as he sang a haunting Welsh ballad. And always, Magpie was beside him, playing his flute in accompaniment.

But when his spirits flagged, he remembered Morgan laying in his coffin, still and grey, and Magpie weeping over him, holding his woolly thrum cap to his heart. Fly would forever know where to find Morgan, but he wondered if he would ever learn what had become of the little sailmaker.

He forced a smile. "I am happy to hear it, Mr. Burgo, as long as you do not completely forget where you are and *who* you are, and wind up leading a mutiny."

"Not a chance o' that, Cap'n! Nay! Me mind's on other things. Like goin' after the prize. Don't really care who she is, but I've a hankerin' fer a juicy Yankee frigate like the *United States* what brought down our *Macedonian* last year or — or that *Constitution* what brought down our *Java* at Christmas. I'd even settle for squashin' one o' them pesky Yankee sloops-o'-war, the *Wasp* or the *Hornet*."

"I am pleased to see that you have not forgotten the names of our humbling naval defeats, Mr. Burgo."

"I won't never forget. With me old *Remarkable*, I brung in nineteen prizes and I'm aimin' fer glory on this cruise, Cap'n." Prosper gritted his teeth. "Just watch me go."

"I admire your confidence," said Fly, unable to share in it. "And, aye, a prize would be most appreciated as long as we do not have to face the power of an American fleet to secure one. I am not certain I could bear those odds again."

Prosper waggled his right hand in the general direction of the *Lady Jane* and *Expedition*, the former sailing two points off the starboard bow and the latter sailing two points astern. "I kin tell ya I don't have no confidence in them two."

"Why is that?"

"The guns on that little twig ... that mail packet couldn't blow a polliwog out o' water and that *Expedition*, for all o' her seventy-four guns, mark me words, she'll be a lumberin' elephant in battle, just like the *Amethyst* were. What's more, I reckon if we ..."

Fly, who had been gazing thoughtfully at their sailing friends while Prosper grumbled away, turned back to learn the reason for the sudden trailing off of his sentence. Following the track of Prosper's widening eyes, he realized that Mrs. Jiggins had returned to the deck, evidently done with tea and Mr. Ludlow. She was still wearing her cascading fruit bowl upon her head and twirling her white frilly parasol upon her shoulder in a manner that could only be interpreted as flirtatious. Acknowledging them with her nodding berries and plums, she strolled past the helm toward the taffrail, calling out: "I declare, gentlemen, there is *nothing* more pleasurable than cruising on a fine September day."

Prosper's mumbled response was spoken to no one in particular. "Well, *I* kin think o' somethin' else what's more pleasurable."

Fly was aghast to see his helmsman suddenly rejuvenated, his head swivelling about so he could delight in Mrs. Jiggins's weaving progress along the quarterdeck.

"Mr. Burgo, I suggest you exercise caution with that one. It was one thing to have taken up with Meg Kettle, quite another to set your sights on Mrs. Jiggins. She's no laundress, you know. She is a noblewoman."

Prosper dropped his head to one side and jiggled his eyes as if inviting Fly to take a look at her retreating figure. The winds, however light they might have been in Fly's estimation, were strong enough to salaciously grope the folds of Mrs. Jiggins's muslin gown, displaying the corpulent curves of her bottom and thighs, providing them both with an exhilarating spectacle rarely seen upon a Royal Navy frigate.

Prosper poked his tongue into his cheek and grinned. "Well, Cap'n, right about now I'd say she don't look so high-born."

CHAPTER 16

FRIDAY, SEPTEMBER 24
10:00 A.M.
(FORENOON WATCH, FOUR BELLS)
ABOARD HMS *INVINCIBLE*

"Wine? At this early hour?" Leander smirked as he reached for the goblet of Bordeaux that Fly had poured and pushed toward him across the great cabin table. "Have you taken leave of your senses, or been adversely influenced by the liquor and laudanum addictions of our lost friend, Captain Prickett?"

"What matters the time of day? As I have seen neither hide nor hair of you for the past four days, not since our unfortunate supper with Mrs. Jiggins and Mr. Ludlow, I felt we should celebrate our reunion with a drink." Fly raised his own goblet in a silent toast, and then sank back in his chair to study his friend. "You appear to be well, old fellow. The worry lines around your mouth have eased up and you have less of the outward aspect of a street-seller. Have you managed to add two or three pounds to your bony frame? Oh, and have you been able to find your missing silver buckle?" He leaned over the side of the table and frowned as he inspected his friend's black leather shoes. "Ah! Excellent! So you have!"

Prior to responding, Leander took a moment to indulge in his wine, his eyes focused on the rolling walls of misty grey beyond Fly's chair and the galleried windows of his cabin. "I am pleased with your assessment, especially knowing I have shaken my resemblance to a street-seller. And yes, I do believe I am slightly heavier, owing in good part to Biscuit's caregiving. He has personally seen to my having received three squares a day, even gone so far as to carry a tray to the hospital if I do not make an appearance in the gunroom."

"What is keeping you from the gunroom? Must you stay behind to protect the honour of the woman you keep in your dispensary?"

"I cannot leave Mr. Duffy alone with Emily for fear he will over-medicate her."

"And do your fears extend beyond him drugging her with too many tonics?"

Leander shrugged, refusing to meet Fly's bright, expectant eyes. "It is not just Mr. Duffy who concerns me. You have a young midshipman named Cadby Brambles who has taken to stopping by the hospital all too frequently and is making a nuisance of himself. He has even confided in me that he believes Emily fancies him."

"Extraordinary! What encouragement has she given him?"

"She may have smiled at him once or twice when he stood gawking at her through the open doorway."

"You cannot blame our men, Doctor. The Royal Navy throws them together for months on end, usually without the company of women, so when they do see an agreeable one they often get so *very* silly."

This time, although their eyes met, Fly charitably shortened Leander's embarrassment by halting his spreading smile. Pulling his chair nearer to the table, he soberly clasped his hands upon its gleaming surface.

"Ah! Here it comes," said Leander, his stare guarded.

"Whatever do you mean, Doctor?"

"Whenever you assume that particular posture, I fear you are going to ask me a favour."

"I do hate that you know me so well, but, aye, I do need a favour. And now that you shall owe me until the day you cease to breathe, I must ask." Fly took a deep breath before launching into his explanation. "You see, Mrs. Jiggins is very down in the mouth as her little scheme to paint pictures on deck with your aunt has been spoiled by the unceasing drizzle of the past few days. Consequently, she is searching for some form of entertainment and has asked when next we might have a party here in my cabin. I have put her off for the time, but I cannot do so indefinitely. Her persistence is dauntless."

"Have you now become the *Invincible*'s officer of entertainment?"

"It would seem so. At this rate I may be forced to hand over both the keys to my cabin and my command to Prosper Burgo. The truth is ... if I am to arrange another grand supper ... I shall require proficient assistance with Mrs. Jiggins and her nephew."

"Are you asking me to clear my social calendar?"

"Yes, and I wondered if your father and Miss Braden would care to join us?"

"The last thing Aunt Eliza expects on this voyage is to receive an invitation to one of your banquets, and I'm afraid she lacks enthusiasm where Mrs. Jiggins is concerned. She is a creature of habit and is already at her most comfortable eating her meals at the little table in the forepeak. And naturally, my father would not dare leave her alone. For my own part, I cannot pretend to like Mr. Ludlow, but since I am indebted to you forever, I shall join you."

"*That* is a relief!"

"And if you are agreeable," Leander added, "perhaps Emily could, as well."

Fly's stare rounded with interest. "Is she much improved, then?"

"She is, and quite eager to end her imprisonment in the dispensary."

"Ah! Then we had better hold fast for the fun begins! Or should I say: the fun resumes?"

Leander raised his eyebrows as if feigning innocence.

"Do not pretend to misconstrue my meaning, old fellow," said Fly, his eyes bright with mischief. He pushed his chair back so he could cross his legs. "May I now conclude that your fears of Emily contracting bronchitis or some fatal disease were unfounded?"

"Not completely."

"Your distinctive brand of caregiving enabled her to make a miraculous recovery, is that it?"

"She was ill with a cold and fever when she came aboard. She did require rest and proper care and —" Leander stumbled around for words, knowing he looked as defenceless as a cornered animal.

"I confess ... I do love seeing your ears turn red, Doctor."

Leander took a deep breath and held it before exhaling. "Captain Austen, in some evil way I do hope you will develop a strong appetite for the company of either my aunt or Mrs. Jiggins on this voyage so that I may take advantage and tease you ferociously."

"I may be all smiles and jokes now, but there will soon come a time when we must sober up. We shall have to answer for our kidnapping of your princess. Back in June, it was by chance that we found ourselves with her aboard the *Isabelle*. One does not turn his back on a wounded woman cast adrift in the ocean between two belligerent ships. *That* state of affairs could not be helped. *This*, on the other hand —" Fly allowed his words to resonate and the gentle patter of rain on the windowpanes to encroach on their thoughts.

Leander regarded him sidelong, chewing his bottom lip. "If you were to argue that we were already put to sea when Emily's whereabouts first became known to you, it — it would not be far off the truth, given how she made her way to us."

"Oh, there shall be no need for me to lie."

"Why? What is your plan?"

"My plan is simple. I shall turn *you* over to the authorities when they come clamouring for answers ... or to Emily's family, whichever comes first. So, while we are cruising upon the Atlantic and making merry with our eminent guests over tea and cakes, I suggest you give some serious thought as to how you shall fabricate your defence."

Leander compressed his lips and tightened his hold on the stem of his goblet.

Relenting, Fly softened his tone. "Have you told her yet about Magpie?"

"No," he replied sadly, "but she has been asking to see him ... and Mr. Walby."

"I do not envy you that task." Fly cleared his throat. "There is one further subject we must tackle; one which has given me little peace at night."

Leander drew backwards, his glance vigilant once again.

"If Emily has recovered, I must move her out of your hospital; otherwise, you shall soon be rocking a cradle, and I cannot have that." Fly was heartened to see the corners of his friend's mouth rise in amusement. "And since space on the *Invincible* is in short supply, she shall have to share a cabin with one of the other two ladies." He slowly reached for the wine bottle to give them both a generous top-up and then observed Leander from under his arching eyebrows. "So, my question to you is ... which one shall it be?"

10:00 A.M.
ABOARD HMS *EXPEDITION*

Like a portent of doom, a drum rolled in the distance.

Magpie broke out in gooseflesh as he stepped onto the forecastle, lugging behind him a necessary bucket like a tumour of grotesque proportions. His head shot up to search the waves beyond the bounds of the flying jib sail, expecting to see the two ships that were still trailing the *Bloody Flux* on their journey. Maybe they had been enemies all along and were now darkening their doorstep, thirsting for battle, their long guns heated up and ready to wreak havoc. But the sea was empty, the two ships nowhere to be seen, leaving Magpie perplexed. The drums then were *not* a call to beat to quarters.

Looking aft, he was shocked to see the entire crew assembled on the quarterdeck, standing tense and hushed as if the captain were about to bore them all by reading aloud the Articles of War. Was it a roll call? An inspection? If so, no one had bothered to inform him of it. But then no one ever bothered with him in the first place. It was painfully evident that fellowship would be denied him on this voyage and that in order to survive he would have to fend for himself in all matters.

Anxious to learn more, Magpie hurried to complete his task. At the forecastle railing, he held his breath and hurled the revolting contents of his bucket over the side, making certain the wind and misting rains sent them flying out over the grey-marbled waters and not back into his face. With the load of his bucket lightened, he narrowed his eye to scan the decks, always on the lookout for Trevelyan — or rather *Mr. Bumpus* — who would surely be easy to spot, towering head and shoulders above the others. But there was no sign of the man's scarred and shorn head in the crowd. Believing the coast to be clear, Magpie pushed in among the ordinary seamen huddled together on the larboard side of the quarterdeck to learn what on earth was going on. Through a tangle of tattooed arms and torsos, he glimpsed a line of grim-faced marines in their scarlet jackets — raised up on the poop deck above the crowd, their bayonets fixed to their muskets. On the quarterdeck below, with his officers and midshipmen at sombre attention a few yards behind him, the captain of the *Bloody Flux* stood alone. Magpie had learned his name only yesterday, spoken irreverently on the lips of the ship's cook while he was doling out the men's rations of grog. *Uptergrove*. It was a name Magpie was quite certain he had heard before, but could not for the life of him recall when and where. In his full-dress uniform with his bicorne hat worn fore and aft on his head, his shoulders pulled back and his chin jutting upward like a bowsprit, Captain Uptergrove's stare was fixed upon something that Magpie could not see; his countenance as unreadable as a plank of oak.

The drumming ceased and a booming shout cut the air. "Bring him to the gangway!" A few minutes later, a second shout was heard. "Bo'sun's mate! Give this man fifty!"

There followed a disturbing cracking sound and a cry of agony that turned Magpie's guts to liquid. He nearly lost his grip on his bucket. Spotting the round hat of Mr. Huxley closer to the front of the assemblage of sailors, Magpie squeezed his way toward him. As Mr. Huxley was the only person on the *Bloody Flux* who had ever spoken to him — even if his communications were less than desirable — Magpie hoped he might explain what was going on.

"What is it, sir?"

Seeing who it was tugging upon his belt, Mr. Huxley frowned with disapproval and gave Magpie a shushing-up. But then, in a rare moment of generosity, he leaned down and supplied him with an answer under his breath. "Wot? Are ye a simpleton then? Didn't ya hear the call to witness punishment? 'Tis a floggin'! Ain't ya never seen a floggin' afore?"

Magpie had heard stories of floggings — floggings carried out with cat-o'-nine-tails before the crew of a single ship, as well as floggings 'round the fleet where the offender is bound to two capstan pawls in a ship's boat and his humiliating punishment is carried out in front of boatloads of men from a number of ships. But he had never before witnessed one. Stretching and angling his neck, he was able to get a better view of the proceedings.

Stripped of his ragged shirt, the victim had been bound spread-eagled to a section of grating turned up on its end. His ankles and wrists were fixed to it with spun yarns, and his trousers had slipped halfway down his buttocks. He looked starved and frail, and Magpie felt himself welling up at the sight of the ugly lacerations that had already disfigured the white, meagre flesh of his back as if he had been branded with a farmer's iron. The boatswain's mate, who had the responsibility of executing the punishment, was a big fellow with big arm muscles. Magpie cringed seeing him winding up his full force, throwing the cat over his shoulder to let fly another hissing, devastating lash.

"Nay, sir, I ain't never."

"Well, ya better watch closely! It's what ya'll git if the cap'n ever finds turds in his lavatory."

Magpie felt as if he had a mouthful of sun-baked sand. "Who is he, sir?"

"A damned Yankee ... one o' the few what agreed to sail with us just so's he could avoid going to rot on a prison hulk in Plymouth."

"What's he done, sir?"

"Theft, though he fiercely denies it." Huxley woefully shook his head, looking uncommonly warm-hearted. "Unlucky sod! Normally, ya git thirty-six lashes fer theft. Uptergrove's ordered fifty."

Magpie shrank against the tumult of another thwack of the whip, another scream for mercy, and the sight of the poor man's back, sliced up and bleeding badly. "Won't — won't that kill him, sir?"

"Nay, but what he does git will keep him sore fer life 'cause the bo'sun's mate's usin' a thieves' cat."

"What's that, sir?"

"Do ya know nothin' at all, then?" he snapped before relenting with a grunt. "It's a mean whip what's got bigger and harder knots on it than a cat-o'-nine-tails. All the more painful. Now git outta here with that reekin' bucket o' yers or I'll chuck ya both over the side and ya'll have to petition a ride to the River Styx on the suckery tentacles of a kraken."

Magpie trembled at the sound of that. "What's a kraken, sir?"

"Off with ya now," said Mr. Huxley, dismissing him with a rough shove.

A dozen hard-fisted men sent Magpie stumbling backward through the crowd. He emerged shaken and bruised on the empty side of the deck, feeling manhandled as if he had just run the gauntlet. Retrieving his dropped bucket, he looked out upon the misty sea, terrified of the thought of being thrown overboard and lost in those endless, unforgiving swells. Not so very long ago he had fought the waves alone with nothing to hold on to, out of his head with terror, fearing he would be pulled under by a horde of sea creatures. Nay! He would never survive it a second time 'round.

Another forlorn gaze toward the mustered Bloody Fluxes ended in Magpie swallowing hard. Standing dangerously near to him was Trevelyan. Keenly aware that his life depended upon remaining undetected, Magpie prayed Trevelyan would not notice him now. This time, however, there seemed little worry of that. Unlike Captain Uptergrove, Trevelyan's emotions were laid bare on his clouded features where a deep flush had invaded right up to the shorn prickles of his hairline. His attention was riveted to the sad clearing on the quarterdeck, but he was fidgety, and kept hitting his thighs with his fists. Magpie could see an ugly, throbbing vein in his neck, and swore that behind those awful, blazing eyes of his, he was plotting an unspeakable murder.

Turning on his heels, Magpie broke into a run, his bucket flying behind him, desperate to reach the relative safety of the lower decks and flee the soul-piercing cries of the poor Yankee who was bound to the grating — mangled, spent, and weeping.

CHAPTER 17

Emily followed the midshipman Cadby Brambles down to the mess deck from the dispensary, careful not to bump into his back end, which, displayed as it was in his relaxed dress of close-fitting, cream-coloured trousers, reminded her of formidable loaves of bread. His movements were jerky and clumsy, and every so often he either knocked into an oak post or made an unexpected rotation as if to make certain she was still behind him and had not been spirited off by one of the many sailors who had made a display of wetting his lips as they had passed by. Her pillowcase of belongings was draped over his broad shoulder, concealing his drooped head, and as such he resembled a homeless hunchback, a taciturn one who had said nothing to her beyond his initial grunt of "Follow me, Miss." As they threaded their way through the inescapable sailors, the parts of Mr. Brambles visible from his open collar on up were infused with high colour, and his breathing was all gasps and hiccups, leaving Emily concluding that he was either very nervous or had caught her bad cold and would soon be forced to occupy the cot left empty by her release from the hospital.

Reluctantly, Leander had left her in Mr. Brambles's care after informing her that, despite her unrelenting cough, the worst of her illness was behind her and she was therefore free to go. "As long as you eat regular meals, remember that sleep is an important commodity, and avoid contact with unsavoury varieties of noblemen, there should be no further episodes of fainting or fever," he had advised while attempting to maintain a straight face. Emily hated the thought of leaving the hospital. Hearing Leander at work through the delicate fabric of the dispensary walls had filled her convalescing hours with joy, even though they had had little time to talk given the constant stream of patients and the hordes of sailors that had descended upon the hospital, some bearing food, others carrying dispatches, most coming for no particular reason than to be a nuisance. But now Emily was ready to return to a more normal existence, and her mind was brimming with ways in which she could make herself useful to both Leander and Captain Austen. Moreover, she could not wait to be reunited with both Magpie and Gus Walby. It was her hope that the three of them could take up together as they once had on the *Isabelle* and spend their leisure hours reading Jane Austen's *Pride and Prejudice*. Such sentimental thoughts impelled her to look for the beloved volumes in her laden pillowcase, travelling in front of her on Mr. Brambles's shoulder. Seeing the outline of their raised spines was reassuring, clearly a harbinger of good things to come.

Nothing today could deflate Emily's buoyant mood, not even the news that she would have to share a cabin. Leander had provided no further details, only that he hoped *they* would get on. But as there was only one other woman on board — no one had informed her otherwise — she had not questioned him, taking it for granted that her roommate would be his Aunt Eliza. And how wonderful! When Leander and his father were two of the most affable individuals she had ever met, how could their female relation be anything but a cut from the same fine cloth? She smiled, recalling the expression in Leander's blue eyes when they had parted in the doorway of the hospital, and his promise that he would seek her out once she had had a chance to settle in. The *Invincible* was now four days into her journey from Portsmouth, too far to turn back, yet far enough away from those who had plotted to keep them apart. Ahead of them were endless days at sea. Her quiet burble of laughter sent Mr. Brambles whirling 'round to check on her.

"Is everything all right, Miss?"

"Quite all right, Mr. Brambles," she replied, beaming up at him.

Remarkably, a torrent of questions began pouring from his red lips like milk from a tilted pitcher, his head eagerly swinging fore and aft as he picked his way along their route, his sudden boundless enthusiasm giving Emily little chance in between to provide answers. Was a warm smile all that was needed to melt a frozen tongue?

"Have you ever sailed before, Miss? Are you comfortable on the *Invincible*? Do you have family in England? Have you ever travelled to Ipswich in Suffolk? That is where I am from. Did you know that my father is a baronet? Do you like music and dancing? Have you ever been to the theatre in London? By chance, are — are you married?"

"Goodness gracious! Where would you like me to begin?"

They had descended the ladder and were now ambling past the middy's berth — a protracted, box-like compartment with its own door and a sizable, open window which overlooked the cluttered interior of the mess deck. Inside, around a table and amid a great deal of shoving and nose-grabbing, an unruly gaggle of boys was attempting to organize a game of backgammon. Spying the distinctive figure of Mr. Brambles in their midst, one of them called out, imploring him to come and play. But when his pleas were repulsed — Mr. Brambles turning his back and *bread loaves* on them in a crude display of superiority — the boy's retaliation, shouted out in a girlish, sing-song voice, was swift and destructive.

"Brambles wets his bed at night! Brambles wets his bed at night!"

The subsequent eruption of youthful howls and laughter rattled the *Invincible*'s oak hull. Emily had to bite down hard on her lip to avoid being drawn into its uproarious vortex. Having lost his zeal in retrieving answers to his myriad questions, a visibly shaken and silenced Mr. Brambles quickly retreated away from the obnoxious midshipmen and rushed Emily toward the back half of the mess deck where the canvas cabins of the officers lined the ship's walls. While accelerating her pace to keep up with him, she glanced around with interest.

The area between the cabins constituted the gunroom and was distinguished by a long dining table — best described as warped wooden boards mounted on trestles — where the officers and other esteemed crew members took their meals. In places, it was deep in shadow, there being no gunports on this deck, and the only natural light came from the gratings and open ports on the gun deck above. The table was set for supper, the oil-lanterns already lit and placed at intervals along its centre board, and though the dining hour was a ways off, there were a few men sitting around it, some writing letters, some reading books, all of them looking up the minute Emily entered their hallowed refuge. Making a statement by flinging his shoulders back, Mr. Brambles strode past the amused onlookers at the table and on down the line of cabins, stopping finally at the last door on the ship's larboard side. His pouty cheeks red and patchy with humiliation, he seemed unwilling to lift his eyes to hers.

"It is this one, Miss," he mumbled, unslinging the pillowcase from his shoulder and stuffing it into her waiting hands before dashing off. Emily watched him go, little surprised that he wound up back at the middy's berth. After a heated display of fist-waving and screaming for bloodshed, he leapt into the air like a flying squirrel and swooped headfirst through the berth's open window. As Mr. Brambles had sailed cleanly out of her range of vision, Emily was precluded from witnessing the ensuing rumpus; however, she had no trouble hearing it — nasty words and threats shouted at the limits of lungs — and neither did the officers seated around the table, much to their disgust, though not one of them shifted a muscle in an effort to suppress it.

Turning away with a smile, Emily rapped upon the canvas frame of her new cabin. Receiving no answer within, she tugged on the flimsy door which jumped open, nearly striking her in the head, and peered into its dimly lit perimeter. From previous experience on the

Isabelle, she knew not to expect a commodious chamber arranged with soft pillows and downy quilts — the comforts of her rooms at Hartwood Hall and even the Brigantine Inn were now just faded impressions — but nothing could have prepared her for *this* scene.

The cabin was a bewilderment of boxes and chests and lockers. Those not stacked to the deckheads appeared to have taken a direct hit of enemy fire, their lids blown off and the contents blown asunder. In truth it was more probable that the owner had hurled them into the air in a fit of passion and remained indifferent to the fact that much had landed upon the scummy timbers of the floor. Emily could not advance into the cabin without trouncing on an elaborate hat or a satin shoe or a stack of underclothing. Contributing to the souring of her stomach was the pervading aroma of the enclosed atmosphere — a potent mixture of lavender water, perspiration, and decomposing fish.

"There you are, my dear! I have been waiting for you."

Aghast at finding such disarray, Emily did not immediately see her roommate, concealed as she was behind the criss-cross of the two slung hammocks. Dressed in little more than a sleeveless chemise, she was bent over, rummaging about in a large, leather trunk exiled to a gloomy corner. Her appearance gave Emily such a start, for in the poor light and her state of undress, she bore a frightening resemblance to her former adversary, Meg Kettle, the *Isabelle's* laundress. Emily watched guardedly as the woman selected a gown from the trunk, pressed it to her bosom, and then engaged in a tussle with the hammocks, pushing and elbowing them out of her way as she came toward her. As the woman had not inherited the slimness of her family's male line, Emily's inquiry sounded dubious.

"Are you Miss Eliza Braden?"

"Wot? No, no! Did they not tell you about me?" Clucking with surprise, the woman took a few more unbalanced steps that brought her out from the shadows of the hammocks and into the light of the candle-lantern hanging near the cabin door. Even before her facial features had come into clear focus, the sight of the eerily familiar necklace, glittering beneath her double chin, ignited the fierce return of Emily's headache.

The woman wagged her head in mock disgust. "Upon my soul! Can it be that you do not recognize me? Is it because you have found me *deshabille* ... with my hair unadorned?"

Emily's pillowcase dropped to the floor with a dull thud. She started to cough. Sensing the strength in her legs was about to abandon her, she reached out to steady herself on the solid backbone of a chair, the seat of which was draped over with a number of silk shawls. Her benumbed voice fell to a whisper. "I do not understand. This — this cannot be possible."

Smiling sweetly, her head falling sideways upon the naked flesh of her shoulder, Mrs. Jiggins enunciated her ardent reply with a dramatic flair. "Oh, but, my dear ... it is!"

3:30 P.M.

Leander and his father had taken up residence on the carved oak bench that stretched across the stern of the *Invincible,* wrapped in their outdoor clothing to ward off the sputtering rain that dropped overhead from clouds amassing like an army in the brooding sky. Old Dr. Braden's brown Carrick coat and broad-brimmed hat had proven much more effective against the elements than Leander's dusky-red banyan made of silk damask, purchased recently in Portsmouth for a song in the same shop where he had found his new spectacles and the silver-plated spoon. Nevertheless, as long as the rain behaved and refrained from drenching him with a downpour, he figured he could survive long enough to hear what it was his father had wanted to discuss with him in private, away from the avid eavesdroppers who roamed the lower decks.

Biscuit had just presented them with welcome mugs of lukewarm coffee — insisting they had been steaming-hot when he had first run them up from the galley. Rolling his mug between his palms in an effort to extract its dwindling heat, Leander found entertainment in watching Biscuit scampering around with his coffee tray. He looked like a jester with his shock of hair rain-slicked against his head, hopping from side to side to maintain his balance on the slippery planks of the quarterdeck, and all the while reciting poems of inspiration in a loud, lusty voice for the benefit of the poor beggars on watch, most of whom — like the skinny midshipman with his arms pinned to his sides, shivering in his light jacket and pantaloons — were unsuitably dressed for the weather.

In addition to the coffee, Leander welcomed the respite from the nasty smells and crowded conditions below deck. Inhaling the bracing tang of the sea, he marvelled at the men standing barefoot a hundred feet above him on tiny footropes, the winds tugging on their hair and clothing as they rolled and bound various sails to the yards. Over at the helm, Prosper stood in his striped jumper, unfazed by the weather, his hands on the wheel, looking out to the white line of the western horizon. Holding his head on a tilt, he appeared to be lending a sympathetic ear — or perhaps half an ear — to Mr. Philpotts, the purser, who paced restlessly in small circles beside him, bundled almost beyond recognition in his layers of waterproof clothing, waving his arms around in angry animation as he unloaded his sundry complaints of the day. Out on the ocean, the *Invincible*'s travelling companions drifted in the distance, both of them still out there, though nothing more than watery-grey ghosts on the waves — the *Lady Jane* sailing ahead of them and the *Expedition* behind as expected given the great difference in their tonnage. In the presence of Prosper Burgo and friends on the sea, Leander felt a much-needed warming surge of reassurance.

Curious to know why he had wanted to speak to him, although not in the least bit surprised as they had seen little of one another since their departure from Portsmouth, Leander turned to study his father, who was sitting on the bench with his legs crossed, leisurely sipping his coffee. "So, tell me, Pa, are you harbouring any regrets about having joined us on this crossing?"

Old Dr. Braden smiled fondly at him. "Not so far. But then I haven't yet experienced the joys of tripping down a ladder or smashing my forehead on a beam."

"Once I have you helping out in the hospital you will discover that those are common injuries for men of the sea."

His father murmured with amusement. "And then, of course, I have not yet experienced stormy seas, although Captain Austen did warn me the Atlantic can get awfully ugly at this time of year." He leaned backwards to shoot worrying glances at the sky.

"Regrettably, being on a ship is somewhat like life itself. One cannot be promised smooth sailing the entire time."

"Then I shall not expect it."

Was it his aunt, wondered Leander? Did his father have concerns regarding her? "And Eliza? How is she faring?"

"She does not complain — well, not to me, anyhow. Perhaps she worries that if she did I would ask Captain Austen to cast her off on the first ship we meet returning to England." He peered up at Leander from under his broad-brim. "Sister or not, she is an enigma, that one. She carefully guards her emotions. Always has."

"I am still recovering from the shock of finding her on board. I suppose we shall never know what possessed her to leave the comforts of her cottage on Mile End Terrace." Leander gathered his coat together at his neck to guard against the strengthening winds. "At least I was able to relieve her anxieties of becoming Emily's cabin mate."

His father grinned. "*That* would have been the death of her. Given her modesty, can you imagine her plight in having no privacy with which to change into her nightgown?"

"Could that be worse than her knowing that, beyond the delicate framework of her cabin, the decks are overrun with men?"

A twinkle jumped into his father's faded blue eyes. "Who knows?"

They shared a laugh and then fell quiet to drink the last of their coffee. When his father spoke again, he had smoothed away all vestiges of mirth. "While she has not expressed her feelings on the subject, Eliza does seem most unhappy that Emily is on board."

Leander, too, had felt the bite of his aunt's chilliness. "I know. But then how could Eliza ever compete for our affections with a gregarious Princess of England in the picture?"

"Perhaps —" His father seemed distant all of a sudden; his squinting gaze strayed with some newfound interest toward the quarterdeck's larboard rail. Puzzled, Leander turned his head to find that he was observing the movements of Shipton Ludlow. The man had made an appearance on deck, in all likelihood to get some fresh air and a moment to himself, away from Mrs. Jiggins. Dressed in his daywear — a snuff-coloured frock coat, nankeen breeches, and Hessian boots — with a silver-headed walking stick thrust under one arm, he was attempting to take some exercise, walking with his head down and a hand pressed to his top hat to keep the bullying winds from tearing it off. Leander hoped Mr. Ludlow would not see them sitting on the stern bench and decide to head over in their direction for a friendly chat.

Setting aside his mug, Leander's father uncrossed his legs and inched forward on his seat, his eyes still locked upon the lonely walker in the nankeen breeches. "We have discussed Eliza, but I am more interested in knowing how *you* feel about Emily being on board?"

"Despite my initial anxieties in terms of how she arrived here, I do not think I have to answer that one, Pa. You *know* my feelings where she is concerned." When his father did not return his smile, Leander frowned. "Why? Have you suddenly joined Eliza's camp and concluded that any kind of a future with Emily is impossible?"

"I only want to caution you, my son." His father's reddened hands gripped the edge of the oak bench on either side of him as he drew in a long breath. "It was only last evening ... quite late ... that I had the honour of being introduced to Mr. Ludlow. Before then, I had not so much as seen him on the ship. Last night he was in the company of your helmsman, Prosper Burgo. They were just leaving the gunroom as I was heading to my cabin for the night. I am guessing they had both been enjoying a glass or two of wine with some of the officers, for they were both flush-faced and in jocular moods."

Leander felt himself tensing up. "Don't tell me you were encouraged to drink with them before bed! And having found Mr. Ludlow charming and articulate, you have come to the conclusion that you rather like the man."

Old Dr. Braden raised his hands in surrender. "On the contrary. I do not like him at all," he said calmly. "In fact, I did *not* like him the very first time we met."

Leander's mouth fell open and swiftly clamped shut again. "Pray! When was it that you *first* met Mr. Ludlow?"

"In late August."

"What? Where?"

"At Hartwood Hall."

"Hartwood Hall!" Leander's rousing exclamation was dampened by a fierce lashing of rain.

"You will recall me telling you that, whilst I was staying in Hampstead, I received an invitation to dine there on a Saturday night, along with young Gus Walby."

Nodding quickly, Leander urged his father onward, his thoughts jostling one another in his head.

"And how we had arrived at the Hall full of great anticipation — Mr. Walby so excited to spend time with Lady Fleda Lindsay, exploring the service tunnels under the house — but ended up leaving there completely devastated, Emily shamefacedly seeing us off at the door because our host, who had been most *unpleasant*, had chosen to stay behind in the dining room to eat his dessert."

"Yes! Yes, I remember you telling me, but I — but I thought that was —" Leander tried to contain his burgeoning alarm. "I am obviously not following you, Pa. At what point did you meet Mr. Ludlow? Is he a friend ... a relative of the Duke and Duchess of Belmont who just happened to be present with you that evening?"

His father's sober gaze wandered absently over the woven pattern of Leander's banyan. "God knows he must have known he could not maintain the ruse indefinitely, but the truth is ... the truth is ... Mr. Ludlow is passing himself off under an assumed name."

Leander froze, entrapped in silence as this thudding revelation took root. He sat rigidly, blinking, raindrops streaming from his hair into his eyes and his slack mouth, unaware of the ship's bell tolling the end of the watch and the gunshot-cracking of the sails on the mizzen. It was some time before he came to life again and then only to seek out the solitary walker on the wind-swept deck, moving now at a snail's pace along the gangway of the ship's waist, still fighting to keep his hat on his head.

4:00 P.M.
(AFTERNOON WATCH, EIGHT BELLS)
ABOARD HMS *EXPEDITION*

Trevelyan had taken his place at the end of the narrow, creaky bench, leaving him bunched up as usual against the side of the ship. He listened to the chatter of his six American messmates as they ate their foul-smelling supper of salted pork, sauerkraut, broken biscuits, and beer. His clerking duties having kept him away from the table until now, his mates were eager to bring him up to speed with the latest gossip. They spoke in hoarse whispers, spitting with heated anger into their wooden plates, careful lest their words be overheard by the Englishmen who surrounded them, absorbed in their own conversations at their own mess tables. Normally, Trevelyan made no attempt whatsoever to enter into discourse, his mates not seeming to mind as they had formed a strange, reverential affection for their "Mr. Bumpus" and had grown accustomed to his reserved manner and pompous preference for literature over their jokes and camaraderie. Even now he had a book with him. The Henry Fielding novel he was still trying to finish up was on his lap, tucked away for safekeeping inside the woolly thrum cap he had found abandoned on the orlop deck. He had planned to read the novel while eating and complete it before returning to his desk in Mr. Croker's office; instead, he found himself more interested in what his mates had to say about yesterday's flogging.

"Have you seen him yet?" he asked in his cool, dispassionate voice, staring at the iron rings that held together the wooden slats of his beer mug.

"We did finally! Poor bugger. He looks like he were roasted on a spit. His lacerated back's puffed up like a black pillow and he's delirious with fever."

"I heard him moanin' last night up in the sick bay, Mr. Bumpus. Ya could hear him right through the floorboards."

"Me, too! Gave me the tremors. I couldn't sleep none."

"Hard to believe Uptergrove didn't give him a few more lashes just to shut him up, ya know, maybe knock him unconscious."

"Or kill him outright!"

"He's a decent man — hard-working, obedient. He didn't deserve none o' this."

Trevelyan realized his hands were slippery with sweat. "What was it he was alleged to have stolen from Uptergrove's cabin?"

"No one can say. No one knows for sure."

"Some think it were Uptergrove's quill pen."

"Others think it might o' been one o' his prized pictures. He's got quite a collection, ya know. I seen 'em once."

Aye! Trevelyan, too, had viewed the collection, for he was often admitted to the great cabin to confer with Uptergrove over reports, lists, and documents. They were pretty, but not one of them worth filching.

The most intimidating mate of the lot — a heavily tattooed fellow with a bald, lumpy head — suddenly burst into gruff laughter. "Well, I'll wager it were Uptergrove's shoes, the ones with them thickset heels what enables him to stand tall on the quarterdeck."

The others joined in on the ridiculing, adding their own Uptergrove insults to the banter, but there was an edge in their laughter and it soon died away. They all returned to the business of eating, shovelling their food into their mouths with wooden spoons and tarred fingers, chewing with their eyes cast downwards in an outward show of respectful compassion for their pitied mate.

Trevelyan wiped his sweaty palms on the woolly thrum-sheathed book perched on his knees. The glaring, yellow light from the oil-lantern swaying above the table hurt his eyes. Closing them, he leaned his head against the ship's rocking side, flinching with the brutal memory of his own torture. God knows he had tried to bury it in the deepest trenches of his brain, but its stark echo was unceasing and unbearable. Those humiliating lashes ... knotted leather on naked flesh ... inflicted endlessly, over and over again ... mutilating his back ... scarring him forever. But there was someone else whose pain awakened acute responses in him, whose misery had only intensified his own and tilled the breeding ground of hatred for those who had brandished the whips.

Little Harry.

As always, his lonely figure came wandering into the fore of the quiet darkness behind Trevelyan's tightly shuttered eyelids. His sweet face was blotchy from crying; his mouth trembled with fear, and his stick-thin arms reached out to him in supplication. *Thomas? Help me, Thomas! Please, please, help me!* Trevelyan could only push his little brother away, forcing him back to the outermost reaches of his memory, begging him never to return. Withdrawing in hopeless sorrow, Harry vanished into the black emptiness, giving him no such promises.

An angry growl beside him succeeded in pulling Trevelyan back to the present, setting him free from his silent agony ... for the time, anyway. His eyes flew open just as the monstrous fists of his tattooed mate came down hard upon the table, eliciting a jig from the wooden mugs and plates, but providentially, no sideways glances from the English sailors sitting around them, thanks to the flow of beer and ale, and the crescendoing noise level in the mess.

Massaging his smarting palms, the tattooed mate leaned in toward them all. With his eyes narrowed upon Trevelyan, he lowered his gravelly voice. "When we git our chance, we're gonna do somethin', Mr. Bumpus. We don't know what yet, but we're gonna do somethin'. That puny Uptergrove's gonna rue the day he flogged one o'ours."

Trevelyan nodded his approval and then shrank back against the ship's side. "Aye! And when you do," he muttered to himself, gritting his teeth against the old pain in his body, "I'll be right there with you."

CHAPTER 18

"**A**re you going to sit down, Emily?"

Fly stood uncertainly next to his desk, where he had been working away on a letter to his wife, not knowing what to make of Emily's sudden appearance in his cabin. She seemed distraught, standing there in front of the dining table, her cheeks ablaze with high colour, her eyes fixed upon the pieces of creamware and pewter, which Biscuit and Mr. Beef had just set in preparation for the special supper. Her hands played absently with the skirt of her gown, the hem of which was soaking wet, and her hair was undressed, falling in tangles of pale gold around her thin shoulders. She looked younger than her nineteen years, much like Fly's six-year-old daughter after an afternoon spent fording streams and traipsing through fields of wildflowers. He sincerely hoped her disposition was not the unhappy result of one of his men having said or done something inappropriate.

Had she not just been released from Leander's hospital? Surely nothing could have happened as yet.

It was raining steadily now and the waves were much angrier than they had been earlier in the day. Glancing out the galleried windows, Fly gave a passing thought to the *Lady Jane* and the *Expedition*. They were invisible in the black torrent of the sea, but he prayed they would both prove to be sound and weatherly, and manage to easily pilot through the storm, which by all predictions would increase in ferocity over the coming hours. The ship rocked beneath his boots. He wondered for how much longer the dishes would stay rooted to his dining table. Maybe he could cancel this little supper, and order everyone to their own cabins until the weather had settled. God knows he had no appetite for the idle chit-chat of his *exalted guests* — the title he now generously and regularly applied to Shipton Ludlow and Arabella Jiggins.

"If you don't sit down, the waves may soon drop you to the floor." Fly's smile did nothing to soften the haunted lines around Emily's eyes.

"I shall stand, thank you." She stepped closer to the reliable sturdiness of the oak table and suppressed a cough.

Returning his quill pen to its inkwell, Fly hustled his unfinished letter into a desk drawer, and waited for her to speak. Had Leander informed her of Magpie's disappearance? No, no. It seemed her attitude suggested shock more than sorrow. "Our guests will soon be arriving," he said, feeling a twinge of impatience, "so I recommend you tell me why you are here; otherwise, you shall have to do so in front of an audience."

She clasped her hands on the front of her gown and seemed to summon courage with a lift of her head. "I wonder if you would allow me to share a cabin with Miss Braden. I know we have not yet been introduced, but I believe we would be more ... suited to one another."

"Have you taken this up with Leander?"

"I have gone searching, but I — I cannot find him."

"Ah! In that case ... my answer is no."

She looked up sharply. "Please! Will you not reconsider?"

"Emily ... Miss Braden's cabin is no bigger than a ditty bag. Mrs. Jiggins's cabin, on the other hand, is what I would consider generous in size, second only to my own. It was initially assigned to my first lieutenant, but he nobly vacated it for her sake. I am not going to make changes now; therefore, you will just have to make do."

"May I return to the dispensary?"

Fly clenched his jaw. "No!"

"Then I thought I might sleep on deck."

"You shall do no such thing." Fly took an aggressive step toward her. "I should not have to remind you that it is not within my duties to appease unauthorized passengers when they find fault with their accommodation. Experience has taught you the seaman's life. Deal with it."

Despite her shaken look, Emily managed to defy the ship's dreadful lurching and maintain her balance.

"What is it, exactly? Do you have a quarrel with Mrs. Jiggins? Or have you discovered that she has an ax buried in one of her many trunks and fear she may use it on you tonight when you blow out the candle?"

She looked up at Fly. "Did she, by chance, know that I was on board?"

"How could she have when *I* didn't even know?"

"Captain Austen," said Emily, pausing to take in air. "I know you are not happy with me being here —"

"Frankly, I am not! But now that I can do nothing about it — unless I choose to leave you in the Azores — we must try to get on and hope in the meantime that your family does not hunt us down, because if they do, they will most assuredly expedite Dr. Braden and me to the gallows."

Emily's eyes drifted away from his. She reached out for the Windsor chair with the cracked bottom, her knuckles tightening around its curved top rail. "I am afraid they have already succeeded in hunting me down."

Fly wavered beside his own chair, glowering with suspicion, but try as he might, he could not ignore the succinct knocks shaking his door, begging his attention. Expelling frustration, he gave his blue jacket a tidying tug and strode across the floor to answer it, not in the least surprised to find Leander standing there. His hair was slick with rain; his clothing soaked through to his skin, and there was an untamed expression in his eyes as if he had just seen Davy Jones perched in the rigging.

"Well, old fellow, wonderful to see you draped so elegantly for our supper." Fly's greeting was tight with sarcasm. "At least your timing is impeccable."

Leander swept distractedly past Fly as if he had not heard his flippant remark. "I am so glad to find you both here. I wonder if I might have a word."

"Make it quick." Fly crisply pulled his door shut. "Mrs. Jiggins and her nephew shall be along presently."

"It concerns her nephew," said Leander quietly, shooting a nervous glance at Emily. "Perhaps it is best if we all sat down."

"Why ever not?" cried Fly, gesturing theatrically toward the table.

Her eyes round with fear, Emily searched Leander's face as she lowered herself into the Windsor chair. "Her nephew? Mrs. Jiggins has a nephew on board with her?"

Leander looked quickly in Fly's direction. "As I think it unwise to risk having them show up and overhearing our conversation, might we delay supper?"

Fly's lips thinned in a frozen smile. Retracing his steps, he reached out for the door, his mouth in the ready position to shout out for a messenger who could convey their altered plans to Biscuit and guests alike, but upon throwing it open, he was intercepted.

Laughing in delight at his sudden appearance, Mrs. Jiggins blew into the great cabin on the arm of Mr. Ludlow like a ship with her sails billowing with wind, bringing with her a dense cloud of lavender water.

"Lord above! How does a lady manage to stay upright on this ship? Will it be necessary to always have a man to guide me about?" Espying Leander, she ramped up her sparkle of excitement, helped, no doubt, by the diamond necklace at her throat which had caught and held the lantern lights. "Dear Dr. Braden! So wonderful to see you again! Perhaps I could entice *you* to take me back to my room after supper, so I shan't twist my ankle on the ladders and fall headfirst to my peril." Hit with a tantalizing thought, her smile broadened. "Oh, but just think, should that happen, you could take care of me in your hospital. And I understand your attention to the ladies is beyond reproach."

Leander was at a loss for words and most likely horrified by the possibility.

Linking his arms across his chest, Fly looked back at Emily, who was turning around on her chair in order to see the new arrivals. In spite of his vexatious mood, he was curious to witness any interaction with her *unsuitable* cabin mate; at the same time, he did not want to miss seeing her response to the dashing Mr. Ludlow. Was this not the first time the two had come face to face? When Emily's eyes flitted past Mrs. Jiggins and landed squarely upon her nephew, Fly received no reward for his curiosity. Emily's face had gone white to the lips.

4:30 P.M.
ABOARD HMS *EXPEDITION*

Tired, his belly howling with hunger, Magpie tiptoed across the floor of the great cabin toward the door with his bucket and lantern, terrified of disturbing Captain Uptergrove whilst he was supping. If he did, surely it would result in an angry outburst and a lecture, or worse still, an immediate flogging witnessed by the crew. Sitting alone at his dining table in one of his roomy, red velvet chairs, eating his lamb and potatoes by flickering lantern light, Uptergrove looked like a despairing schoolboy who was being punished for some misdemeanor, but as he was the one who had requested an immediate scrubbing of his lavatory — the second one of the day — he must have been aware of Magpie's presence. And, sure enough, at the first creak of floor timbers, Uptergrove turned his head around, his deadened eyes devoid of surprise as he looked him over.

"Is it clean?" he asked solemnly, his nostrils flaring.

"Aye, sir, as far as I can see, given the mean light in there."

"And are *your* hands clean?"

Magpie nodded vigorously, hoping he would not demand an inspection.

Uptergrove ripped a bread roll in two and placed one half of it in his mouth. Chewing thoughtfully, he stared at his galleried windows, but as the storm had blotted out the early hour, there were no views of the sea, only the reflection of his cabin and its contents.

Magpie resumed his tiptoeing, believing that Uptergrove's silence meant dismissal.

"How did you lose your eye?" he asked abruptly, his dull gaze still directed toward the windows.

An invasion of fluttering nerves struck Magpie's stomach, shoving aside his pangs of hunger. On that awful night when he had been pressed into service on the *Bloody Flux*, he had told Mr. Huxley he was a farm labourer, not a sailor. What if Huxley had shared this information with Uptergrove? Nay! Magpie couldn't trust anyone, not yet, anyway. He didn't dare tell the truth, even though he desperately wanted to.

"It were an accident I had, sir, with — with a pitchfork."

More silence prefaced the arrival of his unsympathetic reply. "I see."

The groaning *Bloody Flux* careened just then as if she had been kicked by a giant foot, and in a shocking contrast of sounds and responses, one of Uptergrove's prized paintings and its supporting easel were upended and came crashing to the floor. Magpie jumped out of his skin. Uptergrove simply went on chewing, disinterested in surveying the damage. Setting down his bucket and lantern, Magpie scrambled to set them upright for him. Carefully, he gathered up the oil painting — a pretty stone cottage on the banks of a blue lake, encircled with big purple hills in the bright distance — and slid his fingers over its frame in search of cracks and chips in the fine woodwork.

"No harm done, sir," he said, sighing with relief as if he had been responsible for the accident.

Uptergrove inclined his head slightly. "Place everything over there, under the windows."

Magpie did as he was told, aware of the snarling, petulant sea winds on the other side of the glass as he gently lay the painting alongside the folded easel on the velvet cushions of the bench seat. From the corner of his eye, he saw a side-blown flute lying abandoned on one of the end cushions. It was beautifully carved and made of bamboo, and Magpie itched to pick it up in his hands. He had not given his own flute a thought for a while now, lost as it was on the *Amethyst* along with

Captain Prickett and the others, all prisoners now and in the hands of the Americans. He wondered if the sullen Uptergrove played the flute when he was alone, and whether he had been doing so when his cook had brought in his supper.

Unable to linger by the bench seat any longer without raising suspicion, Magpie shyly looked over at Uptergrove for further instructions, but the captain was now cutting his meat with a knife and fork, and seemed to have forgotten he was even there. Magpie waited a moment and then went to collect his bucket and lantern, holding his breath as he crept again toward the exit, anxious to be away. He had almost made it out the door when Uptergrove's voice made a chilling return.

"Be careful in this storm."

"I — I will, thank you, sir."

"You would not want to lose your other eye."

"Nay, sir."

"It would be a shame to end up in a poorhouse."

"I wouldn't much like that, sir."

"No. Well. Off you go. I will look for you early in the morning."

His hand on the door latch, Magpie glanced one last time over his shoulder, his eye falling first upon the nest of grey, wiry hair on the back of Uptergrove's head before straying toward the great cabin reflections on the darkened windowpanes. The scene looking back at him sent a cold rush of wind down his neck and a tocsin ringing between his ears.

Uptergrove's eyes were watching him, closely.

5:00 P.M.
(FIRST DOG WATCH, TWO BELLS)
ABOARD HMS *INVINCIBLE*

Pleading a relapse of illness, Emily had glided past those who had gathered together in Captain Austen's cabin for supper without saying a single word to Mrs. Jiggins and her nephew. It would have been unthinkable for her to have stayed. Had she, there was no doubt she would have staged a hysterical performance of indignation and re-crimination alongside a cast of vulgar words no lady should ever utter, let alone be acquainted with. But having no desire to degrade herself in front of Leander and Captain Austen, she had forcibly sealed her lips upon her anger — ready to erupt like Vesuvius — and held her head high until the distance of a full deck had separated them. In the turbulent wake of the shock, she had stumbled about, reaching out for anything fixed to the ship, negotiating the undulating ladders and gangways through a blur of hot tears.

Emily had no idea how she had reached the mess deck, but she sought refuge there behind the nearest oak column to sweep together her broken pieces. Weakened by the rapid thumping of her heart, she felt incapable of making the last leg of her journey to her cabin, espe-cially as it meant bypassing the middy's berth and the dining table in the gunroom, both of which were overflowing with rollicking boys and men. Could she flee past them all without fomenting suspicion? In their open berth, she could see the young midshipmen snacking on hunks of cake and playing a rousing — though otherwise orderly — game of backgammon. And presiding over them all like a crowing rooster was Cadby Brambles, who appeared to be reigning over the farmyard once again. Farther on, she could see Prosper Burgo doing much the same amidst a circle of officers and men that included Mr. Philpotts, Mr. Duffy, and dear old Dr. Braden. Prosper swayed before them at the head of the gunroom table, a tin cup in one hand, holding his audience enthralled — no doubt with tales of heroic escapades on the east coast of British North America. From her vantage point, Emily could not discern if his jerky movements were the result of the heaving sea or of having imbibed copious quantities of drink. But it made her worry. If not Prosper, who then was steering the ship?

"Em!"

The owner of the cheerful squeak was Gus Walby. Spinning around, Emily found him roosting on a three-legged stool in a small, lantern-lit oasis between two long guns, his faithful crutch behind him, propped up against the side of the ship. Beside him sat an older woman dressed demurely in a ribboned mob cap and homespun gown, the colour of which was obfuscated by shadows. She had a linen shirt draped across her knees and was mending a hole in one of its sleeves. On the floor next to her front-laced half-boots were a number of items, among them an etui for her sewing paraphernalia, what looked like a canister of tea, and a wooden tray with a raised border that safeguarded two earthenware mugs from the forceful thrust of the waves.

"Come sit with Miss Braden and me."

Brushing away the tears burning her cheeks, Emily stepped toward them. Miss Braden nodded almost imperceptibly before rounding upon Gus. "Mr. Walby! She is not *Em*," she chastised, her lips contorting with disdain around her words. "She is *Your Highness*."

Emily was about to gently protest, to explain to her the deep friendship she had forged with Mr. Walby on their journeys on the *Isabelle* and the *Impregnable*, but something in the woman's stern demeanor — and the knowledge that she was Leander's aunt — stopped her. A rush of blood warmed her face when she realized that Gus was not going to properly introduce them. But then, perhaps the poor lad was unaware that they had not officially met.

Miss Braden leaned forward on her stool so that she could see around the heavy gun carriage and down the length of the deck. "I was hoping my brother would join us for tea, but evidently he is still sewn up with the men in the gunroom." Her mouth compressed in a sober line. "What is tea when there are spirits to be had?" Reaching down to the tray, she picked up one of the mugs and handed it off to Emily, giving her a cursory glance — the familiar shape and colour of her eyes arresting Emily's notice — before reapplying her attention to the linen shirt.

Murmuring words of thanks, Emily drank the tea down. The comforting warmth appeased her prickling throat that wanted to cough again, and filled her empty stomach that would now remain so until morning. A third stool had been pulled into their small circle, most likely reserved for old Dr. Braden, who had regrettably discovered livelier avenues of entertainment away from them. She was only too happy to sink down upon it now that standing both vertically and with dignity was becoming increasingly difficult. As Miss Braden seemed indifferent to advancing their acquaintance, Emily turned toward Gus. She had been conscious of his close observation of her and could see that his eyes were cloudy with compassion. He must have known she had just received a devastating surprise in Captain Austen's cabin. Surely, Miss Braden knew, as well. In fact, everyone on the ship presumably knew that Lord Somerton Lindsay was on board, come as a special envoy as a favour to her family to cradle and protect her lest she fall prey to the men on the *Invincible*; come as a spy, along with Mrs. Jiggins, ready to record every step she took, every word she spoke, forever on the lookout for her missteps and indiscretions. Had they already informed her family of her whereabouts prior to their embarkation? Ensuring that the moment they landed in Halifax — or Quebec or Bermuda or wherever it was they were headed — her Uncle Clarence and his minions, defying time and travel, would be waiting for her on the decks of the *Impregnable*, keen to clap her in irons, and triumphantly proclaim their victory over her *unmanageable* behaviour. Perhaps Captain Austen's suggestion of leaving her in the remote islands of the Azores was not such a bad idea after all.

Emily tried to set aside her troubles and summoned a brave smile. "Why aren't you having fun with the boys in the middy's berth, Mr. Walby?"

Gus's face awoke from its pitying gaze. "I have had my fill of them. They are far too rumbustious for my tastes."

"What about Cadby Brambles?"

Gus made a succession of scowls. "He is the worst of the lot, and always saves the largest pieces of dessert for himself. And if he does not get his way, he is prone to tantrums."

"Shocking!" gasped Emily, draining her tea.

Miss Braden lifted a double-lensed, single-handled prospect glass from her lap and examined her handiwork before furtively turning it upon Emily, allowing it to linger there until her subject confronted her with a direct look.

"His mama must have spoiled him," said Gus, shaking his head, sounding so wise for his years. "It might teach him a lesson if he were to feel the sting of the birch on his bottom."

"I am sorry he has not proven worthy of friendship," said Emily, "but I fear you keeping company with we ladies will have you grown old before your time."

Her remark elicited an indignant sniff from Miss Braden's quarter.

"Oh! Not at all! I enjoy your company." Gus gave Miss Braden a wary glance as if uncertain whether to include her in his sentiment. "What I would like is to read with you again — when you have the time, of course. I did so like that book written by Miss Austen. Magpie did, too. He never stopped talking about it."

"Well then, let us form a reading circle on this voyage and invite Magpie to join us."

While her suggestion resonated in their private nook between the long guns, a drastic transformation took hold of Gus. He went quiet, and his probing stare beneath his furrowed brow gave her a scare. What had she said to upset him? Did he consider her remiss, disrespectful of Miss Braden, to whom she had not extended the invitation? Emily was on the cusp of putting things to right when Miss Braden suddenly piped in.

"You are referring to Captain Austen's delightful sister Jane, are you not?"

"Yes, I am!" said Emily, forgetting Gus and Magpie for the time.

"Did you know that we were acquainted with her in Hampshire? We were practically neighbours there in the old days," she said, looking up from her mending, the hint of a premeditated smile on her face, as if wise to her agitation.

"Yes, Miss Braden. I have been so informed."

"My mama used to invite Miss Jane's mother to drink tea with her when it was convenient for Mrs. Austen to steal away from the busy hive of the Steventon Rectory. I often joined them."

Emily's smile was a watery one. Had Miss Braden spent the better part of her years drinking tea and mending shirts?

"Sometimes," she went on, blissfully unaware of Emily's melancholic presumptions, "Mrs. Austen would bring along Miss Jane and Charles, her youngest, so they could play together in the back orchard with Leander, who was often visiting with my brother and his wife. They were all so close in age — those young people — and all so endearing." She held the linen shirt up to the lantern light for a final inspection, and with a nod of satisfaction bent over to retrieve her etui. As she tucked away her needles and thread, she shot a sly glance at Emily. "Were you aware that Miss Jane was and still is a favourite of Leander's?"

Emily's face grew hotter. "I have heard him say such nice things about her," she replied evenly. "Mr. Walby and I are great admirers of her writing."

Tipping her mob-capped head to one side, Miss Braden smiled and swiftly added, "And so am I."

Dear God! Would this day ever end? Emily longed for her bed. The reality of having Mrs. Jiggins as a cabin mate no longer seemed a harbinger that her world was coming to an end. She looked at Gus and tried to muster her flagging enthusiasm. "Shall we plan to gather together tomorrow evening to begin our reading of *Pride and Prejudice*? Will you alert Magpie for me?"

Gus's hesitant reply was hindered by the appearance of Cadby Brambles, who had stumbled upon their peaceful oasis, flush of face and reeking of grog.

"Ah! Mr. Walby!" he cried, far too loudly. "I was wondering where you'd gotten to." Recognizing Emily among the stool-perched trio, he gulped. His scarlet cheeks darkened, and when he looked at Gus again, his rounded glance was a blend of wonder and hostility. Soon, however, remembering his manners, he steadied himself against one of the gun carriages and attempted a graceful bow. "Ladies!"

Emily stood up.

"Oh! Are you heading to your cabin, Miss? Seeing as I have been apprised of its location, might I accompany you?" Mr. Brambles staggered toward her, unwittingly including her in the sphere of his nasty breath. "Be on your guard, Miss. There are drunken men roaming these parts. They are lurking everywhere."

At that precise moment, from away down the deck, Emily could hear Prosper Burgo's inebriated acclamations successfully cutting through the general hubbub.

"Gentlemen! Drink up! To our sweethearts and wives! And may all our ladies be as accommodatin' as the buxom Arabella Jiggins ... not rigid-rumped like that other mob-capped woman we got on board."

Peals and chortles of boisterous laughter followed on the heels of his indecent toast. Miss Braden's throat-clearing harrumph was equally as loud. She must have had the *pleasure* of overhearing Prosper, as well, for she vigorously began gathering up her scattered possessions in — what Emily figured was — her determination to rescue her brother from the debauched Invincibles before their toasting plummeted any further into disgraceful territory.

"You are quite right, Mr. Brambles, and I believe *one* of them is standing before me." Emily pushed past him. "I am off to search for Magpie. You didn't happen to see him in the middy's berth, did you?"

"Wot?" Mr. Brambles appeared more dumbfounded than usual. "Magpie?"

Emily swung toward Gus, whose complexion had paled. He fidgeted on his low stool and turned away from her to study something upon the timbered floor. Her confidence waning, her jangled nerves as unstable as the *Invincible* warring with the waves of the Atlantic, Emily's voice was timid. "Mr. Walby? Is it possible Captain Austen has him mending sails below on the fore platform?"

"MAGPIE?" exploded Mr. Brambles. "Miss, if you're talking about that uncultured clod with the green eye patch, you need to know — he's *long* gone. You won't be seeing him again."

Emily sank back down upon the stool, staring at Gus's bowed head, fearing his explanation. When he finally lifted his eyes to hers she could see they were filled with tears.

"Oh, Em!" he cried woefully, "I'm so sorry. I — I thought you knew."

CHAPTER 19

SUNDAY, SEPTEMBER 26
5:15 A.M.
(MORNING WATCH)

D read flowed through Fly's veins. What was it he had just heard? Throwing off his blankets, he sat up in his cot, wiped his eyes and blinked into the darkness, wondering at first if he were dreaming; waiting for the familiar shapes of his dining table and desk to come into bleary focus if he were not. Had morning come already? There was no welcoming glimmer of dawn peering in through the galleried windows; no shouts or stirrings to indicate human life beyond his quarters. But how swiftly his head cleared! Defiant fists of rain pounded upon the dark windowpanes; the wind howled like mourners at a wake, and from far below the steady, grinding sound of the ship's pumps hit his ears. He was awake, all right; though dwelling in a nightmare, for the *Invincible* was still labouring in the grip of an autumn storm.

Insistent knocks shook his door — Fly instantly identifying them as the rousing racket that had awakened him — and from the other side a familiar Scottish accent called out.

"Cap'n Austen?"

"What is it, Biscuit?"

"Sorry to bother ya, sir. Kin I trouble ya to come on deck?"

"What is the time?"

"Between two and three bells in the morning watch, sir. 'Bout a quarter past five."

"Is there anything wrong?"

"Might be, sir. The officer o' the watch said he'd feel a sight better if ya was to come and have a look. It's beyond his ken."

Unhappy at the thought of leaving the comfort of his cabin to be whipped about by the wind, Fly swore under his breath before steadying his response. "I'll be right there," he said, yelling out an afterthought: "Have strong coffee on hand!"

It had been well past midnight when exhaustion had overtaken him and he had dropped into bed, having consumed too much wine and without changing into his nightshirt — things he despised and rarely did, thankfully. Already dressed, he had only to feel around for his boots and rain cloak before setting off, arriving on the quarterdeck in no time. Without delay the cold, shivery arms of the black night wrapped around him. Foaming waves roared past the *Invincible*'s rails, pummeling her hull like a blacksmith hammering upon his lump of iron. The air crackled in a frenzied rush of sounds. He could hear her masts straining and moaning as if in the agonies of childbirth, and the foresail bitterly complaining that it alone was doing all the work. Hurrying toward the helm to stand with Biscuit and Prosper Burgo, he balanced himself against the binnacle that housed the lighted compasses and looked around, his face and hair already drenched in rain.

"*Where* is the officer of the watch?"

Biscuit placed a mug of black coffee into his hands. "Gone below fer a spell, sir. He said he were goin' to git the carpenters' latest soundin' report on the pump well."

"Why? Are we taking on too much water?"

"Some, but nothin' to worry at. Not yet, anyway, sir."

A loud guffaw burst out of Prosper. "More like yer officer o' the watch went below to heave-ho, Cap'n."

"Heave-ho?"

"He said he weren't feelin' so good. Betcha he's spewin' his biscuits into a bucket right about now."

"Oh, I see." Fly quickly gulped down his tepid coffee before icy spoondrift managed to dilute it. "Tell me, Mr. Burgo, was he drinking with you in the gunroom last evening?"

Prosper peered into the blusterous night, his fingers locked around the handles of the wheel; his wispy curls whirling around his ears like a waterspout. "He might 'ave bin. I don't rightly know. I were just there to provide the gents with some evenin' amusement. But either way, Cap'n, it ain't me fault he can't hold his grog."

"Go and get him at once!" Fly demanded of Biscuit, who lumbered off, hunched over against the savage wind. Exasperated, he turned back to Prosper. "Now then. Where away?"

Prosper twisted his neck and nodded in the general direction. "Over there! Two points off the starboard bow. Kin ya see them lights blinkin'?"

Fly studied the watery speck of light, appearing and vanishing and appearing again like a reef marker in the murky distance. Lights were normally doused at night to keep a ship's position secret from enemy forces, so what could this mean? "Hand me your night-glass, Mr. Burgo." Setting down his mug upon the binnacle, Fly squinted through the large lens of the brass and leather telescope, his view hindered by the inverted image it afforded. Most men-of-war were equipped with a framework of lights that could be hoisted up the yards to signal intelligence to sister ships, but this — whatever it was — appeared to be a solitary light.

"Have you seen any flares, Mr. Burgo? Heard any gunshots?"

"Nay! Nothin' at all, Cap'n."

"What is our present speed?"

"We're scuddin' along at nine knots."

"Any soundings?"

"Nay! Ain't been any at all, and I've bin here at the wheel since midnight."

Fly arched his eyebrows. "Do you not require sleep?"

"Sleep? Hah! Who else d'ya got on board what knows how to steer a ship in this bloody rumpus?"

Unwilling to acknowledge the annoying truth, Fly pressed on, grim-faced. "If there have been no soundings, then we can rightly discount the possibility that the winds have pushed us prematurely upon the island of Corvo, and that what we are seeing is a false fire or — or the stern lantern of a Portuguese merchantman."

"In my experience, Cap'n, it usually takes two weeks of sailin' before any chance of raisin' the Islands o' the Azores."

"Ah, but then you, Mr. Burgo, are able to push a ship as no other — storm or no storm — and are quite convinced we can cross the Atlantic in record time."

Fly's compliment wrested a grin from Prosper's pursed mouth. "She's blowin' hard and pushin' us southward o' our course, but I don't figure we'll be seein' the Azores fer a bit yet — not unless these compasses is broke and our dead reckonin' is off."

Fly chewed on his lower lip, at a loss to sufficiently explain the mysterious light. But now the officer of the watch had returned and was reluctantly being conducted along the quarterdeck by Biscuit who — despite the wind's reign of terror — was now strutting like a guardsman holding sway over his prisoner. Scowling, Fly raised his hand to hold them at bay a moment, and then stepped closer to Prosper to air his frustration.

"I should have guessed it was Cadby Brambles who had abandoned his post! He is sorely testing my patience."

"If ya had more lieutenants, Cap'n, ya could leave off assignin' watch duty to the younkers ya have on board and to the likes o' Cadby Brambles. He's a hangdog wretch, that one!"

Fly contemplated Prosper's self-assured profile, and quietly mumbled thanks to the Greater Being for the accident which befell the *Prosperous and Remarkable*. A dozen lieutenants could not possibly match the seaworthiness of the privateersman from Canada.

"Right then, Mr. Burgo. Bring us up to that light. I need a closer look."

"I'll do me best, but ya gotta know the winds will fight us every knot o' the way."

"No doubt! But by all reasoning, it is coming from either the *Expedition* or the *Lady Jane*. And my guess is ... one of them is in trouble."

6:40 A.M.

Emily quickly braided her hair. She was certain she would go crazy if she stayed another minute in her cabin. The mess deck was a furnace of heat. And the smells circulating throughout — sour breath, sweat, and urine, not to mention Mrs. Jiggins's damnable lavender water — pressed upon Emily's chest like a slab of cement, leaving her lungs depleted of oxygen. Worse still had been her dark dreams. They had stalked her throughout the night. Not surprisingly, Magpie had been in every one of them — always in the agonies of drowning — and she had been an impotent onlooker, crying out and imploring the sailors standing idly by to rescue the little lad. No one would chance it except for Leander, who had managed to lower the skiff into the water all on his own. But the powerful waves had cruelly dashed and overturned it, sucking Leander beneath them, leaving Magpie alone in the cold, cruel ocean, screaming as the *Invincible* sailed farther and farther away. Not even wakefulness could guarantee freedom from the appalling dream scenes. They had cornered her like a frothing beast, rendering escape impossible.

Slipping on her shirt and trousers as quietly as possible, Emily tried her best not to cough or trip over a trunk. She could not risk disturbing Mrs. Jiggins. Last evening, she had feigned sleep when the woman had burst through the cabin door all aquiver following her supper with Captain Austen. Emily had successfully thwarted chit-chat then, but now — after such a night — she felt even less inclined to engage in conversation, knowing it would result in verbal warfare. Attending to the final button on her shirt, she glanced over at her cabin mate, swinging in her cot like a child tucked away in its cradle. As her breathing seemed blissful, she was surely dreaming of dinner parties and the attractive men upon whom she might set her cap, totally oblivious to the devastation she had wrought with her appearance — and that of her *nephew* — upon the *Invincible.* How tempted she was to give Mrs. Jiggins's round, drooping rump a good, swift kick before she left her cabin.

Once safely on the other side of her door, Emily waited for her eyes to adjust to the shadows on the mess deck. An oil-lantern swayed above the gunroom table. Its illumination enabled her to see the jumble of sleeping sailors in their hammocks, tightly packed together like fish in a barrel, their snores and wheezes rising and falling with the ship. The hour was surely an early one for there was no one moving about in a bleary-eyed race to fetch the morning rations. Aside from the snoring, the groaning of oak timbers, and the howling wind in the distance, all was strangely quiet. As she mapped out the best route around the hammocks in order to reach the companion way, she heard a door close and the sound of approaching steps. A man, swilling on a tankard, emerged from the gloom. Seeing her, he briefly paused, but said nothing at all as he resumed his steps toward the table. Pulling out the chair beneath the oil-lantern, he dropped down heavily upon it. His frilled, loose-fitting shirt was informal. She had never seen him without a coat and starched cravat. The shadow of a beard darkened his jaw and the wavering light distorted his features, awakening Emily's childhood notions of the legendary, black-faced Hampshire poachers.

"Mr. *Ludlow!*" Her smile was derisive.

His eyes flicked up at her, but he did not take the bait.

"Are you drinking away your sorrows with strong liquor, regretting you ever longed for an adventure at sea?"

"I harbour no regrets. Indeed, the respite from Hartwood Hall has been refreshing."

"Goodness! Given the heat and smell of this deck, your description is amusing." Emily teetered toward him, reaching out for the edge of the warped table. "I admit I am astonished that the storm has not confined you to your cot. I would have enjoyed hearing you crying out for salt beef and mustard to cure your seasickness."

"Then I am sorry to disappoint you."

"I do hope you brought along enough clothes for the voyage. If I remember correctly, the last time we met, you were in such a hurry to return home. I cannot imagine you had a trunk packed away in your barouche in the event that things did not go your way."

"I thought it wise to plan ahead," he replied, unwilling to meet her gloating expression.

"That *is* fortunate! I wonder though, has anyone informed you that you shall be responsible for your own laundry and mending? I highly doubt your Mrs. Jiggins can be relied upon to help you out."

He smiled to himself. "Well then, perhaps *you* can do it! Didn't needlework form the basis of your education?"

"Oh no! Why would I agree to that when you shall provide us with such entertainment as you try to solve the mysteries of a needle and thread?" She leaned in over the table. "What's more, now that you are here and so full of gusto to play at being a seaman, I am keen to witness how well you fare when the guns start firing, when the ship is pumped full of holes and the decks run red with blood."

Flexing his fingers around the tankard, he finally lifted his hardened eyes to hers. "How interesting — when I can say the *very* same about you."

A piercing whistle sliced through the jagged silence that followed. Emily flinched at its suddenness. To her it had sounded like a gun blast. Turning around, she could see the boatswain, holding his lantern high, wading into the sea of sleepers.

"Up all hammocks ahoy!" he bellowed. "Beggars awake! Look lively! What're ya waitin' fer? Yer ma's teat? Tumble up! NOW!"

A vapour of moans and curses seeped from the men's hammocks. And yet, before long, their occupants exploded into action, goaded on by the boatswain who continued his morning reveille by heaping abuse upon all laggards. Hammocks were flipped and stowed, lanterns were lit, shoes were sought, and stiffened limbs attempted to fill trousers and shirts. Emily looked on, knowing her hopes of gaining the ladder were now dashed. There would soon be a herd of men trampling up the rungs. Eager to leave Lord Somerton to his wine, loathing the displeasing feel of his eyes on her, she sought the strength of an oak post and stood helplessly by, wondering if she could withstand returning to her cabin.

"Reef up the foresail!"

"Heave to! Heave to!"

"All hands on deck!"

"Lower the boats — fore and aft."

Everyone stopped in their tracks. Ears were cocked to these new shouted commands that came from above through the amplification of the master's trumpet. The men eyed each other in their confusion. Lowering the boats? What was all that about? Questions were fired around their number with alacrity; reasons put forth and discarded. Emily tensed up. Had someone fallen overboard? Had her nightmares of Magpie drowning become a horrific reality for one or more of the Invincibles?

The boatswain was quick to dispel the chatter. "Ya heard the orders! Somethin's afoot! Now git a move on!" he bawled.

Behind Emily, the doors of the cabins opened one by one. Senior, junior, and petty officers poured out onto the deck, some of them carrying lanterns. They fanned out around the gunroom table, their faces rumpled with concern. Emily spotted old Dr. Braden among them, his sister, already dressed in her mob cap and homespun, holding on to his arm. Mrs. Jiggins could be heard, loud and clear, even before she jumped into view, her cheeks as white as Cornish pasties, swaddled in bedclothes with a turban plopped hastily upon her head to conceal the curling papers in her hair.

"What's going on? Are we sinking? Are we going down? Oh! I fear I have the staggers! Where is Dr. Braden? I must have a tonic of opium and camphor at once."

But there was no sign of Leander.

That was it. Emily was going up with the men — herd or no herd. She gave Lord Somerton a withering glance. He was standing now as if unsure of what to do, how to react, his expression pleading for an explanation. Masking her own alarm, she refused to do anything to allay his.

"I think it best you stay below, Lord Somerton."

"Why?" he asked, his eyes shining in the lantern light.

"Because I am quite certain you will only get in the way."

8:30 A.M.
(FORENOON WATCH, ONE BELL)
ABOARD HMS *EXPEDITION*

Magpie tried to squeeze his way through to the starboard rail, but there was an unbroken wall of men standing there like links of a heavy chain, and no one seemed keen to break it so that the lad with the eye patch and offensive bucket could have a look. Undeterred, he continued searching for an opening, keeping his eye prudently averted from the fore shrouds where two naughty midshipmen, upon Captain Uptergrove's insistent orders and despite the fierce weather, had been seized up for hours. Magpie could not bear the sight of their shivering bodies nor hear their whimpering pleas to be released. What was worse, they had been put there as punishment for nothing more than a minor misdemeanour. Mr. Huxley had lowered his hard-nosed guard long enough to tell him that the boys had been accused of "a bit o' rumbustious play while stagin' a mock battle durin' their leisure time."

It was now widely known among the crew that Captain Uptergrove possessed a wicked temper. Already, Magpie had seen much evidence of it. And they had only been at sea for a week! The Bloody Fluxes often whispered that Uptergrove "was a floggin' cap'n, the worst kind." But there was no time to dwell upon that now, especially when — little more than a lob of spittle from their starboard bow — there was a ship going down.

Locating a secure spot for his shoes and bucket near the ship's bell, Magpie decided to take his chances on the bowsprit. There, he could get a clear view not only of the foundering vessel, but of that second, larger ship which had come through the storm to her aid. He chewed on his lip as he mulled things over. By chance, were these the two ships he had seen sailing close to them ever since they had left Portsmouth? Were they travelling to the Barbary Coast and the River Styx, as well? Did they possess names on their sterns as foul and ugly-sounding as the *Bloody Flux*?

Inching his way along the bowsprit, he was careful not to go beyond the figurehead on the prow. Should there be any unforeseen listing beneath him, it might save him from being pitched overboard. Locking his legs around the solid length of oak, he lifted his shirt — already soaked through with spoondrift — and removed the spyglass he had found earlier, abandoned on the forecastle on top of a crate, home to a nervous hen. Hopefully, no one had seen him take it. He didn't want to be seized up to the shrouds and tortured alongside the weeping midshipmen.

The winds had died down and the waves were not running as high as they had been earlier. But the sky was still an unbroken, moody mass of grey, similar in colour to the nest of wiry hair on Captain Uptergrove's head. It seemed to begrudge the arrival of morning, unwilling to give the sailors sufficient conditions with which to carry out their rescue mission. Would those clouds soon drop their cold needles of rain upon them once again? Magpie hoped not. An attempt to reach the survivors might then prove impossible.

Out on the sea, the poor little ship had careened over on her side, exposing her copper-plated hull. Her sails had been torn from their braces and stays, and her twin masts bobbed in the water like storm-shattered limbs of a tree. Many of her men — excluding those thrashing in the water, struggling to reach the boats battling their way toward them — were clinging to her larboard rail as her starboard side was already submerged. Others were trying to escape through her unwieldy gunports. Magpie hated hearing their cries for help, and was so grateful he could not clearly see their faces. But oh, how he shuddered in sympathy, knowing something of their terror.

Behind him on the quarterdeck, Captain Uptergrove shouted for the remaining boats to be manned and lowered from their skid cradles. Through the spyglass, Magpie watched the same being done on the large ship that had come to assist, her crew running around, colliding with each other in their attempts to swiftly reach their various stations. Oh! And there was their captain! He stood out from all the others — an imposing figure in his billowing rain cloak and blue bicorne, worn amidships upon his head. From across the water, his orders to his men were inaudible, but as he moved around the quarterdeck, his arm-waving and finger-pointing suggested they were much the same as Uptergrove's. Magpie kept the spyglass trained upon the unknown captain, determined to avoid looking upon the harrowing scenes in and around the little sinking ship, worried — if he glanced in her direction — he might catch sight of bodies drifting upon the waves, lifeless and terrible.

When the bustle on the decks had swallowed the captain up and he vanished from view, Magpie began scanning the stem-to-stern arrangement of his ship. To be sure, she was a fifth-rate frigate: three-masted, flush-decked with one continuous deck of guns above the waterline. She looked solid and weatherly, and — and — he fumbled with the spyglass, nearly dropping it. What a knuckle-head he was! How could he not have noticed before now? There was a Nelson chequer painted upon her hull! Her gun deck was yellow and her gunports black, giving her the look of a sailor's checked shirt and ... a certain familiarity. With trembling fingers, he held the spyglass aloft once more, his innards thrumming with emotions that seemed to soar on unseen wings high above the fore royal yard. Until he knew for sure, he could not leave the bowsprit. Endless, anxious moments dragged by while he waited for the ocean currents to nudge the frigate around so that he could look upon her stern, so full of fear that, at any second, Uptergrove would sneak up behind him, seize him by the neck and demand his privy be scrubbed before the noonday meal.

"Please, please hurry up!" he urged the sea waves.

For once good fortune had landed in his lap. Was there someone nearby, willing to give him a hug? There — there it was — her name, painted in gold lettering upon a black background in the upper curve of the stern, just above the windows of the great cabin! Magpie jumped up on the bowsprit to laugh and whoop. He could not care less if the winds carried him overboard or if his jubilant dance was frowned upon by those Bloody Fluxes who, on account of it, might have been distracted from the tragedy of the sinking ship.

It was true, he could not read. He had no literary skills whatsoever, but he knew *that* particular word, having seen it a dozen times while standing on the Portsmouth wharves in the days before they had left England. Sitting there in the Atlantic, no farther away than a broadside's sweeping reach, was the *Invincible*. And that unknown captain he had followed with interest around her quarterdeck was none other than Captain Francis Austen!

9:00 A.M.
(FORENOON WATCH, TWO BELLS)

Trevelyan could not believe his hard luck. To be sure it was as rotten as the timber planks of the foundering *Lady Jane*. Unable to handle the overnight throttling of wind and waves, she was going down, and in doing so she had cozily brought the crew of the *Invincible* within a stone's throw of the *Expedition*, leaving *him* standing face to face with his enemies.

He pushed away angrily from the fore-rail. He was weary of watching the madness unfolding around the *Lady Jane*; besides, he harboured no sympathy for the well-being of her stricken crew. As far as he was concerned, they could all perish in the ocean. It would serve them right for endangering him by summoning the *Invincible* and the *Expedition* to the deathbed of their enfeebled ship. Indubitably, if he were to tarry at the rail, that clever devil, Captain Austen, would eventually espy him. Maybe the grave academic, Emily's Dr. Braden, would be the lucky one to capture the biggest prize of all, or — Trevelyan laughed aloud — even Emily herself.

He ground his teeth together. Above all things, he did not fancy returning to a prison beneath the waterline. Perhaps the woolly thrum cap he was presently wearing upon his head would throw them off his scent should one of them — with the assistance of a spyglass — be studying the faces of the spectators pushing up against the *Expedition*'s rail. He might be deficient of good fortune on this day, but what a small stroke of luck to have found the thrum cap abandoned in the hold on the morning they had left Portsmouth, and to have no one report it missing. Could it be relied upon to serve him well? He crossed his fingers in the hopes that, to all lookouts, he would be identified as the *Expedition*'s carpenter, not Trevelyan the traitor, the condemned criminal who had magnificently eluded the bumbling Royal Navy and the gallows at Newgate Prison.

With renewed determination to remain undiscovered, he set off toward the clerk's office where much work was awaiting his attention. But something on the bowsprit caught his eye. He stopped short to gape. A curly-haired imp was jumping up and down, his face glazed in smiles, one hand intertwined in a clutch of knotted ropes to keep him from falling into the Atlantic. How preposterous, mused Trevelyan, that the boy's demeanour should appear jovial and celebratory, and entirely out of line with the sombre events of the morning. Oh, hell, what did he care? Shrugging it off, he returned his thoughts to the myriad assignments Uptergrove had asked him to complete before the day was over, knowing that the adjoining of men from the crew of the *Lady Jane* to their own would increase his workload tenfold. But a slight turn of the boy's head did not escape his notice. Neither did the round patch of green that covered up one of his eyes.

Trevelyan stood there completely stunned as if someone had accosted him and slammed the barrel of a gun into his chest. A wave of repugnant memories nearly felled him. Moving his hands over his thighs, he felt for the ragged holes where two portentous dirks had once done serious damage and began cursing like a tinker, knowing full well he was not mistaken. It was that foundling ... that mongrel ... that puny sailmaker from the *Isabelle* who had wielded those dirks and spewed vomit all over him in a seedy Charleston tavern.

And wasn't it just Trevelyan's luck that the mongrel and he were so intimately acquainted with one another?

CHAPTER 20

H aving relieved yet another survivor of his anxiety and seen to it that he was provided with a blanket, Leander took some time for himself beside the ship's bell where the master of the sandglass was about to strike the half-hour. Fatigue washed over him in successive waves like those that endlessly crashed upon the rugged Cornish coast. He longed for a chair. If he closed his eyes, would he be able to open them again? From the moment Fly first realized the *Lady Jane* was in trouble, Leander had been on duty, and from the looks of it, it would be hours before he was reunited with his bed.

Leander examined the activity around him on the weather decks. Another boatload of survivors was being helped aboard. There was quite a crowd of them now. Wherever space could be found, they sat quietly with their thoughts, some of them still shaking from their unexpected swim in the Atlantic, others curled up and sleeping off their ordeal.

Mr. Duffy and Mr. Philpotts were busy distributing grey wool blankets. Gus Walby was recording their names in the ship's muster-book. Leander's father had jumped in to assist with brief examinations of the men and to bandage up those who had been knocked about while trying to escape, their jumpers and trousers red from the hemorrhaging of head and leg wounds. Hovering near to him was Aunt Eliza in her mob cap, looking stiff and uncomfortable in the presence of so much masculinity. And there was Emily. Leander hated her being out in the cold morning, but he could not help smiling. Her shirttails and long braid of golden hair were flying in the wind, and in her buff trousers she blended well with the seasoned sailors. With ease, she moved among the Lady Janes, holding high Biscuit's prized Sheffield-plate coffee pot, offering smiles and words of encouragement as she filled up their mugs and cans. A flush-faced Cadby Brambles was glued to her side, holding plates laden with cheese and biscuits, seemingly gratified to be moving about with her, shooting haughty, look-at-me glances at the unsuspecting Gus Walby whenever the two crossed paths.

Of all the scenes playing out upon the decks of the *Invincible*, there was one that struck Leander as absurd. Their two passengers were relaxing on the stern bench in their Sunday best, engrossed in the rescue operation as if it were a masquerade at the Vauxhall Gardens. Fortified with the tonic to ease her staggers, Mrs. Jiggins appeared intoxicated, cackling with delight as she eyed the new crop of men coming on board from behind her fan of bright colours. Beside her, Lord Somerton sat slumped and glowering, his eyes following Emily's progress around the deck. Leander's first instinct was to stride over to their snug corner and task them with onerous chores, but his annoyance was dampened by the appearance of Biscuit, who scurried past him — head into the wind like the figurehead of a ship — clutching a suspicious bottle in either hand.

"Biscuit! Did you steal those from the spirits' room?"

"Nay, Doctor! It's from me own store o' rum ... what I use fer makin' me special biscuits. Ya gotta know ... coffee ain't enough fer these lads. They've lived through a shock. A wee dram will bring 'em 'round agin."

"No doubt! But once those bottles have been drained, might I suggest you see to boiling up a cauldron of soup? Our numbers may swell considerably before noon and they must all be fed something hot," said Leander, sighting two more of the *Invincible*'s boats, pulling toward them, packed to the gunwales with glum survivors.

"No worries, sir! I left Jim Beef in charge o' vittles — should be plenty o' pea soup to go 'round ere long."

Biscuit cheerfully scampered off to dole out his warming splashes of rum, leaving Leander alone to assess the wisdom of serving spirits to the newcomers. High above his head, a litany of distinctive mutterings interrupted his tired thoughts. Glancing upward, he spotted the afore-mentioned Mr. Beef, swinging easily along the ropes of the standing rigging like a monkey at play. As if cognizant that he now had an audi-ence in the ship's doctor, Mr. Beef shored up his mutterings.

"Straight down to the old locker with all o' yas," he howled, casting an evil eye over the ruins of the *Lady Jane*. "Untold terrors be waitin' there: flesh-eaters and phantoms and swarms of eels! Ah! Death and woe!"

Leander rolled his eyes in frustration as he brought them down to deck level once again and found Fly standing in front of him, looking as limp and spent as an old shoe.

"Dear God, Lee! Do you think I am hell-fired? Was I born under an inauspicious constellation of stars?" Bewilderment glazed his eyes. "I did *not* set sail on a Friday, and I have yet to see Mother Carey's chickens! But here we have it! Another misfortune! And we have only just left England."

"It is not your fault that the *Lady Jane*'s pumps could not keep up with the storm."

"No, but I somehow feel responsible for her aged oak timbers. Our fleet is full of ailing ships, and we have no other choice than to push them to their limits. The Admiralty saves the very best to fight the French while we are expected to ward off the Americans with the rotting dregs."

"If her timbers were in such bad shape, is it not ironic that she beat us back to Portsmouth during our last cruise? The gales we lived through then did not seem to hinder her whatsoever."

"No," said Fly, as if his thoughts were miles away. His bloodshot eyes slid away from Leander and came to rest upon the half-submerged *Lady Jane* where the last of her crew, hoping to escape a watery end, were clinging to her upturned keel. "The truth is I can use the extra men and I am certain Uptergrove can, as well, but the loss of another ship and her cargo! The least I can hope for is that some of it shall be saved. But there is little time left to do so. She's going down fast."

As Leander's first concerns were for her survivors, he did not question the *Lady Jane*'s cargo. "There are not enough blankets to go around. These men must be sent below to warm up. I have already asked for the portable stoves to be lighted on the mess deck."

"I hope you and your father have checked them over for lice and open sores and various diseases before we unleash them upon our own men."

"We have and will continue to do so." Leander gave him an indulgent smile. "And could you please have a word with Mr. Philpotts? He is so cranky and difficult, but he must scrounge up some dry clothes for them; otherwise, I fear they shall all come down with pneumonia."

"You are such a prophet of doom," Fly said wearily.

"To the same degree as our friend, Davy Jones?" Leander gestured above his head.

Fly watched in wonder as Jim Beef climbed ever higher on the rigging. "Nay! Not as bad as that!" he huffed. "Right then, I shall do battle with Mr. Philpotts so long as you ask Biscuit to quietly slip me a cup of cheer, or whatever it is he has in those bottles."

Leander ambled toward the break in the starboard rail where the latest group of survivors stood huddled, waiting to be told what to do. As he sidestepped the Lady Janes reposing on the quarterdeck, he glanced across the water at the *Expedition*. She was no longer a dreamy speck floating on the ocean. Having heaved to so near to them, her crew had come into focus. It was now easy to discern the officers from the ordinary seamen, and the men from the boys. His eyes were drawn to a small face framed in dark curls, sandwiched between two grumpy-looking jacks at the rail and struggling to see what was going on.

"Upon my soul!" he whispered as ghostly fingers flitted across his heart.

Quickly, he skimmed the quarterdeck for Fly, hoping, but unable to find him. Neither could he see Emily; a sea of grey wool blankets had swallowed her whole. And Biscuit? He was too far away, out of earshot. Hurrying toward the *Invincible*'s rail, he searched for the small face on the *Expedition*, desperate for another look — a closer look — but the jacks had kicked the boy away from the rail as if he were a vessel of bubonic plague. For a while Leander stayed stock still, his heart leaping in his chest, fervently hoping the little head would reappear somewhere else along the side of the ship.

But it never did.

Reluctantly, he moved on, chiding himself as he put one foot in front of the other. "False hopes, Leander. Nothing but false hopes."

10:00 A.M.
(FORENOON WATCH, FOUR BELLS)

"Oh, I am much improved and enjoying myself immensely," cried Mrs. Jiggins with glee, fluttering her fan before her rosy, steaming cheeks.

Somerton curled his lips in disgust. "You are tipsy! Anyone looking at you would think you had poured a can of whiskey over your morning porridge."

"Have you no sympathy for my nerves, young man?" Mrs. Jiggins pouted as she made pat adjustments to her draped silk turban. "If I am to survive weeks of having to totter like an old cart around this ship, with no opportunities to organize balls and with no one to dress my hair, and then — and then on top of it all be forced to witness the horrors of shipwrecks, I am going to require regular tonics."

Somerton said nothing at first, knowing full well — though hating to admit it — that he could have used something to calm his own nerves. He had no interest sitting in the midst of such vexing ship-sinking scenes beyond his inherent need to make certain the timbers of the *Invincible* were seaworthy and did not break apart like those of the *Lady Jane*'s. He wondered again how his youngest brother, Octavius, had managed to tolerate the life of a seaman before his untimely death.

"You should have stayed in bed to sleep it off."

"And miss all this excitement?" Mrs. Jiggins beamed at the Lady Janes as they came stumbling on board. "Oh, so many lovely ones!"

Somerton's eyes bulged in their sockets. "To what are you referring?"

"Why, all these men, of course! They make me feel scrumptiously alive."

"I cannot believe you are hungering for jack tars with grey teeth and greasy bodies."

"My word! That Prosper Burgo is glancing my way again." Mrs. Jiggins waved her fan flirtatiously at the helmsman who was striking a jaunty pose at the ship's wheel, with one hand on his hip and an unmistakable leer on his face.

"Good God! The man looks like a beet-red fox in trousers! And — I might add, having once had the misfortune of standing close to him — he is so redolent of onions."

"But Captain Austen claims he possesses many redeeming qualities."

"Such as?"

"He did not actually say."

"Aha! Well, I would say there is a dash of rascality about Mr. Burgo."

Mrs. Jiggins covered her mouth with her lacy-gloved fingers and giggled.

Somerton glared at her happy profile. "And here I thought it was bad enough that you had set your cap upon the ridiculous Duke of Clarence."

"Oh! Tush! When did I ever?" She flicked her fan at him and sat forward on the bench, her eyes earnestly searching the ever-widening flock of men before her as if she were trying to locate someone in particular. "Now there is one man I *truly* admire."

Following her dreamy gaze, Somerton was dismayed to find it had landed upon Leander Braden. "You cannot be serious! That rack of bones? He's a featherweight, as light as a kite. I'm surprised the wind has not yet carried him off."

"Not only is he lithe and graceful —" she paused to suck in a mouthful of air "— he has magnificent bone structure! And those eyes of his! Striking! I do believe he can see directly into my locker of private thoughts."

Somerton's resentment scaled new heights as did his desire to deflate her turbaned head. "I believe he cannot."

"And how would you know?"

"He would have jumped overboard by now."

"Fiddlesticks!" she wheezed, striking him in the arm with her fan.

"Really, Arabella, must I remind you that you are here as a favour to the Prince Regent and his family?"

"Do not stress yourself! I shall epitomize the perfect chaperon."

"You shall be more than that. You will teach Emily to be a lady, befitting her birth."

Mrs. Jiggins lent a touch of drama to her slurred words. "I shall be her mother and governess, her director and protector."

"And when you are done with her," continued Somerton with urgency, "she will understand the folly of being an adventuress and marrying beneath her station."

Whisking her attention away from Dr. Braden's bone structure, she arranged her features in a prim mask of sincerity. "So long as you do not insist that I try to convince her to marry your brother, Wetherell. Any woman would hang herself from the bedpost before riding below the crupper with him."

Somerton wrinkled his nose in disgust. He could not stomach her vulgarity. And here, within days of embarking on the *Invincible*, she had already embraced the coarse vocabulary of Prosper Burgo. Thank goodness he no longer had to play at make-believe that they shared a kinship.

"So why are *you* on this ship, Lord Somerton?" she asked, thrusting her glistening face into his.

He quickly glanced away. "I, too, am here on behalf of the Prince Regent."

"Oh ho! Did you think you could pull the wool over my eyes?"

"Your tonic has made you nonsensical."

"Has it?" she asked vacantly, cocking her head to watch in admiration as Dr. Braden accepted a mug of coffee from Emily. It was some time before she spoke again, and when she did, her voice was robust with resolve. "Well, know this! I have a scheme up my sleeve of which you shall approve wholeheartedly."

Having noted the exchange of affectionate smiles between Leander and Emily and wishing he could overhear their whispered words to one another, Somerton's reply was testy. "Pray, do tell!"

"All in good time, Lord Somerton!" Crushing her fan against her bosom, Mrs. Jiggins hooted with sudden glee. "Blessed day! The sun is finally peeking through those atrocious clouds. Now where in the world is Miss Braden? Can you see her? There — there she is with her brother! I must go to her and tell her to prepare for our first painting circle after luncheon."

With astonishing agility, she hopped up and was away, leaving Somerton alone with his peevish thoughts. Slouching against the stern bench, he pulled down the brim of his top hat and launched *sotto voce* curses at the doctor and his lady.

1:00 P.M.
(AFTERNOON WATCH, TWO BELLS)

Leander peered over his spectacles in order to make a positive identification. Was that really the captain he was seeing, squeezing his way into the disorderly hospital, trying to keep a bowl of pea soup firmly in his grasp to avoid an errant elbow or head from upending it? Could it be? Was that soup actually destined for *his* consumption? Weaving his way toward Fly, Leander took delivery of it with a surprised but appreciative smile.

"Captain Austen, have you forsaken your duties as our leader to bring sustenance to overworked doctors?" he asked, bolstering his voice to be heard over the din of chatter.

"Biscuit placed it in my care as I was passing through the galley. He was worried that you had not eaten anything today. Now, I do apologize for neglecting to bring a spoon; however, I do have some bread for you." Reaching into the breast of his jacket, Fly produced an overbaked, green-speckled roll and handed it off to Leander. "It looks like something you would see doled out on a prison hulk, but I am certain it will soften up nicely in the soup."

Accustomed to the inferior quality of shipboard victuals, Leander did not blanch. "Did Biscuit manage to entice Jim Beef down from the shrouds and back into the galley to help out?"

"No! The last I saw of Mr. Beef, he was nesting on the main top like a prodigious raven protecting his young. However, Biscuit did manage to secure some assistance from a most surprising quarter."

Leander raised an inquisitive eyebrow as he tasted his soup.

"Your Aunt Eliza."

"Wonders never cease!"

"I doubt she will relinquish mending for full-time employment in the galley, but she jumped at the opportunity to help out as a means of evading Mrs. Jiggins and her proposal of an afternoon painting circle."

Leander rolled the tension from his shoulders. "England has just lost another ship and Mrs. Jiggins can think of nothing but her own pleasures." His eyes wandered to the square of sea afforded through the nearest open gunport. The weather had changed dramatically while he had been labouring in the hospital. Gone were the low-hanging, black mists and the cresting waves. They had been driven back by a legion of golden clouds. "Well, I'll be damned! Mother Nature! She unleashes her winds to destroy our ships and take lives, and then sends the sun out to play to taunt our calamities." He looked back at his friend. "Please tell me Mrs. Jiggins has not set up her easels and pots of paint on deck."

"Do not fear! To keep her out of the way, I insisted she set up her circle in my cabin."

Leander whistled. "You run the risk of permanently losing your cabin to her and her many schemes. Take care!"

"You are probably right. Mrs. Jiggins will most likely be the cause of my death. How wise our Royal Navy is to discourage *women* on board while at sea."

Ignoring Fly's meaningful glance, Leander set down his bowl on the only uncluttered corner of his desk and began stuffing pieces of the stale roll — the ones as yet untouched by mould — into his hungry mouth. While he ate he watched Fly appraise the situation around them. There were at least thirty Lady Janes spread out on the hospital floor, some in a state of undress, all awaiting their examination.

Another twenty or so were jammed into the dispensary. Ameliorated by food, warmth, and a sound ship, they appeared to be in good spirits, sharing and commenting upon each other's versions of the shipwreck. Not one of them seemed ruffled by the strident demands of Mr. Duffy, who displayed extreme agitation as he went about recording names and medical histories into a journal, and no one paid heed to Mr. Philpotts, who huffed and puffed in annoyance as he distributed articles of dry clothing. In stark contrast, Leander's father went about his work — taking pulses, assessing wounds, and peering down throats — with a quiet competence.

Fly directed a scowl and an order at the agitated surgeon's assistant. "Mr. Duffy, we could do with more balm and less bark, thank you." He crossed his arms upon his chest to indicate his displeasure, but tempered his voice for Leander. "So then, Lee, what do we have here?"

"A few broken legs, the usual cuts and bruises, some anxiety and indigestion, disorders of the bowel and — naturally — a few cases of lues venerea."

"Naturally!"

"Which vastly pleases Mr. Duffy, who has informed the victims that they must pay for their treatment."

"Wicked scoundrel!"

Leander was quick to challenge him. "Ah, but is his greed any worse than allowing Biscuit to charge the men for a spoonful of slush to spread upon their bread?"

"Given the rancid state of our butter and cheese, I feel his slush fund is justified." Having completed his appraisal, Fly edged his way back to the hospital door. "By the way, Mrs. Jiggins was hoping that *you* would join her circle, but I see I was right when I informed her that you would be held captive down here until we raise Halifax ... should we make it that far."

"As she knows of your interest in sketching and mapping, how was it *you* managed to evade her?"

"I was all but forgotten when she succeeded in nabbing a bigger prize."

"A prize bigger than you, Captain Austen?"

"Aye! Your Emily!"

"Good God! I would have thought Emily had bolted to the galley along with my aunt."

"On the contrary. She seemed quite agreeable." Fly abruptly put an end to their banter. "My main purpose in coming here was to let you know that I shall be meeting with Captain Uptergrove as soon as we are able to lash our ships together. It is imperative that we discuss the distribution of these men and determine which one of us shall be responsible for writing the necessary communications. And then, of course, an inventory of all that has been salvaged of the *Lady Jane's* cargo must be carried out. I may be gone for some time."

"Did you want me to accompany you?"

"No! Though it grieves me to think that I cannot trust any of my young lieutenants, I am leaving you and Prosper in charge. Gus Walby can come with me. It will be an adventure for the lad. But while I am away, might I give you a word of advice?"

Concerned by the shadow of gravity darkening his friend's features, Leander stooped toward him, curious to know what he had to say.

"Have your father keep an eye on things here for a while and go swing by my cabin."

"I am afraid Mrs. Jiggins would find me a most untalented and uncooperative student," said Leander in protest.

"Perhaps, but you would not want to be outshone by Lord Somerton, would you? His character may be questionable, but he is — what I believe the ladies would call — a handsome gentleman." Fly gave him one of his slow-dawning smirks. "And, in my opinion, his clothes are much smarter than yours."

CHAPTER 21

1:30 P.M.
(AFTERNOON WATCH, THREE BELLS)
ABOARD HMS *EXPEDITION*

Magpie emerged from the great cabin privy with his fingers crossed behind his back, but it soon became apparent that his gesture was all for naught. Captain Uptergrove was still scribbling letters at his dining table, his greying head hunched over his quill pen. It had been Magpie's hope that ship business would have called the captain away long before he had finished up with his cleaning, especially as everything was in an uproar with the *Lady Jane* having gone down. He didn't like being alone with Uptergrove. There was something about the way the captain stared at him — or beyond him — that gave Magpie a creeping feeling as if there were a ghostly figure wavering in his small shadow. What's more, Magpie was itching to get a good long look at the new oil painting Uptergrove had on display. The pretty cottage by the lake was still there, but now beside it, on an easel of its own, was a gilded portrait of four young children:

two girls and two boys, the youngest one just a toddler in skirts. Even though Magpie had only caught a fleeting glimpse of the painting upon entering the great cabin, he had instantly been smitten by the family's happy expressions and the warmth of their surroundings. There was a saucy cat and a caged bird in it, too. And the older boy was playing a flute! He wondered if it might be the very same one that the captain kept on the cushions under his galleried windows.

Uptergrove lifted his flinty eyes from his letter and peered at Magpie through the ornate branches of his silver candelabrum. "Well?"

Magpie set his bucket down gently to keep it from rattling upon the polished oak floor. "Sir?"

"Is it clean?"

"Aye, sir."

"And your hands?"

"Oh, very clean, sir," he hurried to say, holding them up for inspection.

"And did you sprinkle the rosewater about in there as I asked you to?"

"I did, sir."

Uptergrove's pale gaze would not relent. It rolled over Magpie as if he were a joint of salted beef available for purchase in the victualing yard. To escape its unwanted scrutiny, Magpie turned aside and sought comfort in the family portrait. His chest swelled with longing. The children seemed so content. One of the girls was curtseying in her yellow- and pink-flowered gown and the littlest one was clapping his hands, perhaps in reaction to the tune his older brother was playing on the flute. And, aye! Magpie was sure of it now. It *was* the beautifully carved, bamboo flute sitting on Uptergrove's window cushions. And the cat — oh, my — he had such an amusing expression upon his furry face as if he were plotting to eat the bird in the cage. And on the carpet by the wee one's feet, there was a magnificent, silver fruit bowl, stuffed with glistening apples, plums, and cherries. And the room in which they had all come together looked so cozy and inviting, full of rich furnishings and stuff, the likes of which Magpie had only seen once in his whole life ... at Bushy House, the home of the Duke of Clarence.

"My children."

Magpie was embarrassed by his impertinence. "Yer a lucky man, sir."

"Yes. I believe so."

There was no pride or fervour in Uptergrove's voice; it sounded strangely empty, as if he were speaking of his squat-bottomed inkwell ... not his family. Magpie waited for him to say something more, digging his toenails into the soles of his shoes as he watched him trying to sharpen the nib of his quill with a penknife.

"Do *you* have a family?" he asked, finally discarding the pen and pulling a new quill from a bundle of fresh ones sitting on the table by his forearm.

"Nay, sir! I weren't nothin' but one o' Mr. Hardy's climbin' boys in London."

Uptergrove's eyebrow shot up in a half moon. "In London? Whereabouts?"

"I don't rightly recall, sir. All's I remember is there were a lively fish market nearby."

"I thought you said you had been a farm labourer ... that you had lost your eye to an accident with a pitchfork."

Magpie's stomach went all queasy, as if he had been caught stealing the apples from the fruit bowl in the oil painting. "Oh, that were later on, sir, after I were done climbin'."

"I am certain Mr. Huxley had said something about you having a mama."

"She — she weren't me real ma, sir. She only took me in 'cause she felt pity fer me."

"I see."

The way Uptergrove licked and then flattened his lips made Magpie queasier still. He despised himself for his lies. If he should ever receive an opportunity to reveal his story, how could he tell the captain that he was really a sailmaker; that a splinter of oak from the warring *Isabelle* had destroyed his eye, and that the only family he had ever known was on the *Invincible* ... the very ship that was now tacking on the ocean, a few hundred yards from their aft end. Surely, he would be punished with a tremendous whipping for telling such fibs. Or maybe Uptergrove would have him — would have him shot on sight!

"You passed the word for me, sir?"

The voice in the doorway caught Magpie unawares. Abandoning his bucket, he sidled behind Uptergrove's children, hoping the vast, red velvet chairs that encircled the dining table would shield his shaking legs from detection, knowing full well the family portrait would not.

"There you are, Mr. Bumpus." Shoving his own chair backwards, Uptergrove stood up. "As soon as our ship is securely lashed to the *Invincible*, Captain Austen and his clerk shall be paying us a visit."

Magpie bit down on his fist. His head started to spin. Captain Austen? Here? On the *Bloody Flux*? Were his ears playing a cruel trick on him? Or were his prayers about to be answered? Dear God, what did Mr. Bumpus think of it all? Had he wet his trousers? Had a lump of bile lodged in his throat? Was that why he was awfully slow to reply, and when he finally did so, he sounded as if he had fallen ill with the croup?

"And how may I be of service, sir?"

"First off, I shall require a clerk to be present at our meeting. There is much to discuss, and thus much to record. Secondly, I wonder if you could arrange with my cook for something special to be brought in … fruit and cake, perhaps, and something to drink."

Again, there was hesitation on Mr. Bumpus's end. "Would you like coffee or —"

"I know Captain Austen is fond of good French wine."

"Very well, sir, I shall see to your refreshments and tell Mr. Croker his presence is required in your cabin straightaway."

"Why tell Mr. Croker anything at all, Mr. Bumpus?"

"I — I am only his humble assistant, sir. He would be most unhappy to think he had missed out on such important business." His afterthought was swiftly uttered. "Besides, I understand Mr. Croker is quite eager to make the better acquaintance of Captain Austen."

Uptergrove responded with his usual "I see" and then they both fell quiet. To Magpie, who was trying so hard to stay still, the silence seemed interminable, like a half-hour turn on the quartermaster's sandglass when one is on duty. Over the racket of his anxious heart, he strained to listen for clues that might reveal the men's attitudes and movements. One of them — probably Uptergrove — made quite a noise clearing their throat, but there was no further exchange of words, nothing to indicate their conversation had come to an end. A chair scraped against the floorboards. Boots shuffled near the door. A quill pen began scratching on paper. Soon, distinct voices from the quarter-deck began infiltrating the great cabin. Someone called for the grappling hooks while someone else angrily ordered the livestock pens to be cleared away. Beyond them, muffled voices roared in unison.

Magpie slowly emerged from behind the painting, his eye darting around the room. The doorway stood empty. Uptergrove did not look up from his letter, but the contraction of his mouth and his curt nod seemed to signal dismissal. Retrieving his bucket and fearful of making the least sound, Magpie tiptoed toward the exit. If he were forced to swim across the Thames River, the distance would not seem quite as far and dangerous. Bypassing the back of Uptergrove's chair, he concentrated on the floorboards in front of him, knowing that freedom would soon be his. But as he drew nearer to the door, he made a terrifying discovery. Mr. Bumpus had not fully departed. He was lingering by the binnacle, pretending to have business with the helmsman, evidently in no hurry at all to carry out Uptergrove's orders. Like a dreadful scene in a dream, Bumpus slowly swung his grinning face around and their eyes met, locking into place like the cocking of a matchlock musket.

The bucket fell from Magpie's grasp with a deafening clatter, depositing its heap of soiled rags squarely at the captain's feet. Feeling a choking sensation in his throat, Magpie stared down at the reeking abomination on the floor and waited for the grim knell that would end his life.

3:00 p.m.
(AFTERNOON WATCH, SIX BELLS)
ABOARD HMS *INVINCIBLE*

Emily heard the tolling of the ship's bell and wondered how much longer she could withstand being imprisoned in the great cabin, at the mercy of Mrs. Jiggins's undisciplined tongue, which babbled like merry sailors in anticipation of their grog hour. Up to this point, she had been — in her humble opinion — a model of endurance, nodding respectfully throughout Mrs. Jiggins's dissertation on the picturesque, and accepting both her brush-stroke corrections and artistic notions of seacoasts, promontories, and crumbling castles. But now, her foot tapping was wearing a hole in the floor planks, her bottom had numbed upon her rigid chair, and she was desperate to flee. As to where, she had yet to work out. The foul odours and bedlam in the berthing deck held no appeal, and Captain Austen had forbidden her from assisting in the hospital while Leander was determining the health of the Lady Janes, saying he could not risk her "seeing the men without their trousers on." If only there were a quiet place on the ship where she could hide away and be alone with her turbulent thoughts.

Mrs. Jiggins's three other students only served to exacerbate Emily's desire to escape. Lounging at their easels in a semicircle before her, they half-heartedly toiled away on their artwork, delighting in making her ill at ease, or so it seemed. It was unpleasant enough that Lord Somerton was stealing glances at her from around his canvas, especially since he had snubbed the group with his scowls and tersely spoken monosyllables. Though sitting there in a crisp linen shirt and intricately knotted cravat, one ankle resting upon the opposing knee, he looked more like a Romantic poet than a man of property and privilege. Then there was Cadby Brambles. He was just ridiculous. Who had allowed him time off for such pursuits? Why he was making no attempt whatsoever to hide his glances. Openly and annoyingly, he gawped at her like an infatuated schoolboy, mooning grins ruffling his face whenever their eyes met. Really! Had he never seen a woman before setting foot upon the *Invincible*?

Surprisingly, the worst of the lot was Eliza Braden. Released from her soup-making duties in the galley, she had slipped soundlessly into the great cabin and asked permission to join them, only to be met with a burst of enthusiastic applause from Mrs. Jiggins and her claim that they were now indeed a "splendid party!" Miss Braden was still going to great lengths to avoid looking in Emily's direction, although at one point, she had lifted her double-lensed prospect glass with the intention of evaluating her work, but instead, had slid it past her canvas to do a sly inspection of Emily from top to toe. Between her ghastly magnified eye — a veritable cyclops — and the mob cap that framed her pointy face like the fanned tail of a peacock, she was a terrifying sight to behold. Through it all, Emily could not help feeling ashamed, believing the goings-on in the captain's cabin to be absurd. Why, any outsider who happened upon their little scene of domestic bliss would never guess that a tragedy had played out that morning on the sea, the repercussions of which were still being felt beyond its cloistered walls.

Casting off her emotions, Emily gazed critically upon her artwork. Having abandoned her paintbrushes and her attempt at a mucky-brown castle, she had — when Mrs. Jiggins was not looking — started over with a sheet of paper and a pencil. This *new* subject was much more suited to her tastes. Taking up her little lump of rubber, she made a few corrections, shaded here and there with her pencil and then leaned back against the hard spokes of her chair to admire it. She was still smiling when Gus Walby appeared in the cabin's entranceway, politely alerting all of his presence with a quiet clearing of his throat.

"Come in, come in, Mr. Walby! Are you here to join us?" asked Mrs. Jiggins, her cup overrunning with joy.

"I am afraid I cannot take the time just now, ma'am. I was just looking for the captain." The air trilled with Mrs. Jiggins's deflated sigh of disappointment.

Cadby Brambles's face shot up above his canvas. "Why not? What must you do that is so very important?"

Gus looked well pleased and smart in his new coat of cerulean-blue serge. "Captain Austen has asked me to accompany him when he meets with Captain Uptergrove on the *Expedition*."

Storm clouds replaced Mr. Brambles's foolish grins of yore. "Why would he ask you and not me? I am senior midshipman! And I do not require a stick to help me get about."

Emily flinched. Somewhere inside her, a match was struck.

"At least take a moment to look at our creations, Mr. Walby, and tell us which one of us is destined for greatness," cried Mrs. Jiggins, steering Gus toward her own canvas.

Gus's eyes roved reluctantly over her work. "It — it is very nice indeed!"

Mrs. Jiggins blushed with pleasure. "Do you know, Mr. Walby, that my childhood governess was so impressed with my talent, she adamantly believed I was a descendent of Joshua Reynolds? Oh, wait! Or was it William Hogarth?"

The murmurs of approval around their circle were muted. Gus looked helpless, for it appeared he was not acquainted with Messrs. Reynolds and Hogarth.

Mr. Brambles snatched up his canvas and held it protectively against his barrel chest. "I forbid you to look at mine, Mr. Walby."

Lord Somerton stood up, his unkind laughter startling Gus who, it seemed, had taken no notice of him until now. Was this the first time they had come face to face on the ship — the first time since that fateful evening at Hartwood Hall which had ended in tears and humiliation? Emily's eyes narrowed as she watched Somerton stride dismissively past Gus and over to view Mr. Brambles's work for himself. Chin projected, hand on hip; he stood there like an imperious magistrate about to pass judgment on a beggar who had been caught stealing bread.

"Is that because you are afraid Mr. Walby might return to the middy's berth and tell the boys that you tried to paint a picture of Emeline? Or, at least, I *believe* it is her. The forehead is too pronounced and you did a rather poor job of the nose. Try making it less squashed the next time so that there is less of a resemblance to a platypus."

Mr. Brambles turned plum-purple and could not bring himself to look at Emily. Miss Braden lifted her prospect glass again, only this time it was Lord Somerton who fell under her scrutiny.

"Now then, Mr. Walby, come along," said Somerton, waving his hand impatiently in the air as if he were addressing a servant boy. With reluctance, Gus followed Lord Somerton's long strides around the cabin, but chose to stand well back when the older man planted his feet behind Emily to critically eye her work.

Knowing what was to come, Emily braced for it.

"Mrs. Jiggins! Come quick!" Somerton cried out, sounding the alarm bells. "It appears Mr. Brambles is not your only student who has blatantly ignored your lecture on the picturesque."

Awakened from a reverie of admiration for her own work, Mrs. Jiggins flew at once toward Emily's easel, carried on the wings of her Kashmir shawl. One glance left her reeling. "Emeline! We agreed to concentrate on watercolours today! You have made a sham of my very first lesson!"

Emily was unshaken by her outburst. "I am not fond of watercolours and have no talent for them, as you can see," she said, referring to the messy heap of castle stones, dripping with splatters of dark paint on her discarded canvas. "If truth be known, I have always preferred sketching to painting."

Somerton drew closer and laid his hands upon the curve of her chair. "Why paint crumbling castles when you have found obvious inspiration in sketching the ship's doctor?" He lifted one hand and snapped his fingers together in quick succession. "See, now? I have already forgotten! What's his name again?"

Emily reached out for her pot of brackish watercolours sitting on the edge of Captain Austen's dining table, pleased to see a flash of anger in Eliza's grey eyes and hear her reply with such crisp enunciation.

"His *name* is Leander Braden."

Cadby Brambles swivelled toward Emily and blinked at her as if she had just crawled from the sea. "Wot? Why would you sketch a portrait of *him*?"

"Well, I think it is very good," chirped Gus, leaning on his crutch, his bold smile darting between Somerton and Cadby.

"What is this fascination you uphold for our low-born doctor?" insisted Somerton, his voice full of scorn. "I daresay it is unnatural and must be exorcised. The sooner the better."

Emily's blood was in full uprising. She had had enough. Leaping from her chair, she made an abrupt turnabout, colliding at once with Somerton. The contents of her paint pot flew upward before making a violent landing on his chest, mortally wounding his shirt in a destructive shower of mucky-brown. The spectacle sent incredulous gasps and stares looping 'round their semicircle. Miss Braden plucked up her prospect glass; Mrs. Jiggins clutched at her breast, her words frozen on the silent *O* of her mouth. Cadby Brambles's eyes grew wider still, and Gus squeezed his lips together to deaden a snuffle of laughter.

Somerton, his arms outstretched in the air, was in high dudgeon. He threw a scorching look at Emily. "What the devil? You odious minx! Anyone with eyes can see you did that deliberately!"

Stamping his foot like a petulant child, he frowned around the room, as if expecting to see the circle of witnesses nodding in agreement. Unfortunately for him, there was no extension of sympathy. The only response was an outburst of laughter, which only deepened his crimson flush of anger. Believing Gus was responsible for the added mischief, he glared like a demon at the boy. Emily quickly moved in to shield him just in case a punitive punch was thrown. She had no idea which one of them had laughed, but frankly, she did not care.

"I am sorry, Lord Somerton, I did not know you were prowling so close behind me," she said, letting her eyes roll unapologetically over his stained shirt. "Perhaps, in the future, you should learn to keep your distance."

CHAPTER 22

4:40 P.M.
(First Dog Watch)
Aboard HMS *Expedition*

Gus Walby wrested his eyes from the cut-glass decanter of ruby-red wine in the centre of Captain Uptergrove's table, a thing of beauty with the candles glinting upon its fluted base and pineapple-shaped stopper. It was so hard to concentrate on his note-taking. He was feeling heady and could hear his heartbeats. Was it simply his excitement and pride of inclusion with important men and their important business? Was it the heavy air in the great cabin that reeked oddly of roses in addition to the staleness emanating from Uptergrove's clerk, Mr. Croker, who was sitting beside him? The man smelled like an unwashed boot, his hair was greasy and sprinkled with white flakes, and he grunted in agitation whenever the captains' instructions got ahead of his notations. Or was it that Captain Austen had told him, as they were crossing the gangway onto the *Expedition*, that he had a surprise for him when they were done with Uptergrove? Gus concluded it was a whirling combination of everything.

Adding to the mix were the distractions all around him. Earlier, beyond the shuttered door of the great cabin, Gus had heard the boatswain's mates call out, "All hands to play," and now the rousing music and the joyous voices of the Expeditions made him long to be out on the deck, mingling with them. But even within the great cabin itself, there were so many fascinating things to see. How he would love to examine Uptergrove's paintings and peruse the titles of the leather-bound books on his shelf, and maybe even get a closer look at the bamboo flute — so poignantly reminiscent of Magpie — lying on the cushions under the windows. Would there be time for all that when their business was done? He really hoped so.

Stealing a peek across the table, Gus could see that Captain Austen was subdued and had scarcely paid attention to the wine and the segments of orange that a servant had placed before him. Uptergrove, on the other hand, seemed unperturbed by the gravity of the occasion. He had drained his glass in one go, staining his teeth red with drink, and licked his index finger to scoop up his cake crumbs, his features betraying no emotions whatsoever. He hadn't even smiled upon welcoming them aboard his ship. Presiding over all from the comfort of his blood-red chair, he reminded Gus of a grey snake, confident and dominant in his surroundings, but, if need be, quite prepared to strike.

Uptergrove's dull eyes slid toward his clerk, who had his head down over an open ledger, his quill pen furiously scribbling curlie-wurlies of black ink over the page. "Croker! Read that salvage list out to us," he said sharply, settling deeper into his chair to listen, his hands clasped in a meditative steeple against his mouth.

"Aye, sir!" Croker's hands shook as he flipped back through the pages of the ledger as if his life depended upon the speed with which he located the correct one. When found, he lifted the whole works to his myopic eyes and cleared the rattle of phlegm from his throat. "Ninety-one men saved, eleven unaccounted for, including captain, master, and surgeon; all dispatches from Admiralty lost; two chests of specie recovered, four chests of silver and three of gold lost; two mailbags recovered, unknown number lost; thirty-two muskets recovered, approximately five hundred lost; eight hens, two goats, two sheep, three hogs recovered, all other livestock lost." He read on for some time, point by point, detailing the status of every last thing that had once been stowed aboard the *Lady Jane*, his voice strengthening dramatically for items recovered and fading away to an emotional whisper for those lost, ending it all robustly with: "Forty-one crates of wine and spirits recovered, none lost."

"We should take some comfort that not all wound up on the bottom of the sea," said Uptergrove impassively.

Mr. Croker let out a nervous giggle of laughter, but no one shared his amusement.

"It is evident what was deemed of importance to the men as their ship sank beneath them." Captain Austen tinkered with his fork, his unseeing eyes falling upon the uneaten orange. "The loss of the *Lady Jane*'s captain and the Admiralty's dispatches is most concerning. We have no idea what those dispatches contained. Let us hope that copies were made and sent out on other ships heading west. If not, pray we can redeem ourselves by catching a Yankee ship and sailing her into Halifax with the help of a prize crew. It has been four months since Broke's *Shannon* defeated the *Chesapeake*, too long a time since we have celebrated a significant naval victory."

Uptergrove pursed his lips as he deliberated. "Even better would be capturing this Thomas Trevelyan we spoke about at length whilst you supped with me in Portsmouth."

A sarcastic smile broke through the weary lines on Captain Austen's face. "Imagine the money and honours that would be showered upon us all if we were to succeed on that score — not to mention a baronetcy and a golden sword worth a hundred guineas!"

Uptergrove smiled in return, though the pleasure behind it did not reach his eyes. "May I refresh your glass?"

Captain Austen twisted in his chair so he could see out the galleried windows. "Thank you, but I think it best we no longer delay. I gave my men permission to stand down for a short while only. Come the Second Dog Watch, I would like to be away, with them back at their posts and somewhat sober." He rose haltingly to his feet.

Gus scrambled to collect his quills and papers, shooting a regretful glance at the bamboo flute that was destined to remain forgotten on the cushions under the windows.

"Agreed, Austen. I shan't have my men grow soft. As much as it grieves me, they have a tendency to abuse grog and behave reprehensibly." There was a disdainful twitch in the side of Uptergrove's face as he lifted the decanter, pulled out the stopper, and poured himself more wine.

Captain Austen arched an eyebrow. "Troubles already?"

Uptergrove nodded soberly as he pushed away from the table and strolled with them toward the door, twirling his wineglass. "I have had enough of delinquents this week. At present, I have barred one from the entertainments. He is standing on a stool near the bowsprit and shall go to bed without food or drink."

"What was his crime?"

Uptergrove's eyes hardened. "Let me just say he was most careless with a necessary bucket."

"I am sorry to hear of it, but at least your men now know where you stand on discipline," Captain Austen said, sounding unconvinced that the crime fit the punishment. He reached out to shake hands with Uptergrove. "Thank you for your hospitality. We shall speak again soon. In the meantime, sail close."

Captain Uptergrove made his farewells — to the exclusion of Gus — and instructed the sentry standing outside his cabin to see them safely through the energized crowds of Expeditions and across the gangway, back to the *Invincible*. Following in Captain Austen's path, Gus did his best to admire the sights and sounds around him without losing his footing. Fiddle and hornpipe rang clear through the bracing air, inspiriting jigs and reels on both ships. Sailors and landmen linked arms for a turn around the decks or conversed with one another over the rails. Tumblers of grog were passed around and fervently shared. Groups of men formed choirs and sang smutty songs, their voices tipsy and raucous.

"You see how music and dancing can lift a mariner's spirits, Mr. Walby," said Captain Austen, seizing Gus by his waist and heaving him down from the gangway and onto the quarterdeck of their own ship. "And both so beneficial for one's overall health."

"I believe so, sir," said Gus as he resettled the cradle of his crutch under his arm and stood proudly alongside his captain to delight in the lively scenes around them.

He had never known Biscuit and Prosper Burgo to throw caution to the wind and break into circles of unbridled dance; in fact, he didn't even know they had it in them. But as far as their present audience was concerned, clapping, cheering, and foot-stomping them on from all corners of the *Invincible*, they were an uncontested sensation. Their partner, by turns, was Mrs. Jiggins. The vigorous exercise had infused her complexion with high colour. She was as red as a raspberry! But she happily tolerated Prosper and Biscuit's trampling toes, neither man seemingly aware that the dance required the careful execution of certain steps and figures.

Not far from the stage was a group of familiar onlookers. Old Dr. Braden, his demeanour tranquil and amused, was smoking a cheroot in the company of his sister. Miss Braden was rigidly arranged on a vegetable crate, her hands busy darning a pair of stockings, though, every so often, she would raise her prospect glass, squint at the dancers, and show her approval with a nod of her mob cap and a smile that nicely transformed her permanently pursed lips. Inclining against the bulwark, Emily stood alone, the wind playing with the loosened tendrils of her braided hair. She seemed sad, unmoved by the entertainment around her, disassociated from the rowdy crew of the *Invincible*, like a lovely sea nymph found snagged in the fishing nets and forced to live among a school of octopuses, uncultured and overpowering. Gus wondered if she was thinking of Magpie, knowing he of all people should be here, front and centre, taking pleasure in playing his flute. Of course it came as no surprise that Cadby Brambles and Lord Somerton were hovering close by, a couple of skeletons at the feast, both poised to ambush any and all unbefitting suitors who dared to come near to Emily. Mr. Brambles was too drunk and lovesick to dare ask her for a turn around the deck. And Lord Somerton, despite having togged up in a fresh suit of clothes, was bereft of good breeding, and therefore had likely destroyed all chances of her ever agreeing to dance a jig with him. It was no wonder he looked as grumpy as an unfed bear.

Gus was still watching the fun when he thought he heard his name being called. Captain Austen, who was riveted next to him, laughing at the antics of Biscuit kicking off his shoes to impress Mrs. Jiggins with his sublimely pointed hairy toes, did not seem to have heard it. Mystified, Gus peered into the crowds of sailors all around him. But there was no one singling him out or hurrying toward him. Perhaps the words had been uttered by a passing bird, its native squawk sounding eerily similar to the cry of his own name. Perhaps it was the hornpipes, the sound created somewhere between the rise and decline of their resonating notes of music. Then again, it could have come from Mrs. Jiggins. As she hurtled headlong around the deck, all hips, quivering flesh, and laughter, she was generating some very peculiar whoops and nickers.

Ah! But there it was again, more desperate sounding now as if one of the youngsters was in trouble and required assistance. Gus glanced around again, slowly this time, absorbing the action on the ship. To him, everyone seemed content and utterly engrossed in the amusements, even Jim Beef, who was scaling the shrouds, gazing down with satisfaction upon both ships as if he were a king standing on the castle keep, and the sailors his vassals, celebrating a festival in the courtyard below. And when Captain Austen turned to look at him, a generous smile enlivening his face, the distant cries were dismissed and forgotten.

"So then, Mr. Walby," he said, opening his blue woollen jacket to dig around in its breast pocket, "since dancing is not for you today, perhaps *this* will lift your spirits."

Gus could only gape at the treasure held out to him, his heart thumping faster at the sight of his name in calligraphic print. A letter! A coveted letter! In his entire life, only once had someone presented him with a letter, but never had one found its way to him at sea. He glanced up eagerly, hoping to hear an account of its incredible appearance, so pleased to see that its bestowal had afforded pleasure to a man such as Captain Austen.

"We, too, were able to salvage a sack of mail, Mr. Walby. I found it among the first handful of letters I was able to sort through before our meeting."

Accepting it reverentially as if it were one of the chests of coins recovered from the *Lady Jane*, Gus barely noticed when his captain quietly slipped away to tell the boatswain to sound his silver whistle and order the men back to work. Ripping open the red wax wafer on the outer sheet of paper, his fingers and eyes fumbled nervously for the return address: *Hartwood Hall, Helena's Lane, Hampstead Heath, London.*

Fleda! Lady Fleda!

The swelling excitement in Gus's chest threatened to snap his breastbone in two and spill his twitching innards all over the oak planks of the deck. He couldn't wait to hear what she had to say. But he had to be careful. He could not risk making a scene; otherwise, he would be noticed, especially by the little middies that, like him, had no loving family and therefore no prospects of receiving a letter at sea. They would surely gang up on him and stick their grubby pennies in his face, demanding a fair exchange for his letter so that they could make believe they were missed and adored and special to someone in the world.

Desperate for a private place where he could eat up Fleda's news without being knocked upon his hindquarters, Gus hastened toward the bow, thinking he might find a moment's peace in the officers' roundhouse. His destination was within reach, the unread letter burning a hole in the palm of his hand, when someone leapt in front of him, deliberately blocking his way. Quite prepared to order whoever it was to shove off, Gus wilted when he realized it was the bullyrag Lord Somerton. With that patrician sneer of his plastered upon his face, he leaned aggressively toward Gus, pinning him against the foremast like a highwayman on a dark country road, determined to steal his valuables, murder him, and dispose of his body in a desolate copse of trees. Bravado failing him, Gus felt the letter slipping from his damp fingers, sputtering in horror as it sailed with abandon beyond his reach.

What happened next was a big blur of anguished cries and pitiful attempts at retrieval while the treacherous wind entertained itself at his expense, him staggering about on his crutch, trying to elude the dancers and drinkers, begging for help from all quarters. What Gus would never forget were Lord Somerton's heartless howls of laughter beating him like thwacks from a horsewhip as he held on to the rail and sobbed, watching his coveted letter descend between the grappled ships and executed in the ruinous waters below.

5:20 P.M.
(FIRST DOG WATCH)

Magpie didn't think he could stand much longer. He thought he might soon faint dead away. The shooting pains in his legs were unbearable. His bound wrists and feet had gone numb and the necessary bucket tied around his neck like a cowbell was so disgusting, it was hard trying to convince the contents of his stomach — such as they were: a bit of maggoty biscuit and some weak tea ingested early that morning — to stay put and not erupt through his mouth and nose for all to see. Already, he was the butt of jokes and pranks. The Bloody Fluxes seemed incapable of leaving him to his punishment. Oh no! They preferred to poke him with pawls and throw grog at his red face and massage pea soup into his hair and give the legs of his stool a fierce yank, hoping to see him crash to the deck in a heap of shame.

Crippling despair invaded Magpie's mind. His lips were a mess of blood from biting back his humiliation and disappointment. Only yards away were his friends and yet they did not know it. And in a matter of minutes, the grappling hooks would be released, the gangway eased back onto the deck of the *Invincible* and the two ships would part. Maybe forever! Upon their arrival and departure from Uptergrove's cabin, he had, with a brimming heart, glimpsed Captain Austen's blue, gold-edged bicorne moving tall through the crowds of men and, bobbing behind him, Mr. Walby's blond head. He had called out to Mr. Walby the first opportunity he got, when his tormenters had finally grown bored of their hateful pranks. He had prayed that Mr. Walby might hear, had even seen him scouting around as if trying to locate the source of the cries. But Mr. Walby hadn't seen him tucked away ignominiously at the bow of the *Bloody Flux* on his stool, screened by towers of rope and groupings of men waving about their tankards of ale. Now his friend was heading toward the far side of his ship, farther and farther away, where the whimpers of a despairing lad could not possibly be heard.

A big sob burst through Magpie's mouth. He thought of Emily. Surely he would be long dead before she ever learned the truth about his melancholy end. He tried to stand taller on his stool and imagined she was there on the *Invincible*, and that she was the one who found him suffering on the *Bloody Flux*. Rallying those around her, she was able to stop the removal of the hooks and gangway, and raced aboard Uptergrove's ship, blue-striped skirts and golden hair flying in all directions, demanding he be freed at once. Hats were flung and shouts of huzzah went up everywhere the moment an emotional Captain Austen realized he was alive. Biscuit called for a roast-beef banquet with three courses to celebrate his return. Uptergrove, his grey face wreathed in smiles, learned that he was not a farm labourer after all, but a sailmaker, and a good one at that. Emily helped him down from his stool, unburdened him of the bucket, and brought a cup of water to his blistered lips, her brown eyes shining, searching his face with such tenderness.

Magpie's whimsical reflections came to a savage halt. His creeping flesh shuddered with unease and then stiffened. He didn't dare turn around. Someone had drifted unseen from the throngs of merrymakers and was moving around behind him, wedging himself into the small space between his stool and the curved bulwark of the bow. Creaking steps paced back and forth. Coattails brushed against the back of his legs. There was some fidgeting and shuffling and noisy, uneven breathing. Magpie gasped. Something, razor-sharp and shocking, was pressed into his back, pinching him right above his knotted hands. A mouth, soured with vapours of grog, found his ear. "You call out one more time to that Mr. Walby, and I will sink this into you so far it'll come out the other side, dangling your blood-soaked liver."

It was all too late now. The whistle had blown. The music and dancing stopped, the games abandoned, the tankards collected, and everyone scattered, scurrying back to their stations. No one noticed the piteous lad on the stool or seemed to think it curious that Asa Bumpus, the assistant clerk, was hanging over him like a bank of glowering clouds. If they had, would they have cared to know why Mr. Bumpus was muttering words of death and disembowelment, and biding his time until the ships had safely cast off from one another?

Magpie's failing courage broke down. He began to weep. If only he still had Morgan Evans's woolly thrum cap and could hold it against his face to comfort him and catch the tears coursing down his cheek. The *Invincible* was preparing to leave, taking with her the only ones who could liberate him from a journey to the dark side of the earth with Thomas Trevelyan. Chin trembling, he watched her pull away, setting out on the next leg of her journey amidst a rumble of rebelling oak timbers. Oh, to see a friend, someone he knew, before she disappeared into the pearly-grey obscurity of the distant horizons.

His watery eye skittered up the *Invincible*'s mizzenmast and came to rest on the topmen, labouring there on the crossjack yard with blocks and clewlines, unfurling the square sail to harness the wind. But he was soon distracted by a lanky sailor, standing barefoot on the top platform, his arms outstretched to the wind, admiring the sea and the ships. Had the sailor not heard the whistle, ordering all hands back to work? His long hair, pulled free of its queue, floated upward like a peacock's crest of feathers; the billowing, balloon sleeves of his shirt its fanning tail. His upturned nose, a tremendous beak, sniffed the salty air with satisfaction. Dropping his arms, he latched one hand to his hip, the other holding fast to the topmast shrouds, and, quite unexpectedly, swung around to gaze back at Uptergrove's ship. In no time at all he spied Magpie sniveling on his stool. Tilting his head sideways, he scrutinized him thoroughly, his round eyes bulging from their sockets, his black brow see-sawing in snatches of curiosity and confusion.

Magpie could neither wave at the lanky sailor nor plead for help, given that Asa Bumpus was skulking behind him, fixing to run him through if he so much as let out a peep, threatening to fry up his liver and devour it in front of him should he "have the audacity to survive the initial impalement." So, he did the only thing he could think of. He smiled at him. And before the sailor resumed his surveillance of the seas, and the widening distance between the ships dimmed his remarkable features, he reacted in a way that caused Magpie's laden breast to trill with hope.

He smiled back.

CHAPTER 23

As soon as Leander's wind-tossed head appeared at the edge of the fore topmast, his handsome features overspread with good humour, Emily relieved her tension in a sigh and mumbled words of thanks to her maker.

"There you are!" Her voice was shaky as she took his knapsack and offered him a helping hand while he hauled himself up onto the oak platform. "I feared you might falter upon the shrouds and be left suspended by a leg with no one about to rescue you."

"I am, by no means, a natural sailor," he said, slightly winded from his perilous climb. "That feeling of falling backwards is not one I shall ever embrace."

"The trick is not to look down."

"I shall keep that in mind the next time … should there be a next time."

Emily rearranged her wool blanket, still warm from her bed, across the platform as Leander crawled beside her. Safely situated, he pulled the fluttering folds of his banyan around his outstretched legs and raised a mirthful eyebrow. "I swear you shall be the death of me yet, Emeline! It is one thing to have you here on this ship, where you need constant protection from lugworms and coxcombs. It is quite another to suggest we drink coffee together one hundred feet up in the air like two eagles in an aerie."

"Do you worry about me, Doctor?"

His eyes locked on hers. "What do you think?"

Emily stared at her hands, clasped nervously in her lap, hoping he would not notice the advancing colour on her cheeks. "When it comes to climbing the ratlines, Doctor, it is I who must do the worrying!"

"It is comforting to know there is someone on this ship looking out for my welfare," he said, awarding her a fond smile. He reached for his knapsack, flipped it open and began rummaging about inside, his face darkening with dismay. "Evidently, our coffee did not enjoy the climb up either. Much of it has spilled." Carefully, he removed the tin containing the coffee from the knapsack, unknotted the string holding down its sopping-wet, brown paper lid and expectantly peered inside. "Ah! Not all is lost! There's at least a mouthful or two for each of us!" Pouring unequal portions into the two earthenware mugs he had brought along with him, he placed the more generous one in Emily's cold hands. From his coat pocket he then produced a small amount of grated sugar, wrapped in a square of linen, and the little silver-plated spoon he had purchased in Portsmouth and held them triumphantly before her. "Good news!" he said, adding sugar to her coffee and giving it a stir. "You shall not be forced to eat Biscuit's burgoo this morning. He was so anxious for us to dine like proper lords and ladies that he raided Mrs. Jiggins's superior store of rations on our behalf."

With keen interest, Emily watched him reveal their feast, one item at a time, setting it all out in the sheltering space between them where all would be safe from molestation by the wind. When the knapsack was empty, they both conducted an appraisal of their breakfast. Thanks to Biscuit's careful attention to packaging, nothing had been sullied by the spilled coffee. Nonetheless, the cheese did look awfully yellow, the curled slices of ham a bit dry and the oranges somewhat shrivelled. To compensate for their shortcomings, there was a generous slab of apple-cinnamon cake. Leander was obviously of the same mind. Forsaking all else, he cut a slice of it, arranged it nicely on a napkin and offered it up to her.

"How does Mrs. Jiggins merit having a cake made just for her?" she asked, accepting it with an appreciative smile and setting it down on her thigh.

"Apparently, it has become a favourite of hers."

"No doubt, given her choices at mealtimes. But I wonder. Is Biscuit hoping to woo her by way of her stomach?"

"Possibly! He might consider it the only advantage he has over the dashing Prosper Burgo."

Emily gaped at him. "Prosper? Dashing? I think not!"

At the expense of the Messrs. Burgo and Biscuit, they made a few jokes, homing in on the men's dancing skills, or lack thereof, before falling silent to eat and drink. Wriggling her toes in her leather shoes, Emily crossed her trousers-clad legs at the ankles and sipped her coffee. She smiled upon the sea, purring around her like a cat stretched out blissfully upon a warm hearth. She marvelled at the views from their enchanted aerie on the platform. The *Invincible* had set a northwest course, her canvas hauled up and trimmed so she could sail as close to the wind as possible. Ahead, just off her larboard bow, the *Expedition* was in plain sight, voyaging unworried like a self-assured guide in enemy territory. Beyond her stern, the crimson dawn slowly bled into the sky's paling darkness, dimming the stars and the setting moon. Dreams of Magpie drowning had not stalked her sleeping hours; Mrs. Jiggins had refrained from snoring the whole night through, and for the first time in ever so long, Emily was alone with Leander.

Eagerly, she seized all opportunities to glance sidelong at him whenever his handsome profile was turned from hers. Her eyes traced the outline of his well-formed nose, and the raised veins, flowing with blood and life, on the back of his capable hands. How she longed to catch one of them up in her own hands and hold it to her breast; sweep away their breakfast, curl up against his body, and rest her head upon his chest to listen to his heart. Would his beats be sprinting as hers were?

"You shivered. Are you cold?" Leander set his mug down and began stripping off his banyan. "You are welcome to my coat."

"No!" She spoke a little too quickly, lowering her eyes, relieved he could not read her mind. "No, I am plenty warm, thank you."

He hesitated and his brow crept up as if he did not believe her. His eyes on her, he continued to remove his banyan. He spread it over her lower body, tucking it under her knees, looking rather pleased with himself. Settling back against the topmast, he gazed straight ahead, beyond the tip of the bowsprit, toward the still-dark, empty horizon, and went quiet, his fervid expression collapsing into contemplation. "On the subject of advantages, would you ... would you say that I might have one over Lord Somerton?"

Emily smiled to herself, elated to hear him open the door to such bewitchment. There was no denying, her first instinct was to say to him that he did indeed, that by comparison Lord Somerton was a mere donkey to his sleek stallion or the doldrums that slacken the sails to exhilarating winds that send them cracking. Instead, she allowed him to stew in anticipation while she hesitated on the threshold, enjoying a piece of cinnamon-sprinkled apple and chasing it down with the last of her coffee.

"I cannot tell forthwith," she finally said, frowning as if an answer to his question involved much calculation. "I could suggest you advance yourself by taking painting lessons with Mrs. Jiggins. She has much to say on the picturesque and is overjoyed to impart her knowledge on unsuspecting students; albeit, highly critical of their clumsy attempts to achieve anything worth looking at."

Leander picked up an orange and tossed it into the air a couple of times. "And was she highly critical of your attempts?"

"I assure you, everyone was, except for dear Mr. Walby!"

"In that case, I insist you show me your work. Perhaps, I shall prove to be a more affable judge."

There was something worth investigating in his voice. Emily looked him over with suspicion, noting his sudden interest in the brightening sky, his flickering grin, the one he could not wholly discipline, inciting her curiosity. She laughed and broke into applause. "Aha! So it was you who paid us a furtive visit that day! I wondered whose hearty laugh it was. Try as I might, I could not convince myself it had come from the lips of your Aunt Eliza." Adding, with a drawn-out hyperbole of sympathy, "Poor old Lord Somerton!"

To Emily's ears, Leander's laugh was every bit as impassioned as hers had been. It was disarming and joyful, and how nicely it crinkled the outskirts of his blue eyes. Afterward, when the wind had snatched away its lovely notes, he grew thoughtful again and looked at her in a way that made her heart wobble like the puddings Biscuit boiled up for the young middies. Twisting his body toward hers, he reached for her face, his eyes falling upon her mouth. He slipped his arm around her shoulders, pulling her close to him. She heard the quickening of his breath and felt a catch in her own. Closing her eyes, she let herself be kissed, thrilled by the warm ruggedness of his face against hers, the brush of his mouth on her cheek and throat and lips, the gentle stroke of his hand on her back, the musky scent of his skin and muslin shirt. She delighted in his moan of pleasure and her own dizzying sensations, colliding inside her as their tongues found one another, overcome by the reality that it truly was Leander Braden beside her, not simply another spectacular fabrication of her daydreaming mind.

"You there! You there! Woe and despair!"

The words, powerfully spoken, separated them at once. Emily recoiled as if she had been rudely slapped awake. The speaker stood above them, his long arms and legs hooked onto the foremast shrouds like a spider in his knitted web. He gaped at them, his eyes sliding from one to the other, as if weighing their suitability as food for his breakfast. Clambering down the ropes, he landed with a lurching thud on their crowded platform, his bare feet, blackened with tar and red with cold, straddling Emily's ankles. The wind agitated the begrimed strands of his hair and the tails of his mouldy, claw-hammer coat, sending them swirling wildly around him. Now the stranger had the bearing of a biblical prophet on a blustery mountaintop, about to proclaim his divine displeasure at finding them sitting together, touching one another inappropriately. Emily's face steamed. But how was Leander able to maintain his composure? He did not appear embarrassed at all, addressing the man as easily as he would a patient in his hospital who was complaining of a scraped knee.

"Good morning, Mr. Beef. How may I be of service?"

Contrary to Emily's fears of vulgar proclamations, the prophet jabbed a bony forefinger at the *Expedition*, making certain their eyes followed his before he delivered his curious message again. "Woe and despair."

Leander inclined toward Emily. "Do not be afraid," he whispered. "It seems to be a favourite recitation of his."

Violently, Mr. Beef swivelled about, his eyes growing large and hostile as if he had overheard Leander and misinterpreted his innocuous words. Parting his swollen lips, he threw his head back and howled phrases wavering with emotion at the sky. "Suffering and torment. Pain and misery. Punishment and humiliation. Woe and despair."

Leander held up his palms in an attempt to pacify him. "I shall do what I can to assist you," he said gently, "but only if you help me to fully understand."

His urgent reply came post-haste. "He stands there. In punishment."

"Who is there?" Leander half shook his head. "Who do you mean?"

The smoking coals of Mr. Beef's fervour gradually cooled. He gazed blankly at Leander and then again at the *Expedition*, still a picture of tranquility, slumbering on the pink-granite waves. He stayed silent. Perhaps he had forgotten or he could not say. Pain cracked his heavy features. His shoulders contracted and sank. He dug his fingers into the mouldy fabric of his coattails, and for a moment, Emily thought he was going to cry. Then he tried again. He lifted his face to the wind, a crazed expression inflating his eyes. But this time he wasn't indicating the *Expedition*. This time he nodded east, toward the red rising sun.

6:30 A.M.
ABOARD HMS *EXPEDITION*

Trevelyan dragged the woolly thrum cap from his head as he approached the forecastle gangway. He lowered his eyes in deference to the dead sailor who was laid out in his hammock on a spare grating, likely the same one upon which he had been mercilessly flogged. There was a round lump at the dead man's feet, a 32-pounder that would pull him through the countless fathoms to the bottom of the Atlantic. Hunched over him, working diligently by the light of a guttering candle-lantern, the ship's sailmaker sewed him into his canvas coffin, concealing him forever behind a thick seam of English-made twine.

"When did he die?" Trevelyan asked his messmates who had gathered on deck in their thin clothing, the only men caring enough to quit their warm beds and give their friend a send-off before the rest of the crew awakened and began shuffling through their daily routine.

It was the tattooed fellow with the bald, lumpy head (Trevelyan had never bothered to learn his name) who answered him, the others presumably too sorrowful to speak. "Just after midnight it was. I've seen men survive plenty more lashes than what he got. Poor beggar was just unlucky; his organs couldn't handle the beating."

Trevelyan peered down at the dead man's body. His silenced lips and shuttered eyes were lost in translucent shadows of purplish-blue; the hidden scars on his back would still be weeping, barely scabbed over, but no longer troublesome and throbbing with pain. "Where is the chaplain?"

The tattooed mate seethed with anger. "Uptergrove won't trouble his chaplain none to perform a decent burial service. He won't even allow our dead friend to lie in state awhile between the guns with the ensign draped across him."

"Is that further punishment for his alleged thievery? Or because he was an American?"

The mate's lips curled in disgust. "We'll never know now, will we, Mr. Bumpus?"

As macabre as it was, Trevelyan could not resist another glance at the corpse. The motionless face, devoid and deprived of life, was an agonizing reminder of little Harry. He winced as the sailmaker poked his needle through the septum of the dead man's nose. Should it happen he was only sleeping and awakened underwater, absolute death would come swiftly. The prospect of that final stitch struck cold dread in all seamen facing their end, officers and jacks alike, the timid and the stout-hearted.

Thomas? Help me! Help me, Thomas!

Trevelyan hastened away from the mourners and the sad heap of canvas, and strode toward the ship's starboard rail before the ghostly pleas of his younger brother could inhabit his head and reduce him to a weeping, pitiful mess. Shrugging deeper into his coat, he shoved his hands into his pockets and gulped the bracing air. He looked westward, blinking away hot tears, aware of the pains wracking his body ... in his legs, his feet, and across his back. He was rapidly becoming an old man, a cripple, a shipwreck. Where was the vitality of yesterday? Where was the man who had stood tall and formidable on the decks of USS *Serendipity*, striking fear in his crewmen and adversaries alike?

He swung his head toward the east. There the views were radiant, more reassuring, and the small sturdy clouds reminded him of young adventurers, sailing fearlessly on mystical seas, through waves of coral and burnished-gold. Solid, weatherly, and silhouetted against the new day, Captain Austen's *Invincible* trailed the *Expedition*. What were the chances of another ferocious gale stirring up the Atlantic, intercepting his ship and taking her down to join the *Lady Jane* in her watery grave ... before he himself went down? A sarcastic snuffle was his answer. How many more days of tedium before they spotted land? How much longer could he keep up the ruse that he was Asa Bumpus of New Bedford, Massachusetts? Already, a close call had scared him half to death. That little mongrel with the eye patch had damn well nearly succeeded in alerting the Invincibles. What if another need should arise for the two ships to convene and the mongrel was given a second chance? Only this time, *he* was not fast enough to intercede.

Trevelyan broke into a cold sweat.

Behind him, his American mates grunted as they lifted the grating and shambled to the ship's side. There, in unison, they mumbled the burial prayer. Long after "we commit his body to the deep" had been uttered, it lingered in the atmosphere like the beating wings of a bird that had lost its way and was afraid to leave the permanence of the ship. A dreadful pause preceded the final splash. He didn't look. He didn't want to think about the dead man's descent into darkness, sucked downward by the weight of the cannonball, or what he would meet when he finally stopped falling and entered the auld place. He heard his mates straining as they replaced the grating and their creaking steps on the ladder as they made their way below. He did not follow. For a long while, he stayed near the rail, steadying his nerves, jamming his terrible grief into the floorboards of his mind and trying his best to nail them down. He was alone, save for the faceless helmsman at his wheel and the sleepy lookouts at their posts. It was a blessing that no one could see the spreading stains under the arms of his shirt or perceive the queasy state of his mind.

How curious that he should be the first to notice the topgallants of the ships, taking shape against the blood-red dawn. He saw them before the lookouts did, before their raucous cries of "sail ho" warned the dreaming crew and destroyed what peace there was in the early morning.

CHAPTER 24

9:00 A.M.
(Forenoon Watch, Two Bells)
Aboard HMS *Invincible*

Leander padded along the quarterdeck, heading toward the knot of Invincibles gathered on the stern, their eyes and spyglasses fixed upon the eastern horizon where the mystery ships had come up with the sun, carried upon its celestial fingers of gilded red. A terrible hush had descended upon the *Invincible* as if the entire crew had perished from an outbreak of typhus and the wind was holding her breath. Beyond the initial shouts when the ships had been sighted, there had been no drum and fife beating the men to quarters, no rolling out of guns, no dousing of the galley fires, no scuttling of livestock into the boats, and no removal of bulkheads, obstructions, and inconveniences. The sailors on the yards and rigging, and those lining the gangways and railings, were subdued, motionless, watching and waiting for the word. Even Prosper Burgo, who normally would be boasting of past glories and imminent prize money at a time like this, was respectfully muted, clinging fiercely to the ship's wheel, teeth gritted, eyes squinting forward.

A pulsating anxiety drummed in Leander as he drew closer to the stern. He spotted Fly at the base of the mizzenmast, scanning the sea with the spyglass that seemed an extension of his left eye. In attendance with him were five of his senior officers, the captain of the marines, Gus Walby, and the midshipman Cadby Brambles. Mr. Walby was kneeling as best he could on the stern bench beside his discarded crutch, his elbows on the taffrail so he could keep a steady lookout through his own glass. Leander noted the lad was fully engaged in his duty and did not appear agitated by the jealous mutterings of the more senior Mr. Brambles, who was spitting mad that a crippled clerk should be included in a gathering of such eminent men.

Leander crept up behind Fly and waited until he had lowered his glass before pestering him with questions. "How many are there?"

Fly continued to peer eastward. "According to Mr. Walby, there are two of them. I have never met a young person with such sharp eyes as his." He smiled admiringly in Gus's direction.

Leander pocketed his hands in his greatcoat to defend against the buffeting wind, recalling the moment he had covered Emily's shoulders with his banyan following their scramble down the ropes. "Do you think we can keep ahead of them?"

Fly gave his neck a vigorous massage. "I wish I knew the answer to that, Doctor. One of them seems to be more weatherly than the other. I would feel much better if they would just veer off and sail toward Santo Domingo."

"Should they prove to be foes, at least we shall be faced with much better odds than the last time." Leander sounded more gallant than he felt.

"Aye, as long as a few more ships do not show up this afternoon." Fly stepped away from his officers, and turned to eye Leander. "What is different about you this morning, Doctor? You seem uncommonly nimble. Given the circumstances, I should expect to find you in your surgery, throwing your instruments around as you prepare for battle."

"Already done! My knives and gags are set out, the pitch is boiling, the sand scattered, and my operating table is covered with blood-stained sheets. I am open for business."

"Impressive! But my guess is your present mood has nothing to do with your efficiency." Fly studied Leander carefully, from his throat to his hairline. "Your colour is high and your eyes are bright. Do you have a fever, Doctor?"

Leander chewed on the inside of his mouth; his mood was bouncing all over the place.

As expected, Fly pressed on. "It is a shame I cannot ask Mr. Walby to scale the mizzen. It would be helpful knowing what flags those ships are flying so that we could all scurry about and make our preparations. I wonder. May I ask you to go up the mast?"

Leander would have no part of his baiting. "Why ask me when you have a ship full of topmen at your disposal?"

"Because the gossip around here this morning was most extraordinary. I just about choked on my coffee." Fly's direct gaze was now boring holes in Leander's skull. "I understand you have become quite adept at climbing the ratlines."

Leander met Fly head-on, despite knowing his hot face presented a pretty picture for mockery. "And who is it that has taken such an interest in my affairs?" He was met with firmly sealed lips and silence. "Ah! You are going to be difficult. All right then, by chance, was it Mr. Beef?"

"Mr. Beef? Whatever gave you that idea, Doctor? Why our resident madman cannot even string together a complete sentence." There was a slight shake to his head as he relaxed his stance and softened his piercing stare. "For pity's sake, my friend, be careful."

"Captain Austen! If you please, sir!"

The lively shout that tore the shroud of stillness on the *Invincible* made Leander jump. Fly, however, did not flinch. He allowed his own words to linger between them before giving his blue jacket a fastidious tug and striding away toward the taffrail, calling out: "Yes, Mr. Walby! What is it? What do you see?"

The officers and others crowded around the young lad, anxious to hear what his sharp eyes had learned of the ships. Leander, his skin prickling beneath his greatcoat, stayed where he was and slumped against the solid mizzenmast to observe from afar.

Gus swung around on the stern bench, waving his spyglass, eyes ignited, pink excitement on his cheeks. He searched among the expectant faces for his captain. "Sir! One of them just hauled up her colours."

Fly calmly looked eastward. "And?"

"I am almost certain of it, sir!" he cried with a quick gulp and swallow. "She's an American frigate."

9:05 A.M.

Emily was only too happy to accept Arthur Braden's invitation to join his sister and him at their little table in the forepeak. For ages now she had been wandering dazedly about the *Invincible*, alternately smiling and wringing her hands, Leander's banyan around her shoulders to ward off the chill of the strengthening winds. She did not know where to go. She didn't want to hear what had been discovered of the trailing ships, and she definitely did not want to return to her cabin for fear of finding Mrs. Jiggins there. If she couldn't be with Leander, would it not be a comfort to sit awhile with his family? Emily spent a brief moment ruminating. Perhaps not ... given her early-morning tryst on the topmast. Her face was already heating up as she took a place on an empty sugar cask beside Miss Braden.

"You look like you could use a drink." Old Dr. Braden winked and was all sincere warmth as he held up an earthenware pot and poured tea into a creamware cup for her. Emily reacted with sincere appreciation, for only had she been blind could she have missed the pursed disapproval settling in beneath Miss Braden's mob cap. Was it her unladylike appearance the woman censured — the braided hair, checked shirt, scarf, and loose-fitting trousers — or this sharing in the tea which obviously had been brewed from her own cherished tin of leaves and not simply swept up from the leavings on Biscuit's galley floor? It could not be anything else, could it?

Emily clutched Leander's banyan around her. "Thank you. Tea would be lovely. Perhaps it will keep me from seeking out your son and begging him for a tonic of laudanum." Her words threw Miss Braden's features into a profound scowl. Emily shook her head, loathing herself for saying such a thing.

She had only taken one mouthful of tea, any attempt at conversation not yet begun, when Mrs. Jiggins showed up, banishing the stink of rotting fish with her wafting aromas of orange flowers, dazzling the dimly lit darkness of the lower deck in her swishing exhibition of peach silk and ostrich feathers. When no invitation to join them was extended, Mrs. Jiggins went ahead and found herself something to sit upon. Spying a barrel in the shadows beneath a row of hanging fire buckets, she lugged it over to their little table, dropped down upon it quite heavily and blew through a succession of exhalations to ameliorate the discomforts of her exertion. One would think she had single-handedly raised the anchor! She then reached for the last of the creamware cups, frowned at the substantial chip in its rim, decided it was acceptable, and held it out for old Dr. Braden to fill.

"Now then, I have had a word with Mr. Biscuit," she said cheerfully, innocent of the stares around her, "and he has agreed to bring us a lovely lump of apple cake to eat with our tea."

"I daresay he did," Miss Braden said *sotto voce*. Emily was amused by her notes of sarcasm and to hear her add, "And will you be delighting us again this evening by dancing on the deck?"

Mrs. Jiggins scooped up Miss Braden's hand, lying limp and unsuspecting on the table, and gave it a tremendous squeeze. Snatching her hand back, Miss Braden's horrified expression was a true testament that never before had she been mauled in such a way. Mrs. Jiggins, however, did not seem to notice the affront and chattered on in her happy manner. "I do hope so. It was ever so much fun on Sunday. I have not yet recovered from the thrill of it all. And Mr. Biscuit and Mr. Burgo are both desirous to have me teach them more intricate dance steps."

"No doubt." Again, it was Miss Braden, mumbling between her teeth.

Mrs. Jiggins paused for contemplation, cradling her teacup on her lap. "I am planning another painting lesson this afternoon in Captain Austen's cabin." She beamed at old Dr. Braden. "And I do hope you will consider joining us this time? If there are any stirrings of greatness in you, I shall bring them out for all to see."

Arthur Braden parted his lips, but there was a delay in his reply as he looked helplessly around the table. "Have you ... have you not heard, Mrs. Jiggins? It is believed we are being followed by two —"

Mrs. Jiggins, her feathers nodding vehemently, would not hear him out. "Oh, I have, I have, Dr. Braden. It is on the lips of everyone on this ship! This is why I have come at once. It is imperative we discuss this morning's unsavoury business with great calm and bestow upon Emeline the wisdom of our collective years."

Miss Braden lifted her prospect glass to her eye. It grew alarmingly large as it locked upon Emily. "What do you mean by unsavoury business?"

"I shall enlighten you post-haste, Miss Braden." Mrs. Jiggins turned to face Emily and rearranged herself to exhibit earnest care and concern. "You must know by now, my dear, why Lord Somerton and I made this incomparable sacrifice and agreed to take this journey with you aboard the *Invincible*."

Knowing full well what was coming, Emily's measured retort was swift. "No! In fact, I do not. I cannot imagine what possessed Lord Somerton. I had wondered if he was considering a career in the navy, perhaps starting out as a midshipman along with all the other little lads, and then sword fighting his way up the hierarchy with the hopes of becoming Admiral of the Fleet one day. But he is so soft, so well-fed, coddled all his life by his mama, really. I cannot imagine he would survive a week on a ship if he were forced to labour at the pumps and scrub the decks on his hands and knees. How dreadfully he would suffer from hernias and blisters and bruises." She arched her brow at Mrs. Jiggins. "You, on the other hand ... I believe you are hoping to make a conquest and are presently compiling a list of men with whom you are in ardent pursuit."

Behind her prospect glass, Miss Braden quietly sniggered. Old Dr. Braden's thin shoulders tensed up; he kept his sights fixed upon the nervous bounce of his steepled fingers on the oak table. Mrs. Jiggins was aghast; her peach feathers, quivering atop her head, supremely ruffled. She glanced uncertainly from one table mate to another to glean their reactions, pleating knots in the skirt of her silk gown with her unoccupied hand. Her laughter, when it came, was loud and awkward.

"Nonsense! Tush, Emeline! How can you be so flippant?" Abruptly, she stood up, knocking her head against one of the oil-lanterns, mowing down two of her feathers, and glared into the shadows of the lower deck. "Upon my word! Where is Mr. Biscuit with our cake?" In a swish of crackling silk, she then unloaded a portion of her exasperation upon Miss Braden. "And why is it you always wear a mob? As far as I have been able to learn, you are not married!"

Setting down her prospect glass, Miss Braden made a determined show of taking up her sewing, a huge pair of footed woollen drawers with a buttoned closure and frontal flap. Her rejoinder, when she finally dished it out, was an icy one.

"No, but apparently you are … or you were. Did you send him to an early grave, Mrs. Jiggins?" She jabbed her needle into a gaping hole of frayed threads in the derrière of the drawers. "Perhaps I should lend you one of my mobs so you can do away with those ridiculous turbans and plumages you seem to favour so highly. The ones that make you look like a —"

Mrs. Jiggins's spine stiffened on her barrel as she waited in horror for Miss Braden to disparage her. Old Dr. Braden quickly intercepted. Reaching across the obstacles of teapot and crockery, he gave his sister's forearm a warning squeeze and emphatically repeated Mrs. Jiggins's inquiry regarding the Scottish cook. "Yes, yes, where is Biscuit? It would be helpful if he were to come along with our cake … right about now."

When Biscuit did materialize from the darkness of the deck, a spring in his step, whistling a rendition of "Can of Grog" and carrying the lump of cake on his best silver tray, he was attacked forthwith by an irate Mrs. Jiggins.

"It's about time, Mr. Biscuit. We are all famished here! Another minute and you might have found us all dead upon the floor for want of food!"

Biscuit stopped in his tracks. Above his tray, his grin went stale and he gawped at Mrs. Jiggins with his one good eye as if he had never seen her before.

But there was no time for further recrimination and scolding.

Overhead, the hollow drums began to thrum and the familiar orders, the ones that made Emily's blood run cold, the ones she had known would come sooner or later, were expelled through speaking trumpets and lusty sets of lungs from all corners of the *Invincible*.

"We shall beat to quarters!"

"All hands clear the ship for action, ahoy!"

"Signal the *Expedition* at once!"

"See to the livestock!"

"Lower the boats."

"Remove the bulkheads!"

"Release the guns!"

"Look lively, lads! Pull together now!"

Everyone froze at the little table in the forepeak as the *Invincible* thumped with heavy footfalls. All at once everything descended into deafening disorder, hurry and bustle, noise and distress, the ship shifting, rolling, clattering, and bumping with the chaos. Emily's mouth went dry; she closed her eyes in despair. Old Dr. Braden and his sister were grimly silent. Any courage Mrs. Jiggins might have possessed crumbled away at once. She grabbed on to Biscuit's thigh and shrieked, "What is it now? Whatever is happening?"

Biscuit gazed upward at the deckhead, trying to balance his tray of cake, plates, and cutlery while a deranged woman clung ferociously to his leg. As he listened, his face grew increasingly resplendent. "Right then, ladies! Ya better come with me and I'll leads ya to the Lady's Hole," he said, doing a cheerful turnabout. "Ya kin all hide in there."

CHAPTER 25

Magpie held his bucket of smelly rags and brackish water close to his chest as he emerged from behind the curtain of the quarter-gallery privy. Finding the great cabin empty, he whistled a sigh of relief. Captain Uptergrove made him jittery with those all-seeing eyes of his and his cold-hearted demeanour. Had Magpie found him quietly scribbling notes at his desk or at his table, spooning soup into his thin-lipped mouth, he was sure to have tripped on the edge of the rug and brought great misery upon himself once again. He had paid dearly for his punishment of three days ago. His legs and lower back were still pained from his hours of standing on the stool, so much so that it was a chore getting through his day, bending and lifting and hauling stuff around. What was worse, a large number of the Bloody Fluxes poked fun at him whenever he trudged past them on the lower decks, calling him Bucket Boy, Cyclops, Simpleton, and Stool Fool. But the worst of it had been the complete crushing of his spirits. He had been so close to friends and freedom. So close! Nay! Another bout of such torment could not be borne.

As Magpie stepped past the window seat on his way out, his eye fell upon Uptergrove's bamboo flute. It was still lying in the same position on the soft velvet cushions beneath the galleried windows, still untouched and forgotten. Shooting a nervous glance over his shoulder at the cabin door, his heart pounding beneath his ribs, he set his bucket down and picked up the flute, turning it over and over again in his trembling hands, admiring its intricate scrolls and carvings of fruit and flowers. It was the most beautiful flute he had ever seen in his short life. How he longed to place his lips upon its mouthpiece, cover its tiny holes with his fingers and play his favourite tune, the one about the grazing sheep. But he didn't dare. However lovely his music might be, its notes would set off an alarm, alerting the burly master-at-arms who was sure to come bursting into the cabin to arrest him for breaching the peace.

Carrying the flute in his hands like a newborn, he drew toward the gilded portrait of Uptergrove's four children. All of them were still beaming with happiness. Had they ever known misery? He didn't think so. They lived in an exquisite house with exquisite furnishings and had toys and pets to play with. Their bodies were plump, their cheeks red and rounded with good health. Their bellies never went hungry. There was that glorious silver fruit bowl at their feet, available to them at any time, heaped with tempting apples, plums, and cherries, fruits Magpie had never even tasted. And, he thought ruefully as he fingered his green eye patch, they were all handsome children with two good eyes in their heads.

Magpie lifted his face to the rays of warm sunlight streaming through the galleried windows. He closed his eye and pretended he was one of Uptergrove's children. Dwelling in that lively room was blissful. The saucy cat purred as she circled his ankles. The bird chirped secrets to him from her fine cage. His two sisters placed glistening plums in his hands, assuring him he would find their sweetness and texture to his liking. His older brother begged him to play a tune on the flute while his wee brother, the one still in skirts, gleefully clapped his hands and gurgled with laughter. And then Magpie's daydream took an extra delightful turn. The drawing room door suddenly opened and in rushed their mother, all swishing skirts and smiles. She was pretty and fair and full of fun just like Emily, and anxious to hear of their morning adventures. Seating herself on the leather chair, she gathered them all around, the wee one scrambling for a place of pride upon her lap. Magpie looked around at his family, his breast swelling with joyful emotion like never before. He felt as happy as he had been the time Emily had hugged him close to her.

Lamentably, in his real world, it was the great cabin door that opened. There was no pretty mother standing there, no reassuring sound of rustling silk, no tender words of greeting. It was just the opposite. Boots stamped and stopped short on the threshold. A thudding silence choked the room. The atmosphere shifted as if a cold bank of fog had seeped through the cracks of the oak timbers. Magpie's heart was in his mouth. He was still cradling the flute and there was no time to cast it aside or to hide. Uptergrove had caught him red-handed.

"What are you doing, boy?"

The question was terse, loaded with outrage. Magpie could feel his face rapidly draining of any colour it might have had. A quick glance at Uptergrove's hard, unwavering eyes was all he could manage. He lowered his head in shame.

"I'm so very sorry, sir. I know I don't got no right to touch yer things. It's just … it's just yer flute's so very beautiful. I weren't tryin' to steal it, sir, if that's what yer thinkin'."

Magpie crept to the stern bench, expecting to be kicked or feel the thwack of a cat-o'-nine-tails. Nay! Uptergrove would want to discipline him before a mean, jeering crowd, all shouting those cruel names that made him feel worthless. He would whip him senseless the same as that ill-fated American who had died in the night from shock and putrid infection. Trying to control the shaking of his hands, Magpie returned the flute to its home upon the velvet cushions. Near tears, he picked up his bucket. He was too afraid to meet Uptergrove's horrible eyes, but he could still see his captain's hand flexing and clenching on the door latch, and sunbeams glinting off his Hessian boots. More excuses spilled from his mouth, but they were feeble-sounding and thick as porridge.

"Ya see, I were missin' me own flute, sir. It ain't nearly as nice as yours though. I don't know where mine's got to. I lost it. But I promise ya, sir … I won't never, ever touch yours again."

As he waited breathlessly for Uptergrove to respond, Magpie heard a rising roar of excited voices in the distance. The appearance of a flush-faced lieutenant in the doorway provided a reprieve. The awful silence skittered away into the corners of the cabin. Curious, Magpie looked up. Uptergrove had turned his back to hear the lieutenant's message.

"Sir! A signal has come from the *Invincible*."

"What have they learned?"

"They are quite certain one of the ships is an American frigate."

Uptergrove's response was swift and unaffected. "Then we must be prepared. Turn our head toward the enemy and sound the drums and fife at once!"

"Aye, sir."

The lieutenant sped off to relay his orders like a discharge of whirling chain shot.

Turning again, Uptergrove gazed at Magpie. His features were no longer set with flinty anger and suspicion. They were puffy with fatigue and sadness. The fringes on the epaulettes of his uniform sagged like thirsty flowers; his shining boots had lost their lustre and suddenly looked too large for him. A heavy smell of unhappiness had supplanted the stench of Magpie's bucket.

"What is your name, boy?" asked Uptergrove, not unkindly.

Magpie had to moisten his dry mouth before answering. "It's Magpie, sir."

"And your last name?"

"I don't got one, sir."

Uptergrove nodded, his eyes scudding around the room, landing finally upon the gilded portrait of his children. For a long time, he stared at it, saying nothing. And when at last he broke free from his reverie and raised his face, a plaintive sigh escaped his parted lips.

"I am sorry, Magpie," he said, his eyes blinking and unsteady. "I hope you will find it in your heart to accept my sincerest apology."

Lifting his bicorne hat from its peg on the wall, he gave it a quick dusting and departed, disappearing from view on the quarterdeck just as the drummer and fifer summoned the Expeditions to their battle stations.

11:15 A.M.
ABOARD HMS *INVINCIBLE*

Leander was sitting lost in thought alongside his operating table in the cockpit, located in the after part of the orlop deck. His medical ledger was spread open across his knees and his quill pen was locked in his fingers, but it had been a long while since ink had met paper. If it had not been for the rousing throat clearing, Leander might never have been aware that someone was standing nearby, awaiting his attention. His eyes having first alighted upon suede buckskins and fine leather top boots before moving on up to his visitor's face, he knew at once who it was. Snapping his ledger shut, he quickly stood up, trying to exile the thought that the man before him might have guessed the distant planet his mind had been exploring.

"Lord Somerton! To what do I owe this honour?" he asked, hoping he sounded nonchalant.

Somerton wavered before him, hands gripping the lapels of his double-breasted cutaway coat. "I wondered if you might require some assistance here ... perhaps now or at any time in the coming hours."

Leander was amused. Someone must have informed Lord Somerton that, during a naval battle, being safely stowed away in the cockpit, below the waterline, was the safest place of all to be. "Did you have anything particular in mind?"

Somerton peered into the eerily lit spaces around him, taking in the cluster of hammocks, the shelves of tonics and rum, the sand scattered upon the floor, and the sharpened tools lying neatly upon the blood-stained sheets between them. "Not exactly. I do know that you are short of men and could probably use an extra pair of hands."

Leander considered his options. "You could help to carry the wounded down here for treatment."

Somerton recoiled as he digested the suggestion. "But that would mean going near to those who will be engaged in the fight."

"Yes."

"I would be in the midst of musket balls and cannon-fire."

"Yes!" retorted Leander. He tossed his ledger and quill upon the operating table and removed his spectacles, hooking one of its hinged sidepieces onto his open-collared shirt. "I would suggest you change your clothing, unless you do not mind getting those you presently have on smeared with body parts. You may not be able to rinse them clean later on."

Somerton's astonishment grew into suspicion as if he was weighing the possibility that Leander had just mocked him. "I shall see to my clothes at once," he said tartly. "But, I wonder, might there be something I could do down here? It would be no bother at all for me to collect medicines and dressings for you or fetch soup and water for the injured."

"Or hand me the tourniquet and my knives while I am amputating arms and legs?"

Somerton swallowed. "I suppose I could do that."

Leander studied him a moment. "Forgive me, Lord Somerton, it is not that I don't appreciate your kind offer to help, but perhaps you are unaware that there is a hiding place on the *Invincible*. I understand that Biscuit has already taken the women there."

Somerton's cheeks coloured with indignation. Like a litigating lawyer, he swiftly shot back. "Whilst on the *Isabelle*, were you at any time acquainted with my youngest brother, Octavius Lindsay? If I remember correctly, he was a second lieutenant."

Leander waited until he could hold Somerton's fleeting glance. "I was well acquainted with your brother."

"Then tell me, during a battle, what was *he* expected to do?"

Leander was a long time in replying, unable to fully recollect how much Somerton had been apprised, if at all, of his brother's ignominious end. He could give a brassy answer, but he chose to tread carefully on the subject.

"Your brother stayed close to Captain Moreland on the quarterdeck."

"I see." Somerton glanced away to stare at Leander's surgical tools on the table, brows knitted as if trying to identify the inherent purpose of the more obscure ones.

"You are welcome to help here … in whatever capacity you so choose," said Leander reluctantly. "But be forewarned. The cockpit of a ship during a battle can be an ugly and terrifying place."

Somerton looked up and snorted as if reacting to a joke. "Surely, Doctor, if a woman such as Emeline can tolerate it, I can, too."

11:40 A.M.

Captain Austen had given Gus Walby permission to establish his station on the stern bench, at least until the inevitable battle had begun, before lead peppered the air between and around the warring ships. Mr. Philpotts had loaned him a portable desk and a fat cushion so he could sit and work in comfort. He had been left with instructions to complete a watch-bill and dash off a few letters for Captain Austen while he waited for the ships to draw closer. And when they came upon one another, it was paramount he keep a sharp eye out for the names emblazoned on the enemy sterns. It all made Gus feel very important and enabled him to forget that he was no longer a midshipman. Being Captain Austen's clerk came with all sorts of unimagined benefits. He was proud of his little clerking office near the great cabin. He had been proud to accompany his captain to his meeting with Uptergrove on the *Expedition*. And he was proud of the cerulean-blue serge coat Miss Braden had sewn for him. It kept him warm and made him look just as smart as the uniformed men who came together on the quarterdeck, consulting their maps and charts, speaking solemnly with one another. Certainly, in Gus's mind's eye, it made him look an equal to Cadby Brambles, who, at the moment, was strutting around the deck, sticking his tongue out at Gus whenever the coast was clear. Undoubtedly, the loss of Fleda's letter still caused severe heartache, but when Gus concentrated on the positive aspects of his life the emotional wound scabbed over and became somewhat easier to abide.

Before long he spotted Biscuit, scurrying toward him with a laden wooden tray, his whiskery face aglow with smiles.

"Mr. Walby! Are ya ready to do battle? Are ya ready to take an American prize? Is yer cutlass close at hand?"

"No, Biscuit!" laughed Gus. "But my spyglass is."

"Ach! Bless ya, Mr. Walby. If it weren't fer yer eyesight we would still be in the dark regardin' them ships." He set his tray down beside the portable desk on the bench, took from it a steaming mug and placed it in Gus's hands. "Now here's a cup o' chocolate fer ya. And while yer waitin' to see what that other ship be, I've also brung ya a buttered muffin and a cold slice o' mutton. Just holler if ya need somethin' more." He placed a fist to his forehead in a respectful salute and hurried off to prepare other trays for those in need of some warming sustenance as they whiled away the waiting hours.

Gus was soon honoured with another visitor. He had gulped down his chocolate and was peering through his spyglass (so eager to be able to report another tidbit of information) when old Dr. Braden eased himself down upon the bench. "You look quite self-sufficient here at your post, Mr. Walby," he said, casting admiring glances around Gus's station.

"I am, thank you, sir." Remembering his manners, Gus gestured toward the tray. "Please help yourself. I am far too nervous to eat."

Old Dr. Braden patted his stomach. "You are generous, but at the moment I am overstuffed with tea and apple cake. I would, however, suggest you try to force something down. We never know when we shall see our next meal."

For a while they sat companionably, keeping their thoughts to themselves as they contemplated the growing shapes beyond the *Invincible*'s bobbing bowsprit. Old Dr. Braden was the first to speak again. "I was just wondering where I might find you when ... when it all starts. Will you still be positioned right here?"

"Oh no, sir, by then I'll be standing on the quarterdeck with Captain Austen, taking notes for him."

Old Dr. Braden's smile looked uncomfortable. "Yes, of course you will be." He twisted his lips. "Well, if you need me I shall be in the cockpit with Leander and the irascible Mr. Duffy."

"Then I shall come and visit you the first chance I can, sir."

"Even though Leander and I may press you into service?"

"That does not worry me in the least, sir."

Old Dr. Braden extended his hand toward Gus. "Good luck, my boy."

"Thank you! You, too, sir."

They shook hands, holding one another's gaze, Gus seeing the gleam of worried concern in the doctor's old eyes. And as he watched him push himself up off the bench, gather his coat around him and walk slowly toward the companion way with his head down, Gus was surprised by the size of the lump forming in his throat.

CHAPTER 26

1:00 P.M.

(AFTERNOON WATCH, TWO BELLS)

Emily hoisted her candle-lantern for the little group with whom she had travelled to reach this forlorn area on the aft platform of the orlop, in the oppressive space just forward of the ship's rudder. Cadby Brambles had been charged with leading them here through the rumbling excitement on the decks as the crew cleared for battle and the enemy ships loomed larger by the minute. It still surprised Emily to witness scenes of vivacity: the joking, the back-slapping, the well-wishing among men about to confront mortal combat. Even the purser, Mr. Philpotts, normally sulky and objectionable, had an animated grin upon his substantial face. How could they act this way when her spirits were anything but exuberant? She could not control the careening of her heart beneath the folds of Leander's banyan. But it helped knowing *he* was nearby, on the same deck as she, beneath the waterline, beyond the range of splintering oak and exploding shot.

Biting her lip, Emily watched Mr. Brambles dump his burden of blankets and pillows in an oily corner and struggle to lift the slimy grating from the hatchway at their feet. Beside her, Miss Braden was fingering her leather etui and tin of tea, her eyes growing wide beneath her mob cap as she, too, observed the huffing gestures of Mr. Brambles. Even in the murky light, Emily could see that her face was as pale as paper.

"Are you quite all right, Miss Braden?" she whispered gently, sensing a kinship of anxiety between them.

"Of course!" snapped the older woman, embracing her treasures to her breast as if worried someone would steal them away. "Why wouldn't I be?"

Mrs. Jiggins, who had already expressed her dissatisfaction at being led into the "foul-smelling entrails of the ship," especially as she was forced to leave her paint-box and canvases behind, was beside herself when Mr. Brambles finally exposed the yawning void in the floor.

"Upon my soul, young man!" she gasped, her hands fussing with her straw bonnet that concealed all but a salty-brown fringe of hair above her eyes. "You cannot mean that this is where you intend to hide us. Surely this is not the place Mr. Biscuit had in mind."

"Aye, ma'am. This is the Lady's Hole," a winded Mr. Brambles replied, tossing the grating on top of the bedclothes and wiping the slime from his hands on his white breeches. "Captain Austen ordered me to bring you all here."

"Shine the light in there, Emeline. I must have a thorough look inside," instructed Mrs. Jiggins, gathering up her skirts. Emily obligingly stepped forward with the lantern so that Mrs. Jiggins could make her critical inspection. "For goodness' sake, Mr. Brambles! There is no proper floor! How can you expect us to manage in such a tiny wedge of space?"

Mr. Brambles's eyes jumped around their small circle. At a loss for words, he shrugged his shoulders and looked baffled. But in no time at all a second disturbing thought struck Mrs. Jiggins hard, usurping her worries of confinement.

"There wouldn't be any bats down there, would there, Mr. Brambles?"

"Nay, but you might see a rat or two, ma'am. This hole is just behind the bread room and the rats love it there. The bad smell is most likely their nest and droppings."

"My word!" was Mrs. Jiggins's withering response. "What about spiders? You know … the big ones with hairy legs?"

"Don't be absurd!" Miss Braden frowned reproachfully. "How could spiders possibly end up on a ship at sea?"

"Oh, but they can, ma'am," said Mr. Brambles. "They fly in on their silken webs. I am more than certain we took on an army of them in Portsmouth and again while sailing close to England."

"I do declare!" Mrs. Jiggins pulled a lavender-infused handkerchief from her bodice and fanned herself. "It is imperative I speak to Captain Austen about the wisdom of stuffing ladies into a spider-infested coffin. You will have to extract our cramped remains from there with a crowbar!"

Mr. Brambles glanced sharply at her. "With due respect, ma'am, it doesn't matter where you are during a sea battle."

"I beg your pardon, Mr. Brambles?" Mrs. Jiggins stared at him, her head lodged on one side as if someone had snapped her neck in two.

"Should the *Invincible* be blown to bits, ma'am, it won't matter a crumb where you are hiding. We shall all go down together."

"Where to?" croaked Mrs. Jiggins, her brow deeply furrowed with alarm, her handkerchief flying much faster now.

Mr. Brambles hesitated, seemingly unable to provide her with a satisfactory answer.

Emily lowered the lantern. "They call it Davy Jones's locker, Mrs. Jiggins," she said, one hand clasping Leander's banyan to her throat. "It is otherwise known as the bottom of the sea."

2:00 P.M.
(AFTERNOON WATCH, FOUR BELLS)
ABOARD HMS *EXPEDITION*

Magpie watched one of the powder monkeys, a boy no bigger than himself, retrieve a cartridge of gunpowder from the gunner and scuttle past him into the shadow-infested warren of the orlop. It was his turn next. The gunner gave him a hostile going-over from behind the dampened curtains of the handling chamber, the place where the cartridges were made up in pouches of flannel and stored in orderly rows on a wall rack.

"Well? C'mon! Git a move on! This ain't no time to have yer head up yer arse!"

Magpie stepped forward and peered up at the gunner. Locked behind panes of glass were two large oil lamps that flanked the chamber's doorway. Their meagre illumination cast the gunner's fearfully misshapen face in a terrifying light. A portion of his cheek and jaw were missing and one of his eyes ... it wasn't really an eye ... it was a filmy, milky-white, messy thing. Had the man, somewhere in his past, been hit with a fragment of hot canister or, even worse, had a cartridge of gunpowder exploded in his face? Magpie felt weak with worry. Already, he had lost one eye in combat. Should an accident with the gunpowder befall him he would have no face left at all.

"I ain't familiar with the routine, sir. I ain't never carried a cartridge afore."

The gunner swooped down upon Magpie, showing him the full horror of his corrupted eye. "Who sent ya down here, then? Shouldn't ya be cleanin' the cap'n's heads or somethin'?"

"It were the cap'n what sent me, sir."

"Aha! Did he elevate ya from bucket boy to powder monkey? Ain't sure which one's worse!" Leaving Magpie at the curtained aperture, the gunner sauntered off toward the shelves. He took down a pouch of powder, carried it to a roughly hewn table and inched it slowly into a tin box shaped like a cylinder. "Ya gotta be damn careful with this stuff," he said, enclosing the works with a lid and handing it off to Magpie. "Don't get it near a spark or open flame o' any kind. And for God's sake, don't stumble on the ladders! 'Cause ya wouldn't want to lose yer other eye now, would ya?"

Magpie hurried away from him and ducked through an archway into the carpenters' walk. For all his inexperience in carrying the cartridges, he did know it was best to access this passage to the upper decks. It led along the ship's side and would minimize potential collisions with short-tempered crewmen. But the platform here was not made of solid planking and almost immediately the heel of his shoe got wedged into a section of porous grating. While trying to wiggle it free, terrified of upsetting the cartridge, he realized he was not alone. He quit squirming and snapped his head up to listen to the invisible speakers, whispering on the other side of the thin wall.

"Wait 'til we're in the thick o' battle."

"No! Think of it. Too many sharpshooters and heated guns. Best to wait 'til nightfall brings an end to the fighting."

"Aye! And Uptergrove reclaims his cabin."

"We'll have to get rid of the helmsman."

"How?"

"We'll figure that out later."

"What about weapons? What d'we got?"

"Aye! How many guns did ya manage to steal?"

"Shhh! Hold up! Shhh!"

The whisperers fell silent as footfalls were heard, running on the platform in their direction.

"Quick! Scatter! Someone's comin'!"

Magpie, his empty eye socket throbbing with pain, waited until the men had skittered away into the deep hiding places of the orlop and the coast was clear. The waiting left him stuck to the clammy wall of the ship like a web-footed salamander, his heel still wedged in the grating. He gripped the wire handle of the cartridge for dear life, too terrified to even set it down. Perspiration trickled down his face and slipped into his open mouth. Who were the whisperers? And what was it they were fixing to do come nightfall?

The first blasts of cannon-fire came with a warning of imminent death and woe. They shook the foundations of the ship and Magpie's foot free.

2:30 P.M.
(AFTERNOON WATCH, FIVE BELLS)
ABOARD HMS *INVINCIBLE*

"Mind your note-taking, Mr. Walby!" shouted Fly as he studied the puffs of gun smoke spewing from the front of the nearest enemy vessel. "Half past two. First shots fired. No damage done."

There was a warble in Gus's reply. "Just a little shot-splash, right, sir?"

"Aye!" Fly tapped his spyglass against his leg. It was a relief those bow chasers had missed their mark. But what did it matter? Soon, the guns on both sides would be lined up in perfect firing range. Destruction would surely come then. His men, though unharmed, were rattled. Their mounting anxiety was visible and palpable. He could see it in their gaze, their eyes bright and unfocused; and in their restless movements, hands and feet not knowing quite what to do. Some picked at their nails; some polished their cutlasses while others scratched at itchy places. How many of them were wandering in painful contemplation, wondering if, by day's end, they would be minus an arm or a leg or have their head sheared off and their bloody stump hurled overboard like rancid meat? Those dreadful images ripped Fly apart before every battle.

Shutting the book on his dismaying thoughts, he turned around to search the *Invincible*. Were they ready? Had everything been done? He hoped so. The splinter-netting was up, the yards and masts fixed with iron chains to thwart the destruction of falling debris; the hammocks rolled and stowed into netting along the bulwark. Clutching their ladles and ramrods, the gun crews stood together, sights set on the enemy, their captains itching to light the fuses of their cannons and carronades. The marines were lined up, their muskets aimed at the approaching enemy. They looked reassuring in their gaiters and scarlet jackets with the white cross-belts. His little army.

Off the stern, Fly could see the livestock in the bouncing boats. A few of the hapless creatures had been unceremoniously pitched overboard and drowned. He prayed the ones squawking their discontentment in the trailing boats were not blown apart by bullets and whistling shot. Surrounding them was a motley collection of articles that had once belonged to the *Invincible*: soaking tubs, harness casks, puncheons, and pieces of furniture. They bobbed in the waves like carefree swimmers. Fly abhorred the necessity of throwing things overboard to make way for the guns. Such waste! And still so early in the journey. At the end of this day, if he was fortunate enough to survive it, his fervent hope would be to find a chair or two remaining in his cabin alongside his trunks of clothing and uniforms. But then, when the winds of battle had died away, it was not unheard of for a sailor to find himself without any possessions at all, everything having been sacrificed to the sea.

Fly turned back to Gus. The lad was leaning heavily on his crutch and smiled up at him, but Fly could tell he was trying hard to quell a sick stomach.

"Are we quite ready, Mr. Walby?"

"I believe so, sir."

"Right then, stay close to me."

"Aye, sir!" Gus began jotting down the necessary notations in the logbook, using the flat surface of the binnacle upon which to write.

Fly's glance fell on the waves of yellow hair on Gus's lowered head and the small, pale hand that held the quill pen. He wondered again if he should send him below on some fabricated errand, perhaps to see how Leander or the ladies were getting on, but the lad was smart. He would harbour suspicion. Negotiating multiple decks with a crutch was not an easy thing to do. With a firm shake of his head, Fly looked at Prosper.

"Bring me in close, Mr. Burgo, and let us hope we get off the first broadside."

"The wind ain't in our favour, Cap'n, but with a spot o' manoeuvrin' I'll change that fer ya." Prosper's ruddy face was etched in determination. "I'm gonna git us a couple o' prizes today! I'm gonna make ya forget that day with the *Amethyst* … the day we lost Morgan Evans."

"Bless you for your confidence, Mr. Burgo," Fly said, knowing sadly and full well that nothing could ever erase the memories of that horrendous August day.

The shadow of the first ship fell across the forecastle of the *Invincible*. Fly saw her gunports up, the barrels of her cannons agape like confounded mouths, her crew fussing around her guns, ramming home the powder cartridges, scrambling to light the fuses in their race to win the day. There was her captain, his officers, his men, his small boys. There was the ensign flying from the stern of their ocean home, stars and stripes proudly rippling in the wind.

Hundreds of arms flew up around Fly. Pumping fists and cheers of huzzah rent the crisp fall air. The sails of the *Invincible* crackled and snapped their lively, inspiring reply. Beneath his blue uniform, Fly felt a spreading warmth. He took one deep breath and bellowed the culminating order for which they had all been waiting.

"Fire!"

CHAPTER 27

Leander's surgery table was already occupied by a sailor whose name he did not know. The man lay in agony before him, his glassy eyes fixed on the deckhead. He had taken a cruel hit to the groin and was muttering incoherently between bites of a blood-soaked biscuit he had pulled from his pocket. A queue of men waited on the floor for their turn to be seen. In the deafening noise, their moans were inaudible, though Leander knew they were likely mumbling shocked nonsense or pleading for water. The ship rocked and shuddered, threatening to throw Leander off his feet. If not for the sand beneath his shoes, he would have been on the floor with the wounded. He glanced over his spectacles at his father, who stood across the table from him, trying to stem the flow of blood with a wad of bandages and a brown sponge. The look that passed between them was rife with meaning. It was doubtful the man could be saved. With a spasm of impatience, Leander searched the cockpit for his assistants.

Mr. Duffy had left some time ago to return to the scenes of battle. Having lost sight of Lord Somerton, Leander assumed the man had gone into hiding. He was, therefore, astonished to see him suddenly emerge from the obscure regions beyond the cockpit.

"We need fresh bandages, Lord Somerton," said Leander, harbouring no interest in questioning his conspicuous absence. "Fetch them, please."

Somerton answered with a sullen nod and crept hunchbacked toward the supply shelves, sidestepping the sailors collapsed and broken on the floor like old chairs. When he approached the table, he blanched and swallowed, his eyes jumping at the sight of the muttering sailor, lying in creeping pools of gore. Old Dr. Braden hurriedly exchanged the soiled bandages for new ones and immediately applied them to the gushing wound. Somerton gazed at the dark-red horror that had been foisted upon him, his nostrils flaring in disgust as if it were a pile of excrement.

"What am I supposed to do with *this*?"

Leander heard him, but did not look his way. Instead, he leaned closer toward his patient to examine his shrapnel-peppered wounds. "Dispose of it in the bucket by the dispensary door, and while you are at it, bring me more sand for the floor."

The sand was summarily fetched and scattered around his shoes, though done so in a petulant silence. Leander did not care.

Soon Mr. Duffy was back. He came waddling backwards into the cockpit, his armpits wet with perspiration, the ankles of another victim of war in his firm grasp. His blaring shouts alerted all of his presence. "Doctor! There's plenty more where this one came from. Cap'n Austen needs 'em cleared from the deck. They're startin' to pile up like turds in a bucket."

Leander grimaced at the distasteful description and stood up straight, careful not to strike his head against the lanterns. He looked squarely at Somerton. "Go with Mr. Duffy."

Somerton's face darkened. His tongue rolled slowly about in his mouth. His eyes put up a challenge, but, in Leander's estimation, he made a wise decision by saying nothing in return.

4:00 P.M.
(AFTERNOON WATCH, EIGHT BELLS)

"How much longer, Emeline?" whined Mrs. Jiggins, mopping her brow and dabbing at her eyes with her handkerchief that, regrettably, no longer smelled of lavender. "My feet are numb. My back is knotted like two half hitches and I cannot breathe in here. It smells like some-one has set the Billingsgate Fish Market on fire." Her eyes were large in her glistening face.

"It is just the smoke from the guns," Emily shouted in her ear. She sounded reassuring, but was rapidly tiring of Mrs. Jiggins's complaints. She wished someone was around to reassure her. Their hiding place was as hot as a coal fire. Her damp clothes clung unpleasantly to her skin. The thunderous reverberations impaired her ears. And every time the *Invincible* shuddered from an explosive hit, she held her breath, won-dering if their hole would soon be flooded with seawater. "Why don't you try to get some sleep, Mrs. Jiggins?"

"Sleep? With all this knocking about? My insides are scrambled eggs! And this noise? I cannot hear myself think! Never in my life have I heard such outrageous pandemonium … not even at the Prince Regent's drunken soirées."

"When it is all over, you might find yourself deaf for days," said Emily, tugging on her shirt to keep it from sticking to her hot skin. "The men often do."

Miss Braden, who astoundingly was buttoned up to her neck and still wearing her mob cap, finally broke her self-imposed silence. "Could you *please* move over, Mrs. Jiggins? You are practically sitting on top of me."

"I am afraid to, Miss Braden. Look at that frightening crack in the timbers over there. If I were to move … well, I fear that is where the rats enter from the bread room." Mrs. Jiggins let out a long wail. "How much longer will it be, Emeline?"

"I have no idea, Mrs. Jiggins. Sea battles are not games with fixed rules and time limitations. It may be our misfortune to have to hide here for some time to come." Emily looked up into the darkness be-yond the grating. "It will be night soon. If we have not sustained too much damage ... if no victory has been declared ... there is a possibility we shall continue fighting for days."

Mrs. Jiggins took up her whinging again. "I simply cannot go on this way. I shall be completely numb in five more minutes."

"Try!" snapped Miss Braden, wrenching her skirt out from under Mrs. Jiggins's bottom. "'Tis far better than the alternative."

Mrs. Jiggins finally acquiesced. "I suppose you are right. I do not really have a desire to meet this man they call Davy Jones. He sounds like a degenerate." She eyed Miss Braden's tin of tea. "A cup of something warm might soothe my nerves."

"Are you not overheated enough already?" Miss Braden's disbelief grew vexatious. "Oh, I see! Were you hoping I would jump up; trot along to the galley, fire up Biscuit's stove and bring back a pot of boiled water for you ... while balls of lead are flying every which way?"

"Well, no, I never would have assumed —"

"Good! Because I do not share my tea with strangers!" Miss Braden stashed her tin away under a mildewed blanket.

Mrs. Jiggins was aghast. "Strangers? I thought we were —! How can you possibly consider me a stranger when we have spent hours baking in here like bread rolls in Biscuit's oven?" She briskly propelled her handkerchief over her face and the flabby skin of her neck. "My word! This is worse than being tortured at the Tower."

"And how would you know?"

"Well, I ... I have read of such accounts in novels!"

"For goodness' sake, *will* you move over?"

Mrs. Jiggins put up a resistance. "No! I will not! I will not abide rats crawling into the bodice of my gown."

"Ha!" spat Miss Braden. "There's little room in there for anything, let alone a clan of rats!"

Mrs. Jiggins sniffed. "Maybe *you* should move over. In that mob of yours, you shan't notice those spiderwebs by your head."

The *Invincible* jounced like a bucking horse. Mrs. Jiggins shrieked. Miss Braden prayed to Peter and Paul. Emily clapped her hands over her ears. Another hit. Another shower of lead. Had it penetrated the heavy oak walls this time? Had it brought death in its wake? Were Fly and Gus and Biscuit still safe? Was Leander overwhelmed in the cockpit, unable to get to the wounded fast enough, anguished when he could not preserve a life?

Emily picked up Leander's banyan, pulled it on and cast aside the blankets and baskets of food to make space beneath the grating. Clambering onto her knees, she reached up and struggled to move the cumbrous square that covered their hiding hole.

Miss Braden pawed Emily's back. "What are you doing?"

"Emeline!" Mrs. Jiggins shimmied up the slanted walls of the Hole, knocking her straw bonnet askew on her head. She tottered forward to grab a handful of Leander's banyan. "Where in heaven's name are you going?"

"Do not fret. I will come back," Emily said, adding only in her head, "at some point."

"Wot? You cannot leave us alone in this place! What if we are discovered and molested by marauders?"

"Throw our cheese and biscuits at them, Mrs. Jiggins. That should knock them out cold and keep them at bay." Groaning under its weight, Emily shifted the grating just enough so she could leap out of the hole. Once she had gained the platform, she leaned over to peer down at the ladies. The dim light stippled their ashen faces, their trembling expressions suggesting this was the final farewell before they were sent on their way to Mr. Jones's ocean locker. "You have food and water and light. All you need," said Emily, lugging the grating back into place with a jarring thud. "Just please ... while I am gone ... try not to kill one another."

4:30 P.M.
(FIRST DOG WATCH, ONE BELL)

Fly was hoarse from yelling. His throat was raw and parched. He was broiling hot and in desperate need of water. The smells of smoke, gunpowder, and blood were abominable and overpowering. They filled his brain as if he had been submerged in a pond of weedy, brackish water. And the noise! The unrelenting barrage of thunder! If only he could deaden it the same way his gun crews did ... with scarves bound tightly around their heads. But if he were to follow their lead, how would his men single him out on the decks? For them, he had to stay visible.

Fly squinted through the nearest gunport at the American frigate, sailing one hundred yards away on the blue waves, tacking and wearing in chimneys of black smoke, assuming position to deliver another devastating broadside. Of the two enemy vessels, she was the lethal one. As far as Fly could ascertain, the other one had not even come close enough to fire off a shot. But then, as yet, Uptergrove's *Expedition* had not been of much help. Fly prayed that would soon change. If they were going to win the day, they would require a full complement of firepower. He watched the gun crews go through their paces, vociferously urging them to pick up their speeds, roaring instructions and advice where needed, and all the while bitterly regretting the scant time he had given them to practise their drills. But like most captains, he was not in favour of clearing the ship for action when the ocean was serenely empty and free of imminent danger.

Mr. Duffy and two of his helpers suddenly walked out of the prowling smoke, nearly knocking Fly over.

"See to these men!" Fly rasped at them. "Take them below at once. I want nothing in the way of the guns. And, please, when you return to the cockpit, pass the word for the carpenter. I must have a damage report and know if we are taking on water in the bilge."

It was then that Fly realized Lord Somerton was among their small group. The man had on his best coat and breeches as if he were expecting to banquet in the great cabin. Without delay, Mr. Duffy and his other assistant dashed off to execute their morbid tasks. But Lord Somerton remained rooted, imperiously staring down Fly, completely unaware that, in the midst of battle, a captain's time was precious.

"How can you see anything with all this damn smoke, Mr. Austen?" he said, using his finely tailored arms to drive off the offensive air. "I shall soon be covered in soot and resemble a chimney sweep."

"'Tis an inevitable side effect of war," muttered Fly unsympathetically, peering out the gunport.

"So then, where shall I begin?" Somerton gazed critically around the upper deck, his face soured as if he had eaten a slice of lemon.

Withholding his ill humour, Fly jerked away from the gunport and did a swift look-about. As the smoke cleared, he grew more anxious. Already, there was so much ruin and so many casualties. One in particular, a forgotten child splayed upon the planks beside a starboard gun, caught his eye and left him reeling. Fly dragged himself heavy-footed toward him. Crouching, he lifted the boy's wrist to feel for his pulse, but knew he would find nothing there. A round of double-headed shot had opened the boy's bowels, probably killing him instantly. His middle was dashed to pieces, his organs splattered across the floor and the gun carriage. But death had spared his face. It was untouched, unlined, and unburdened. Gathering up the weightless body in his arms, Fly handed him to Somerton, taking particular care to cradle the little head of tawny hair against Somerton's chest.

"You can start with this one."

"Shall I take him to the cockpit?" Somerton was impassive and pitiless as if he were holding a bundle of soiled laundry, not someone's beloved son.

"Nay! Dr. Braden can do nothing to help this child." There was a catch in Fly's throat. His eyes briefly met Somerton's cold ones before he turned away. "Say a prayer for him and then throw his poor remains overboard."

CHAPTER 28

5:00 P.M.
(FIRST DOG WATCH, TWO BELLS)

Gus Walby blew a big sigh of relief when he spotted Captain Austen striding toward the quarterdeck. It saved him from undertaking an arduous journey down the ladder to find him, one that was sure to reap further trauma. What's more, Gus believed that in the presence of their fearless captain, fewer men would be felled at their stations in a hail of bullets. All had descended into frightening chaos whilst the captain had gone below to assist the crews on the gun deck. If it had not been for the protection of the binnacle — the box that housed the compass — Gus himself might have gone down. As he observed Captain Austen winding his way through the smoke, he was all pins and needles. But, to his chagrin, the captain was taking a circuitous route to the helm. He paused to inspect the condition of the sails, stopped here and there to shout an order, ducked now and again to dodge splinters, and grabbed and downed a proffered ladle of water from Biscuit. Gus fiddled with the big brass buttons Miss Braden had laboured to affix to his serge coat, exhaling in exasperation. There was consequential news to be relayed and he was busting to tell it.

As the Invincibles let fly another screaming broadside, he hugged the binnacle. Seconds later, the enemy ship returned fire. It sent Gus careening into Prosper Burgo's skinny legs like rolling shot.

"Look here, young Gus, ya gotta stand tall on the deck," Prosper shouted into the blare, giving him a hand up, seemingly unfazed by the unexpected thumping. "Here comes yer cap'n."

When Captain Austen finally arrived at the ship's wheel, Gus was brushed off and vertical. The captain looked dishevelled and terribly sad, which made Gus worry that, from his superior perspective, things were going badly. He had abandoned his bicorne. His breeches, cream-coloured and gleaming that morning, were blackened with soot. He was bleeding from a cut above his ear and the front of his jacket was smeared with entrails.

"Mr. Burgo," said Captain Austen, struggling to be heard over the roar, "how is she holding up?"

"As long as her masts are upright and her rudder intact, she flies over the waves," Prosper shouted. "So don't come here and tell me her hull's been smashed in and we're sinkin."

"At present we are still afloat, Mr. Burgo. All appears to be well and sound, except for the loss of ..." Captain Austen redirected his eyes at Gus. "Do you have a name for me yet, Mr. Walby?" There was an irascible edge to his inquiry.

Gus stepped out from behind the binnacle to point at the nearest enemy vessel, the one that had inflicted much damage on their sails and men. "She's the *Liberty*, sir," he said proudly. "The same ship we encountered during that storm on the American coast in June."

Captain Austen followed Gus's eyes out to sea, his grimness lifting. "Well, I'll be! Her return to service was exceedingly swift."

"And, sir! I have a second name for you!"

Captain Austen's eyes fluttered with surprise.

"The other one ... well, you are not going to believe it, sir! She's the *Amethyst!*"

Prosper howled with laughter. "The *Amethyst?* Ya mean the ship what once belonged to Cap'n Prickett, the oaf with the arse wind what knows no limits? Mighta helped him and us some if he'd used his pocket thunder to power his sails when we was faced with that Yankee fleet a while back."

Gus stifled a giggle and looked up at Captain Austen, searching his solemn profile for evidence of excitement, hoping the news would elicit a smile from him. "She may be flying the wrong colours, sir, but it's her, all right!"

Prosper snorted disdain as he tugged on the handles of the wheel. "The way the *Amethyst*'s bin slackin' off in this fight, I'd say they still got Prickett and his whey-faced crony, Bridlington, callin' the shots."

Captain Austen's hand fell lightly upon Gus's shoulder. "Will wonders never cease? And here I thought the *Amethyst* would be safely sailing in American waters by now." His anxious stare brightened as he turned to give Prosper a flying clap on the arm. "Stay on them, Mr. Burgo, throughout the evening, throughout the night. We cannot afford to lose them."

6:20 P.M.
ABOARD HMS *EXPEDITION*

Having delivered another powder cartridge to his gun captain without incident, Magpie was rewarded with the words, "Ye kin stand down fer a while now, lad." It was growing shadowy. The sun was leaving her sky, beautiful and unaffected by the last bellows and cries and explosions of the engagement beneath her. Where the sea had been riven with shot-splash and dying men, she was a radiant pool of gleaming crystals and rose-tinted waves that regally carried away the debris of battle, including the enemy ships.

For a time, it appeared, the Americans had retreated. The gun crews on the *Bloody Flux* cheered and boasted of their auspicious hits, though neither side's cannon-fire had brought the other to its knees. Relieving his thirst around the scuttlebutt, Mr. Huxley was overheard proclaiming, "There'll be no victory on this day. Sure as I know it, we'll be fightin' again at first light."

Magpie hated to think this might be true. It made his chest thud in a painful way and his stomach go all queasy. He wanted those enemy ships to sail away and, by dawn, be crushed on an outcrop of sea rocks or have fallen off the earth. Granted, he was not an admirer of the *Bloody Flux*, but it distressed him to no end to see ragged holes in her sails, swathes of her woodwork in pieces, and weaving rivers of blood on her decks. It left him questioning whether it was ever possible to cross the ocean without calamity … without gales and foundering ships and vicious swabs that wanted to kill you.

Magpie went off in search of Captain Uptergrove, locating him easily near the bowsprit, standing in the company of a scraggy-faced lieutenant with his spyglass aimed at the American ships. He rehearsed his words as he waited an endless while for Uptergrove to notice him wavering there.

When it came, the captain's greeting was flat and uninspiring. "What is it?"

"Beg yer pardon, sir."

"Yes?" came the inevitable beat of impatience when Magpie had trouble unloading his thoughts.

He swallowed the stuffing in his mouth. "Is Cap'n Austen's *Invincible* gonna be all right, sir?"

Uptergrove looked askance. His eyes roved over Magpie as if he had never seen him before. It was easy to guess what he must be thinking. How would an insignificant lavatory boy know the name of the *Invincible* and that of her captain? Magpie was grateful when Uptergrove's roving came to a stop.

"Aye. I believe they will both live to see another sunrise." He raised a finger, signalling for Magpie to wait a moment. Turning aside, he mumbled a message into the ear of the lieutenant, who nodded and immediately set off, hurrying toward some unknown location. Upon returning his attention to Magpie, he unexpectedly swerved and winced in pain, his hand trembling as it reached down toward his right thigh.

Magpie gasped at the alarming tear in Uptergrove's breeches and the weeping of dark red down his leg. "Why, sir!" he cried. "Ya've bin injured real bad."

"'Tis nothing but a flesh wound."

"Maybe yer doctor should see to it, sir."

Uptergrove displayed no emotion. "We have no *doctor* on this ship. We have an idiot who calls himself a surgeon. As tragedy would have it, his true love lies with liquor and opiates, not saving the lives of seamen."

"At the very least, sir, ya needs to wrap somethin' 'round that real tight. Is yer officer fetchin' a bandage fer ya, sir?"

For a moment, Uptergrove looked incredulous. "No. I sent him on a mission of a different nature."

"Would ya mind me suggestin', sir … ya need to see Dr. Braden. He'll take care o' ya. He'll know what to do."

Uptergrove tapped the top of his spyglass against his chin. "And where," he snuffled, "shall I find this Dr. Braden … out here?"

"He's on the *Invincible*, sir! He's Captain Austen's friend. They grew up together in Hampshire. He's a doctor, not a butcher. He did his schoolin' in Edinburgh, sir, and he took real good care o' me when I lost me eye."

When Uptergrove's eyebrows arched up and froze in disbelief, Magpie's hand swiftly stoppered his mouth. But the mistake was made, the damage done. Now Uptergrove would know he had been lying all along about being a farm labourer and having a poor old ma and losing his eye to an accident with a pitchfork. Now he would face the gallows for sure. Terror crippled his brain. He couldn't remember the reason he had gone looking for the captain in the first place. On tenterhooks, he waited for the master-in-arms to show up. He waited for those chilling words, "Clap this boy in irons," to erupt from Uptergrove's sour mouth. But how strange! The captain had wandered away from him and was peering once again through his spyglass, watching the progress of the retreating ships.

Slowly, Magpie backed away, his eye anchored to Uptergrove's nest of wiry hair. If he ran off without making a sound, surely, given all that was going on, he would be forgotten. Three or four steps into his escape, he slammed into the returning lieutenant, who did nothing to help Magpie's cause by bleating: "Hold on, now! Where do you think you're going?"

"I weren't goin' nowhere, sir," said Magpie, trying to steal a look past the lieutenant's big bulk to gauge Uptergrove's reaction.

"I ran out of breath fetching this for you," he muttered, his scraggy face overcast with annoyance. "Here! Take it." He dumped a small box in his hands.

Dumbfounded, Magpie stared down at it. "What's this, sir?"

"Haven't a clue, but the captain says you were to have it."

Magpie stared at the box with wonder. Would it disappear if he took his eye off it? He had seen boxes like this one before in Captain Austen's cabin and once, long ago, at the home of the Duke of Clarence. They came from elegant shops and when you opened them you would find a pair of gloves or a neckerchief or a gentleman's fob nestled among sheets of tissue paper. But Magpie wasn't a gentleman. He had no use for gloves and fobs and such things.

The lieutenant patted Magpie on his bottom and spun him around. "I have a notion the captain needs his privy attended to at once," he muttered before hustling him along the forecastle, "and inside that box you will find nothing more than cleaning cloths."

His curiosity deflated like a battered balloon, Magpie took several listless steps before risking a glance back at Uptergrove. There he was, still at the bowsprit, his spyglass now limp at his side and the lieutenant nowhere to be found. The *Bloody Flux* was tacking on the waves and the dying light of day had spilled upon him, creating a silhouette of his lonely figure. Magpie had no idea that he was gazing in his direction and was, therefore, rattled when his name was shouted. Stopping dead, his eye swept back and forth over the forecastle, expecting to see the master-at-arms closing in on him, flexing his arms before tackling him to the ground. But the only person around was the captain.

"There will come a time, Magpie," Uptergrove said, friendliness in his voice, "when I shall invite you to my cabin and ask that you play for me."

11:30 P.M.
(FIRST WATCH, SEVEN BELLS)
ABOARD HMS *INVINCIBLE*

Emily sat swaying on a four-legged stool at the table, entranced by the speed at which Leander's quill pen flew over the pages of his medical journal. The only light in the cockpit, a flame in a stark, black iron lantern, hung between them. In the deep, dark spaces surrounding them, the stillness of the ship was broken by the whimpers of feverish dreams and the lulling creak of the hammocks and cots. Sheer will kept Emily from shuttering her eyes for the night. She longed for a bath of warm water to soothe away her cares; soap to scrub away the grime on her face and hands and fingernails, and the pervading smell of death. It amazed her that Leander was even able to retrieve the words that had to be recorded in his journal, the names of the wounded, descriptions of their injuries and treatments, tonics administered, and surgeries performed. He had been on his feet all day, dispensing orders, teaching and labouring over the mangled bodies of Captain Austen's men. Twice she had fetched a clean shirt for him, but this newest one was speckled with blood and dried swathes of it still clung to his forearms where the sleeves had been rolled to the elbows.

Behind Emily's stool, old Dr. Braden was curled up on the floor, sleeping soundly like a shepherd's dog, completely exhausted from the day's work. Emily had brought him food and water and made him a bed from a mattress she had dragged from an empty cot. Overpowered by his need for sleep, he had gratefully accepted it, taking care not to blanch at its stained, emaciated condition. Emily mused briefly about Lord Somerton, wondering where he might have found a nook in which to lay his head. Her imagination led her straight to a bed of mouldy straw in the hog's pen.

"Leander," she said softly, pushing a plate of cheese and cold mutton toward him. "Here. Eat something before you faint away."

With a final flourish of ink on his page, Leander closed up his journal. Despite the day, he had a smile for her, mournful and weary though it was. Helping himself to a piece of meat, he leaned back against the spools of his chair. "You should try to get some sleep, Emily."

"I do not know where to go. Our cabins have not yet been restored to us."

He nodded thoughtfully. "You could always join Mrs. Jiggins and my aunt in their hiding place."

"I could, but I am guessing that is where Lord Somerton has sought refuge."

"Ah! Yes, I did wonder where he had disappeared to."

"Were I to go looking for him, I would most likely find him snoring alongside the ladies in that stuffy hole of theirs," sneered Emily.

Leander looked amused. "Out of all this tragedy, our fellow man still provides us with some laughter and diversion." Returning the untasted mutton to its plate, he gazed at her in earnest from across the table. "Thank you. For your help. And for being here. The things you saw today ... things no woman should ever have to see ... and yet you managed to get on so very well."

A visitation of those horrors crashed through Emily's brain. The stumps of shattered limbs, the torn throats, blood everywhere, the screams of the men, especially as the pitch rose ever higher. Her heart had travelled at dangerous speeds the whole time, completely ungovernable. But Leander did not need to know about that — he would surely send her away otherwise — nor of the wine she had secretly asked Biscuit to bring to her, and the moment she had had to excuse herself to vomit and weep in a corner away from the cockpit.

"It was not as hard as it was the first time ... on the *Isabelle*," she said truthfully. "I tried to follow your lead ... yours and your blessed father's. I drew strength from you both. If you could stand there and face such misery and calmly act and know what to do for each man, I figured I could do my small part without complaint."

Leander's smile was gentle. "It was evident to me that the time you spent among the library of medical books at Hartwood Hall was well served."

"I did manage to fit in a reading of *Robinson Crusoe*, as well, Doctor."

"And did Crusoe the traveller have strange and surprising adventures?"

"He did indeed! As have we!" Emily added the last bit with a small laugh.

"Then if we are shipwrecked on this voyage, I shall look to you for direction." He went quiet for a time, one ear cocked to the men's sleepy mutterings behind him. The smile lines around his mouth suddenly tightened. Emily wondered if the horrors of the day were passing wretchedly through his mind. "It is never easy," he said, staring down at his journal. "I try to give each man my full attention and hope I can help each and every one. And over the years, I have found I have grown somewhat numb to it all. Unless, of course ..." he said, clearing his throat.

Emily finished his thought. "... unless the person placed before you is someone for whom you hold great affection."

His eyes briefly met hers. Rising quickly from his chair, he stepped away to secure two blankets for her from a cupboard in the wall. Emily watched him move slowly around the cockpit, the weight of responsibility on his back.

"Go get some sleep or you will be a hindrance and a nuisance to me tomorrow," he said as he offered up the wool blankets.

Reluctantly, Emily slid off her stool to accept them, knowing there was truth to his admonition. "What about you, Doctor?"

"I will stay here. This will be my bed," he said, patting the back of his chair. "More, I fear, will die in the night. Even stout-hearted mariners long for the support of loved ones when they give up their hold on life. At the very least, when the time comes, they shall have a friend at their side."

Overcome with emotion, Emily could only speak in broken whispers. "When my time comes, it would be a great comfort to me to have you near."

Leander reached out to stroke her cheek and the braid of hair that fell across her shoulder. Gazing at her, he drew a long breath. "Take your blankets, but, please ... do not go far away."

Emily wiped the tears from her eyes. "Unless you decree it, Doctor, I promise I never shall."

CHAPTER 29

Thursday, September 30
3:30 a.m.
(Middle Watch, Seven Bells)
Aboard HMS *Expedition*

Magpie stirred once the quartermaster on duty flipped over his sandglass and began tolling the bell. The contented murmur of the sea rushed along the length of the hull below him and he could hear the soft mumbles of the men on watch. They were consoling sounds in the night, but not potent enough to wipe from memory the brutal hours of yesterday. He picked at and brushed away the sleep from his good eye, adjusted the patch over his bad one and blinked into the darkness around him. Against the brilliance of the Milky Circle and various celestial bodies, glittering sweeps and pinpoints in the sky, the ship's masts and sails were small and black and insignificant. The sky afforded the only means of light for those awake as orders had gone round during the First Watch to douse all lanterns, except for the flame that kept the compasses illuminated. Magpie could see the outline of the helmsman at the wheel and an animal sniffing around his heels — a goat, perhaps. Beyond the helm, human shadows floated around the weather decks, going about their duties, and a few feet away, the sentinel, charged with guarding Uptergrove's cabin, was asleep, slumped and breathing through his mouth against the door frame, his musket lodged in the crook of his arm.

The wind abruptly made its presence known. Its gusts and moans shivered the yards of canvas and cut Magpie to the core. His teeth began to chatter uncontrollably, his entire body was gooseflesh. Hours ago, before bedding down near the captain's cabin, he had come up empty in his search for a makeshift blanket — an empty flour sack or a scrap of spoiled sail. If only one of those toiling shadows would come toward him to offer up a worn Kersey jacket or Morgan Evans's woolly thrum cap or his special old blanket, the pond-green quilt that Mrs. Jordan had given him long ago to keep him warm at sea. Their reward would be a handsome one: his week's ration of oatmeal and ale. But then he remembered. And for a while he was able to forget his misery with the cold night.

Pushing his upper body from the clammy timbers of the deck, he snuggled in against the limber wall of canvas, stretched his legs out and vigorously rubbed warmth into his benumbed arms. Reaching for the box that Uptergrove had gifted him, he placed it on his thighs and wiggled off the lid. He gazed upon the bamboo flute, lying like the king's crown on its plush bed, a pouch with golden drawstrings made of the finest, softest leather. His fingertips traced its intricate scrollwork and caressed its tiny carvings of fruit and flowers. He swept it up, box and all, and embraced it against his heart. The smile on his face was so big it hurt! If he tried, he was certain he could walk on air. What had possessed Uptergrove to part with it and give it to the boy who cleaned his toilet, the little liar caught fabricating details of a life he had never lived? Maybe the captain had gone mad, much like Jim Beef of Bedlam, and would take up shroud-hopping and shrieking when his leg had fully healed. Magpie laughed to himself and wondered if his desire to join Uptergrove's children in their cozy drawing room would, one day, prove to be something more than mere wool-gathering. Happiness flowed through him, inspiriting him to leap up and entertain the men on watch with his favourite tunes. But as yet no order had come from

Uptergrove to do so. Besides, until then, Magpie needed to keep his whereabouts a secret. Until the crew was summoned from their beds and daylight rendered night crimes and misdeeds impossible, he must remain an unheeded shadow of the night.

Magpie put his priceless gift in its leather pouch, pulled the draw-string closure, and placed it back in the box. He set it lovingly beside him like a faithful puppy. Curling up in a tight ball against the canvas, he tried to gain more sleep before the sun came up. He had just drifted off when advancing footsteps roused him. Their approach seemed stealthy and sinister and out of place. Surely, whoever it was had no legitimate business with the captain at this hour. Eagle-eyed now, Magpie peered around the edge of the canvas wall. The worrying outline of two men rose up against the dim light of the night sky. One was stout and muscular, the other slim and long-legged. Starlight glinted off a bald head and exposed the woolly worms of a carpenter's thrum cap. The men crouched beneath the short ladder that led up to the poop deck and huddled together to talk.

"If not now, when?" There was urgency in the first low-pitched voice.

"I shall get word to you," was the calm reply.

"Do the others know?"

"Aye! They have all received their instructions."

"What are our chances of this bein' successful?"

"Excellent, I believe."

"How kin ya be so sure?"

"Injuries have weakened Uptergrove. He has taken to his bed."

"So?"

"For God's sake, man, without him, there is no leadership around here."

After that, the wind carried off their voices so that Magpie could hear nothing more than a muffle of their conversation. Aware that their words were not meant for his ears, he stayed near the wall, hoping the darkness would keep him sufficiently cloaked and concealed. The sentinel snored on, oblivious to the presence of interlopers near the great cabin. The goat lost interest in the helmsman's boots and wandered off in search of more captivating aromas. The ship's bell sounded eight times, ending the Middle Watch. The topmen climbed slowly down from the yards. Magpie could see the grey shadows of those waiting to replace them gathering near the shrouds. The bald-headed man and his thrum-capped friend concluded their rendezvous. Easing themselves out from under the ladder, they stepped to within a foot of Magpie. It would have been easy to seize their ankles and shout for the sentinel. But the men's parting words killed any desire he had for heroism.

"Right then! I'll wait fer the word," said the bald man in a gruff whisper. "I know what I gotta do, Mr. Bumpus."

As they scuttled away in opposite directions, Magpie sat still, holding the boxed flute against him like a life preserver. A cup of reality had been dumped over his head and its icy drizzle chilled him to the bone.

7:00 A.M.
(MORNING WATCH, SIX BELLS)
ABOARD HMS *INVINCIBLE*

Emily was nearing her destination when she sensed someone coming toward her on the orlop platform. Throwing her lantern out in front of her, she came face to face with the last person she had expected to see in this part of the ship. He was an unkempt vision. The buttons on his shirt were undone, exposing a far-reaching thatch of white hairs, and the wispy curls around his ears were standing on end as if something had frightened them. As well, there was a strong essence of liquor about him. Had the ship not still been operating in battle-station mode, Emily would have guessed he had spent the night carousing or been soused in a barrel of brandy.

"Mr. Burgo!" she laughed nervously. "Who, pray, is steering the ship?"

"Well, I gotta sleep sometime, Miss," he said, making a half-hearted attempt to hide something behind his scrawny frame, but no attempt whatsoever to cover up his nakedness. "Did ya think I were on duty right 'round the clock?"

"No, of course not, but under these appalling circumstances, I believe we would all breathe easier knowing you were at the helm."

"Thankee, Miss!" He grinned with his eyes screwed closed. "I'm headin' there now. And when ya hear them blusterin' guns go off agin, ya'll know this old hound's got two hands latched to the wheel." In his solemn execution of a departing bow, he tripped over his boots. Smiling apologetically, he excused himself and lurched sideways into the gloom.

Alone again, Emily heard howls of unbridled laughter and sprightly whispers coming from the dead area near the stern. An orb of light danced and flickered over the Lady's Hole, casting the grating's shadow and that of two grotesque heads against the aft wall. Intrigued, Emily pushed on, picking her way around the mounds of sharp-edged furniture brought below for safekeeping, wary of faults and breaches in the floor beneath her feet. A waft of stink, curiously similar to the one Mr. Burgo had carried with him, curdled her stomach. Squatting down beside the Hole, Emily gazed wide-eyed at the glistening faces that jumped and squeaked with excitement at the sight of her.

"Emeline! My dear girl, we thought you had abandoned us forever. How long has it been since you left us here to languish in the dark and fend for ourselves?" Mrs. Jiggins's throaty greeting was generously convivial. She was bare-headed and her shockingly short, salt-brown hair was slicked back from her forehead and tucked in behind her ears. To Emily, she bore a striking resemblance to Meg Kettle as the woman had often looked at the culmination of her laundry days.

Miss Braden proved an even bigger surprise. Her mob cap had been tossed aside, probably at the same moment as Mrs. Jiggins's straw bonnet, and her gown was opened at the neck to reveal the existence of a bosom. Her graying curls were pinned atop her head and untidy strands clung to her cheeks. She smoothed down the wool blanket, spread communally over their legs, and held up a pewter plate loaded with little sugar-sprinkled cubes of gelatin. "Would you care for some Turkish Delight?"

"Where in heaven's name did you get that? I do not recall seeing anything of the sort in our food basket," asked Emily, recovering from the startling expression in Miss Braden's offering. At what point in the night had the woman untied the stays binding her carefully measured voice?

Miss Braden suppressed a giggle. "Our amiable Mr. Biscuit stopped by with the treat. He said we deserved a little royal spoiling."

Emily set the lantern alongside the grating, knelt down and got into a cross-legged position. "Biscuit? Are you telling me that, in my absence, you had more than one visitor?"

Their smiles evaporated and their cheeks glowed with guilt.

"Whatever do you mean, Emeline?" asked Mrs. Jiggins, stuffing a handful of the sugared confection into her mouth.

"I just bumped into Prosper Burgo! As I doubt he was down here patching up holes in the hull, I was wondering ..." Emily left her words dangling in the air as she scrutinized the two of them through the square apertures in the grating.

Miss Braden did not know where to look, but Mrs. Jiggins promptly replied, chewing and talking around her Turkish morsels. "Oh, my dear, you see, Mr. Burgo feared for our safety. He assured us he could not adequately conduct his duties at the helm, valiantly chasing down the enemy, until he knew for certain our throats had not been cut. So he came to see us and kindly brought along ... ah, um ... one pitcher of ... what did he call it, Miss Braden?"

"Negus! He called it negus!" slurred Miss Braden.

"Yes, that was it. Wine and hot water mixed with lemon, sugar, and spices! Lovely stuff, Emeline!"

"Is there any left?"

There came a swift "nooo" from Miss Braden's quarter.

Mrs. Jiggins lifted the blanket, produced the pitcher, and tipped it upside down to show the contents had been spent.

Emily leaned forward, hands gripping her knees. "And while here, did Mr. Burgo help you drain the negus?"

Neither one answered at first. Miss Braden fingered the edge of the blanket. Her eyes were wide and watery as if she had lifted her prospect glass to them. Denuded of her mob cap, she looked like a frightened young girl. "You won't tell Arthur and Leander, will you, Emeline?" Her plea was whispered.

"No! No! Especially not Leander," added Mrs. Jiggins, about to cry. "I so wanted to creep into his cabin at night, crawl into his hammock, and kiss him on the lips. How will I ever win his heart if he knows about Mr. Burgo?"

At first, Miss Braden looked at Mrs. Jiggins dazedly, as if she had not understood her meaning, her face twitching as she digested this plum of dark intelligence. Emily braced herself, waiting for her to explode and rake Mrs. Jiggins over the coals for entertaining such indecent thoughts. Instead, Miss Braden dissolved into laughter, howling and dashing away a sudden outpouring of mirthful tears.

"You? Trying to crawl into my nephew's hammock? Why you would get one fat leg up on the canvas and have my poor boy flipped and sprawled upon the floor. Kissing, indeed!"

A shamefaced Mrs. Jiggins was silent as she waited for Miss Braden to regain control of herself ... which took longer than expected.

Emily made scolding sounds with her tongue. "If you two promise to behave yourselves, I shall not breathe a word about what I saw and heard down here. I shall stay as silent as the grave."

Mrs. Jiggins reached up and wiggled her bejewelled fingers through the grating. "Bless you, my dear. That would be best for everyone."

Angling her head, Emily sharpened her tone. "But if you don't ..." she threatened, enjoying their subservient glances for a bit longer than she should have. Jumping to her feet, she asked if they wanted to leave the Hole for some coffee and a stretch.

"Oh, no!" said Mrs. Jiggins, hitching the blanket up around the general vicinity of her middle. "We are both settled in here so deliciously." She smiled sweetly, first at Miss Braden and then up at Emily. "But thank you, my dear, for stopping by to visit us."

Emily was confounded. Perhaps she had heard incorrectly. But, no! Neither of them moved a muscle and their eyes, blank and surprisingly sober, signalled it was time for her to leave. Promising to check in on them later, Emily collected her lantern and tiptoed away, pausing a few feet on to eavesdrop on their negus-laden whispers and giggles.

"Do you think we fooled her, Eliza?"

"Yes! I am quite sure we did, Arabella."

"Good! Now! Where is that second pitcher?"

"Right here, my dear!" was the exuberant answer.

"Splendid! Drink up, my friend!"

The last thing Emily heard was the triumphal tinkling of crystal goblets.

7:30 A.M.
(MORNING WATCH, SEVEN BELLS)

"Did ya manage to catch some winks, Doc? 'Cause it sure don't look that way." Biscuit made his inquiry as he presented Leander with a mug of coffee and placed it in his cold, stiffening hands. "If ya don't mind me sayin' it … yer a man sucked dry o' life. And if yer not careful, they'll be throwin' ya overboard, mistakin' ya fer one o' yer desiccated cadavers."

Leander meditated as he warmed his hands on his mug. The morning was damp and autumn-chilly, and his breath steamed in the salt air. "Remind me next time, Biscuit, to stop you before you offer up unsolicited opinions on my appearance." Despite his tangy retort, he relented with a smile, being ever so thankful for the beverage.

"Ach, Doc!" said Biscuit, balancing his wooden tray on upturned fingers while his free hand had a vigorous scratch of the area close to his crotch. "I looked in the mirror this mornin' whilst tryin' to shave. I ain't no prize meself!"

Was it possible Biscuit was even in possession of a mirror? Surely, the man's heavy crown of orange hair had never known a comb, his tangle of nose hairs had never known a trim, and his grey, crooked teeth had never been acquainted with a toothbrush and powder. "You shall not hear me utter any words of unequivocal agreement."

Biscuit's laugh came deep within his belly. "At least someone on this ship thinks I'm a prize."

Leander looked suspicious. "And who might that be?"

"Yer aunt! Miss Braden!" Biscuit flashed an impish grin. "I gave her some Turkish Delight early this morning."

Leander's lips opened in disbelief. "I am afraid I have no idea what that is."

Biscuit, having quit his scratching, was preparing an explanation when Lord Somerton approached and, uninvited, drew up between them.

"I daresay I agree with the cook," he declared, pilfering one of the mugs from the coffee tray. He shrugged off Biscuit's glare of disapproval and watched the cook trudge off in a huff.

Leander was on his guard. "In what way?"

"In referencing your appearance, of course, Doctor!" Somerton's eyes, black and cold as onyx, met him straight on. "I would highly recommend you seek a few hours of bedrest before it is too late."

Leander's lips tightened on his percolating anger. "Did you become a doctor overnight, Lord Somerton?"

"No," he answered with a slow smile, "but I understand we shall be hard at the fight again today and you, of all people, need your wits about you."

"The idea of sleep is a nice sentiment, but, for a ship's doctor, not always easy to come by." Coffee in hand, Leander left him and made his way toward the stern. He hoped the man would tire of him and search elsewhere for companionship. To his annoyance, Somerton followed. He was like an insufferable guest at a party with whom the others were loath to be seen unless they were willing to annihilate their social standing. Silently, Leander scoffed at this comparison, knowing Lord Somerton, given his wealth and privilege, would never experience isolation of any kind at a festive occasion. *On land, that is*, he added in his head to make himself feel better.

Leander shaded his eyes against the rising sun poking mischievously over the far horizon like a child who wanted to play games and could not understand the concerns pressing on the mind of his reluctant father. For a time, he watched the *Expedition*, still whirling in the night mists, thrumming on the waves just off the *Invincible*'s starboard quarter. Bouncing a fist against his mouth, he moved his attention to the enemy vessels. They were sailing west, well ahead of the *Invincible* and, much to Captain Austen's mounting frustration, outside the bounds of striking distance. If Leander's excited sources were to be believed, that those two ships were, in fact, the *Liberty* and the *Amethyst*, it was staggering news indeed.

"Having witnessed something of your routine in the cockpit yesterday, I was mulling over your plight, Doctor."

"Were you?" Leander looked down at Somerton, secretly pleased he surpassed the man in height, if nothing else. "How curious when you seemed to be in hiding most of yesterday."

Disregarding the slight, Somerton continued his spirited drivel. "I see you as a mere vassal on this ship and, as such, it struck me! Rather than settling for old King George's Navy, why not join the militia?" He assessed his suggestion's effect on Leander with an over-the-shoulder glance. "The militia would provide you with a smart uniform and one of those tall shako hats … oh, and a sword, of course! I am certain you would like that! I do believe you might even look rather dashing in tight-fitting trousers and Hessian boots."

Resentment welling, Leander seethed at Lord Somerton's elevated profile before looking back, unseeing, toward the *Expedition*. "It may be a happy pursuit of yours, but I have never been one to bother much with fashion." As soon as he said it, he could feel critical eyes travelling over his worn overcoat and breeches, and down to his shoes where one of his silver buckles had again gone missing.

"That is quite evident," Somerton concurred with sarcasm. "But just think how you could put your regimental splendour to good use."

"How so?"

"Why, the ladies, of course, Doctor!"

"The ladies," Leander repeated with a frown.

"Men in the militia have it easy. There is always plenty of time for picnics and parties and balls. As women of all ages are besotted with gold-braided red coats, you would be welcomed into all the best drawing rooms across England."

"That is precisely what I long to achieve," muttered Leander on the edge of his mug.

Somerton folded his arms on his chest and leaned back to study him as if sizing him up for a new suit of clothes. "You do possess the necessary stature. You are perhaps a snip too thin, but given your fearful episode of starvation at sea, I suppose there is nothing for it. However, my good man, your youthful attractions are not long for this world. I would highly recommend you leave behind this revolting occupation you have chosen for yourself and sign up with a regiment before the inevitable decline." The last bit was proffered with one of Somerton's distinguishing smirks.

Leander wanted to hit back hard. *Why is it, when you have no profession of your own and no wife, not even a whiff of one, and you tend to value entertainment above hard work and industry, you have not signed up yourself?* But Leander said nothing, electing instead to file his rejoinder away in his arsenal, for now. An exchange with Somerton would only descend into a verbal sword fight and Leander had no strength to carry a sword. How grateful he was when Biscuit made a return visit to inform Somerton that a bite of hot breakfast was awaiting him below. How particularly satisfying it was spying Biscuit's furtive wink, indicating a little artifice on his part.

Left blissfully alone, Leander sought refuge on the stern bench. He leaned his head back against the time-worn oak of the taffrail. His eyes, heavy and gritty as if they were full of sand, closed at once. He listened to the sound of the ruffling wind, enjoyed the sensations of being lifted and gently dropped on the waves, and soon found himself falling victim to his imagination. It transported him, not to the enchanted aerie on the lofty platform of yesterday, but to the tiny, bleak garret of his aunt's cottage on Mile End Terrace. Magic had transformed its cold austerity. The narrow, rickety beds and ancient bedclothes had been replaced with a velvet-flounced quilt, pillows sheathed in fox fur and the warm, fragrant presence of Emily. She lay beside him, her unplaited hair scattered like strands of golden thread across the pillows, her dark, liquid eyes smiling up at him. Clear, beautiful, poignant notes of music played around them as Leander reached out to embrace her. Somehow, though, the music was not in harmony with the fantastical scene he had created. They filled him with a deep sadness, not the expected exultation. Emily's smile faded. She melted away and then vanished altogether, taking the warmth with her. Outside the cottage, the wind moaned like a child who not could find his mother. It rattled the small panes of glass in the room's circular window and the trough under the eaves of the roof. Another woman appeared, one he had known and loved long ago. She stood quietly in the doorway, clad in a ghostly-white chemise, and gazed at him with pale, feverish eyes. In her arms she carried a dead baby and held it out to him like an offering, hoping he would accept it.

Leander's eyes shot open. He sat up straight on the stern bench and glanced wildly around him, recognizing nothing at first. For all he knew he had been plucked up and placed on a Spanish galleon in a long-forgotten century. It took a bit before he realized he had fallen asleep. As the fog cleared, he was left with a sickening sense of loss.

His wiped the dampness from his face and struggled to battle emotions he had long since buried.

Gradually, his heart resumed its normal rhythm and the darkness of his dream fell away. He grew aware of the *Invincible*'s crew around him, relaxing at their battle stations, chatting around the scuttlebutts, savouring their mugs of coffee, eating their portable breakfasts of cheese and biscuits, sharing their predictions on the day. Way on high, Jim Beef was clambering around the shrouds of the mizzenmast. Leander squinted up at him in wonder, amazed at the man's confidence in a place he himself was not. But it did not seem Mr. Beef was enjoying his regular, pleasurable hike around the ropes. He was flailing one arm about and wrestling with the footropes as if fighting an intruder, his coal-black hair and coattails flying at odds around him. Suddenly he stopped his fight and stared down at Leander. The second their eyes met and locked, he pointed at the ship that sailed alongside the *Invincible* like a well-trained dog. Leander wanted nothing more than to be left alone, to find an empty cot and sleep a dreamless sleep. But in Jim Beef's huge, untamed eyes, there was a message.

Leander again heard the sweet sounds of a flute, advancing faintly through the hum and bustle of the Invincibles and the rush of the sea. His skin prickled and the hairs on the nape of his neck rose up. A chill, like the one that had filled his aunt's garret, walked right through him. They were the same elusive notes that had come to him in his dream. Something wrenched his memory, painfully, as if he had taken a punch to the side of his head. His mind's eye saw the curly-headed child being shoved rudely away from the rail of the *Expedition* on the day the *Lady Jane* went to the ocean's floor. He thought of Jim Beef's shocking, early morning intrusion on the platform yesterday; his agitation and struggle to make himself understood.

"*He stands there. In punishment.*"

"*Who is there? Who do you mean?*"

The madman had not been able to say. He did not know his name, though he recognized him as the boy he had saved from Mrs. Kettle and her menacing knife in the black bowels of the *Prosper and Remarkable* a month ago to the very day.

Finally, Leander understood. Finally, it all made sense. He could not move, could not speak as he strained to hold tight to the flute's music. It was not coming from the *Invincible*. It was coming from the *Expedition*. And the tune? He knew it and knew it well. It was the favourite of the little sailmaker's ... the one about the grazing sheep.

CHAPTER 30

Magpie lowered the flute and looked over at the sunlit corner by the windows where the captain's hammock was gently rocking. It was silent save for the soft creak and moan of its tarred ropes pulling on the deckhead. He was too fearful to approach it, but from where he stood he could see something of Uptergrove's face. The captain's eyes were closed, his grey hair had been swept from his forehead and his skin had a sallow aspect to it like an old powdered wig. He hadn't spoken in a while. Was he asleep then? Had he heard the tune before drifting off? If so, had he liked it? Magpie was hopeful. He had been overjoyed to play it for him, so happy to respond to his whispered request: "Play something pretty for me, Magpie." So happy to prove he had a measure of refinement and a skill or two beyond scrubbing toilets. Maybe, when Uptergrove awoke, Magpie would tell him he was also quite good with a needle and awl, and sewing up first-rate jib and square sails. That was sure to impress him.

He gazed around the great cabin with a big sigh. Sadly, it was no longer great. It had been stripped of its fine furnishings and books, and the walls had been laid bare except for a uniform jacket, hanging on an iron peg like a wet towel. Uptergrove's coats and trousers, his hats, boots, and swords had all been removed. His beautiful paintings had been packed away and placed in the hold for preservation against the guns. Magpie missed seeing the happy faces of his four children, their saucy cat, and the little bird in its cage. He thought their company might help to calm his nerves and the roiling of his belly. The only thing overlooked was a cut-glass decanter with a stopper shaped like a pineapple. It was lying on the oak floor beside the captain's hammock. A single shaft of sunlight, peering through the east-facing windows, was dancing on it, highlighting its contents of blood-red wine.

Magpie scratched his cheek and pulled on his ear. He asked himself if he should stay or go. He didn't really want to stay. Truth was he was worried someone would come looking for him and throw him out, shouting at the top of their lungs that he had neglected his duty of carrying the cartridges for the guns. Moreover, he was deathly afraid that the barking Mr. Huxley or haughty Mr. Croker or, heaven forbid, the dangerous Mr. Bumpus, would come storming through that flimsy door, seize him by the scruff of the neck, and abuse him. But no one at all had come in to check on the captain and see to his leg wounds in a while. Perhaps they had forgotten about him, being all too preoccupied with preparations for the second encounter with the American ships.

Unwilling to leave the captain on his own and praying he would soon wake so they could talk, Magpie stayed put. Replacing the flute in its dear box, he tucked it up under his arm and tiptoed toward the quarter gallery. There, he took up watch, sitting cross-legged on the floor, beside the curtain that hid the lavatory. He would wait. For what, he was not exactly sure. But he would wait.

8:50 A.M.
Aboard HMS *Invincible*

Emily hurried to the *Invincible*'s stern, a hand pressed to her exploding chest as she dodged the sailors, livestock, and guns in her path. She would have come long before this had Leander been able to locate her. But he never thought to look for her in Biscuit's galley, or expected to find her organizing baskets of food and bottles of ale to take around to the men. His blue eyes gleaming with excitement, he had revealed his suspicions in her ear, worried that anyone else should hear lest they prove woefully inaccurate. The two of them had set off together, intent on keeping a vigil at the rail, but Emily was forced to finish the journey alone after Leander was intercepted by an urgent message from the cockpit. There were surgical concerns that neither Mr. Duffy nor old Dr. Braden felt confident enough to address on their own.

Once on deck, Emily went straight to the stern bench where she found Fly Austen, dressed informally in white breeches, shirt, and waistcoat, the sea breeze tousling his dark hair. He was overseeing Gus Walby, who was tearing apart the flag locker, searching for specific signal flags. Gus, his fingers deftly unravelling the flags and then discarding the wrong ones, looked over at Emily and gave her a fond smile, full of unspoken meaning. Cadby Brambles was there, as well, oozing puffed-up importance, for he had been assigned to watch for any communications that might come from the *Expedition*. So far that morning, all was quiet.

The conditions were now favourable for a fight. The sun had burned off the mists, the breezes were rising, and the *Liberty* and the *Amethyst* were bearing down on them. Even from afar Emily could see their square sails swollen with wind and their resolute bows dividing the waves.

"Captain Austen, how much time do we have?"

"Very little," was his grim reply.

"Pray, sir, tell me in terms of minutes and hours."

He wrinkled his brow. "An hour, perhaps."

Emily fought to gather her wits. Everywhere she looked, there were eyes. The men waiting for the action to begin, those sitting high on the yards and below by the cannons, had torn their attention from the enemy vessels to fix their curiosity upon her. She met their stares with smiles, knowing they deserved as much, for surely their conflicted feelings were the same as hers. She watched the group of sailors working to lower the *Invincible*'s boats to be towed behind the ship. Clucking around them was the purser, Mr. Philpotts, mopping his brow and fretting for the safety of the livestock being loaded within. At the wheel, Prosper Burgo looked keen and alert, the effects of his clandestine visit to the orlop purged and forgotten. He swivelled his head to give her a sailors' salute.

"Might I have your permission to take the jolly boat, sir?"

"And just where are you planning to go this fine morning, Emily?"

"To the *Expedition*, of course," she answered, surprised by Fly's question. Was it not obvious or was he being facetious? "If I take Leander and Mr. Beef with me, and maybe Mr. Brambles, I could be there and back in no time."

Hearing his name, Cadby Brambles piped up. "Oh, I cannot go, Miss," he insisted, turning white and looking as if he might lose his breakfast at any second. "Captain Austen needs me here to record all communications."

Emily's hopes sank. She was certain, if anyone, he would be willing to help her. "Then I shall go without Mr. Brambles," she boldly told Fly.

Directing a warning glance at the midshipman to foil his unsolicited remarks, Fly gently took Emily by the elbow and steered her to the side of the ship, away from the two young men.

"There are no guarantees, Emily," he said firmly. "We are going on the mute observations of a madman."

"No! No! The day the *Lady Jane* went down, Leander thought he might have seen him at the rail."

"Every ship carries its quota of orphans and unwanted boys. Seen from a distance they must all look alike."

Emily's eyes blazed. "What other flutist, sir, are you acquainted with that knows the tune 'Sheep May Safely Graze'?" she snapped, regretting her tone as soon as she saw the frightening protrusion of his eyes.

"There are times I admire your headstrong qualities, Emily," Fly said after a ponderous moment. "This, however, is not one of them."

"How is it you do not care?" she asked eventually.

"What gives you that impression?"

"If you did, I believe your desire to find out if he is actually on that ship would be as strong as mine."

"The *Expedition* is not going anywhere," he replied dismissively.

"How can you possibly know that with those guns pointed at us? Please! I … I beg you."

Fly drew himself up and spoke to her as he would a newly recruited ropemaker who had failed to learn the ropes, despite his attentive mentoring. "I am not certain you fully understand. Take a good look around you! What do you suppose we are doing here? Readying ourselves for a Sunday picnic? We are going to war! And there are many lives here to consider." His voice grew fierce. "And my friend, Leander, is not going anywhere regardless of the fact that you would unthinkingly place him in harm's way. I came far too close to losing him once. I shall not risk it again."

Emily coloured and went silent. Fly turned away from her and stared out over the rail. It seemed an interminable while before he spoke again, the fierceness eased but still boiling beneath the surface.

"Mr. Walby has some knowledge of the signal flags. He shall send a message to Uptergrove."

"And if he does not answer?" she asked weakly.

"Then we shall have to wait until the end of the engagement and I will take the matter into my own hands. If I have to, I shall row that jolly boat across the distance myself."

Emily leaned against the bulwark, wringing her hands, broken. "I am truly sorry, Captain Austen. I do not possess the strength you do. I cannot bear another battle."

"You have no other option."

He was about to leave her, but something gave him pause. He gazed toward the *Expedition*, considered her for a moment and then, with something approaching sympathy, he looked down at Emily. "Here. Take it. I do not need it at present." He offered her his spyglass. "Perhaps, with any luck, you might spot the little lad."

With those words, he marched back to the locker to check on Gus's progress with the flags. "Mr. Walby! Are you ready to send your messages? Come, now! Look lively! We do not have all day. Tomorrow, I shall charge you with a complete reorganization of this locker. That shall be your first task of the new day."

Emily only heard Fly's robust shouts of admonishment. She knew nothing of his struggle to fight back tears.

9:30 A.M.
(FORENOON WATCH, THREE BELLS)

Biscuit gave a loud grunt as he tossed the grating aside and peered into the Lady's Hole. It was so dark in there he figured he had just un-earthed a medieval grave. Fortunately, though, its occupants, stirring now from the noise of his arrival, were still alive. He went to retrieve his oil lamp from the cask of water upon which he had left it while deal-ing with the grating, and shone it overhead. Two groggy, sweat-soaked heads popped into view.

"Oh, Mr. Biscuit!" prattled Mrs. Jiggins. "Thank the Lord! Such perfect timing! Have you brought fresh candles with you? Ours has been vexatiously extinguished."

"I sure did, ladies!" he chirped, pulling a bundle of them, tied in string, from the nether regions of his red flannel shirt.

"And have you brought us anything else, my good man?" asked Miss Braden, whose behaviour was almost giddy.

"I came here for no other purpose," Biscuit chuckled, giving them a finger-signal to wait a moment. Leaving the ladies, he darted back to the same water cask and soon returned, hefting a gift basket over their heads. Pleased with their delight, he knelt on the platform and passed it down to them, instructing them with good humour to be careful with the contents.

Miss Braden, oohing and aahing, examined the proffered wares through the magnification of her prospect glass. "What have you brought us?"

"Knock-me-down, curse o' Scotland, and three glasses fastidious-ly cleaned with the tails o' me shirt." He named the items with such gusto; one would think he had presented the ladies with the keys to Windsor Castle.

"My word! You shall have to translate for us poor ladies who know nothing of liquor and spirits," said Mrs. Jiggins, her eyes shining in the lamp light.

"I brung ya a pitcher o' beer and decanter o' whiskey!"

Mrs. Jiggins clapped her hands together most enthusiastically. "Lord bless you! And here I was suffering from such a thirst."

"And have you left anything for the men to drink?" asked Miss Braden with a sly smile.

"Nay! Not a dram!" Biscuit teased with a wink.

Distant cannon-fire riffled the air. The ladies, rather than scream and exclaim, continued to give the basket their full attention.

"Whatever shall they drink after their fighting is done?" Miss Braden serenely pulled a glass from the basket.

"Canna worry about that now, ladies. 'Ere! Quick! Hand me up one o' them glasses!"

Forthwith, whiskey was poured all around and soon in everyone's eager grasp. Biscuit raised his glass to give the Thursday toast. "A bloody war and a sickly season."

His mouth was about to be rewarded with a first tasting when he noticed the ladies had gone quiet and their brows had wrinkled like two scraps of corduroy. "I do not like the sound of that, Mr. Biscuit," protested Mrs. Jiggins. "Do you think you could try again?"

Clearing his throat, Biscuit lifted his glass into the darkness. "A nip o' whiskey afore the battle." He paused to let a slow smile form on his glistening lips. "And let it be said, we didna waste a drop."

10:00 A.M.
(FORENOON WATCH, FOUR BELLS)
ABOARD HMS *EXPEDITION*

Trevelyan took shelter behind the red-jacketed marines and their smoking muskets at the larboard rail, his ears ringing with the tremendous noise of the long guns. He looked around with satisfaction. The sounds and smells of war! They reminded him of another time, when he was commanding the *Serendipity* and those on board did his bidding; when the best food and wine were brought to his table by a bowing servant; when men that had raised his ire trembled beneath him and begged for mercy; when the prospect of returning to England to claim his inheritance still burned in the forefront of his mind. God willing, he would get there again. He would flee before Francis Austen and the grave academic, Leander Braden, discovered him existing right under their noses. He would get his revenge, but this time it would be complete.

Trevelyan scoffed as he watched the sailing master, the first lieutenant, and a few other lackeys prancing around the quarterdeck, trying to lead the Expeditions, completely out of their depth. Mr. Croker, the *masterly* clerk, was among them, exacerbating the situation with his red-faced screaming and agitation. To Trevelyan, the gun crews and their captains had a better grip on things. They were quick to worm and sponge and then load their guns, and knew to wait for the roll of the ship before firing off so as not to waste the shot in the sea or in the sky. *Good*, he thought to himself. Uptergrove had drilled them and taught them well. At least there was no immediate worry that the *Expedition* would be beaten, boarded, and taken a prize. That kind of nonsense had no place in Trevelyan's plans. His fervent eyes flicked toward the great cabin. It had been left intact. Was Uptergrove still in there? How unwise if he was! Had *he* been in command, those walls would have come down at once and Uptergrove dispatched to the hold. *For safety reasons, of course*, he added with a grin.

Something, a bullet, an arrow of oak, perhaps, whistled past Trevelyan, missing him and smashing into the leg of a bare-chested, pimply youth holding a rope rammer. His subsequent screams meant nothing to Trevelyan. He made no effort to assist the boy; instead, he skirted the mess of spilling blood and ducked behind the boats that were still secured to the ship's waist. There, he plotted his next move. Perhaps, soon, it was time for the assistant clerk to pay a visit to the great cabin and see how the captain was faring. As the Expeditions, officers, sailors, and landmen alike, were busy at their guns, trying to recapture a measure of glory for the Royal Navy, who among them would think something was amiss should they see Asa Bumpus entering the captain's quarters?

CHAPTER 31

10:40 A.M.

Magpie leapt up from the floor where he had been sitting and waiting for the longest time, and hurried to the captain's hammock, ignoring the stiffness in his legs. Uptergrove was finally awake. He must have been drugged earlier on; otherwise, it would have been impossible to sleep with cannonade repeatedly slamming the ship the same way a maid beats dust and dirt from a carpet. Now Uptergrove seemed aware of the explosions, the shouts, the cries, and the snapping wind urging the sails of the *Expedition* onward. Seeing Magpie approaching his bed, he blinked several times as if trying to place his face among his crew.

"How long have we been at it?" Uptergrove's question was posed so quietly that Magpie had to lean forward to hear it.

"'Bout an hour or so, sir."

Uptergrove tried to swallow. "Water, please," he whispered with difficulty.

"Oh, sir, there's no water 'round here, but I got some wine," he said, bending down to grab the decanter from off the floor. He held it up for him to see.

Uptergrove nodded.

Magpie looked around helplessly, realizing there was a further problem. "I don't got a cup fer ya, sir."

Uptergrove tried but could not raise his head from his flat pillow. He cleared the phlegm from his throat. "The stopper has a tiny hollow in it. Pour the wine in there and place it to my lips. I shall take but a little at a time."

Magpie followed his instructions, but as he held the stopper in his shaking hand, he was baffled once more. How could he get the wine to the captain's lips when his head only reached an inch above the hammock's edge? He glanced around the cabin again, wishing he had overlooked a chair or a stool, something to raise him up to Uptergrove. But nothing had been left behind.

Sensing his predicament, Uptergrove offered a suggestion. "Hop up on the window seat."

Magpie was extra careful climbing onto the seat's cushions, petrified by the thought of dribbling the wine all over the captain's chin and blankets. But it was the perfect height. From here he had no trouble leaning over the captain's hammock. "May I, sir?"

Closing his eyes, Uptergrove nodded again and allowed Magpie to cradle his head with his hand and feed him the thimble of wine. When Uptergrove had taken it, Magpie settled back on the cushions to keep an eye on him just like Dr. Braden did with his own patients.

"I wanna thank ya, sir."

One of Uptergrove's eyes popped open. "Why are you thanking *me?*"

"Fer the present, sir." He cast his one eye toward the lavatory entrance to make certain his treasured box was still there. "Ya see, Captain Austen got me a new pair o' shoes!" He clicked his heels together. "And Dr. Braden made me an eye patch!" He patted the green circle over his lost eye. "And the Duke o' Clarence gave me a big supper once."

"The Duke of Clarence?" Uptergrove's eyes were both open now.

"Aye! Emily's uncle."

"Who is Emily?"

"She's a princess, sir, and she loves Dr. Braden. I'm hopin' they git married one day."

"Dr. Braden? Is he the same fellow who is on the *Invincible* with your Captain Austen?"

"Aye! One 'n' the same, sir."

"My, you do have stories to tell me."

"But I want to tell ya, sir, I ain't never had a present like that flute." Magpie suddenly hopped off the window seat and went to get the box, worried it would get up and walk away on its own if he did not keep it close to his side. Once he had settled in again, wiggling his bottom comfortably on the cushions, he took the flute out of its box and soft leather pouch, and lifted it proudly so that Uptergrove could see it. "Why, sir, it makes me so happy, I feel like cryin'."

"No need for that. I am pleased my son's beloved flute has found a new owner."

At the mention of his son, Magpie perked up. "Oh, the picture, sir!" he cried, unable to get his excited words out fast enough. "I do so like that picture o' yer children with the funny cat and bird and all. Thinkin' o' that bowl o' fruit makes me hungry!" He rubbed his belly and smiled. "And yer wee boy is so adorable! And I seen yer older son holdin' the flute in it. Was he tired o' playin' it, sir? Is that why ya gave it to me?"

Uptergrove peered up Magpie. He did not answer right away, but when he did, there was a catch in his voice. "Yes. Yes, he was getting tired, very tired."

"Well, when ya git a chance to, sir, could ya thank yer son fer me? Tell 'im I'll treasure it fer always. I'll learn to play that song ya wanted me to earlier, sir, the one about Amazin' Grace."

Uptergrove said nothing. He glanced away to stare at the blank, white wall of his bed and brushed something from his cheek. But a moment later, when a sequence of brisk knocks struck the cabin door, he tensed and looked up at Magpie, fear written on his face.

All the excitement of the flute and lovely chat with the captain was forgotten as dread flooded Magpie's gut. He didn't like the urgent rap of those fists on the door. It sure didn't sound like the surgeon come to redress Uptergrove's wounds.

"Sir! Sir! Don't answer the door," he pleaded before realizing it would be impossible for Uptergrove to do so. Lying in his hammock, he was powerless. "I gotta tell ya quickly what I heard in the night." His words froze in his throat as the door shook again. Knowing it was too late to explain anything, Magpie excused himself, scooped up the flute, pouch, and box in his arms and fled from the window seat. He made for the lavatory, praying to Saint Paul and God in his heaven that the din of the guns and muskets would bury the sound of his bold dash across the cabin.

He had just pulled the curtain shut and crouched down beside Uptergrove's toilet when the door jumped open with a bang.

10:45 A.M.
ABOARD HMS *INVINCIBLE*

Emily cowered in the rounded bow of the forecastle, shielding her head with her arms, terrified that at any second an explosion of splinters would find her hiding place. Fear had paralyzed her, rendered her as helpless as the goats and sheep drifting behind the ship in the unarmed cutters. The ladder that would lead her to safety was a distance of a thousand feet, or at least it seemed that way. She had found a semblance of shelter behind a harness tub of salted beef and pork, a fortuitous find, given Captain Austen's meticulous rules pertaining to the clearing of decks before battle. Meant for disposal over the ship's side, time had run out and it had been left behind. For this she was eternally grateful. Still, she was trapped, with no recourse, forced to clamp her ears and bear hardship until the thundering guns, hundreds of them, stopped firing.

As the universe whirled fantastically around her, hurling hideous scenes at her feet, Emily feebly told herself it was all a dream. But her eyes could not be fooled. Above her, a dead topman hung upside down, entangled in the running rigging, his blood draining from him, pooling and then scuttling around the forecastle. A marine no older than herself had fallen from the fore platform right in front of her,

316

his body broken upon the arch that protected the ship's bell. He was still clutching his bayoneted musket, his pride and joy, its bright finish polished with care before the encounter. His glassy eyes gaped at her, wounded surprise upon his smooth face, as if accusing her of pushing him to his death. Emily grabbed handfuls of her shirt and buried her face, desperate to forget his terrible eyes.

For too long a time she had lingered on the weather decks, holding tightly to the captain's spyglass, sweeping it back and forth over the *Expedition*, willing Magpie to come into view. She had planned to go below when the ships were close enough to begin launching broadsides, but having failed to catch a glimpse of his curly head, she could not bring herself to leave. Did he even know she was on the *Invincible*? Was there anyone on those battle-ravaged decks of the *Expedition* keeping an eye out for him? The indisputable answer had chiselled away at her. So she had stayed, in plain sight by the *Invincible's* rail, praying he might see *her* and take courage.

Captain Austen, enraged at finding her in the thick of battle, had wrested the spyglass from her fist and yelled at her to get below. But that had been ages ago. He had since disappeared in the melee, invisible among the others in his soot-infested shirtsleeves and waistcoat. Black smoke had knocked out the sun as if it, too, were an adversary. It was so thick and obfuscating, Emily could not see the aft end of the ship. Where was Prosper Burgo? At the helm, she told herself, plotting the *Invincible's* course. She imagined him there, his nose lifted contemptuously to the recommendations of the sailing master, doing it his own way to bring the ship close enough to let fly at their foes. Gus Walby was nowhere to be seen, either, but surely he was near the ship's wheel, choking on the smoke and frightened, but obediently scribbling down disordered notes in the journal for his revered captain.

In all the chaos, one man stood out. Biscuit had long ago abandoned his rounds with the coffee tray and had joined the lines of marines at the starboard rail, some shooting, some kneeling to reload. Biscuit stood among those aiming their volley fire at one of the enemy ships. He carried a blackened musket and looked every inch a soldier in a bright red flannel shirt. The sight of him eased the anxious thudding of her heart ... somewhat. Soon another familiar face appeared. Near the guns on the starboard gangway, Lord Somerton sauntered out of the smoke in his dusky coat and trousers, an extension of the swirling cloud itself. He was hunched over, but his eyes were alert, vacillating around him as if he were hunting for something in particular. It was unfathomable that he was here on deck and not stowed away in the hold with the barrels of ale, shaking in his Hessian boots, a pipe of Madeira and stash of cheroots to tranquilize him. Whatever was he doing skulking around in the line of fire?

Emily did not have to wait long to find out. She saw his eyes light on the marine splayed across the arch of the ship's bell. Hastily, he moved toward him, safeguarding himself behind fighting sailors whenever possible. Arriving there, he yanked the musket from the youth's hand, disposed of it by the chimney head, and hefted the man's limp body up and over his shoulder like one of those barrels Emily had pictured him hiding among. At first, she thought he was simply employed in taking the wounded to Leander in the cockpit, doing his part like everyone else. But Somerton did not head for the ladder that would ultimately lead him there. He staggered past it and away from the action, lugging his burden toward a section of the larboard breast-work. Removing the man from his shoulder, he negligently dropped him against the hammocks, stowed in the netting there, steadying him with a leg while he took a moment to catch his breath. It was more of a struggle for him hiking the marine up and setting him on the side of the ship. A dreadful chill swept through Emily, but comprehension came far too late. The deed was over and done with before she could scream in protest. Somerton had shoved the man backwards and was leaning over the rail, watching his descent to the waves.

Her stomach heaving, Emily covered her mouth. She had heard stories of dead seamen being hurled overboard, usually those that were in bits and pieces, but never had she witnessed such cold-blooded brutality. To be tossed away in such a heartless manner, considered insignificant and worthless, denied the dignity of a funeral. The young man had not even been seen and pronounced dead by Leander. What if there had still been life in him?

Emily could not bear it. Huddling against the harness tub, she wept.

Somerton wiped his hands clean on his trousers, a smirk of satisfaction on his lips as if he had fought off a sea monster bent on devour-
ing the crew. He resumed his hunt for his next victim. It was not long
before he found Emily. An eyebrow shot up and his hands flipped his
coat back to land on his hips. "Well, well! What do we have here? A
little princess!"

Emily hated his disgusting smirk. She wanted to claw it from his face.

"Your Highness! Do be careful!" he shouted with fervour. "Or, I
fear, you shall be next."

A dead calm settled over the *Invincible*. Though smoke still curled
and stalked the decks, everything else had come to an abrupt stop as
if the ship had insisted on a moment of rest. Gus Walby was suddenly
there, standing before her on his crutch. She blinked up at him, a welcome apparition in a nightmare, and felt a warm surge of relief. But
there was no smile on his lips. His pale face was racked with worry and
he looked years older than his tender age.

"Gus!" she cried, wiping tears away with her shirt.

"Em! Come with me!" he said, stooping to pull on her arm. "We
must get you below before the guns sound again!"

Emily seized his hand and climbed to her feet, prepared to face the
stretch of deck they would have to traverse to gain the ladders. Leaning
heavily on one another, sidestepping streams of running red and shapes
that writhed in pain, they hurried as fast as they could. Emily was
vaguely aware of the wind wailing in the sails like a requiem for the
dead and the distant crack of gunfire.

11:15 A.M.

Fly's luck was changing. Finally! The tension drained from his shoulders as he stood back to admire the magnificent sight, his eyes stinging from the smoke, but his face beaming, bolstered by the jubilant
men that crowded around him, hoping to shake his hand. They had
succeeded in taking down the *Liberty*'s mizzenmast with a direct hit.
Hearing the ominous crack of oak, they had all held their breath as the

mizzen wobbled and the American sailors beneath fled in terror lest she fall on them. Huzzahs burst from hundreds of throats, his included, as she finally fell, toppling over her larboard quarter with a tremendous crash and upheaval of saltwater. The *Liberty* was crippled. Sailing would be impossible now with that dishonourable mast dragging her down like a sea anchor.

For the longest time, the Invincibles had made no headway. Fly knew his men had not been well drilled. For that he accepted some of the blame, but the inaccuracy of their aim had him tearing his hair out. So much of their shot had gone awry, into the sea or whizzing past the enemies' sails, inflicting minimal damage. The waste of ammunition had him cursing, and not always under his breath. Despite all that, and though he would never say, he believed he had played a hand in their reversal of fortune. Commandeering one of the starboard 18-pounders when its captain had been struck down, Fly had led its crew. Positioned well beyond the recoil range of the gun, he had ordered the fuses lit, peered along the barrel to line it up and waited for the ship to roll before pulling the lanyard that ignited the charge. The memory lifted his sagging spirits. But then, who really cared? A victory was a victory. And no one person could ever do it alone.

Now if only the *Expedition* could make quick work of the *Amethyst*, this day would belong to England. On that score, Fly's confidence sadly wavered. In fact, he was mystified. The two ships, both 74s and bearing equal gun power, were fighting one another, but without heart or grit. They reminded him of reluctant medieval lords and their legions of men, coming late to the battle, hoping to find the fight over and victory declared, others having done the work for them.

The minute the cheer went up, Prosper Burgo elbowed his way to Fly's side, assuring him straightaway that the wheel had been given over to a trusted younker. Shooing the crowds of happy men away and back to their stations, Prosper led Fly toward the stern. His ruddy face was caked in soot and wreathed in smiles. Engorged veins embossed his bald crown, the result of raucous shouting and cries of glory. He gave Fly a lively clap on the back, which nearly sent him flying, not to mention vexing the tender skin of the burns he received when Trevelyan set the *Isabelle* afire. But Fly forgave Prosper his blatant act of insubordination as nothing in that moment could diminish his mood.

"Well, Cap'n! We got ourselves a prize!" Prosper cried, punching the air around him as if boxing an invisible opponent.

"Aye! I believe so." Fly nodded, stepping back to set his sights on the *Liberty* as the *Invincible* circled around her.

"And ya'll be lettin' me form the prize crew?"

"Let us not count our *prize* chickens before they hatch, Mr. Burgo. There is still much to do. As the *Liberty* is not going anywhere for the time being, I would ask that you return to the wheel, post-haste, and bring us alongside the *Amethyst*. I am not pleased with Uptergrove. His fight has been lethargic. I feel certain he has left his midshipmen to lead the charge."

"I tell ya! That Prickett ain't in a gaol like ya think. He's still aboard the *Amethyst*, fightin' gingerly like a Thames ferryman, hopin' to keep his sails aloft and hull in one piece."

"A nice sentiment, Mr. Burgo, but if that were true, our Captain Prickett is going after the wrong ship. He would be directing his weak cannonades at the *Liberty* ... not the *Expedition*."

"Suppose yer right." Prosper's smile faded as he considered Fly's logic. "By the bye, did Uptergrove ever get 'round to answerin' yer signals regardin' our wee sailmaker?"

"No. Not a word back," said Fly, finding and pulling a small splinter from the back of his hand and blotting the beads of blood with his shirtsleeve. "However, keep in mind my message contained no requirement for immediate action. When there are enemies on the doorstep, a ship is a beehive, not the best time for mustering the crew." It was Fly's turn to shoo away Prosper, though he did it good-naturedly. "Go to your post, Mr. Burgo, and bring me in close to the *Amethyst*. The Americans had no compunction in going after us with their greater firepower when we last met. Let us go after them now. Two on one!"

Prosper leapt nimbly in the air, hollered an ear-splitting huzzah, adding further to Fly's deafness, and strolled happily off. Fly watched him kick the younker from the wheel and take back command, digging in his feet, determined as ever. Alone again, he gazed ponderously over the watery battlefield as the *Invincible* sailed by the *Liberty*. The respite was over. The men were all back at their stations, reloading, ready to have another crack at it. The powder monkeys scurried about, lugging fresh cartridges from the hold. The marines and sharpshooters knelt on the platforms and squinted down the short barrels of their muskets. Occasionally, one of them went off. Fly smiled with pride. "One opponent down, another to go," he said to himself, feeling more hopeful than he had an hour ago. He snapped open his spyglass and raised it to his left eye, keen to assess the damage done to their potential prize.

Somewhere in the distance, a woman screamed.

CHAPTER 32

11:20 A.M.

Leander wrenched his spectacles from his nose and peered up at the deckhead, listening to the sounds coming from above. For a brief time there had been a pause in the engagement; only the edges of muffled conversations and the odd crack of musket-fire had filtered through to the orlop. But now the big guns were at it again, their broadsides rattling the timbers around him. He stood amongst the carnage in the cockpit, hemmed in by buckets of water, linen bandages, and brown sponges, and the old chest that held his surgical instruments. It was a hellish scene, straight from Dante's *Inferno*, the darkness, the deficient ventilation, the sickly sweet smells of putrefaction, and the severed limbs at his feet, quivering grotesquely as if they were still attached to their hosts. And the casualties! There was an endless queue of them, weeping and pleading for his attention. The break in gunfire only brought new ones through the door. Where was he supposed to tell Mr. Duffy and his helper, Jim Beef, to set them down? Where? For a moment, Leander sunk low as if he had fallen through the hull and were drowning in the black water beneath the *Invincible*, suffering the punishment of keelhauling. Already, he had lost count of the wounded and of the dead and dying, their numbers having spilled far beyond the cockpit. And his fatigue ... it was immense and overbearing. Would he last through the hours until the dawn of tomorrow without collapsing? Could he manage the intricacies of securing waxed thread ligatures to arteries and blood vessels? Though he tried to dismiss it, even castigated himself for it, a familiar question swooped through his mind like a tormenting bird. Why, at that supper two weeks ago in Portsmouth, had he buckled under the weight of Fly's persuasive personality?

"It is so damn dark in here; I can hardly see what I am doing. Pa, could you fetch more light?" He shot a cursory glance over the operating table at his father, who immediately looked around, bewildered and uncertain. "There, there in the dispensary cupboard," Leander grumbled, unable to curb his impatience, though goodness knows his father did not deserve to be treated thus. With no word of complaint, he was working as hard as he could. Over his shoulder, Leander addressed Mr. Duffy and Mr. Beef, tempering his voice this time. The last thing the poor souls on the floor needed to see was their surgeon in hysterics. "Set them down wherever you can, perhaps in the cable-tiers and wing berths. Give them water before you go and, for God's sake, please find yourselves more help. Where the devil has Lord Somerton gotten to?"

Mr. Duffy's reply was too casual for Leander's liking. "Likely playin' a game o' solitaire somewhere 'round here, sir."

Leander swore under his breath. He gazed down at the man lying on the blood-soaked sheets on his table, delirious, repeatedly mumbling, "Bear a hand, Doctor." Like Morgan Evans, he was a carpenter. He even looked a bit like Morgan and there was little doubt he was near to him in age. Every bone in the young man's right hand and wrist had been shattered. It would have to be amputated post-haste.

"What about the ladies, then, Mr. Duffy?" Leander asked, in a stranglehold of melancholy. "I believe they are still in the Hole at the stern. Have Emily and my aunt come straight here. Do not bother yourself with Mrs. Jiggins."

"With due respect, sir," said Mr. Duffy, helping himself to a sponge from one of the buckets and dashing it over his face and neck to clean away the sweat. "Your Emily's on the fo'c'sle."

Certain his ears had failed him, Leander's head snapped up.

"Last time I saw her, she was sittin' near the bowsprit."

"Doing what, exactly?"

"I dunno, sir." Mr. Duffy was not in the least bit concerned. "Shellin' peas, mayhap!" Like a simpleton, he found humour in his own witticism. Having lost interest in the conversation, he sidestepped arms and legs, and eyed the slumped men on the floor as if determining which ones were still conscious. "Listen up, mates! I'm here to tell ya good news! Just now we brung down the *Liberty*'s mizzen. It's hangin' over her quarter like a cow's lazy tongue. And now her steerin' don't answer!"

A few fists pumped the air. A cheer rose up, lacking its usual verve, but a cheer nevertheless. Someone called out, "Victory!" Another shouted, "For the prize!" Mr. Duffy clucked proudly as if he had single-handedly slayed the enemy. Leander had no heart to rejoice. He was at a loss to know what to do about Emily. Wild-eyed, he glanced across the room at his father, who was returning from the dispensary with two more lanterns. Having overheard Mr. Duffy's shocking revelation, his father nodded, his old eyes gentle and concerned, and swiftly gave the lanterns over to a loblolly boy for lighting.

"No, Pa, you are not going anywhere," Leander said firmly, reading his mind. "I cannot afford to lose you."

His father met his glance evenly, kept his mouth shut, and prepared for the amputation.

Leander put his spectacles back on his nose, telling himself over and over that Emily would manage ... she was resourceful. But it did little to alleviate the shaking of his hands. He frowned at the hulking shadow that fell across his table. It blotted out what little lantern light he had, plunging the carpenter's mutilated hand into darkness. Leander knew before he had looked up that Jim Beef had fallen in beside his father. Had he come forward, hoping to help as he once had with Morgan Evans? To hold the patient down while the teeth of his saw sliced through bone marrow? Or had he, too, seen Emily on deck and was here to proclaim, "Death and woe?" Leander studied Mr. Beef, searching for clues on his gaunt face. His unruly hair was pulled from his face and tethered in a queue, accentuating his prodigious nose and the unblinking eyes that bobbed and stared emphatically back at Leander. Mr. Beef let out a low, grunting laugh and hurried to the door, his glowing eyes never leaving Leander.

As he picked up the tourniquet and prepared to apply it to the young carpenter's arm, a burble of emotion and gratitude escaped Leander's lips.

11:20 A.M.

"Dear God!" Emily fell on her knees and raised her arms to the sky, imploring.

There had been musket-fire. But it seemed so far away. Gus had been beside her, steering her to safety, squeezing her fingers, whispering words to keep up her confidence. The next thing she knew there was a queer expression on his face, his eyes wide and unseeing. He gasped as if he had suffered a punch to the belly and staggered a few steps. His crutch hit the deck with a terrible thump before he did. Emily tried to reconcile the prostrate form sprawled beside the wheels of a carronade. No! No! This fallen boy was not Gus. This was someone else's poor child, not one she had ever met or known or loved. Her Gus was on the quarterdeck with Captain Austen, recording the events of the battle, so proud to be near his captain, so happy to have had a chance to return to sea on the *Invincible* and brought there by Dr. Arthur Braden, the man who had been his champion and taken him from his miserable life with his uncharitable Aunt Sophia.

The sight of blood, seeping from his serge coat, mingling with the bloodshed of fallen mates, awakened Emily so violently. Surely the needles of a thousand splinters had cruelly embedded themselves in her heart. A primal, despairing, plaintive scream rose up, fought brazenly to get out, but never left her lips.

"Someone! Please help me!" she cried piteously, every word a struggle.

On her knees beside him, Emily peeled back the short skirt of Gus's frock coat. The spreading stain, darkening his clothes, turning his shirt red and the cerulean-blue of his coat black, indicated he had been hit somewhere in his middle.

Her mind was a muddled mess and refused to co-operate. Fearful lest he be hit again, she stripped off her shirt, her fumbling fingers having no patience for the buttons, leaving her in a chemise that, long ago, she had tailored to accommodate the wearing of trousers. As quickly as she could, she secured the shirt around Gus's small waist and knotted the cuffs, hoping it would staunch the flow of blood until ... until someone carried him down to Leander.

There was a second worrying pool of blood by his head. Had he been hit twice? With gentle, probing fingers, Emily felt the sticky blood crusting his blond hair, but there was too much of it to draw conclusions. Yanking the scarf from her braid, she bundled it into a ball and pressed it to his head.

"Gus! Can you hear me?" Her plea was more of an order, insistent, meant to wake him. But he was sleeping now, his eyes closed, his face placid and untroubled by any pain he may have felt. "Oh, please, my dear friend!"

Emily felt someone kneeling beside her. Here was help, she thought, her shoulders sagging with relief. Looking up, she was dismayed to find it was Somerton, his outer coat discarded, his shirtsleeves and face wet with perspiration. *No wonder*, she thought bitterly, *given his strenuous activities of late.*

Somerton shoved Emily rudely out of the way and pitched the balled-up scarf over his shoulder. "You see? You see?" he cried. "This is the reward for the fool who chooses to assist a helpless princess." Gathering Gus up in his arms, he rose to his feet, grunting with exertion.

Too overwrought to concern herself with Somerton's behaviour, Emily jumped up and pointed toward the companion way. "Take him to the cockpit ... straightaway!" she cried, her words muted by the roar of battle.

"Whatever for?" He scowled at her. "So the good doctor can pronounce him dead and riding the pale horse?"

Somerton set off. For a second time, he passed the ladder down, scurrying toward his favourite place beside the larboard breastwork,

Gus's bleeding head jouncing over his elbow. Knowing at once what he had in mind, Emily raised a scream, but it stuck in her throat.

In desperation, she searched for help. She heard running footsteps and realized they were her own. No one had witnessed the melancholy drama unfolding on the forecastle's larboard side. They were all too preoccupied with their own fight to stay alive. By the chimney head, something winked in the sun's rays that had wormed their way through the blanket of smoke. She remembered the bright finish of the young marine's musket. Within seconds, she had the still-warm barrel in her own hands and was striding toward Somerton. She raised it to her eye, her thumb twitching near the flintlock.

"Stop! I will use this!"

Seeing her with the gun, Somerton howled with laughter. "Insipid woman! You might want to reload it first."

Emily was dashed. Where was Captain Austen? Only his commanding bark would make Somerton halt in his tracks. But he was not there. This misery had to be faced alone. Summoning all the power and menace her lungs could muster, she screamed again.

"GET ... AWAY ... FROM ... HIM ... NOW!"

Arriving at the ship's side, Somerton turned his head toward her, his dusky eyes taunting. "I am only following the captain's orders," he yelled. "Clear the deck of the dead ones, he said. It does not matter the condition of the corpse ... if they are dead ... they are dead." He pressed on and made ready to hurl Gus's languid body into the hungry sea.

Emily rushed toward him, prepared to spear him with the musket's bayonet if need be. Anything to stop him! But the musket fired off, its startling, unexpected crack unbalancing her, throwing her against the bulwark. She watched the ball of lead smash into Somerton's arm, tearing open his shirtsleeve. The spray of blood unleashed was maroon in colour, much like the harvested chestnuts that grew on the trees at Hartwood Hall, was her absurd thought. Gus was dropped like a basket of rotting apples on the deck. Gawking and blinking at his butchered forearm, Somerton grew unhinged, screaming and shrieking, spitting filthy-sounding words and ugly accusations in every direction.

"She shot me! The vile minx shot me! Where is Captain Austen? Alert him at once!" He held his arm to his body, his face a bloated, purple fury.

No one came forward. No one turned from their fight to give them a passing glance. They had both roared their outrage into the wind and gunfire, their drama nothing but an unremarkable scene in a tempestuous production. Emily drew her knees up and huddled in a little quivering ball of misery, shutting out Somerton's caterwauling and the pandemonium of the broadsides. She did not see who took Gus away, nor to where he had been taken. Rocking and weeping, she sat there lost for a long while until something warm was placed around her stooped shoulders. It was dirt-stained and smelled like the bowels of the ship — old cheese, fish, and mouldy oak timbers. But it shut out the late September chill. How surprised she was to find it was Jim Beef's overcoat and him squatting in front of her, grinning boyishly, kindness shining in those wild eyes of his. He said not a word as he picked her up, easily as if she were weightless, and carried her off the forecastle. This time, at least, she knew where they were going.

Peering back at the scene over Mr. Beef's shoulder, Emily's eyes found Biscuit. He had turned away from the marines and was following her path to the companion way, his musket lowered and smoking at his side. There was something about the sober cast of his good eye, the firm line of his mouth and the manner in which he stood there, watching her when no else was. It made her wonder.

11:30 A.M.
(FORENOON WATCH, SEVEN BELLS)
ABOARD HMS EXPEDITION

Magpie silently gave a prayer of thanks to the gods for the booming noise of the battle. Without it, that unknown man dressing Uptergrove's wounds would have suspected there was someone shaking like a half-drowned puppy in the quarter gallery. Surely, he would have been alerted to the resounding hoofbeats of Magpie's galloping heart. And Magpie didn't want any alerting. The man didn't look like a surgeon, an assistant, or even a loblolly boy. His heavy face was too hard and loutish, and unlike Dr. Braden, he wasn't wearing a black apron and spectacles with hinged side-pieces. From Magpie's perspective on the floor, though a disadvantageous one, it did, however, appear the man was competent with the cleaning and dressing of grievous wounds. For Captain Uptergrove's sake, Magpie was most thankful.

Cowering beside the toilet, he racked his brain, trying to invent excuses should the loutish man, or some other detestable character, discover him in hiding. But his ideas were lame. Everyone on the ship knew him as the bucket boy, and yet here he had neither bucket nor cleaning cloths with him. Even worse, the man might accuse him of stealing Uptergrove's flute. What if he did and Uptergrove was too frail to come to his defence? Magpie had given this careful consideration. Taking the flute from the box, he had slipped the golden strings of the leather pouch around his neck and under his arm. Without the extra bother of the box, an escape enacted quickly would enable him to fend off any hostile gangs of Bloody Fluxes.

The ship endured another hit. It writhed like an animal in pain. Magpie flailed about, trying to steady himself against the toilet and the thin oak wall. He didn't even know how well or how poorly the battle was going. What if the Americans had already boarded the *Invincible*; taken Captain Austen and Dr. Braden prisoner, and left Biscuit and Prosper Burgo hanging by their necks on the yardarm?

Footsteps entered the captain's cabin and pattered to the hammock by the windows. Magpie peeked out the curtain again. His galloping heart took off like a horse that had taken a mean slap on its flank.

"Did you give him a tonic?" Trevelyan asked the loutish man, peering down at Uptergrove. "Good! Then you are free to leave," he said, with a fling of his scarred hand. When the door clicked shut, his voice rang loud and clear and cheerful. Too cheerful. "And how are you feeling now, sir?"

Uptergrove's response was softly spoken. The only thing Magpie heard of it was a mumbled "Mr. Bumpus."

Trevelyan locked his hands behind his back. "We are going to have you moved below, sir. You lie in much danger here. How fortunate you are we have not yet been raked from stem to stern."

"And the fight? How goes it?" Uptergrove's voice was still hoarse, but stronger this time.

"I fully expect to win the day, sir."

"Send in Mr. Croker ... and the first lieutenant, if you please. I would like a full accounting of the day."

Trevelyan's cheeriness ebbed away. He no longer sounded like an assistant to the clerk. "I shall send them to you, but only once we have you safely below."

Magpie could not hear Uptergrove's reply and wondered if he had given one at all. An unsettled silence fell between the two men. Gunfire filled the void, louder now. Trevelyan had taken his weight on one leg and was freely tapping the foot of his other. Behind his back, his hands fidgeted with the tails of his coat. Clutching the curtain in a white-knuckled fist, Magpie followed Trevelyan's sudden pacing between the hammock and the door. Was he waiting for help to come and carry off the captain? Maybe. But Magpie didn't feel right. When Trevelyan paused beside the captain's bed, glared down at him with such loathing on his face, and slowly drew a handkerchief from the waist of his trousers with no intention of blowing his nose ... it became too much.

He couldn't remember what sort of sound he had uttered, but it must have been high and hysterical, for immediately it sent Trevelyan searching for its source. His awful, hooded eyes found him at once.

"Well, if it isn't the mongrel! Our own bucket boy!" he said, marching toward the lavatory. "Spying on the captain, are we?"

There was no chance to run or go anywhere. Trevelyan was on him like wildfire, cornering him in the lavatory. Seizing his arm, he hauled him to his feet, nearly dislocating his limb, and struck him brutally across the face on the same tender cheek worked over by Mr. Huxley the night of his impressment. Magpie screamed in pain, trying to wrench free. Trevelyan struck again ... and again, smiling fiendishly as though he enjoyed the feel of each blow.

"Did you think I had forgotten? No! That's your payment for those dirks you sank into my legs."

His hands groped for Magpie's neck. Magpie clawed and kicked at the walls. His throat was closing it, he could not draw air. His vision was blurring. My God! This was it. He was going to die in Uptergrove's toilet. But all of a sudden the strangling hands let go. An ominous laugh rumbled through Trevelyan. Flipping his frock coat open, he showed Magpie the hilt of his cutlass, letting the sight of it sink in before pulling it from his waistband. Spinning him around, Trevelyan grabbed his hair, yanked his head back, and held the cold blade against his windpipe.

"You could call out, Mongrel, but no one will hear. Our Uptergrove's sleeping like a newborn babe."

"I want Morgan Evans's thrum cap back!" Magpie gasped weakly, feeling the humiliation of his bladder giving way.

Trevelyan's laughter was abhorrent. "What nonsense you speak on the brink of death!" He gave Magpie's head another yank. "I cannot promise it will be quick. You shall have the once-in-a-lifetime privilege of watching your blood drain from your ..."

A thud! A dreadful crack! The smashing of glass! The cutlass fell, clattered, and spun away. Trevelyan had a dumb look on his face. He was awash in red, but it didn't look like blood! He gawped at Magpie as if wondering how the bucket boy had managed to wield such a blow, his lips forming curses. Then his eyes rolled back in his head and all six feet of him collapsed on the floor. Magpie's hands flew to his ravaged throat, struggling to suck in air as he blinked at Captain Uptergrove. There he was, hunched over and breathing hard, all grey and white except for the startling patch of blood seeping through his linen drawers. In one clenched fist, he held the jagged remains of the wine decanter.

Magpie burst into tears, so great was his relief.

"Are you all right?"

"A bit bruised, I think, sir," he sobbed, unwilling to tell his captain that he had wet his trousers.

"You haven't much time," Uptergrove said, tossing away the last fragment of the decanter. He glanced with contempt at the floor. "I have only just given Mr. Bumpus a bump on his head." He snorted sarcasm and spoke quickly, breathlessly. "He shall soon be revived. At length, they will come for me. As we speak, there's someone out there, guarding the door. I am afraid there is some kind of sinister plot afoot."

"There is, sir. I were tryin' to tell ya. I heard Mr. Bumpus talkin' with others ... 'bout real bad things."

"I have long suspected as much. Thus, the reason I made him the clerk's assistant ... to keep him close."

"But ya gotta know, sir ... Mr. Bumpus ain't really Mr. Bumpus."

A bright stare of surprise broke through Uptergrove's unyielding expression. "What are you telling me, Magpie?"

"He's a traitor, sir. He kidnapped Emily."

"Your princess?"

"Aye! And burned Captain Moreland's *Isabelle*. He's done a heap o' bad things, sir."

"Do you know his name?"

"Oh!" Magpie exclaimed, realizing he had forgotten the most important bit. "Aye, sir! He's Thomas Trevelyan."

Uptergrove's white hand fluttered to his chest. "Dear God!" he whispered, visibly sinking under the weight of the revelation. "Are you absolutely certain, Magpie?"

"Never so certain in me life, sir. He's Trevelyan, all right. And he knows I know it. Said he'd fry up me liver and eat it if I ever told anyone."

Uptergrove's breath left him in a long hiss. "I suspected something, but not that ... never that." He shot an investigative glance over his hunched shoulder. "I must somehow get word to Captain Austen." He looked gravely at Magpie, who could see his mind hard at work. "Do you have the flute?"

Magpie indicated he did with a pat on the leather pouch.

Slowly and painfully, Uptergrove stepped over Trevelyan's prone body, trying his best to avoid the shards of glass and puddle of red wine. Inside the lavatory, he lifted the sheet of oak with the hole in it that constituted the toilet seat.

"Quick as you can! You can get out this way."

Magpie gawped at the rolling sea and then back at Uptergrove, knowing there was no point in disguising his terror. It had incapacitated every feature on his face. "I ... I can't swim, sir."

"Look! There is much debris in the water. Pull yourself up on something to keep you afloat."

"But the drop alone will shove me under the sea, sir. I may never surface."

"Yes! Yes! You are right." Uptergrove considered this. He leaned against the wall to think, wincing as his eyes searched all around for an answer.

Magpie peeked again over the side of the toilet. Waves thrashed the stern and leapt up at him, beckoning, daring him to do it. He felt as if he were teetering on the dome of St. Paul's Cathedral, about to fall into an angry mob below bent on tearing him limb from limb. It was such a dizzyingly long way down and his first meeting with the Atlantic a few weeks back had not gone particularly well. She was cruel and frightening and could do bad things to you. Her icy fingers were razor-sharp. She could mutilate your body and your mind, making you think that, at any minute, pale arms would grab hold of you and force you to inhabit her hideous world.

"A climbing boy!" Uptergrove said it triumphantly.

"Beg yer pardon, sir."

"You told me you had once been a climbing boy," he said, his eyes feverish now, the patch of blood on his leg spreading, gaining ground. "I assume you know something of tight, unpleasant places and situations and ... chains and ropes!"

"Aye, somethin', sir. Why, what are ya thinkin' of?" rasped Magpie, rock-hard knots of fear cramping his belly.

Uptergrove pointed at the rudder chains that criss-crossed the stern beneath them and then up at the mess of ropes and canvas, the remains of the mizzensail and her backstays, dangling over the ship's side, the consequence of a well-aimed hit. "So, if you can ... try to —" he broke off abruptly and began wiggling out of his nightshirt, dragging it over his head.

Magpie's eye grew wider still. A whoosh of wind sailed up through the hole, tugging on his hair and loose trousers, a warning that once he left the ship, he was leaving behind safety and security ... maybe forever.

"Here! I shall help to the best of my ability." Uptergrove handed him one end of his nightshirt and wound the other around his fingers and wrist.

"A blanket might serve better, sir."

"No time for that!" Uptergrove's face, white as wax, looked determined. "Now ... as soon as you can, grab on to one of those ropes or the chains or whatever else might come raining down on you."

"What if they ain't anchored to anythin' anymore, sir?"

Uptergrove grimly bit his lip. "Let us not think of that."

Behind them on the floor, Trevelyan stirred and groaned.

"Hurry!"

Magpie hooked one leg over the side of the toilet and looked down at the roiling, debris-strewn water, frozen in fear.

Trevelyan was sitting up now, rubbing the back of his head, trying to make sense of the blood he had found there.

"Hurry, Magpie! Go!"

There was nothing for it. Magpie had to believe his chances were good.

"Tell Captain Austen what you have learned here."

Magpie nodded, choking down the dry lump in his throat. "Bless you, sir."

He touched the flute's leather pouch, inhaled the cold rush of the wind and slid from the roughened edge of the toilet, grasping the nightshirt for dear life as Uptergrove sent him swinging into the emptiness.

CHAPTER 33

Leander found Emily curled up against a dusty, coiled rope in the cable-tier, lying back to back on a platform with Mrs. Jiggins, whose snores were louder than the guns. There was a strong smell of rat dirt and blood about it, but it was the only place available when Jim Beef brought her down to the orlop, a weeping mess, asking where Gus was, stammering incoherently, something about Lord Somerton and a musket going off. Leander had given her a tonic, as she was beyond consoling. At the same time, he had administered one to Mrs. Jiggins, although somewhat reluctantly for she reeked as if she had bathed in whiskey. Her wits fuddled, she had come barging into the cockpit like a runaway barrel, with poor Eliza tagging meekly along, a little unsteady on her feet. Mrs. Jiggins had been full of resolve to "save the sailors," but one glance at the butchery on the floor, one breath of the fetid air and she had promptly fainted away, falling flat on her face. Heaven knows what her nose would look like when she was revived. Once his aunt, looking very green, was engaged in helping Mr. Duffy, and Mrs. Jiggins had been towed out of the way, Leander had learned something of what had taken place on deck.

Emily sat up. Her eyes were huge in her face, terror-stricken. She shrugged farther into Mr. Beef's ragged overcoat as if trying to cloak herself and hide from the light. Leander knelt down next to her, amazed at the noises issuing forth from Mrs. Jiggins's mouth. The guns, he noticed, had gone silent.

"Did you manage to sleep at all?"

She nodded, smiled uneasily and brushed a fall of hair from her eyes. "A wink or two. Tinctures of opium seem to do the trick."

"I have only a moment to change my shirt, Emily. I must get back."

Her hand seized his arm, unperturbed that it was viscous with blood. Her shining eyes bore into his, her voice fitful, pleading. "I do not want to hear what you have come to say. Not now. Maybe later, once I have slept for three days. Just not now, please. I cannot bear it."

Gently, Leander peeled her hand from his arm and gave it a sympathetic squeeze. "Emily, I am overwhelmed in the cockpit. I need your help."

She shrank back, pulling the coat around her, and turned her face toward the darkness. "I know he is in there. I cannot see him ... his broken little body." She shut her eyes. "I have no strength. My head is reeling, I can barely stand. I am crippled with unhappiness. Please do not ask this of me now."

Leander tightened his fingers around hers. "I shall be operating on him soon."

She gave a bitter little laugh and looked back at him. "On who? Lord Somerton? You can take his head off for all I care. Goodness knows he does not use it."

Holding her gaze, Leander waited for her anger to abate.

"You mean ... do you mean Gus?" she asked in the merest of whispers.

"I cannot pretend. His condition is most serious."

Emily withdrew her hand. Her frown was distrustful. "But I saw the blood ... on his shirt ... on the back of his head."

"He took a bullet, but his head ... I believe he struck something as he fell and was knocked out."

She gazed past Leander, remembering, and caught her breath. "He was lying beside a gun carriage."

"Perhaps that was it." He could see the weary despair fall from her eyes and the embers of hope taking its place.

"Is he … awake?"

"He is. And asking for you."

Emily buried her face in her hands. Choking sobs shook her slender frame. Leander let her go, let her weep her gentle heart out. He settled in cross-legged beside her, a protective arm around her waist, and smiled sadly when she picked up his right hand, waiting by his knee. She fixed her concentration on it, her fingers stroking his palm, tracing the stains of blood that had dried in the lines of his flesh. Removing Mr. Beef's overcoat, she glanced around, as if wondering where to leave it, and threw it over Mrs. Jiggins's slumbering lump.

"Please help me up."

Distrusting his ability to speak, Leander could only nod. He rose to his feet stiffly and held out his hands to assist her. When their eyes met, he could see her tears and feel the trembling of her body. His insides clenched with sympathy and love for this woman standing before him. Impervious to all resistance, his mind leapt forward for a moment, eager to leave the gloom of the orlop behind and the stark reality that there were men and boys holding on as best they could, hoping he would perform some act of magic to grant them a second chance at life.

Leander could see the snug cottage, whitewashed and thatched, sitting on a knoll of green overlooking a shimmering sea. By now, he knew it well. There was a gaggle of happy children running around, playing blind man's bluff, screaming with pleasure. A dog or two pranced about at their feet. Emily carried a plump toddler on her hip, one hand shading her eyes as she watched over her growing sons and daughters. The setting sun caught the golden light in her unbound hair; the fresh wind lifted it from her shoulders. She smiled, catching sight of him cantering down the road on a chestnut mare in his broad-brimmed hat, his medical bag slung over his shoulder. Dismounting to a lively chorus of squeals and greetings, he bent down to let the little arms wrap around his neck, cherishing the exuberant kisses on his cheek.

Leander felt himself redden. Were the inner workings of his mind revealed in a silly, dreamy expression on his face? Had Emily guessed he had temporarily slipped away, and if so, did she know where he had gone? Did she ever go there, too? Sobering up, he rebuked himself for such thoughts at such a time. He set his brow and jaw, critically, like a butler inspecting his footmen before the serving of dinner, his eyes skimming the naked flesh of her shoulders.

"Perhaps, before I take you to Gus, we should find you some clothes?"

1:10 P.M.

The afternoon sun, having escaped the veils of smoke, beamed her jewelled rays on the glorious scenes. Fly looked out upon them with satisfaction, the palms of his hands drumming along the starboard rail, his body shaking with joy and relief. It was over. The day was won. The *Liberty* was drifting aimlessly, immobilized by her shattered mizzenmast. The sails of the *Amethyst* had been cut to ribbons, no longer able to harness the wind. After circling them for two days like a wary shark, the latter had gone down with little resistance, as if she were eager to return to the English fleet. Maybe Prosper had been right all along! Maybe Captain Prickett *was* still in command on that ship.

Fly's discerning glance appraised the *Invincible*. No. She had not been left unscathed. Her fore and main topgallant yards were down, several of her sails had to be replaced, and a fearsome amount of woodwork, including the hull, needed the attention of the carpenters and caulkers. Hopefully they could all adequately refit at sea and the following days would hum along to the sound of hammers, mallets, and augers, and smell like fresh canvas and paint. Afterward, when they were all pronounced seaworthy again, he would send his prizes back to England where they would be met by his countrymen with huzzahs and celebratory banquets, and the *Invincible* and *Expedition* would quietly carry on to the American coast without, God willing, further catastrophic delays.

Right then! As soon as the smoke cleared from his head and the ringing in his ears abated, he would form the prize crews and communicate with Uptergrove to make certain all was well on his side and inquire again after Magpie. Then his full attention would be handed over to his men ... the ones who had fallen. Sooner or later he had to face the butcher's bill. There would be funerals to arrange and letters to write, but for now, if only for a brief while, he begged leave to rejoice.

Pushing away from the rail, Fly turned, lost his footing on a patch of blood and gore and nearly stumbled over Cadby Brambles, who was working alongside the launch, the only one of the boats left on deck during the battle. Recovering, he gave his jacket a dignified tug and curiously eyed the young midshipman who was bent over, red-faced and annoyed, scratching furiously at something with his fingernails. The two goats that permanently lodged inside the launch looked down at him, their furry expressions indignant as if demanding to know what all those hours of racket and fuss had been about.

"Mr. Brambles! I must say, you did exceedingly well during your first encounter with the Americans."

Abandoning his task, Mr. Brambles spun around, his countenance all agog as if hoping to hear accounts of his great feats of heroism in facing down the enemy. "Do you really think so, sir?"

"You managed to get by without losing your limbs. I don't even see a scratch on you."

Hope faded in Mr. Brambles's eyes. He looked shamefaced, his colour burning as he outstretched his arms to inspect them for wounds he might have overlooked. "I suppose I was lucky, sir."

"That you were. Now, what is it that has frustrated you so?"

"Well, it's *this* thing, sir." Mr. Brambles pointed at a ghastly, bloody, wormy object, the size of a pancake, stuck to the side of the launch like an engorged leech. "Prosper asked me to take it off, because he didn't like looking at it, but I swear someone's taken glue to it." He gave his head an exasperated shake. "Do you know what it might be, sir?"

"Aye! Sadly, I do. I have seen a few of them in my time," Fly said, hurrying on his way, shouting the answer over his shoulder. "It is the lining of some poor fellow's stomach."

He left the youth behind him, heaving and choking his guts out on the deck. Suddenly very thirsty, Fly was heartened to find Biscuit loitering by the rail, staring out at sea. Laughing heartily, he called out to him.

"Biscuit! Quick as you can! Put down your musket! To the galley with you! Grog for all! Make it a double allowance! And serve me first."

"Aye, Cap'n."

"And when we are all satiated, fire up your old Brodie stove. I am in the mood for a sea-pie for my supper."

His vitality was met with a listless salute. Given the auspicious occasion, Fly had expected to see Biscuit wink his good eye, cast out a clever quip, or even break into a lusty song about women and free-flowing ale. But he seemed sad and subdued. Dumbfounded, Fly watched him creep away toward the ladder, the musket still in his grip, shoulders hunched as if he had received a public scolding, not a simple request for food and drink. The mystery was instantly forgotten, as was the prospect of grog and sea-pie, when a huffing Mr. Duffy fell into Fly's path. His flabby chest was stained with blood; his duck trousers sullied with human matter. He appeared to have come from an abattoir, not the bottom of the ship.

"Sir! I think Dr. Braden needs ya in the cockpit."

Fly grunted, having no desire, or stomach, for the horrors of Leander's surgery at the present time. But it was unlike his friend to ask for assistance of any kind, ever. "You *think*?"

"Aye, sir! There's a bit of a drama goin' on down there."

Fly shook his head. The man was testing his patience. Had he imbibed the rum Leander reserved for medicinal purposes? It would not be the first time.

"It's that tetchy Mr. High-and-Haughty, sir," said Mr. Duffy, his weaving eyes unable to conceal his excitement. "And it's him what's playin' the lead role."

1:15 P.M.
ABOARD HMS *EXPEDITION*

Trevelyan sat fretting in the darkness of the orlop deck, staring at the tiny leaping flame in his lantern. He was a shaking, anxious wreck. Fortuitously, there was no one around to hear his unquiet fear. He was alone, save for the person lying comatose in the creaking hammock beside him. He pulled the wad of linen from his head and squinted at it. The bleeding had subsided, but already he could feel the emergence of a bump, an excruciating one. Later, it would form a scar. Trevelyan let slip a rancorous snort. Aye! Another scar! Just add it to the attractive collection of cuts on his hands and face and thighs, and the unseen ones that had cleaved his heart, causing permanent damage.

He glanced at the hammock. What an ugly picture it had been in the great cabin, wrestling the weakened, fearful Uptergrove to the ground and forcing a tonic down his gullet, his mangled leg bleeding all over the place. And later assuring that vapid surgeon that all was well, that he, his trusted clerk, would stay below with the captain until the battle was over. If God had any mercy, he would let the man die. Then again, would anyone on the ship even know if his death had been hastened along with the aid of a pillow?

Twinges of anxiety scratched Trevelyan like sharp talons. Angry words burst unchecked from his mouth. Damn that feckless mongrel to hell. He should have cut out his liver when he had the opportunity to do so. And where exactly had he gotten to? After subduing Uptergrove, he had gone searching, but there was no sign of the eye-patched bucket boy. Trevelyan studied the vague grey outline of the woodpile at his back. Was he hiding somewhere down here? Or, perish the thought, had he somehow managed to flee the ship?

Trevelyan hammered his fist into his palm and screwed his eyes shut. Almost immediately, the pitiful wraith appeared in the shifting darkness behind his eyelids. Refusing to hear his haunting, heart-wrenching pleas, Trevelyan intercepted him.

"Not now, little Harry! But soon. Soon."

His dead brother hung his head and wordlessly withdrew, back into the dismal shadows of his nameless place. Shuddering, Trevelyan locked his arms across his chest, leaned against the woodpile and tried to focus on the coming hours. There was nothing more he could do until the sun set and the men were safely stowed away below deck.

CHAPTER 34

Leander had been gone no more than ten minutes. He returned to the cockpit, full of renewed determination, having left Emily in the gloom by the cable-tier, decently clothed in one of his muslin shirts and awaiting his summons. At the door, his entrance was blocked by Lord Somerton. The man was sweating profusely, hugging his shattered right arm to his chest. Someone, likely Mr. Duffy, had cut away his shirtsleeve and bound the bullet wound in a sloppy tourniquet of bandages.

"Dr. Braden, I have been waiting for hours," he said, his inflection heavy with reproach. "I shall not wait any longer."

A deathly silence reigned over the cockpit. Leander glanced past Lord Somerton's lipless countenance for answers. The men, those who had tortured Leander with their piteous pleas for help, were all strangely quiet. Eliza met and then avoided his questioning eyes, pretending an urgent task required her attention. Mr. Duffy was sneaking out the cockpit's back door. It was his father, washing his hands in a pan of water, whose embittered expression said it all: Lord Somerton had kicked up a disturbance in his absence.

"I shall see to you as soon as I can," Leander said, speaking calmly as he would to any one of his patients.

Somerton flung his healthy arm across the doorway, his face darkening. "No! You shall see to me now."

"Find yourself a place to sit down and rest."

Somerton hissed through gritted teeth. "Do not tell me what to do."

"You would be wise to heed my recommendation. Anger will only exacerbate your condition."

"I will *not* sit down until you have seen to my wounds."

"You cannot snap your fingers and expect to be served here. This is not a tavern."

Somerton exploded like an overheated carronade. "I have never been treated like this in my life ... especially not by an inferior such as you."

Gasps of outrage rippled throughout the cockpit. And then a hush fell again.

Leander stood his ground, refusing to flinch. "I may be a doctor, but I cannot fix your bruised arrogance ... sir."

Somerton seethed, his eyes darting around, challenging anyone who dared to look at him with an egregious scowl. He made a curt gesture at the table where Gus Walby was mumbling and twitching in pain on the blood-soaked sheets. "You have that deformed boy on your slab!"

"What of it?"

"Should not those who are highest in rank take precedence in your operating theatre, Doctor?"

"Every injury is assessed by me. Those with the most grievous wounds are taken first. If the suffering is the same, the order in which they arrived prevails."

"Do you mean to tell me," he laughed, brandishing his good arm in the air, "that if Nelson came walking in here, you would insist he wait his turn while you attended cooks and shoemakers and grog-drinkers?"

Leander lifted his chin. "It is most fortunate that you, sir, are not Lord Nelson."

Somerton raised his fist. His face was so full of hostility Leander was certain he was going to strike him. He was not alone in those sentiments. Rebellious murmurs rose up from all corners; Leander was forced to quell them with an open-palm entreaty for silence.

"Get a hold of yourself, man, and lower your voice. Show some respect for those living out their final moments."

Fear and doubt lurked in Somerton's eyes. He was surrounded by a pack of snarling wolves, parrying without a sword. "For God's sake, my arm is shot up! I am bleeding everywhere," he burst hysterically. "I am the son of the Duke of Belmont, a man of extensive wealth and properties. That boy over there is nothing! Nothing! Why would you ever waste your time patching him up?"

"Because, like all men on this ship," Leander said, pausing for effect, "he is worth saving."

The walls of the cockpit swelled with silence. No one moved. Tongues were left sticking to the roofs of mouths. Eyes were riveted to the confrontation in the doorway. A light touch on Leander's elbow almost went unnoticed. Turning finally, he found Emily there, anger and sadness vying for supremacy in her eyes. Beyond her, obscured in the orlop shadows, he could see the distinctive outline of Fly's bicorne and the glint of gold buttons on his frock. But his friend stayed well back, perhaps recognizing that the situation did not require his interference.

"And her! This woman! She shot me. I demand immediate justice!" Somerton's accusation erupted from spittle-flecked lips, but its poison was undermined by his childish mewling.

"Are you completely certain of that, sir?" asked Emily, her head to one side. "I sympathize with your misfortune, but this behaviour of yours is most peculiar. Come, come, Lord Somerton, you seemed fine on deck ... as long as the blood that was being spilled was not yours."

Linking arms with him, she guided him toward an empty spot in the cockpit, carefully circumnavigating outstretched legs, acknowledging with an appreciative smile those who struggled to pay their respects with a bob of their head or a sailors' salute. Lord Somerton, stunned into silence, yet sporting a scowling face that promised future retribution, dropped to the floor and hungrily downed the drink of water Eliza brought to him. Meanwhile, the injured jacks were on ten-terhooks, watching Emily, awaiting the spine-chilling climax.

Her voice rose up again, clear and undisturbed. "It might help you to know this, Lord Somerton. Your youngest brother, Octavius ... also the son of a duke ... even while clutching his entrails to keep them from spilling out his belly ... he waited patiently for his turn."

Someone started to clap his hands. Others followed, one by one, until the whole cockpit resounded with exuberant applause. Leander shook his head in admiration. Could it be Emily carried sympathy for Somerton as she once had for his doomed brother? Pleading for a re-turn to peace and quiet, Leander resumed his duties, making a mental note to fortify Lord Somerton's water cup with opium the first available opportunity.

Beyond the surgery, through the open door, the orlop echoed with laughter.

At Sea

Magpie's eye flew open on his dreams, the troubling images skittering away like sailfish before he could revisit them. At first, he did not know where he was, too dog-tired and spent to raise his head to gauge his whereabouts. Was the battle finally over? If so, was that pockmarked hull, looming before him, a friend or foe? Maybe it wasn't even a ship. Maybe he was dead and those formidable oak timbers signified heaven, one reserved for sailors, and those beams of milky sunlight were the pearly gates that Biscuit had once talked about. But what about those eerie, supernatural sounds he could not identify? Could it be? Was it the gods, deliberating among themselves, deciding his fate?

He tried to move his body, but a gasping pain tore through his back. Something cumbrously heavy was pinning his legs down. He brought his hands to his face. They were rope-burned and stiffened with cold; his fingernails were broken and bleeding. He remembered scraggy ropes and oily chains; scratching and scraping on wood; his heart in his mouth, and the iron-cold smell of the numbing Atlantic.

To erase the shuddering memory, he gazed upon the sun-soaked clouds floating in the sapphire sky like a mythical giant's serving of mashed potatoes, smothered in melted butter. They reminded him of the roast-of-pork feast and baked bread pudding the Duke of Clarence had once fed him. He thought of Emily, smiling and spirited, reading the story of the Dashwood sisters and their headaches with men. He thought of Dr. Braden, his handsome face gentle and concerned as he went about his examinations. He could hear the ring of Captain Austen's jolly laughter; Biscuit's accented voice, bellowing orders in the galley; and Prosper Burgo branding those around him a scoundrel and a jackanapes. He felt a twinge around his heart as he thought of Gus Walby, the best mate a lad could ever have. They were fine people, his loved ones, and they had all shown such kindness to a low-born sail-maker and climbing boy.

His eye fell from the sky to stare at the battered, sea-weathered walls near his head. He played a game of pretend, fancying that he was one of Uptergrove's children and they were all frantically looking for him. "I am here!" he shouted, reaching out, hoping to feel their eager, grasping hands. But it wasn't warm flesh that he met. It was a strand of wet yarn. Exploring further, Magpie realized he had found the golden drawstrings of the leather pouch. He still had it ... the flute ... Captain Uptergrove's cherished flute. His heart soared with the seagulls, wheeling in the sunshine near the broken yards of the topgallants. He listened to the message being whispered on the wind.

"*Tell Captain Austen what you have learned here.*"

Maybe ... just maybe ... it all meant something.

1:40 P.M.
ABOARD HMS *INVINCIBLE*

Emily could feel eyes on her, but their owners did not sit in judgment. They were the eyes of innocuous creatures like those that watched quietly, curiously, from the blue forest shadows at night. Leaving the sullen Lord Somerton on the floor, holding his head in one hand, she made her way toward the surgery table, her stomach churning from the dreadful stink of blood and wounds and death. She kept the top of Gus's head in her field of vision, afraid to look at the ugly hole in his trembling body. Leander and his father were quietly conferring over the surgeon's chest, selecting the required knives, bullet forceps, needles, and ligature thread from the vast array of instruments. Miss Braden, her smile queasy, her face a ghastly shade of green beneath her iron-grey curls, fell in step with Emily, placed a warm cloth in her hand and gave her arm a gentle pat.

Emily leaned over Gus and smoothed away the damp tendrils of blond hair from his troubled brow. "I am here, my dear boy," she whispered close to his ear.

He wept when he saw her.

"It is all right," she said lightly, groping for the right words to sustain him. "I am familiar with the pain. It is most unpleasant. But soon you will be well. Miss Braden is here, too! And you have not one but two doctors who are going to remove that lead from you."

From the corner of her eye, she could see the long, thin knife Leander was holding in his hand, its steel glinting in the light of the overhead lanterns. Flinching, she began sponging the sheen of sweat from Gus's stricken face.

"I'm a complete wreck, Em! Ruined everywhere! Best to let me sink like the *Lady Jane*," he said, revealing his tortured thoughts in frightened snatches.

Emily looked to Leander for help. His fist was bouncing against his mouth. His eyes were on her, their striking colour evident even in the cockpit's shade. He twitched as if making a sudden return from a distant place, and nodded encouragement.

"I shall have none of that, Mr. Walby, for I believe … I believe you have a great deal more living to do," she said, echoing Leander's thought-provoking words as she lay in his hospital on the *Isabelle*, recovering from her own bullet wound. "And Captain Austen needs his keen-eyed clerk at his side. You *shall* walk again on that quarterdeck with him."

Gus's eyes, edged with dark circles, glowed like black stones in his colourless face. "If I don't make it …"

"You must see yourself there, Gus ... standing tall and proud and useful."

"But if I don't, Em ... I know it is a long way back to England, but maybe you and Dr. Braden could bury my heart there ... in Bunhill Fields ... with my mother. That way ... she won't be so lonely in her little grave."

"Shhh!" Emily stroked his head, unable to keep her composure. Being reminded he was an orphan was too much. Tears fell down her flushed cheeks and slipped into her mouth. "Do you want the leather gag? It may help."

"Yes, please. And if you were to hold my hand, Em," he said, gazing up at her, hope and fear welling in those large, pleading eyes, "it would be a tremendous comfort to me."

Some of the watchers groaned in sympathy. Miss Braden turned and crept away, breaking into a quiet sob. Emily entwined her fingers with Gus's little, brave ones and gave his hand a squeeze.

There was a tremulous smile on his lips as he closed his eyes to wait. "And, if you please," he whispered, "don't ever let it go."

CHAPTER 35

6:00 P.M.
(FIRST DOG WATCH, FOUR BELLS)

Cadby Brambles was in a rotten mood. He was hungry and exhausted and could not believe that Captain Austen had asked him to entertain the ladies at the stern bench while the decks and sides were being swabbed, and the guns damped down. He was expected to stay with them and smile politely until Biscuit could piece together a meal for them in the galley. The ladies! Pshaw! This was punishment, he reckoned, for not sustaining an injury whilst battling the Americans. It was not quite as bad as scraping stomach linings off the sides of boats, but awfully close. He glared at Mrs. Jiggins and Miss Braden, their heads together, the former prattling to the latter who was inexplicably quiet. In fact, Miss Braden did not look at all well. Perhaps her ordeal in the surgery had blanched her complexion. Her small eyes had gone missing in puffy folds of skin and her windblown curls — who knows where that preposterous mob cap had gotten to — gave her a shopworn appearance. Mrs. Jiggins was even worse. She was inexplicably cheerful, evidently ignorant of the news that Lord Somerton, her nephew, or whoever he was, had been shot in the arm. Moreover, it looked as if someone had smacked her face with an iron skillet, maybe hoping to shut her up. Her nose was swollen and purple with bruises, and her bonnet, with its profusion of plastic fruit, was sitting askew on her fringe of hair. What a pair they were: salt and vinegar, odds and ends, flotsam and jetsam, he thought with a wry smile. Now, if Emily had been among them, he would not mind this chaperoning at all. But, oh no! She was much occupied, brooding at the bedside of Gus Walby, cooing and whispering who-knows-what into his ear, counting on her presence being a critical factor to his survival. Had a blast of grapeshot ripped *his* arm off, *who* then would be sitting with whom?

"My art supplies and easels! *That* is the sum total of all I have left," whined Mrs. Jiggins. Her devastation was so immense; one would think she had been diagnosed with an incurable disease.

"Praise the Lord for sparing your art supplies," Miss Braden replied dryly.

"I have gone looking, but was told all but one of my hat boxes and trunks of clothing were thrown overboard."

Miss Braden massaged her temples. "There isn't anyone on this ship who has much to his name."

"But I daresay! Imagine! Tossing my beautiful things overboard without so much as seeking my permission."

"What a shame the ways and means of men on the sea are so foreign to you." Miss Braden's huffed sigh suggested she was a far greater authority on the subject of sailors.

"Without my pretty silks and bonnets, how shall I ever win the attentions of Dr. Braden?"

"I do not think my brother has any interest in forming a relationship with a woman at this stage in his life."

"Your brother? No, no, Miss Braden! It is young Leander who tempts me ... that has me all churned up."

Cadby, who found this information highly amusing, snorted like the *Invincible*'s resident hogs. Mrs. Jiggins shot him a withering glare, but as soon as she heard Miss Braden's insulting cackle, he was instantly off the hook, released from purgatory.

"Good heavens! Have you seen yourself?"

Alarmed, Mrs. Jiggins started patting herself down as if she were on fire. "Why? Why?"

"Your face matches the colours of the fruit on your head."

"Wot?"

"You look as if you were hit with a splat of mulberry jam."

Mrs. Jiggins's hands flew to her face.

"That tumble you took in the cockpit …" Miss Braden paused, remembering, and then laughed even louder. "It has stolen your charming beauty, I wager, for weeks to come. Henceforth, do not be surprised if the ships' oldest goats find no attraction to you."

Mrs. Jiggins let a loud breath go, adjusted her Paisley shawl and knotted her arms across her bosom. "Oh, you may laugh at my plight, Miss Braden, but do not forget … Mr. Biscuit and Prosper Burgo are both smitten with me. Wholly besotted!"

Miss Braden looked down her nose. "Indeed! Is that you or the negus speaking?"

Embroiled in their game of one-upmanship, the ladies seemed to have forgotten Cadby was there. He let them bicker away while his attention happily strayed to the noisy excitement of life beyond the stern bench. The fighting had come to an end hours ago, and yet the Invincibles were a long way from a full recovery. They had managed to secure the *Liberty* to their larboard quarter, but were still in the throes of doing the same with the *Amethyst*. Captain Austen, fed up with the lack of communication from Uptergrove, had instructed his men to go ahead and latch her to their own starboard. It was of utmost importance that the ships be corralled before nightfall, so the prize crews could take command of the American ships, round up their weaponry and snuff out simmering plots of revenge. Consequently, the cutters, barges, launches, and jolly boats, bobbing in a maze of tangled ropes, would have to remain where they were until they could be collected at first light.

One of the jolly boats arrested Cadby's attention. Unlike the others, it was bouncing on the blue waves like an exuberant child seeking attention. He frowned, caught his breath, squinted and stared at it. No! It couldn't be! Surely, he was wrong. It was getting late in the day and he was overly tired. His imagination must have run away with itself or it was the setting sun, playing tricks on the darkening water with its drooping light. Maybe the abundance of smoke and noxious effluvia had damaged his eyesight. Yes! Yes, that was it, he assured himself. Anxious to forget and swab it from his mind, Cadby veered back to Mrs. Jiggins and Miss Braden.

"Ladies! Shall I fetch each of us a can of grog?"

6:10 P.M.

"Tell me first, Doctor … what you will do?"

Somerton had been heavily sedated with a rum tonic. His breathing was shallow and his words were slurry and thick with terror. As Leander tightened the brass screw of the tourniquet to staunch the flow of blood, he considered him. There was no time to expound on the intricacies of the procedure, but perhaps, as a courtesy, Somerton was owed a brief explanation. He was not a man of the sea; the hideous practices of the cockpit were unknown to him. Try as he had to prove otherwise, he was still made of flesh and bone. Debilitating fears and convictions roamed the wastelands of his brain. Soon, like all tested men, he would discover the calibre of mettle coursing through his veins.

"I shall begin by cutting through your skin, tissue, and muscle, right down to the bone, and then peeling back your flesh. A saw will be used to sever the bone. Afterward, your arteries and smaller vessels will be tied up with thread ligatures. The tourniquet will be removed at that point, and your skin folded over the stump and taped with adhesive straps. I will finish by dipping and sealing it in pitch."

"My stump!" Somerton let a quivering breath go. "Do I have any other option?"

"I am afraid not," Leander replied quietly. "If left, your arm will grow gangrenous and you shall die."

Seizing the tin cup from the hands of Leander's father, Somerton lifted his head and downed more of the tonic, most of which spilled down his chin. He knocked away the proffered leather gag and glared up at Jim Beef who stood ready to assist, but had trouble meeting the man's strange, all-seeing eyes. Despite the sedation, the contempt Somerton harboured for the motley men surrounding him like bars of a cage, their grubby, callused hands placed at intervals along his body to hold him down, was written plainly on his face.

"Will that be cold?" he asked, perceiving the knife coming toward him.

"I have heated it in warm water on the hanging stove."

"How very kind of you, Doctor." In bleak despair, he shuttered his eyes and croaked out a final whisper. "Right then. Get on with it."

Silence enveloped the room like a winding sheet. Somerton tensed as the men leaned forward and dropped their weight on him. Leander made the first incision. The high-pitched screams that followed were sufficient to shake the stout-hearted and rouse the battle dead.

8:00 P.M.
(SECOND DOG WATCH, FOUR BELLS)

"So ya see our Emily had nothin' to do with it, sir."

Biscuit ended off the telling of his tale and hung his head. He was sitting on the front few inches of his chair, the seat of which was cracked and wont to catch on the bottom of his trousers, but it was the only one available in the great cabin, its furnishings and accoutrements not yet returned. Clasping his sweaty hands between his bouncing knees, he waited for Captain Austen's verdict. When it did not come, Biscuit looked up at him. He was leaning back on the cushions of the window seat, his legs crossed, peering out at the night. There was not much to see besides an impenetrable wall of blackness that mocked the large whale-oil lanterns and their feeble attempts to illuminate the back of the ship. He shifted around on the cushions as if trying to get comfortable, pinched his nose and traced his fingers along his eyebrows, small gestures that indicated restlessness. It wasn't until the ship's bell clanged that he seemed to remember he had company. He faced Biscuit, his eyes full of suspicion.

"I appreciate you coming here to tell me this. It is serious indeed. But you are a cook, are you not?"

"I am, sir," said Biscuit, dumbfounded by the question.

"Perhaps your marksmanship is not what you think it is."

Biscuit's mouth fell open. How did he respond to that?

"If you hoped to take credit for this, you are too late."

"Credit? Beg yer pardon, sir. I'm right confused. How's it possible I'm too late in tellin' ya such a thing?"

"For the simple reason that Prosper Burgo was here earlier making a confession."

Biscuit sat up straight, his arms falling to his sides. "Burgo? What the devil was he fessin' up to?"

"And in addition to Mr. Burgo," Fly continued, ignoring his inquiry, "I have also heard from Mr. Philpotts, Mr. Duffy, and, if I correctly deciphered what he was trying to say, Mr. Jim Beef of Bedlam himself."

Biscuit was completely baffled. "And?" was all he could say.

"I am afraid you shall have to cross swords for the honour, for they all claimed it was a ball of lead from *their* musket that struck Lord Somerton in the arm."

CHAPTER 36

FRIDAY, OCTOBER 1
BEFORE DAWN

"That food should sustain you for at least four and twenty hours, Doctor."

Emily nodded approval as she took the empty plate from Leander and helped him bed down under his blankets. It was his turn to be taken care of. He had been at it all night, refusing to rest until he had seen and helped every last one of the wounded. She assisted him, stumbling and spent, up the ladders to the newly restored hospital on the upper deck, and into a hammock slung beside the open gunport, the same place she had once occupied. Gus was lying on a cot nearby, quiet and white, but no longer mumbling nonsense and thrashing in a fitful slumber. Plastered and bandaged, the others remained on the orlop under the watchful eyes of Miss Braden and old Dr. Braden, both of whom had managed to steal some rest, and of Biscuit, who boasted he knew "somethin' o' medicine."

"I shall stay here to fight off anyone who dares to interrupt you," vowed Emily, tucking the blankets around him. "My new friend, Mr. Beef, has miraculously found a comb-back armchair for me, which means I, too, shall be sleeping in luxurious comfort."

Leander, his head on his pillow, gazed up at her, assessing her with those intelligent, if somewhat sleepy, eyes of his. "You did well."

"As did you." Emily gazed back, drinking in the angles of his cheekbones and the curves of his lips, rounding up enough threads of courage to seek an answer to a question that terrified her. "Will … will he pull through, Doctor?"

The coveted smile that would put her mind to rest did not appear. "I cannot tell," he declared solemnly. "The good news is … the lead pierced through muscle, not his stomach. But I have seen men leap off the table after an operation and enjoy several more spirited hours of life, only to die later of infection or fever or tetanus. I wish … more than anything … I could allay your fears."

Emily filled her lungs with the sweet-smelling breezes that rushed headlong through the gunport. It helped to ease her gnawing anxiety. "And I wish, more than anything, for an end to storms and shipwrecks and battles. I want to sail to a safe harbour and find a cottage where I can nurse you and Gus back to perfect health."

"What about Lord Somerton?" he asked, with a lopsided grin. "Could you find it in your heart to nurse him, too?"

Emily gave it a moment's consideration. "No. Although I am not entirely heartless. Poor man! His life has been forever changed. It will not be easy for him going forward. Therefore, I shall ask Mrs. Jiggins to keep an eye on him. They may find solace in one another."

"What manner of solace does Mrs. Jiggins need?"

"Never you mind, Doctor!" She arched an enigmatic eyebrow, but could see that Leander's mind had moved on.

"Getting back to this cottage of yours … where is it, do you think?"

"Somewhere by the sea," she told him, adding with a frown, "just not on it."

"Thatched and whitewashed?"

"Perhaps. Or maybe stone."

"But it is sitting on a green knoll."

"Definitely! With oak trees and silver birch all around. And gardens of blue hydrangeas. There must be gardens."

"And will there be room for Magpie, as well?"

"Yes! Always!" she said, tears stinging her eyes.

"And is that what you would like of *all* things?"

Emily wiped her cheeks, his question arousing hope.

"Tell me again ... when shall you turn twenty-one?" His heavy eyelids blinked slowly, scarcely able to open again once they had closed.

She sighed with disappointment. "Not for a very long time, Doctor."

"Oh, well that is not good," he mumbled. "We never know what may happen. Certainly your family would not be pleased. I shall ever after be an anathema. But maybe on the other side of the world ... across an ocean ... they shall never know."

He went so quiet after that, Emily was certain he had dropped off. "Know what, Doctor?"

His eyes flew open. High colour suffused his cheeks. "Would you ever consider marrying a poor old doctor?"

"Perhaps not one quite as old as your father, although he is a dear," she laughed. "Now go to sleep. We can talk at length later when you are well rested and clear-thinking."

"I am thinking quite clearly now, thank you."

"You could have fooled me!"

"But I may never wake up or ... or when I do, more Americans will be spotted on the horizon." He looked up at her, thoughtfully. "I shall go to sleep, but first ... I should very much like to hear your answer."

"What was the question?" she teased, her heart about to burst through her ribcage.

Leander began rummaging under his blanket. To Emily's surprise he produced the little silver-plated teaspoon he had purchased in Portsmouth. "A token of my affection ... and most ardent love," he said smiling, holding it out to her, his eyes growing heavy again. "And this question: Would you, dearest Emeline Louisa Georgina Marie ... would you consider marrying me?"

She reached into his bed, found his hand, brought it to her lips and held it tightly against her damp cheek. "Yes!" she said softly, realizing no one had heard her reply. Leander was already asleep.

Smiling through tears, Emily gazed out the gunport. There was the first light, an orange-gold shimmer, warming that far, far horizon, engraving the beginnings of a pathway on the purring sea. Intermingled with the sough of the morning wind were the distinct notes of a flute.

"Em?" a little voice called out behind her. "Are you still there?"

"I am, my darling Gus," she replied, her breast swelling with renewed hope for the future and all its possibilities.

BEFORE DAWN

Fly Austen meandered toward the helm, his mind overflowing with lists and calculations and questions, all the things that had kept him awake in the night, tossing and turning in his bed. What a reassuring sight to see Biscuit and Prosper Burgo, leaning against the binnacle, chatting leisurely with one another. It was such an ordinary sight, but to him it signified constancy and survival. They had passed the night without incident, despite yesterday's procurement of seamen of ambiguous character. He had half expected a gang of mutinous Americans to accost him at his cabin door, their muskets and pistols trained upon his chest, and convey him to the plank.

As soon as Fly reached the helm, Biscuit favoured him with a mug of coffee.

"Hope ya don't mind, Cap'n. I put a wee dram in it fer ya."

"We shall let it go, this time," said Fly, feigning disapproval, looking around to make certain all was indeed well.

"It's damn parky out here this morning!" griped Prosper, blowing into his hands. "Woulda bin nice if ya'd brought me somethin' warm to drink, Biscuit."

"Quit yer caterwaulin'! Ya remind me o' that high-born whilst he were under Dr. Braden's knife, weepin' and whimperin' like a dog."

Fly felt their eyes on him, bracing for a castigation that did not come, his attention having crept away into the remains of the night.

Emboldened, Prosper risked barking out a question. "Did ya find them spongy louts on board the *Amethyst*, Cap'n?"

"Who do you mean?" Fly demanded impatiently, surprising himself that he sounded so prickly.

"*Who* else? Prickett and Bridlington!"

"No, regrettably, but we did discover some of our old friends who are overjoyed to be reunited. Their numbers shall markedly bolster our prize crews with …" Fly's words trailed off into the cold silence. Handing his coffee mug to Biscuit, he left them at the binnacle and walked to the stern. There, he kneeled on the bench, gripped the taffrail, and blinked into the swirling mists, his flesh creeping, his heart beating uncomfortably. With greater urgency, he then strode toward the forecastle, desperate to see around and beyond the slumbering hulks of the *Liberty* and *Amethyst*, affixed to his ship's quarters. Prosper and Biscuit were behind him, their tread struggling to keep up to his. By the bowsprit, Fly searched the sea within sight, cursing the grainy darkness, imploring the sun to haul itself up and make the world blue again.

"What's wrong, sir?" Biscuit's voice was tentative.

At first, Fly was too staggered to speak. "It's the *Expedition*! She's gone!"

Prosper leapt nimbly over the bulwark and onto the bowsprit. Clutching the foremast stays, he walked along the spar, thrusting his nose into the westerly wind. "Neptune's goblets!" he finally cried. "Why that Uptergrove … that gleekin', rump-fed, good-for-nothin' codpiece!"

Biscuit gave the woolly hairs on his chest a ferocious scratch. "Should we be beatin' to quarters, sir?"

Fighting to understand, Fly shrank back against the ship's side, uncertain whether to laugh or cry. This was his reward for being too hasty in his celebrations. "What good would that do?" He threw his hands in the air. "Sitting here in the middle of the Atlantic, latched to our American prizes like an overloaded donkey? *We* are not going anywhere."

10:00 A.M.
(Forenoon Watch, Four Bells)

Emily awoke to find old Dr. Braden's kindly face floating in front of her, his finger on his lips.

"Shh! Come with me, my dear, but let us not wake Leander and Mr. Walby." He helped her up from her chair and held out his arm. "Do not pump me with questions," he instructed during their brief journey, not once meeting her eyes. "I know only that Captain Austen has requested your presence on the quarterdeck."

His mysterious words, spoken so sombrely, quickened Emily's heart.

A crowd had gathered above deck. When she appeared at the top of the companion way, their murmuring grew less sonorous. Elbows were dug into ribs and eyes glowed with excitement as if liveried trumpeters were about to signal the start of a grand procession. The sun, in a sky as blue as forget-me-nots, warmed the October chill from the air. Emily looked up at the men sitting on the lofty yards and platforms, and around at those standing at the rails of the American prizes, grappled to the sides of the *Invincible*. It was hard to believe she was on the sea. There were so many people about, new faces and old, she felt transported back to Portsmouth Point. Miss Braden in her mob, and Mrs. Jiggins sporting her basket of fruit on her head, shocked Emily by bobbing curtseys as she passed them by. Prosper Burgo rewarded her with a jaunty salute and a brazen wink of his eye. Cadby Brambles blushed like a bush of pink roses as their eyes met and, thereafter, rushed to question Prosper on the meaning of the old ladies and their curtseys.

Prosper's lips curled in exasperation. "Because, ya nestle-cock, our Emily's a princess ... a bloody remarkable princess."

How disappointed Emily was to have missed seeing Cadby's expression as he blurted out astonishment: "Wot? She's a wot?" But up ahead, near the capstan, Biscuit and Captain Austen were waving her onward.

His expression unreadable, his hands clasped behind him, Fly leaned toward her when she reached his side. "We are not yet out of the woods, Emily. I am afraid that many challenges still lie ahead. But for all that, I thought it only right we take a moment to give thanks."

Biscuit's hearty laugh rang out, his crooked lines of gray teeth on display for all to see. Startled, Emily gaped at him as he dashed tears from his whiskery face.

"Ya see, Em, it's like this: we found a fish … in our jolly boat … curled up and sleepin' with the sheep."

The murmuring crowds parted; Biscuit and Captain Austen swept aside. There was Jim Beef, smiling and bowing to the crowds of on-lookers, delighted with the attention and his own importance. Sitting up in his arms, swaddled in blankets, was the one who had gone missing, the one who had left Emily in wretched suspense, anguishing over his whereabouts. He was shivering and clutching a bamboo flute, finely decorated with carvings of fruit and flowers. His green eye patch was gone, exposing the red ruins of his eye. Seeing her, recognition and elation kindled his face. He jumped and squirmed in Mr. Beef's arms, nearly knocking the madman off his feet, and shouted her name.

"Em! Em! Em!"

It was a tune Emily had longed to hear again. Its pleasing notes echoed around the masts of the grappled ships before the wind carried them off and scattered them on the gold-flecked sea. Pressing a hand to her mouth, she hurried toward Magpie, certain her knees would give out. Gazing at him, smiling and frowning by turns, she gently stroked the scarred and puckered skin of his cheek with her thumb.

"Mr. Magpie! *Where* have you been?" she finally demanded, sternly shaking her head.

"Oh, Em! Just wait 'til ya hear!" he said, gulping down excitement, hugging the flute to his heart. "What a tale I have to tell!"

EPILOGUE

"**S**ir! I have come to inform you that Captain Uptergrove has died."

Trevelyan slowly turned from the ship's wheel to see who had delivered the message. He was pleased to find it was Mr. Croker. Saucer-eyed and sweating, the man had a bandage tied around his scrawny neck and was carrying his arm in a sling. Somehow, he no longer looked like the very important clerk he once claimed to be.

"Pity," said Trevelyan coldly, his chin firmly set. He ran his hands along the smooth handles of the wheel and peered into the western sea. "But you see, Mr. Croker, I am much more interested in the horizons. What of them?"

"The officer of the watch says they are still empty, sir."

Trevelyan dismissed Mr. Croker with a curt nod and sealed his lips in a smile. To the sullen Expeditions, he was a fearless lion, a symbol of strength, a leader. But strip away the exterior and they would discover his true self: a weeping, joyful mess, giddy with happiness. His trembling fingers reached around the wheel for Captain Uptergrove's bicorne hat that, earlier, he had filched and set upon the binnacle for safekeeping. He beat it against his thigh to loosen the old grime and plunged it on his shorn head, choosing to wear it amidships. There! He was in command … once again. Looking up at the grey, marbled sky, he welcomed the light rain on his scarred face and blinked at the British colours flying overhead, limp and battle-tattered.

"We did it, Harry," he whispered proudly between fits of helpless laughter. "We did it at last."

AUTHOR'S NOTE

The majority of characters in *Run Red with Blood* are fictional; however, a few of them require a word of explanation.

THE BRITISH ROYAL FAMILY

King George III and Queen Charlotte had a large family. Six daughters and seven sons lived to adulthood, including their eldest son, George, the Prince Regent (later George IV), and their third son, William, the Duke of Clarence (later William IV), both of whom are mentioned in *Run Red with Blood*. George III and Queen Charlotte did not have a granddaughter named Emily. In creating my fictitious Princess Emeline "Emily" Louisa Georgina Marie, I imagined her father to have been a child born to Queen Charlotte between the Duke of Cumberland and the Duke of Sussex, as the queen — who was pregnant most years of her early marriage — had a window of childbearing opportunity between these two sons.

FRANCIS "FLY" AUSTEN

Fly was one of Jane Austen's most beloved brothers. He enjoyed a long life and a distinguished naval career. Many of the personal details I gave to his character are true to his appearance and nature, but I did take literary licence with regard to the experiences I had him endure during the War of 1812. He did fight the Americans, but not as a commander of HMS *Invincible*, and by 1813, he had long since been promoted to captain. I do, however, like to imagine that the well-respected, intelligent, courageous, and humorous Fly Austen in *Run Red with Blood* is very similar to the man who once was.

SHIPS

Although there have been several ships in history known as HMS *Invincible*, HMS *Expedition*, HMS *Amethyst*, HMS *Illustrious*, and USS *Liberty*, the vessels and their crews in *Run Red with Blood* are fictional.

The lines and verses from the songs "We Be Three Poor Mariners," "Spanish Ladies," and Robert Burns's "Scots Wha Hae" that appear in my book are in the public domain.

The following appear in the text and warrant a word of explanation:

Page 12   Three Threads ale was a mixture of one pale and two brown ales.

Page 12   A corsair was a pirate or Barbary privateer.

Page 18   The bo'sun or boatswain was responsible for inspecting the sails and rigging.

Page 19   "Cooking off" is a premature explosion of ammunition due to heat.

Page 22   Portsmouth Polls were local prostitutes.

Page 27   Portsea Island is an island off the southern coast of England that comprises the town of Portsmouth.

Page 32   The Solent is the body of water in the English Channel that separates mainland England from the Isle of Wight.

Page 35 An etui is a small, decorative holder for sewing implements.

Page 42 A letter of marque was a licence granted by a sovereign, giving a ship's commander (often a privateer) the right to commit acts that constituted piracy.

Page 43 Old Boney was a nickname for Napoleon Bonaparte.

Page 43 A cox'n or coxswain is the helmsman of a ship's boat.

Page 47 Powder monkeys were the young lads who carried the powder cartridges for the guns up from the ship's hold during a battle.

Page 51 "Every hair a rope yarn" refers to a rugged seaman.

Page 53 "Beggars should be no choosers" is an old form of "beggars can't be choosers."

Page 55 Marshalsea was a debtor's prison in London.

Page 56 A fribble was an effeminate fop.

Page 63 Slavers were ships that carried slaves.

Page 69 Oakum refers to old pieces of untwisted rope used to caulk ships' seams.

Page 70 Bucks were young men whose chief interest was the pursuit of pleasure.

Page 74 Augusta, Elizabeth, Sophia, and Mary were four of the six daughters of King George III and Queen Charlotte.

Page 78 Bedlam is another name for London's Bethlem Royal Hospital for the mentally ill.

Page 78 Brickbats were pieces of brick used as missiles during riots.

Page 79 Rondy is the short-form for a press gang's rendezvous or meeting place.

Page 79 Landmen were men who had no formal naval training, but had skills required on ships.

Page 110 *Lues venerea* is Latin for syphilis.

Page 114 An antaphrodisiac was a medicine used to dull carnal desire.

Page 120 Chinoiserie refers to Chinese motifs in Western art and was especially popular in the eighteenth century.

Page 130 Skillagalee is a thin, unnourishing gruel or broth.

Page 149 The blacklist was a list of delinquents slated for punishment.

Page 156 A boatswain's starter was a rope used to flog laggards.

Page 157 Jacks were British naval seamen.

Page 160 Mrs. Dorothea Jordan (1762–1816) was an actress who lived with the Duke of Clarence (1765–1837), and bore him ten children.

Page 162 Thomas Rules's Bar in Maiden Lane (1798) is the oldest restaurant in London.

Page 177 Larboard is the old word for the port side of a ship.

Page 202 Spoondrift is spray from wind-whipped waves.

Page 203 A false fire was a light on shore used to lure a vessel to destruction.

Page 214 Vauxhall Gardens, on the south side of the Thames, was a pleasure garden and the place to be seen during the Regency period.

Page 215 Mother Carey's chickens was the name sailors gave to the storm petrel, a bird whose appearance near a ship portended a storm or trouble.

Page 238 "Skeletons at the feast" referred to those who brought gloom to an otherwise joyful occasion.

Page 240 A roundhouse was the officers' private lavatory.

Page 293 Wool-gathering is the indulgence in dreamy thoughts and imaginings.

Page 324　Keelhauling was a horrible punishment by which a sailor was hauled under the keel of a ship.

Page 324　"Bear a hand" is a plea for assistance.

Page 327　"Riding the pale horse" is synonymous with death.

Page 341　Sea-pie is a dish of fish, meat, vegetables, and layers of pastry.

ACKNOWLEDGEMENTS

I could not have reached the end of my four-year journey with *Run Red with Blood* if it were not for the support of a special group of individuals to whom I owe my deepest and sincerest gratitude.

My cherished mentor and friend, Anne Millyard, who has always believed in my tales of the sea; Paula Boon and Dawn Huddlestone, who offered excellent suggestions as I read to them each new chapter in our writers' circle; Kevin Patterson, for designing and creating both my website and wonderful front cover; Sonia Holiad, for happily taking time out of her busy schedule to give my book its first edit; Nancy Beal and Cathy Kuntz, for their literary enthusiasm and camaraderie; the terrific team at Dundurn Press for keeping me on track with my deadlines; and editor Shannon Whibbs, whose patience and diligence propelled me to the finish line.

I would also like to express my heartfelt thanks to Patrick Boyer for his friendship and guidance throughout my writing years, and to my beloved family: Randy, Evan, and Brodie, whose love and encouragement have kept me continually moving toward new horizons.

In the Same Series

Come Looking for Me

In *Come Looking for Me*, a mysterious young English woman named Emily risks a crossing of the Atlantic during the War of 1812 for the promise of a new adventure in Canada. But she never arrives.

Captured by Captain Trevelyan, a man as cold-blooded as his frigate is menacing, Emily is held prisoner aboard the USS *Serendipity*. Seeking to save herself, she makes a desperate escape overboard in the midst of a raging sea battle and is rescued by the British crew of HMS *Isabelle*. Yet Emily has only exchanged one form of captivity for another, and remains in peril as England escalates its fight against the United States on the Atlantic.

On board the *Isabelle*, Emily encounters a crew of fascinating seamen and strikes up unexpected friendships, but life on a man-of-war is full of deprivations and dangers to which she is unaccustomed. Amidst heartache and tragedy at sea, she struggles to find her place among the men until a turn of events reveals her true identity. And when Trevelyan's ship once again looms on the horizon, Emily fears losing the only man she has ever loved and falling into the hands of the only man she has ever loathed.